KING OF THE FRANKS

John W. Currier

CLOVIS

KING

OF

THE FRANKS

For Marian —
You shared part of this journey
of writing — I hope you enjoy it.
Love,
John W. Currier
12-13-97

MARQUETTE UNIVERSITY

PRESS

Library of Congress Cataloging-in-Publication Data

Currier, John W. (John Warren), 1953-
  Clovis, King of the Franks / by John W. Currier.
   p. cm.
  ISBN 0-87462-052-X (pbk.)
  1. Clovis, King of the Franks, ca. 466-511—Fiction. 2. Franks—Kings and rulers—Fiction. I. Title.
  PS3553.U6685C58   1997
  813'.54—dc21   97-21233

© John W. Currier

All rights reserved. No part of this publication may be reproduced, stored in a retrieval system, or transmitted in any form or by any means, electronic, mechanical, photocopying, recording or otherwise, without prior permission of the publisher.

Maps generated using MapIt.

MARQUETTE UNIVERSITY PRESS
MILWAUKEE

The Association of Jesuit University Presses

CONTENTS

PREFACE VII

EPIGRAPH IX

DEDICATION XI

MAP XII

CLOVIS, KING OF THE FRANKS 1

EPILOGUE 324

FAMILY TREE 325

GLOSSARY OF NAMES 326

BIBLIOGRAPHY 328

PREFACE

In the late 5th and early 6th centuries, Rome had fallen and chroniclers were few. Much of the information they passed along to us, whether in the form of story or song, history or fiction, was offered with a specific goal in mind, such as defending the authority of the Church or confirming the power of God. In this time, before France was France, in the days of Gaul, a proud people known as Franks, played a dominant role in the history of that place. The young chieftain, Clovis, became instrumental as Gaul was transformed into France.

The writings of Gregory of Tours give us the most important record of the significant events in the life of Clovis, King of the Franks, though his account is sometimes more fantasy than fact. Still, through his efforts, and the efforts of others, like Fredegar and the anonymous writer of the *Liber Historiae Francorum*, we have the building blocks necessary to construct a story about Clovis.

Readers will face the problem of trying to understand a culture not their own. Some might find it surprising, for example, that in the time of Clovis, married priests could still be found and bishops were occasionally succeeded by their sons. That is but one example of the many and varied dilemmas a modern reader might face when opening a book dealing with the early Middle Ages. Perhaps it is best to surrender to the predicament and move on.

Medieval historians acknowledge how difficult it is to establish a reliable chronology for this time. I have seen the same difficulty and have tried to place the significant events of the story in an appropriate way. Many conversations had to be invented, along with a few characters. All that has been invented, however, is intended to support the spirit of the historical record and is, hopefully, reasonable and entertaining.

In researching Clovis, I discovered a story well worth telling. It is a sweeping tale of romance, treachery, and adventure. It is a story that deserves to be told, not only because of its significance, but also because it is, very simply, a good story.

A word of gratitude is due to Mrs. Terry LaMantia, Mrs. Kathy Nelson and Mr. Jon Rinka whose constructive criticisms helped make this a more readable book; to Mr. Wayne Cody, who has the heart of a poet and was a great encouragement to me throughout my struggles with Clovis; to the kind people of France who were so gracious as I researched there; to Dr. Ian Wood, Dr. Patrick Geary and Dr. Bailey Young who by telephone and post were generous with their insights; to Dr. Andrew Tallon and Marquette University Press for their confidence; and lastly, to my wife, Dr. Lisa Hébert, whose support, critiques, and saintly tolerance of my incessant chatter about Clovis will surely free her from years of Purgatory.

J.W.C.
Hartland, WI
1997

"… the voice of lament was oft-times raised, and men said: "Alas! for these our days! The study of letters is perished from us, nor is any found among our peoples able to set forth in a book the events of this present time.""

"Now when I heard these and like complaints ever repeated, I was moved, with however rude an utterance, to hand down the memory of the past to future generations, in no wise leaving untold the conflicts of the wicked and those who lived in righteousness."

—Gregory of Tours
6th century

for Lisa

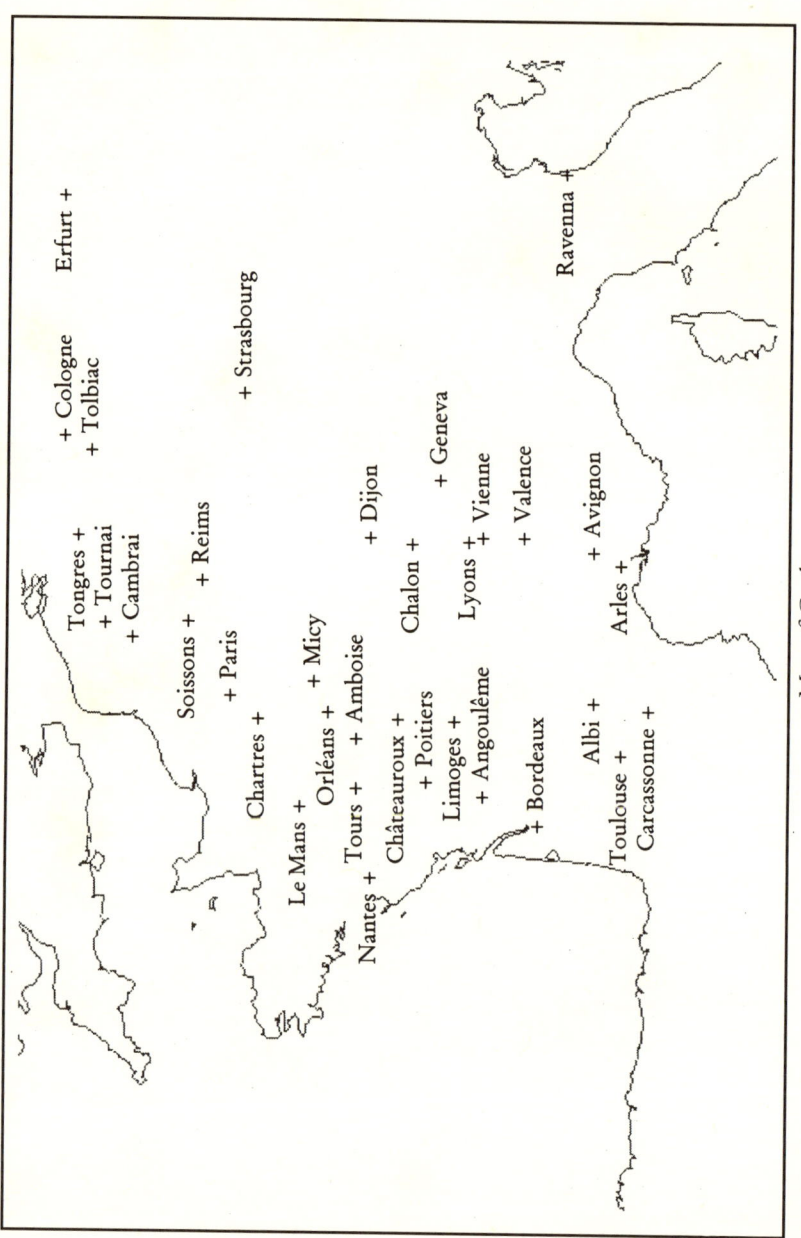

Map of Gaul

Chapter 1

A New Chief Emerges
486-487 CE

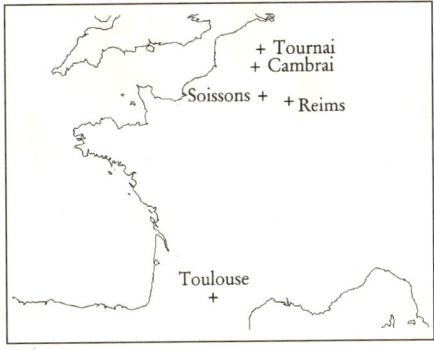

It was the second time Clovis had been to the city of Cambrai; the first he could barely remember: a visit with his father when he was a child. Now he was here on business of his own. He signaled his men to hold and they obeyed, bringing their mounts to a stop. Clovis continued on, pulling up his stallion next to a man who trudged alongside the road, weighed down with a bundle of kindling.

"Friend," said Clovis, "may I have a word?"

The villager stopped, heaved a sigh and turned slowly, frustrated at being interrupted as he hauled his load. When he saw the long braid of blond hair that graced the head of Clovis, however, his eyes widened, his posture straightened and he forgot his irritation. Among the Franks, a braid was the mark of a chief. The man looked at the riders closely, putting the matter of their appearance into a carefully ordered memory. Later, gathering his family to hear the news, he would describe this meeting in all its detail. He would stand before the fire and embellish the account and their eyes would widen too.

"How can I help?" he asked.

"You can help me find Ragnachar, Chief of the Franks of Cambrai."

A frown came across the man's face. "Chief Ragnachar will be where he always is—with his counselor, Farron!" The villager indicated the direction with a sideways glance and a tilt of his head. "In the Great Hall. That way."

Clovis nodded and turned his horse back onto the road, waving for his men to join him.

Clovis was chief of the Franks who lived in the city of Tournai. He was capable beyond his years—and popular with his people. His straight nose, dimpled chin and searching eyes added a special attraction to the Tournai women. That was of little concern to him now, though, as he led his men toward the Great Hall of Cambrai.

As Clovis and his men entered the city, piles of rough hewn timber and stacks of clay bricks indicated new construction sites just inside the defensive moat. Men were working. The town of Cambrai appeared to be prospering. The homes were in good repair, their high-pitched roofs well sealed with bark and sod.

The odors of the marketplace came to them long before the merchant's stalls came into view. The Franks inhaled deeply, enjoying the smell of freshly baked bread. The midday stride of the town was strong. Tradesmen entered and left the city, messengers skirted past them in haste and farmers brought their produce, all bearing witness to the health of Cambrai. Deeper in the town, the number of citizens increased, as did their activity. The townspeople looked vital—fit and well dressed.

Five men rode with Clovis, four of them hand-picked soldiers of the Home Guard, the professional warriors who reported directly to their chief. They were especially large men, of a size that would make the bands of robbers, waiting for easy prey by the main roads, think twice before attacking. And yet, the impression their size made was easily surpassed by the damage their skilled hands could inflict in battle. The men wore tight linen tunics that covered them down to their knees. Rectangular cloaks of green and red, drawn snug around their waists with leather belts, warded off the chill of fall. Their feet were covered with deer-skin boots, tied with straps that wrapped up over their calves.

The fifth man, Gerard, the Captain of the Home Guard, was shorter and stockier than his companions. He had a large nose that was only slightly camouflaged by his bushy mustache. His chin was weak and his thinning hair bore witness to his years. A sterling character and unwavering loyalty to Clovis had earned him not only the position of Captain of the Guard, but also the respect and friendship of Clovis. He had been in the Home Guard for ten years, fighting his first battles under the rule of Childeric, the father of Clovis. Now, Childeric was dead, Clovis was chief, and Gerard rode next to him.

The focus of the administrative life of Cambrai, the Great Hall, was appropriately situated in the center of town. Moving beyond a long row of connected homes and passing by the carts of produce, meats, and baked goods that filled the marketplace, the riders came to the notably large, free-standing building made all the more distinctive by the two guards positioned at the front entrance.

Both guards were unkempt, unshaven, wearing tattered garments, and apparently unconcerned with what was happening around them. One scratched at a scab on his hand while the other picked his nose and then looked at his finger, unable to find anything. But the guards were not so careless as to neglect their duty entirely. As the visitors

Chapter 1 A New Chief Emerges: 486-487 CE

halted their mounts in front of the disheveled soldiers, the scab-picker, without looking up from his hand, demanded, "Who calls?"

"Clovis, Chief of the Tournai Franks," was the reply. At the word, "Chief", the guards stood taller, and looked up at Clovis, straightening their weapons in respect to this ruler of Franks. Clovis tipped his head slightly to his right and said, "This is my commander, Gerard, and these men…" he turned his head to direct the guard's attention behind him, "…are soldiers of my Home Guard. I've come to see Ragnachar."

"One moment," said the second guard as he wiped his hand on his sleeve and entered the building.

Clovis and his men dismounted and tied their horses to a nearby oak.

"I don't expect I'll be long, Gerard," said Clovis as he straightened his cloak. "There's very little to discuss, really. Either he'll join us or he won't."

Gerard reached into a pouch which hung on his belt and withdrew a carrot. He stroked the neck of his horse with one hand, and offered the carrot with the other. "I'm certain he will," he said, calmly. He wanted to offer support to his new young chief. Gerard knew Clovis was capable of great things, he would likely accomplish much more than his father had, but he was inexperienced.

"I suspect you're right," said Clovis, warmed by his friend's confident tone. "If I know my cousin, he won't take long to convince—once he learns there may be profit."

"We'll be here," assured Gerard. The others voiced their agreement.

Clovis patted Gerard firmly on the shoulder and smiled.

Before anything else could be said, the guard who had earlier disappeared returned to usher Clovis into the presence of Chief Ragnachar. The guard held the door open as Clovis entered the hall.

It was a simple structure in spite of its size. It was comprised of only one large room with a beamed ceiling and four windows, two at each end of the hall. The windows let in a considerable amount of light, though the effect was still far short of the brightness of day. Clovis noticed the smell of the room before he could see the details. The walls were draped with skins of boar and deer, and the smell of game was strong. His eyes adjusted rapidly to the dim light of the room and he saw, against the wall, opposite the entrance, a throne situated between two windows. Looking into the daylight beyond, he couldn't tell if there was anyone in the throne or not. Turning to observe the rest of the surroundings Clovis saw tables along the sides of the hall bearing bowls of fruit and vegetables that failed to offset the ripe odor of the skins. Still, the food added a pleasant accent to the animal smell. Goblets were standing ready to be filled with wine. Then Clovis spied Ragnachar, seated at the table nearest the throne.

"Cousin Clovis! Good to see you!" Ragnachar arose and, holding a large apple in his hand, rolled his bulk around the table toward the younger chief. His belly showed between his shirt and his leggings, and he belched loudly before speaking. "I and my man, Farron, welcome you!" He swept his left hand toward a man lounging in a chair close by. Clovis glanced at him and bowed slightly in greeting, thinking that the man looked soft. He had no color to his skin, which made his narrow lips look especially red. "And you remember my brother, Ricchar?" He offered a further gesture, apple still in hand and then, as if the sight of the apple in his own grasp reminded him that the fruit was there, took a large bite from it.

"Of course," said Clovis as he bowed again.

"Greetings cousin," returned Ricchar from his place at the table, his lip curling in sarcasm.

Clovis noticed Ricchar's look and remembered the first and only time he'd met his cousin. The same sneer was on display the day Childeric was buried. At the time, Clovis was too young and preoccupied to know it, but today he decided he didn't like the man. He turned his attention back to Ragnachar and said, "It's been a long time."

"Yes…it has. It was at your father's burial, wasn't it?" Ragnachar paused, recalling an earlier day. The burial of Childeric was not an event to be forgotten. Leaders of the Franks had gathered from all over Gaul. He remembered standing with Chararic and Rignomer, his kinsmen who led tribes in Tongres and LeMans, respectively. They stood at the graveside in Tournai, in the cemetary on the high ground east of the river. Thirty horses were sacrificed in honor of Childeric, all at the same moment so the smell of blood wouldn't cause a stampede. There, along with the others, Ragnachar said good-bye to the most powerful member of their family, hiding his jealousy, impressed by the wealth buried with the dead leader, planning his strategy for dealing with the boy, Clovis, who would be chief in his father's place. The strategy, lacking support from his kindred, had long since been forgotten. Now Clovis was here. Returning to the moment, Ragnachar said, "What was it, five years ago? You've grown since then."

He took a long look at Clovis; he looked like his father. The lines of the young chief were muscular, and his square jaw accentuated a sharp narrow nose. His golden braid lay draped over his shoulder

Chapter 1 *A New Chief Emerges: 486-487 CE*

and across his chest, the end tied with a leather strap. "You're now…in your 20th year?"

"You have a good memory," said Clovis.

"How fast the years go by!" Ragnachar exclaimed, shaking his head. "And tell me, how is your mother?"

"She's well. I expect she'll outlive us all."

Ragnachar laughed. "Good, good. Yes, I'm sure she will." He took another bite of the apple and returned to his memory of Childeric's burial. Basina was across from him, on the opposite side of the grave, holding the arm of her son, Clovis, not quite clutching it, that would have been unseemly, but holding on, trying to offer comfort. She was not a Frank by birth and yet, that day, she was an example to all Franks, for her dignified grief gave strength to all, encouragement that, while the world had changed, it had not ended. He turned to Farron and said, "She's one of the loveliest women I've ever met!"

Farron was silent, but cocked his head and raised an eyebrow in, what seemed to Clovis to be a lewd display.

Ragnachar saw the look of distaste on the young chief's face and interjected, "But we don't have to stand all day. Come…" He led Clovis to the food-filled tables and distracted himself. He took one last bite of his apple before throwing the remains to the floor, then wasted no time in tearing off a chunk of bread from one of the several loaves that were already growing stale. He poured himself a full goblet of wine, offering Clovis nothing. Waving his goblet toward an empty chair, Ragnachar finally invited Clovis to sit.

"Tell me now, what brings you to Cambrai?"

Clovis helped himself to some wine and then settled into the chair he'd been offered. He lifted a bunch of grapes and popped one into his mouth. In a matter-of-fact way he said, "Battle."

Ragnachar's smile faded.

"Battle? Are you warring already?"

"I've been chief for five years, Ragnachar…five years of peace. It's not too soon."

"No, no, I didn't mean to suggest it was." Ragnachar looked at Farron, who shrugged and said nothing. Ragnachar pursed his lips, scratched his eyebrow and thought. After long consideration he continued, "Why would you intrude upon a peace that's been so…so constant?" He paused to belch. "And who would be your enemy? Surely not us?"

Before Clovis could answer, Ricchar asked, "You're not trying to walk in your father's footsteps too soon, are you, cousin?"

Clovis clenched his jaw and turned toward Ricchar as his face began to redden. "My father was a strong and brave man, Ricchar, and you do well to remember him. But remember, as well, he never fought for sport. He wanted to make a place for his people. If it hadn't been for Rome, his reach and rule would have extended much further. Maybe even you would have bowed to him."

"Clovis," said Ragnachar, trying to ease tensions that he could see were escalating too quickly, "my brother doesn't mean to offend. We could all say that our territory would have increased had it not been for Rome. But your brave father, was wise not to fight them. He would have lost."

Slowly and deliberately Clovis turned his face back to Ragnachar, keeping his eyes on Ricchar until his turn was complete.

"Perhaps," said Clovis, making an effort, even as he spoke, to calm his anger, "Perhaps then. But Rome is dead now…or at least dying. The Romans in Tournai see it. They're beginning to join MY army. Rome hasn't shown an interest in Gaul for years." Clovis paused, his look darkening. "And yet a Roman still rules in Gaul."

"Syagrius?"

"Yes."

Ragnachar's eyes widened and he gulped as he leaned forward in his chair.

"You intend to go to war against Syagrius?"

Clovis took a drink from his goblet and as the taste filled his mouth he nodded almost imperceptibly. There was, however, no mistaking his affirmation.

"You can't be serious!"

Clovis set his goblet down and wine sloshed out on the table. "Yes I can!" He spoke with a confidence that nearly persuaded Ragnachar that Clovis was in his right mind. Nearly, but not quite. "Syagrius has no right to rule," continued Clovis. "He governs on a false pretense. He pays no heed to his Emperor Zeno in the East, and yet he sits on the throne at Soissons!"

"But, Clovis, he has the claim of history. His father ruled in Soissons before him." Ragnachar knew it wasn't a convincing argument, and Clovis waved it off as soon as it had been spoken. Ragnachar was distraught by the plan. After all, Cambrai was doing well, better than most of the towns in northern Gaul. He didn't want to put that at risk. Still, he could think of no effective reasoning to dissuade Clovis. And so he asked again, this time with pleading in his voice, "Why must you bring battle to such a peaceful time?"

Chapter 1 *A New Chief Emerges: 486-487* CE

"Yes, indeed, why?" Farron said, sitting up on the lounge chair, as he spoke. "We do nicely, with only rare interference from Soissons. We even trade there. Why should we do anything that would disrupt that?"

Clovis turned toward Farron in feigned courtesy, but when Farron had completed his argument, as if to make it clear that his words had been ignored, Clovis made no expression, gave no gesture, offered no comment and turned his attention back to Ragnachar. "I've already enlisted the help of our cousin, Chararic, in Tongres. His men are hungry for battle. And a share of the spoils were sufficient to convince him."

"Spoils?"

Clovis smiled subtly. "Yes, Ragnachar, spoils. Riches are waiting in Soissons...not to mention land."

Ragnachar leaned back in his chair and, as he thought, he began to stroke his belly. Then, silently, he stood, walked around the table and sat on the edge of it, next to Clovis, stroking his mustache all the while.

"Mmm," hummed Ragnachar. "Perhaps this idea of yours deserves more thought." He crossed his arms deliberately, barely spanning his girth to where his stubby fingers could touch. Without looking around he said, "Farron, might we not benefit from such a venture?"

Farron leaned forward and poured himself some wine.

"Only in victory, my good Ragnachar, only in victory."

Clovis added, "Syagrius employs a considerable number of Franks. We may gain an advantage in them. I don't imagine they'll relish fighting against their brothers for the sake of a dead empire."

Ragnachar sighed heavily and gazed at the dirt floor. "The men do seem restless. They might welcome some warring." He looked at Clovis. "You say Chararic has agreed to join you?"

"So he says."

"Yes, so he says. But I've never quite trusted him."

"Nor have I, cousin," agreed Clovis. "But I do believe we can trust his greed."

"Spoils..." The Chief of Cambrai mused a long while. "I can't bear the thought of Chararic gaining from this," he said, at last.

"He will, you know, if he fights," said Clovis. "There's no doubt of that."

"No, I suppose not," said Ragnachar. He heaved a large sigh. The truth of his own greed was plaguing him. "There are always spoils, even in the smallest campaigns." He sighed again and said, "Can you give me just a moment?"

"Certainly."

As Ragnachar walked to the far end of the hall, Clovis reached for more grapes. Now it was Ragnachar's decision.

A damned inconvenient time to go to war, thought Ragnachar. And yet, his musings continued, it would be a mistake to decline involvement. If Clovis is destined to be at all like his father, thought Ragnachar as he turned and looked hard at the young chief, then it's wise to be his ally. There's no reason to believe that Clovis will do anything other than surpass his father as a great leader and warrior. This young Frank has charisma. Ragnachar admitted it. The minute Clovis walked into the Great Hall he could see it. He has a grasp of the political situation, he's right in saying that things are changing in Gaul. No one imagines that Rome will be conqueror or savior ever again. And, spoils? Spoils! Ragnachar took in a long, deep breath and let it out before he walked back to where Clovis and the others waited.

"It seems, cousin, we'll be splitting the spoils three ways instead of two. You can depend on my support."

Clovis gave one hard grunt of approval, stood and said, "I'll issue the challenge to Syagrius."

Farron was not surprised at Ragnachar's decision. He didn't generally trust him to make wise decisions, but he expected him to make the obvious ones. In this instance the two were one. Still, Farron didn't care for the prospect of going to war.

"Tell me, Clovis," he said, reaching out to brush away a roach that had found its way to the table, "without our help, would you have issued the challenge?"

Clovis turned to Farron, shook his head and grinned, saying nothing.

Ragnachar scowled at Farron, who, when he noticed the look, retreated into the safety of his chair like a scolded dog, licking his lips and offering no further comment. Ricchar, ready to ask the same question, saw the exchange and decided to hold his tongue.

Ragnachar, looked back at his cousin. "I'll get my people ready," he said, and bowed ceremoniously to his new partner in battle.

"I'll return with Chararic soon," said Clovis returning a less ostentatious bow. Then, with no further word, the young chief turned to leave offering only a wave in answer to Ragnachar who called, "Farewell."

Stepping past the guards, the crispness of autumn greeted Clovis. He took in a deep breath enjoying the invigorating chill as he approached his men.

"Any luck?" asked Gerard.

Chapter 1 *A New Chief Emerges: 486-487 CE*

"He's with us."

"Excellent!"

"It was easier than I'd hoped for. Even easier than it was with Chararic." Taking the reins of his horse from Gerard he paused to compare his two cousins. "They're both greedy. You know them, Gerard."

"Oh yes!" said the captain.

"But Ragnachar is not so bright as Chararic. More cautious, but too stupid to avoid being predictable. Chararic, on the other hand, is more of a problem. I need to watch him." Clovis patted his horse on the shoulder. "But for now, they're both with us."

"Excellent!" repeated Gerard. He knew numbers would be decisive in fighting the well-trained Romans. The stories his father told him of Attila's encounter with Rome had taught him that, long ago. Even if Rome was in decline, as people seemed to be saying, Gerard knew they were still deserving of respect on the field of battle.

The men mounted their horses and Clovis took in another deep draught of cold air. "Autumn is a good season for battle, Gerard. The men will stay fresh longer."

"Without a doubt," said Gerard.

The Franks left Cambrai, talking of war.

"He challenges me?"

Syagrius, the only remaining Roman ruler in Gaul, paced briskly in front of the large stone fireplace that warmed the main chamber of his Soissons palace. A fire was crackling, taking the chill off the room, a chill that was deeper with each new autumn day. At the end of every pass, he spun around, sending the tail of his long purple robe flying, tossing up clouds of dust that glowed orange, backlit by the fire. The challenge had only just arrived. The messenger who delivered it was being held for questioning, though there was no expectation that anything useful would come of the interrogation. The King's advisor, Aurelian, who would have to prepare a response to the challenge, stood by watching Syagrius seethe.

"He challenges me?" the incredulous Roman repeated.

Syagrius was a bigger man than Aurelian, and the advisor to the king had learned to stand back when the ruler was angry. An enraged Syagrius had once thrown a goblet, not at anyone or anything in particular, and Aurelian still wore the scar from that tantrum on his forehead.

"The Franks are a deceptive people, Aurelian," said Syagrius, continuing his pacing. "Barbarians! They live in tribes! Not in societies, mind you, but tribes! No kings or emperors for them. No, they rule themselves with chiefs! He shook his head,...barely civilized!"

Syagrius fumed. His usually handsome features took on a grim look. His jaw clenched, his lips tightened, his eyes narrowed, and a frown creased his brow. He stopped his pacing and looked into the fire. He recalled that day when he crested a hill to face the sight of his father's body, shaded by Childeric who stood over it. The corpse was all but unrecognizable, chunks of flesh missing from the form, mutilated by the father of Clovis. Now this insolent barbarian challenged him!

He turned and strode to a chair and sat down hard, his back to his advisor. "Clovis! His father died an easy death!" The muscles in his jaw tightened again as he considered what he'd come to know of Clovis. Since rising to power he'd been building his army. Every little town defeated or held for ransom gained him men and supplies. Syagrius struggled for a strategy that might offer him an advantage in battle. The picture of his father's lifeless form returned to him. "Clovis!" He spat the word.

The tension built in him and the lines in his broad forehead grew deeper. He took in a deep breath, his nostrils flaring, and he jumped up to pace again.

"Good God, Aurelian, these Franks take their enemies scalps!"

Aurelian resented the blanket statement. His wife, Idena, was a Frank. Mixed marriages were not unheard of, but neither were they common. Marrying a Frank had caused him his share of anguish. His own family had questioned the union. But he knew the Franks were more noble than most Romans would admit.

"That doesn't hold true any longer, my lord," he said. "It's been two generations since that's been seen." The correction was one he felt compelled to offer, though it was not received kindly. Aurelian saw the look of growing fury on his King's face, and he stepped backward in caution.

"At least, my lord," he said in a softer voice, trying to make amends for his objection, "the challenge is a decent one. One would think a Roman wrote it."

Syagrius stopped to consider the assertion and turned his gaze to the floor. The glazed tiles that lined the hearth were worn from his pacing. Over the years, many hours had found him here in thought, walking back and forth as he tested the solidity of ideas, the treachery of possibilities, the hope of opportunity. Now the blue and gold squares were faded, no longer glossy. He looked up at his advisor.

"Yes, Aurelian, he was civilized enough to grant us the choice of place and time. Perhaps this is a good thing. If Clovis is defeated, these little excursions he uses to build his army will stop. He can't really believe his savages will stand a chance against the troops of Rome!"

The word "savages" struck Aurelian harder than any goblet Syagrius could have thrown. He winced as he thought of his wife and her family. Though not of the Salian tribe, the tribe of Clovis, they were Franks nonetheless. He would never have thought the word, "savages" had any application. If anything, they were gracious and elegant. They were stately in bearing and had as much a sense of honor as did any Roman he knew—more than most. No, they were not savages.

"We'll accept his challenge, Aurelian," Syagrius said, smiling, "Yes. We'll accept it with relish!"

"Yes, my lord. Where will we meet them?"

Syagrius walked toward a tall window opposite the fireplace. Dwarfed by the carved stone arch, he leaned on a pillar, gazed out upon the gentle slopes that surrounded the city. Soissons rested in a basin, forest all around. "I know just the place," he said, adding a confident smack of his lips. "These Franks are pagans, Aurelian. I know where we might gain an even greater advantage than we already have." His lips peeled back from his teeth, forming a wicked smile that Aurelian didn't see. "Clovis is undoubtedly ready and it won't take long for our men to prepare. Inform them that we'll meet near Coucy...two weeks from today. The sooner Clovis falls, the better!"

From Soissons, the battlefield was a short day's ride north. The hills grew steeper for nearly an hour's ride, then they leveled off into a wide plain. In order to familiarize themselves with the site, Syagrius and his men arrived one full day before the fighting was to begin. Scouts reported that the Franks were nearby, though further details were few. The battlefield was as Syagrius remembered it and his strategy, direct and simple, did not change. His commanders walked with him to high ground to receive their final instructions. Little planning was necessary. Syagrius had chosen this field of war well and his commanders needed little convincing.

A simple camp was established. Few provisions accompanied them. There would be no siege, no prolonged campaign. There was no need to prepare for a long stay.

On the morning of the battle, at the first light of dawn, the troops of Rome assembled, weapons ready.

A lonely stone church stood on the crest of the hill where Syagrius watched his troops gather. The tiny sanctuary had been a landmark in the area for nearly thirty years, inhabited now by a reclusive ascetic who lived off the generosity of God's earth and the occasional gifts of God's children. Stirred by the noisy preparations for battle, the hermit peered down over the army of Syagrius and then out to the plain where many of the warriors would draw their last desperate breaths.

As the sun rose, the church cast a shadow over the men who stood ready now, armed for war. The morning sun climbed, and the rough cross atop the church threw its own shadow, that inched through the ranks of soldiers. Those who needed to vomit away their tension, mostly the newer recruits, had already done so. They were quiet now, contemplating.

Syagrius had no intention of risking his own life, but he was in his battle dress: red tunic, chain mail, armor, and helmet. He couldn't be certain if it was cowardice or prudence that convinced him, but as far as he was concerned, it was enough for the men to see him readied for battle. The years since his earliest fighting on the Loire, and the lingering pain of his father's death by the sword had taught him that life was not to be risked flippantly. He leaned forward on his stallion and looked north, beyond the trees, to where the land began to rise again. In the distance, the shadow of forest land offered a dark backdrop for the day. Looking at the line of trees marking the Roman road that led to Cambrai, he said to himself, "There...they'll come from those trees." There was no doubt about it. Syagrius knew that somewhere, behind the line of oaks, Clovis stood gazing back at him, across an expanse of land that Syagrius knew would serve Rome well. He sat back and smiled, satisfied.

To his left he could look down on his troops, standing in rows, ready for the order to attack. Though he was confident of their skills, he was concerned that almost a third of them were Franks. Would they give their best? Indeed, thought Syagrius, would any of his men give their best? Since the news that Rome had fallen to the barbarian, Odoacer, too many of the men had seemed infected with a sense of futility.

Ten years had gone by since that final blow to the great city of the Caesars. Odoacer, leader of a sufficient army of Germanic opportun-

Chapter 1 *A New Chief Emerges: 486-487 CE*

ists, men who had once looked to Attila, claimed an easy victory from Orestes and his son, Romulus, the boy Emperor. The new rulers moved the affairs of government north, from Rome to Ravenna, and Rome, as his father had known it, was no more. Zeno, in Constantinople, was the official Emperor, but he had little interest in Gaul, and almost no influence as far as anyone could tell. The name, Zeno, was never invoked to lend authority to a cause. Even the attempt to act in the name of Zeno would have met with confusion, or laughter, depending upon where in Gaul one made the gesture. These last Roman defenders in Gaul were feeling more and more isolated and less certain of their mission. Syagrius hoped that the prospect of victory would provide fuel for whatever fires remained in his men's bellies.

The day was clear and crisp. A steady breeze blew from west to east and there was not the slightest hint of haze, even to the farthest horizon. Steam blew from the mouths of the soldiers and the nostrils of the horses. Those on foot stamped their feet to keep warm and to release some of the anxiety that grew with every minute. The dew had not fully left the ground when a murmur of observance arose. Hands pointed north and all eyes followed them to the sight of nearly six thousand Franks coming through the trees onto the battlefield.

Syagrius was well acquainted with the look of Frankish warriors: tall, muscular, physically well-trained. Their light complexion and blond hair fooled no one into thinking they were soft. Nothing could be further from the truth. Syagrius had witnessed them in action against the Saxons and he begrudgingly admitted to himself that, aside from the troops of Rome, they were the most intimidating warriors he'd ever seen—more determined and proud than any people he'd ever known. Their strength in battle was almost legendary and it was certain they would not give up without a good fight.

They were not, however, as well outfitted as the Romans. Nor were they as colorful. A scanty coat of mail and kite-shaped shields were all the Franks had in the way of protection. Aside from that, they wore only leather and the familiar linen or woolen tunics. The Romans, on the other hand, had the advantage of helmets and armored skirts as well as more refined mail and shields.

The Franks were almost entirely on foot, as far as Syagrius could tell. It appeared that only a few commanders, no more than fifty, were mounted on horseback. The men walked out into the open looking completely unorganized and Syagrius smiled as he watched their chaotic approach.

"It looks like easy work today, eh men?" he shouted to his soldiers. Their spirits seemed to rise slightly as the possibility of a rout presented itself. There was joking in the ranks and Syagrius thought the men were standing taller.

"Horsemen, ready!" he commanded.

The men on horseback brought their steeds forward a few steps and focused their attention on their leader.

"Now, Clovis," muttered Syagrius, "we'll see what you're made of!"

Clovis briefed his chieftain cousins. "They'll attack with the horses first," he said, proud of his knowledge of Roman tactics. His father dealt with the Romans on more than one occasion and Clovis had learned Roman strategies from his father's stories. Their tactics were admirable, and no one could deny that the Romans had been successful in their warring. But they were not insurmountable. "My men will take the fore. I've taught them how to deal with horses. My grandfather, Merovech, your kinsman, fought *Attila's* horsemen!" Clovis could see that Ragnachar and Chararic were not convinced. The sight of the Roman horsemen, more numerous than they'd ever seen, conjured images of deadly chaos. A small collection of horses they were used to, but an army of mounted soldiers was too much. With scolding in his voice Clovis said, "I'll deal with the horsemen. Stay in the trees until they've done their worst."

Ragnachar and Chararic willingly agreed.

Clovis looked over his shoulder, then back at his cousins. "My men are taking the field. Make your men ready."

"May the gods be with you, cousin," said Ragnachar.

"Yes," Chararic said, sounding distant and less encouraging, "yes...Gods be with you."

Clovis turned, mounted his horse and, leaving the road, broke through the trees to join his men. His hands started to sweat. Little skirmishes he'd known in the past had taught him a great deal, but this battle was different. This was not another marauding band of thieves or a party of disgruntled Franks. This was Rome.

Ragnachar watched Clovis for a moment, envious of his certainty, and then returned to his men to prepare them for battle. Chararic went to ready his men for betrayal, if the need arose.

Clovis had covered only half the distance from the trees to his troops when he noticed they'd stopped in their tracks and were arguing among themselves. The men in front were refusing to go further, while those in back were trying to push ahead, unaware that there was a problem. When confused and anxious men broke through the paralyzed front ranks, at last able to view the field of battle, their looks turned from those of curiosity to those of horror. Gerard, on his horse trying to rally the men, was having little success in assuring the soldiers. Clovis knew he had only moments. A disorganized look was one thing, but true confusion was another matter altogether. Syagrius would attack as soon as he perceived it. He dug in his heels and steered his horse toward the nearest man.

"The problem!" Clovis demanded.

"Look!" was the simple and frightened reply. The soldier pointed to a point midway between the two armies. And Clovis saw. In the middle of the battle ground lay a circle of Pagan sepulchers. It was holy ground. The men wouldn't want to offend the Gods. Even as his fury at Syagrius grew, Clovis found himself impressed with the tactic. He could see the dismay on the faces of his men and he knew he had to act.

"Don't fear the Gods!" he shouted, riding back in forth before his soldiers. "Odin has given us this day for battle!" He hit the flanks of his mount and rode into the burial ground, bring his horse up to stand between two of the sepulchres. "We'll have the victory," he shouted, "and the Romans will pay for warring here! Have courage!"

The men shook off their panic and began to focus on fighting. Clovis hoped it was enough, for though the Gods might be willing to grant victory to the Franks, he suspected they were not willing to grant them more time for words of comfort. Clovis knew Syagrius would not let this moment pass by without taking advantage of it. His Roman counterpart had watched the Franks enter the field and then stop in fear. It was his cue and he didn't miss it. Six hundred armed and mounted Roman soldiers heeded the order to charge and descended the hill, racing toward the distraught Franks.

Clovis turned from his men to see the horsemen's charge. He looked back at his warriors and gave what he knew would be a critical command, "In groups as I've taught you—twenty square—quickly!" He rode back from the tombs, across the field, repeating the command as he went.

The men crowded into groups as rapidly as they could, protecting their own horsemen, their commanders, who were now on the inside of the groupings. Packing themselves tightly together in a squatting position, pointing their javelins upward and outward, only the outermost men had any freedom of movement. They felt vulnerable to any weapons that might be thrown into their midst but they had been assured by their chief that the horsemen would wield swords and not javelins.

The horsemen arrived just as the hurried shuffling was completed. The Romans broke formation and circled the 15 groups of kneeling Franks, unable to reach more than the outer circle of warriors. When the opportunities presented themselves, when horses slowed or when they drew sufficiently near to the huddled soldiers, the Franks on the fringe, two and three at a time, would strike out at their legs, cutting at the animal's tendons, bringing the riders down to meet the point of a sword.

Unprepared for such an organized response from a band of infidels, Syagrius watched, immobile and amazed, as two-thirds of his horses and horsemen were cut down. What tactic was this from the Franks? Masses of ready targets was what he expected, not obstacles that horse could not challenge nor speed conquer.

As the surviving horsemen retreated in confusion, Syagrius came out of his stupor.

"Attack! Attack!" he shouted.

His foot soldiers, angered by the boldness of the Franks, moved as a trained unit, row upon row, marching resolutely toward the momentarily triumphant enemy.

Clovis was ready and rallied his men. The Franks fanned out to face the Romans. They made a check of their mail, their weapons and their nearest companions, making certain that the men they were trusting to fight beside them had escaped the sword.

At the same time, Ragnachar, looking more than slightly foolish as his broad form weighed down his horse, led his men through the trees. For nearly half a league, the trees issued forth fresh and eager soldiers. Quickly the numbers of the Franks swelled from 6000 to 10,000. The men, already on the field shouted a cheer when they saw their reinforcements coming. Clovis watched their approach with mixed emotions. On one hand, he felt satisfaction that Ragnachar had timed his advance so well. On the other hand, when Chararic and his men didn't appear, anger flared in Clovis, his distrust of the man confirmed.

Syagrius remained on the hill by the church. Watching the addition of Ragnachar's Franks to the field of battle, he took in a deep breath and exhaled slowly. Still, he thought, my troops are well trained and not yet outnumbered. The Romans continued on, marching directly through the circle of sepulchers, now forgotten by the Franks.

Chapter 1 *A New Chief Emerges: 486-487 CE*

The hermit's eyes widened at the unfolding scene as he watched from his perch atop the chapel. His pulse quickened and his face twisted into a mask of pain. Many of God's children were about to die.

Ready for battle the Franks waited, testing their javelins for balance and their franciscas for weight. The francisca, a single bladed throwing ax, was a deadly weapon. Instinctively the Franks knew when the time was right, and, simultaneously, nearly 4000 hand axes went aloft next to another 2500 javelins, landing with devastating effect into the tightly grouped Romans.

Franciscas tore through armor and flesh, embedding themselves into skulls and torsos. Javelins impaled those who had allowed a fatal inch of error as they dodged the weapons. Those felled by the missiles hit the ground, adding a dull drumming sound to the cacophony of screams brought on in the first moments of battle against the Franks. Roman ranks scattered to regroup from the attack. Franks drew their short bladed scramasax swords and ran into the fray.

Syagrius flinched at the first onslaught, and was worried momentarily when he saw his men scattering. But almost immediately his worry disappeared when the battle shifted to the sword. After all, he thought, with swords, no one can match a Roman. This stage of the battle promised to be especially bloody as Franks, brutal as they were, fought against men who were clearly their match, and more, when it came to sword-fighting. Syagrius smiled wickedly, ready to enjoy the slaughter of Clovis.

It was then, as his men pushed the Franks back toward the trees that he noticed a large number of his own soldiers holding back. Nearly one-third of his men were Franks, men he'd decided to place at the rear, to insure that the more enthusiastic, and probably more loyal warriors would take the lead in battle. Franks had never balked at fighting Franks, so there was sufficient reason to think these men would fight with honor now. As the battle raged, however, these Franks stopped at the circle of pagan sepulchers, unable to go further.

"Fight, you bastards!" Syagrius yelled, "You're not still afraid of pagan gods are you?" But his voice wasn't heard. The Franks, the soldiers whom Syagrius had never fully trusted, whom he considered savages, chose not to raise their swords against their brothers—at least not on holy ground.

The hermit stared in wonder at the scene; Syagrius watched in disbelief.

Chararic's men watched the battle from the trees along the road. The Franks were strong, but it was clear that the Romans were the better swordsman.

"We're not going to fight?" one commander asked.

"Not yet," said Chararic, intent as he watched the battle develop. He leaned forward, his mouth open, his eyes squinting.

"It looks like we could help."

"Not yet!" Chararic snapped. "We'll wait..." he hesitated, "...until we're certain that no trap has been laid...that no other Romans are waiting to attack from another direction."

"From where, sir? We can see the whole plain."

"We wait!" screamed Chararic, causing the commander to withdraw. Chararic was not in the mood for defeat and he would hold his tribe back until he was convinced that victory was assured. He watched the battle intently, his respect for Clovis growing as the fighting drew on.

The men of Syagrius continued to pour down the slope on the opposite side of the plain, a thick mass of brown that shimmered with flashes of newly sharpened blades. The front ranks were already in combat when the warrior mass separated in two. Hesitant soldiers, holding back, gave Chararic the confidence he needed.

"We go to help our brothers!" he cried, and Chararic led his men out of the trees and into battle.

Still atop his horse, Syagrius rose to his feet in his stirrups as a new stage of the battle unfolded before him. The horsemen had failed, the order of the ranks had broken too quickly, his Franks were refusing to fight and now, the final blow: more barbarians had emerged from the trees. With a third of his troops essentially out of the battle and with Chararic's 2000 men joining in, the Romans were now seriously outnumbered. The addition of more Franks to the field brought a battle cry from the Franks who were already fighting. With renewed vigor they began to push the Romans back and it became obvious that Rome was going down to defeat. As that realization broke upon Syagrius, he understood as well, that he would lose his throne. He settled back into his saddle, dumbfounded.

The Roman ruler was alone now. The commanders who had watched the battle with him were now in the midst of the fighting, trying to help. Their efforts would be in vain. It would be a short conflict. Battles were rarely prolonged. The weight of the weapons and the energy expended precluded lengthy engagements. The cool

Chapter 1 *A New Chief Emerges: 486-487 CE*

weather on this day had promised that the warring could continue longer than usual, but the defeat of the Romans would come well before exhaustion would.

The sun was high enough now that the shadow of the church was nearly gone from the ridge, called back within the walls of the chapel itself. Only the shadow of the church's cross still fell on the ground. As the shadow crept onward, placing Syagrius at the base of the cross, he surrendered to the obvious conclusion that he must flee. But where? he thought. There is no Rome. Where? The honor of sovereignty was his only hope and he made the decision to flee south to the Visigoths. The last 30 years or so had been generally peaceful with them. Perhaps the new king, young Alaric, would give him refuge.

He noticed the hermit gazing down on him from his place on the church. Even he knows, thought Syagrius. Even he knows it's over. The hermit's countenance offered passivity and nothing more. Syagrius looked away from the man to peer once again at the ever more disturbing scene of the battle. His men were beginning to disperse, running for their lives. His eyes filled with tears of frustration. Knowing no other option, Syagrius turned his horse and bolted, leaving the last sounds of the battle behind him.

It didn't take long for word of the defeat to reach Soissons. Syagrius fled south, driving his horse mercilessly. Skirting Soissons, he stopped in a small village to the southwest, hiring a messenger to enter Soissons and instruct his advisor, Aurelian, or if he was unavailable, the bishop, to make arrangements for getting the royal family out of the city and to a rendezvous in Orléans. Time was critical. Knowing that any delay threatened his own safety as well, Syagrius didn't wait for an answer, but continued south, past Paris and on.

The runner arrived at the palace in Soissons, and was led by a guard to the hall where administrative matters were addressed. The messenger, still sweaty from the journey shivered in the cool room. There were embers in the fireplace, but only the last dying coals of an earlier blaze. The boy paced to keep warm as the wait lengthened.

"Aurelian is attending to an errand, I'm afraid," said a man who broke into the room already speaking, "though you are welcome to wait for him."

"No sir. If this Aurelian is not available, I'm to go to the bishop."

The information brought nothing but a disinterested nod from the man who now pointed the way to the door.

Glad to be moving again, the runner hurried on to the cathedral to deliver the message to Principius, the bishop of Soissons. There, the runner was directed to the Bishop's residence where a well built fire offered warmth as well as welcome. He was ushered into the presence of the bishop in a matter of minutes.

Those who were familiar with Remigius, the bishop of Reims, agreed that Principius looked much like him. They were both lanky, yet dignified in their bearing and both carried the same long, slightly hooked nose and pointed chin. The similarity struck no one as unusual, being that the two men were brothers. Principius was the younger and was glad to live in his brother's shadow. He had neither his brother's ambition nor his talent, but he served well as the bishop of Soissons, administering the business of the Church with sufficient quietude so that the people of Soissons generally did what was required of them with minimal grumbling.

Now, in the garments which commanded the respect of all who came into his presence, the clothes of a bishop, a white robe with gold trim, heavy and elegant in its abundant folds, Principius welcomed the runner whose duties required, it appeared, great anxiousness.

"What is your business today, my son?" asked Principius, kindly.

"Please sir," the boy began, bowing and addressing the bishop in the most formal way he knew, "King Syagrius asks your indulgence and favor. He asks that you send his wife and son to meet him in Orléans. He's going there now."

Instantly Principius knew something was wrong. His look changed from one of gentle and casual interest to one of intense concern.

"Aren't our men in battle? Have they returned?"

"I don't know, sir. I've only just come from my home, west of here, where Syagrius hired me to deliver this message."

"Was anyone with him?"

"No, sir. He was alone. He was in haste and made it clear that the message was urgent."

Principius was certain now that his worst fears were being confirmed.

"Yes,...urgent," he said, his head spinning at the implications. He took a quick shallow breath and sniffed loudly. "You've delivered your message, my son, and you have my thanks. I'll honor the King's request." The boy bowed, thinking his work was done, but as he was rising from the bow Principius continued, "There's another message I'd like for you to carry. Are you up to it?"

"Yes," said the boy, though he was beginning to wish he hadn't become involved.

"This message is for Bishop Remigius in Reims." He paused a moment and looked at the messenger closely, trying to determine if he was ready to hear this message. The boy stood attentive, and Principius saw a lad of character. He believed the boy was not likely to falter under this or any news. "Tell him that Soissons has fallen to Clovis and seek his blessing for our city."

The young messenger's eyes widened a bit but he didn't lose his composure. Principius had him repeat the message once, arranged compensation for him and then sent him out to fulfill his charge.

As the messenger departed, an aide entered the Bishop's chambers.

"Father, a soldier of the guard has arrived and requests an audience."

Principius nodded and frowned. The entire guard had followed Syagrius into battle.

"Sooner than I expected," mumbled the bishop.

"Excuse me?" inquired the aide.

"Nothing. Never mind. Yes, send him in."

Principius already knew what the soldier would say. The Franks would be arriving soon.

Toulouse. Syagrius always imagined he would be here under different circumstances. Now it was his refuge in exile. No news had come from Soissons since he'd brought his wife and son to this place, and he wondered, each day, how his city was faring. As the fall grew into winter, though, Syagrius and his family became increasingly content with their state of affairs. His wife, Rosamund was settling in nicely and Julius had already found playmates in the court. The child king, Alaric II, named for his ancestor who had gained his fame by sacking Rome, received them with honor and provided them with a residence befitting a visiting ruler. Two servants were supplied to maintain the eight rooms and provide for the needs of the distinguished guests. The king of the Visigoths willingly accepted the cost of the arrangement.

Alaric didn't mind paying because, even though the concept of "Rome" no longer carried any substantial meaning, it still had value in the eyes of the general public who remembered the authority Rome once wielded, and the idea of Rome still held a great deal of romance for the young king. Though his advisors had been quick to recommend giving Syagrius sanctuary, even at the young age of twelve, Alaric was not blind to the potential profit of such a course. Even if it was an illusion, Alaric would gain respect from the people if he was seen as an ally of Rome. However, it rapidly became apparent that the advantages of the arrangement were to decay for both Alaric and Syagrius.

Late one winter day, a messenger arrived in the court of the king. Alaric sat on his throne, his black hair framing eyes that seemed set too wide. He was beginning to show signs of manhood. A stray whisker or two hung on his face and his shoulders were already broadening. But in spite of these early signs, Alaric was still a boy. He sat in a throne that was too big for him, surrounded by advisors who were ready to whisper recommendations into his ear. He looked at the man before him.

"You have a message?"

"I bring word to the king of the Visigoths from Clovis, son of Childeric, leader of the Franks, conqueror of Soissons." The messenger was uncomfortable, young and new in the service of Clovis. He was uncertain of his fate, feeling unprotected and isolated. Alaric noted his uneasiness and let him sweat for a moment. The visitor glanced nervously around the room. The throne-room was sumptuous, filled with tapestries, urns and statues that had accumulated from generations of victories. The plunder evoked an impressive list of names: Euric, Ataulf, Theodoric and, among the many, the great king, Alaric I. The surroundings offered a richness few in the world knew. The young king enjoyed the wealth but had yet to fight in his first battle, was yet to claim his own booty. Until that day, he was learning his role as a diplomat, and he especially enjoyed the power to intimidate that came with his title. But enough was enough.

"Go on."

"You have Syagrius, formerly of Soissons, in your care?"

It was not odd that Clovis would have discovered the whereabouts of Syagrius during the last two months. Alaric was not surprised at that. Still, as his whispering advisors constantly warned, there was no need to reveal too much too soon. He leaned back in his throne, looking relaxed.

"And if I do?"

"Clovis demands that you surrender him."

"Clovis demands that I surrender him, does he? Hmmmm."

An advisor leaned over to the young king, whispering, "We have been expecting this, Alaric."

Chapter 1 *A New Chief Emerges: 486-487* CE

The king waved his advisor away and again spoke to the messenger, "Can you tell me why, if I did hold Syagrius, I would want to turn him over to this…Clovis?"

"Even now, my lord, Clovis approaches from the north and he promises to lay siege to the city if you don't deliver him."

A look of concern flashed across Alaric's face; a look that he quickly erased, though without the ease of a more seasoned ruler. With a quick gesture he kept his advisors beyond whispering range. He didn't need them now. He considered the fact that this Frankish chief had defeated trained Roman troops…no small accomplishment. It suggested that he might very well be able to make good on a military threat.

"You'll have my answer in the morning," said Alaric abruptly. Then, in a more congenial tone, he added, "Until then, consider yourself our guest." No reason to be rude, one advisor was constantly pointing out. In time, decency may bring its own reward.

Morning dawned clear and cold, unveiling, as one looked north from the city of Toulouse, a view of 8000 Frankish soldiers gathering along the sparkling dew-covered bank of the Garonne river.

Up early, roused by one of his advisors, Alaric went to the castle walls and took in the scene with bleary eyes.

"Damn!" he said out loud to himself, "I have no quarrel with these Franks!" He thought about his responsibility to Syagrius, a ruler who had sought safety in his court. Put in the same circumstances, he would seek such refuge himself. Yet, he thought, who now, can do me more harm? There was no need for an advisor to answer that question. He turned and called to a nearby soldier.

"Yes, my Lord?"

"Collect two guards and bring them with you to meet me where our guest, Syagrius, is staying."

"Yes, sir." The man bowed slightly and turned to obey his orders.

Alaric watched the soldier until he was out of sight, then he turned to look again at the mass of Franks assembling before the walls of his city. He shook his head in frustration, one last time, before making his way toward the quarters he'd provided for the last Roman ruler in Gaul.

Alaric's creased brow betrayed the disquiet he felt, worry more profound than children ought to know. There was an aide at his side, ready to offer advice if it was required. But that was little comfort.

Being warmly received into the house of Syagrius made his task all the more difficult. Rosamund, having spent most of her life as the wife of a ruler, playing almost no domestic role, had shown noteworthy skill in making the residence comfortable and charming. Adorning every window were linen curtains, drawn back now with white ribbons, allowing the morning light into the room. Sunlight fell on brightly colored rugs which covered the stone floors. The furniture, though simple, was attractive and arranged well. Green and rose tinted glass vases throughout the house were filled with dried flowers. Animal skins graced the walls, making the rooms warm and inviting.

"You're up early, my King," said Rosamund. "Can you join us for breakfast?"

Syagrius rose from his place as Alaric entered his home and, in the same moment, lost any interest in food. He knew immediately, from Alaric's look, that something was wrong.

"No, Rosamund," said Alaric, "I didn't come to eat." He looked at Syagrius and hesitated.

Syagrius didn't have to ask what this early morning visit meant. He saw his royal guardian falter, and he knew.

"Clovis?" he asked.

Syagrius had never imagined Clovis would ignore him. No good conqueror would allow his enemy to live, only to rise up against him later. At least not if there was a way to end the threat. He'd been hopeful, though…foolishly hopeful.

Alaric looked at Rosamund and the boy Julius. The young son of Syagrius had endeared himself to the king. Alaric had thought on more than one occasion that they might have been good brothers. That kind of relationship was not likely now. He looked back at Syagrius, and, with an obvious facial contortion, made his desire clear that they go elsewhere to continue the discussion. The Roman just shook his head, as if to say, "let us deal with this together." Alaric acquiesced.

"Yes," said Alaric, "it's Clovis. He's outside the walls." Syagrius closed his eyes and tightened his lips almost to a smile as he received the news. He sat back down and took in a deep, staccato breath. Unable to look at Syagrius, Alaric stared out the window as he said, "You'll be delivered to him this afternoon."

Rosamund gasped at the words and Julius went to her, confused, seeking the comfort of his mother's touch. Together they waited, silent. Syagrius opened his eyes to look at his wife and son, then back at Alaric. "I understand," he said. "I would probably do the same." He heaved a sigh of acceptance, sat taller and asked, "Will there be a place here for my family?"

"They're welcome to stay," said Alaric, trying to sound helpful. "They will be cared for. I'll see to it."

"I thank you," said Syagrius as he bowed solemnly. Alaric blushed.

"I can't give you much time," said the king. "Use well what moments you have." After an awkward pause the king added, "I'm sorry." He then left Syagrius to be with his family, posting two guards outside his door.

"You could escape! You could go at night and we could…" Rosamund's plea was cut short by the sad smile on her husband's shaking head. There was no escape. Once there might have been, when he could have taken his own life. Though once honored by Rome, now suicide was an escape the Church denied him and one he feared besides. He shook his head again. There was no sense in wasting these last few moments talking about escape. Instead, they spent the last precious hours together, talking about the years they had shared—good years. And they spoke of their son's future. And they held each other and kissed each other and in the end, they all cried.

"I trust your journey's been pleasant?" asked Clovis. He smiled mockingly at his prisoner. "You'll be home soon." Bound in chains that cut into his wrists, fatigued from the three-week journey which took him nearly the entire length of Gaul, a haggard and delirious Syagrius barely acknowledged his captor. His eyes rolled up into his head as he tried to lift his face and then he slumped forward again, saved from falling off his horse by ropes that held him to his mount. Clovis laughed and patted Syagrius on the top of his head with false affection.

Gerard rode behind, respectfully. Childeric had never mocked an enemy so. It didn't suit Clovis, but Gerard knew better than to say anything.

It had been an onerous trip for Syagrius. Much of it had been spent watching his captors pillage and loot the small towns they encountered along the trek north. The churches lost the most as they held more valuables than the people. Still, in spite of that, the people suffered more. Cattle, grain, riches and women were all taken as if they were the looter's own. And the Franks felt no remorse as they increased their spoils. If anything, they felt inconvenienced when they found themselves in need of another wagon. Looting was one of the glories that came with being a soldier. Wealth was only a part of it. The soldiers took almost as much satisfaction in discovering what people would try to hide as they did in taking it from them. Since defeating Syagrius, the Franks had filled wagon after wagon with spoils that would be divided among them when they returned home. Syagrius had watched it all with sorrow. It had been a painful journey.

"No, it won't be long now, Syagrius," Clovis continued to ridicule his prisoner. "Soon your people will know beyond question that you are conquered. Tonight we camp beyond Reims, and the day after tomorrow we'll present you to the people of Soissons."

Syagrius heard the words through a haze. He knew that once he arrived in Soissons, he would be lucky to see more than one sunrise. He thought of Rosamund and Julius, and the fog of unconsciousness engulfed him.

The Franks celebrated in camp that night. The looting of Reims had been particularly rewarding. Of all the churches they'd seen on their journey homeward, the Cathedral of Reims was the largest. And that meant there was more wealth in the town. Aside from the expected jewels and coins, more silver was found there than in any of the other cities they had plundered. Candlesticks, ornate plates, chalices and bowls were snatched up eagerly by the marauding Franks.

A circle of smaller camps surrounded the larger camp of Clovis. The arrangement was efficient and practical. On the edge of one of the outer camps, as men sat eating fresh venison and drinking plundered wine, a guard shouted a warning. Instantly the men rose, swords drawn, ready to fight. Figures of four horsemen materialized as they came within reach of the fire's glow. The horsemen were unarmed, asking only to speak with Clovis.

After a careful look, the Franks decided that the riders were not dangerous, but they continued to watch the strangers carefully, as they led them to the inner camp. A runner went ahead to alert Clovis, and as the visitors arrived, the chief emerged from his tent, warm from victory and wine.

"Greetings friends, how can I help you?"

"You're Clovis?" one of the riders asked.

"I am," said the King of the Franks. Then, with an inquiring look, Clovis asked, "And you are…?"

Chapter 1 *A New Chief Emerges: 486-487 CE*

"I am Maccolus. I and my friends," he gestured to the others who rode with him, "serve the Church of our Lord and Savior, Jesus Christ."

Maccolus was a solidly built man, not fat but husky. His head was balding and he wore a closely cropped beard. Through it, Clovis saw a serene face, a visage of peace, a man of confidence.

"A pleasure to meet you, Maccolus...you, and your friends." He bowed slightly to them. "Again, how can I help you?"

"We beseech you, Clovis, ruler of the Franks, hear a message from Remigius, bishop of Reims."

"I'd be pleased to hear it," said Clovis with a refined graciousness rare among the Franks. His father, having acquired the powerful skill of tact through his own dealings with the Romans, had taught the skill to his son. It was clear that the greetings had passed and diplomacy had begun. "But come," he said, putting on the image of the gracious host, "you must be tired. Let your horses rest and join me by the fire."

Maccolus accepted the invitation for himself and his men. They dismounted their steeds and followed the warrior chief, seated themselves around the central fire of the camp and, for a moment, enjoyed the warmth in silence. Bread and wine were brought out and the priests from Reims respectfully accepted the hospitality.

"Now, this message," said Clovis.

"Yes," said Maccolus through a swallow. He turned to face Clovis and wiped his mouth clean before he continued. "Your men have looted the city of Reims...and the church."

"Yes, I know," replied Clovis "but surely you didn't come here to tell me what I already know?"

"No, no. Nor is this a challenge. You are our ruler now." Clovis smiled at the words. "But I do come to ask, on the Bishop's behalf, a favor regarding the looting."

"Go on."

"Among the many things that your soldiers took from Reims, you'll find a silver bowl that once rested on the altar of the Cathedral. The bowl has special meaning to our people, and Remigius requests that you return it to the church."

"That's all? One bowl?"

"That one bowl would be more than sufficient," said Maccolus. "It was a gift to the people of the church. If you could see to its return, I'm sure the people of Reims would be grateful." The three companions bowed their heads in unison, affirming what Maccolus had said.

"Tell me more about this bowl." Clovis leaned back and made himself comfortable. "What makes it so special?"

"As I said, it was a gift. It was given to the church by St. Martin of Tours, himself." It was obvious by his tone, that Maccolus thought that explained everything.

"I don't know this Martin," said Clovis slowly.

Maccolus barely blinked his surprise and in his next breath said, "He was a warrior, much like you, who saw a vision of our Lord, Jesus. Then, he turned to a life of faith. He fought the heretics and performed many miracles. He's revered among the people, and," as if to remind Clovis of the reason they's come to see him, he added, "the loss of the bowl has wounded us all deeply."

Clovis looked into the fire and considered the request. The name of Saint Martin was unfamiliar to Clovis. But the name of Remigius was a different matter. He's well respected and powerful, he thought. What's one silver bowl in comparison to his favor? But, he asked himself, will the men allow it? After all, it is their booty, not mine. And yet, he mused further, perhaps I've earned a favor or two from them.

He looked up from the flames and into the face of his guest. "Follow me to Soissons, Maccolus, if you're able, you and your men." Clovis looked at the others. "When we get there we'll be dividing the treasures we've taken. And, if fortune grants me the bowl, I'll do as the bishop asks."

Maccolus smiled. "I can hope for no more than that. We'll be happy to travel with you."

"Good," said Clovis as he stood up, "we'll travel tomorrow. Until then, be our guests and have your dinner with us."

"You're most kind, Clovis. Thank you. We accept your invitation." He and his three silent friends bowed in respect to the chief.

Syagrius watched with particular intensity as the sun brought a glow to the eastern sky. He was fond of sunrises. "They're more definite than sunsets...more hopeful," he had once said to Rosamund. They were newly married then and didn't think much about endings. Only beginnings. Now he readied himself for this last leg of his final journey to Soissons. Soldiers were striking camp and beginning to gather on the road, readying themselves to receive the order to march. Clovis oversaw the completion of the preparations, then mounted his horse to lead his troops back into Soissons.

Chapter 1 *A New Chief Emerges: 486-487* CE

He commanded that Syagrius be brought to ride beside him, and the bound ruler was led forward on his horse. The march began. Along the way, they passed by vineyards and meadows, bee hives, and herds of cattle. Syagrius didn't notice. Viewing the sunrise had sapped what little energy he had. He looked gaunt and broken, but was aware of his fate and ready to meet it. Clovis looked long at his captive, acknowledging the strength that Gerard had been respectful of for days. The silence of the Roman impressed him and he thought, the man is not without courage.

In the courtyard before the palace, the citizens of Soissons gathered, having heard news that Clovis, their new ruler, was about to speak. Many of the people waited for their first look at this conqueror. Franks were not unfamiliar to the people, but travel was unusual to most of them. Few had journeyed as far as Tournai and fewer still had ever enjoyed the opportunity to catch a glimpse of this Chieftain.

Inside the palace, Clovis was straightening his clothes in an effort to assure that his first appearance before the people of Soissons would be as effective as possible. Their first look at the new ruler would command respect. Their first look would reveal dignity. Their first look would impress. His attire was not Roman, which might seem odd to a people so long ruled by Rome, but it was distinctive, even among the Franks. A long wine red cloak, fastened with jeweled pins, framed his impressive physique. His long braided hair, full mustache and ever-present francisca at his side, left no doubt that Soissons was ruled by a Frank. Satisfied with his attire he turned to another concern and ordered Gerard to collect Syagrius. "The people must see him," he said.

"Of course, my lord," was Gerard's reply. He didn't understand why Clovis would want this display. He'd never wanted his opponents exhibited like this before. But Gerard was a better soldier than to challenge his chief. He was finding that he respected the conquered Syagrius, but his loyalties to Clovis far outweighed his regard for the Roman. He ordered two guards to retrieve their prisoner.

As Clovis stepped out on the porch, the people quieted. He stood at the top of the steps, between massive pillars and looked out over the crowd. For the span of a long-held breath, ruler and ruled considered one another. No judgments were made. Now was a time to think of possibilities, not facts.

There was a murmur to one side and the people turned to look at what was causing the commotion. Soldiers were clearing a path through the crowd, making way to the stairs of the porch. Syagrius was with them, staggering, stumbling, as he was shoved up the steps. As a child he had played here, now he climbed the steps to be humiliated. His hands, still bound behind his back, bled around scabs that had formed during his journey from Toulouse. He reached the top of the stairs with difficulty and, having regained his balance, looked up into the eyes of Clovis. There wasn't time to speak. Gerard turned Syagrius to face those who were once his people. He'd deserted his subjects and now he lowered his gaze, in shame and in resignation. He expected no compassion from those he had ruled.

Clovis stepped forward and lifted the down-turned unshaven face of Syagrius so the people could see his eyes. They were tired and sad, red from lack of sleep.

The people stared silently at him. Few felt sympathy. His reign had served only the rich. Most denied receiving any benefit from this king. A few quietly voiced their view that it was what he deserved. Most said nothing. None expressed sadness. Clovis felt more for the fallen ruler than did the crowd.

He released his grip on Syagrius and the man's head dropped forward again. Clovis looked at the crowd and said, "From now on, I rule in Soissons!"

The silence that followed declared what Clovis wished to hear—there was no loyalty for the old ruler, and there was respect, if not fear, for the new one. Secure in his authority, Clovis gave the order Syagrius had been waiting for. Turning to Gerard, Clovis quietly said, "Take him. All we required of him now is his head."

Syagrius heard and nodded, having spent many of his last hours in preparation for this moment. He didn't stumble now. His father had died at the hands of a Frank, now he would too. He raised his face and walked back down the steps with the renewed strength and dignity as the certainty of death replaced uncertainty of imprisonment.

Behind the great hall of the palace in Soissons lay a field that stretched to the north, ending at the rim of the basin that blocked any further northward view. There, the warriors of Clovis, Ragnachar, and Chararic gathered. The time had arrived to divide the booty that had been taken during the campaign against Syagrius. Great casks of wine had been opened, much of it consumed, and the men were jovial.

Everyone understood the arrangement. It was custom. No matter what their rank, all the soldiers shared equally in the spoils. It was a tradition long honored by the least to the greatest, even to the chief of the tribe. The commanders represented the soldiers. Each commander would return with a share of the spoils that would then be distributed among their men. It was the job of the commanders to make sure that all got a fair share of the wealth. Grave consequences followed if that responsibility was not fulfilled. Deceit was not tolerated, and more than one greedy commander had met his end at the hands of cheated and angry men.

Fifty commanders heeded the call of their chieftains and filed into the banquet hall of the palace. The room, used for dinners and conferences, could easily have accommodated more than the fifty who collected there now. Near one end of the hall lay the spoils, heaped in a pile to the right of the throne. Clovis stood in front of the riches, watching, as the commanders gathered. As leader of the campaign, Clovis was willingly granted the land that had been acquired in the previous weeks. Many of the commanders expected a portion of the lands to be gifted back to them by a grateful Clovis, but that would come later. Not so with these treasures. This plunder would be enjoyed today.

Holding up his hands, Clovis quieted the men.

"The time has come to celebrate our victories!" Clovis swept his arm toward the mound of silver, gold, utensils, armlets, chains, coins, jewelry, and statues. The commanders cheered. Clovis raised his hands again. "We've all earned a share in the treasure and you have my congratulations and my gratitude!" With that, he offered his most ceremonial bow.

The commanders cheered again as they felt the spirit of victory being resurrected within them. Even a few days can dampen the memory of conquest, allow the fire of battle to fade, but now came the reward, and their enthusiasm was rekindled.

"There is only one thing I ask of my warriors," Clovis had to shout above the din. The men, gathered in a semi-circle around Clovis and their riches, quieted and listened respectfully. "I hope you won't refuse me."

One commander yelled, "Without you, Clovis, we'd have nothing! Ask what you will."

Clovis smiled, reassured, as many of the commanders applauded in agreement.

"I ask only one thing: that you will not refuse to give me, over and above what falls to me by lot, this silver bowl taken from the church at Reims." He pointed to a large bowl that was set slightly apart from the rest of the treasure.

Maccolus and his men stood to the left side of the room, anxious to hear the response to the Chief's plea.

There seemed to be general agreement among the men, but one of the commanders, Dallin, by name, feared that this was the first step toward a greater inequity. Wine increased his greed, heightened his fear that he would not get his due. He shouted, "I don't like it!"

Clovis blinked, but his face showed no further expression. He searched for the mouth from which the voice originated and, finding Dallin, asked, "You would deny my request?"

"Yes," said Dallin, "I would deny it! Nothing beyond what falls to you by lot shall be yours! It is the law of the Frank!" He knew he needed to render the bowl useless so the dispute would be over the custom and not over the object. He stepped forward, raised his francisca and brought it down, splitting the bowl nearly in two. The deformed mass spun across the floor, clanging the entire way, stopping at the feet of the priest, Maccolus. For the briefest of moments his serenity was lost and a look of horror came to his face.

Some of the Franks gasped, but all understood that, as far as tradition was concerned, Dallin was correct. Clovis knew it as well. It was the custom. All would get equal shares today.

Clovis looked into Dallin's eyes. He took in the image of his furrowed brow, receding hairline and closely set eyes. One day, they would face each other again, and he would remember this moment. He would remember this face.

"So shall it be," said Clovis, "but I wish to cast lots for the bowl first." He went to Maccolus and, after giving him a consoling look, stooped to pick up the vessel.

Few wished to challenge Clovis, especially for a broken bowl. Only Dallin came forward. And as fortune would have it, Clovis gained possession of the bowl as part of his share. With bowl in hand, he stood back from the activity on the floor as the commanders cast lots for the remaining riches. He watched Dallin the whole time.

It was two weeks before Clovis made the journey to Reims. It was his last item of business before returning to Tournai. The two weeks in Soissons had been filled with reminders that Rome no longer ruled in Gaul. The story of the defeat of Syagrius was told over and over again in the palace, the market, the stables, in every corner of the city.

Maccolus went home to his bishop empty-handed, assured that Clovis, himself, would come to return the bowl. And on this day, Clovis did come to Reims, attended by Principius, bishop of Soissons, and a small entourage, sufficient to the task of carrying supplies for this short visit. The party rode into the city of Reims from the north, through the great Port of Mars arch, past the imposing Roman architecture of the Governor's Palace, by the Amphitheater and lastly, to the most influential church in northern Gaul. Soon Clovis was addressing the region's most influential churchman, Bishop Remigius.

Seeing Remigius, after having become acquainted with Principius, Clovis couldn't miss the family resemblance, though he thought Remigius was the more striking of the brothers. His features were more exaggerated, his confidence more evident. The bishop was nearly as tall as Clovis, and looked to be about fifty years old. His eyes shone with wisdom, framed with lines of experience. Clovis watched silently as the Bishop's long and graceful fingers straightened the writings he had before him. There was both confidence and purpose in his movements. As Remigius stood and greeted his younger brother, Clovis noticed that the elder Bishop's eyebrows twitched as his whole face climbed into a warm and crooked smile. Remigius then welcomed Clovis with a deep rich velvet voice.

"At last we meet," said the bishop of Reims taking the Frank's hand in his own and shaking it firmly.

"Yes," replied Clovis, "though we've waited too long." Remigius smiled another crooked smile and let his eyebrows twitch again. "Yes, too long," he said.

Then he abruptly became silent and spent the next few moments observing the features on this young man's face. The King of the Franks endured this for only a moment and then, with respect in his voice, proceeded with business.

"I'm sorry, Bishop, but, as I'm sure your man, Maccolus, told you, the bowl you hoped to retrieve from me has been damaged beyond repair." From under his arm, Clovis pulled a bag from which he withdrew the rent vessel.

With great tenderness, Remigius accepted the bowl from Clovis and looked at it with sadness in his eyes.

"I am glad that the bowl's been returned, no matter what its condition."

"I would have liked bringing you something more than ruined goods."

Remigius smiled at the young visitor. He saw in him a great potential. "You're most kind, Clovis. But, truly, the bowl will do." He put it down on the table behind him. "In returning it you've shown your good faith. It will not be forgotten. Now, come, walk with me." He stretched out his arm to point the way.

Few people dared speak to Clovis with the voice of authority. But for some reason, Clovis was willing to accept it from this man. Perhaps it was because Remigius reminded him of his father. The bishop didn't look like Childeric, but his carriage brought back vivid memories to Clovis—memories of his father, who had died too soon. Remigius motioned Clovis to his side and asked Principius to leave them for awhile. The bishop of Soissons excused himself after reminding Clovis that he would make the return journey with him on the next day.

The bishop of Reims led Clovis down a short hall into the nave. They walked along an outer aisle of the church that was lined with paintings of the life of Jesus.

"You've done well, returning the bowl," said the bishop.

"I hold no grudge against the Church."

"No, I'm certain you don't. And I'm certain the people of Reims will appreciate what you've done." There was silence for a moment as Remigius took time to choose his words. "Your rule increases considerably."

"Yes, Bishop, the Gods have been good to me..." Clovis lifted an eyebrow, half curious over the comment of Remigius, half involved in his own concerns, "...but there's more."

"More?"

"More to conquer, more to rule."

"Oh, yes. For an ambitious ruler, there is more, I suppose." Remigius showed a faint smile and took a further moment before deciding to press his agenda. "Many of the people in this region are Christian, you know."

"Yes, so you've informed me," said Clovis. He remembered the letter Remigius wrote to him years before, when he became chief of the Franks. Clovis still kept the letter. "But as I've said, I have no quarrel with the Christians."

"No, nor they with you, I imagine."

"No...none that I'm aware of," said Clovis, "unless it would be for looting their churches."

"That would be reason enough, my friend." Remigius chuckled and Clovis joined him with a noncommital smile.

Remigius decided to pursue his own concerns no further. Building ties between the Church and a ruler took time. This day brought a significant and sufficient step toward a good relationship with this man, that of familiarity. For now, Remigius was satisfied.

The two of them rounded the corner nearest the choir. Clovis looked up to a majestic painting of Jesus seated on a throne, flanked by angels.

"Rule well, then, Clovis, and gain your people's loyalty."

"I fully intend to, Bishop."

They continued around the church saying no more, both lost in different thoughts. Returning to the door of the Bishop's rooms, Remigius broke the silence.

"Now I can tell my people that a gracious ruler sits in the throne in Soissons. That is good."

"Kind words, Remigius. I thank you." Clovis bowed once again before walking from the room. As he departed, keeping an eye open for Principius, whom he imagined would be close by, Clovis reflected on the meeting, impressed by Remigius, angered that he could not have delivered to this man the cherished bowl unharmed. He remembered Dallin and frowned.

On a bright morning in March, 3000 Frankish soldiers, the Home Guard of Clovis, lined up on a broad field outside the city of Tournai. They gathered facing a slight rise that stood between them and the city. Behind them and to their right was forest. To the left, the field stretched for more than two leagues.

It had been a good year for the Franks. Soissons had fallen into the hands of Clovis, and most all of the surrounding region of Belgica Secunda, the northernmost province of the fading Roman Empire, had been secured as small local rulers had been conquered, one after another.

After the defeat of Syagrius, the Franks had returned to their homes in and around Tournai, nearly a week's ride north from Soissons, to spend what was left of the winter with their families. Now, with the arrival of spring, they gathered for inspection.

Clovis arrived at the field on horseback, Gerard at his side as usual. As he rode over the crest of the rise, the troops responded with cheers of "Hail, Clovis!" as they banged their forearms against their shields in tribute. The noise could be heard in the city.

Clovis took in the tribute and smiled. These men had proven themselves against Syagrius, showing their strength, skill, and loyalty, and

Clovis was glad that he'd taken the time and effort to instill some sense of discipline among them. For five years, after his father had died, Clovis worked to further what Childeric had begun, teaching his army the lessons of Roman soldiering, impressing upon them the danger of never changing their way of warring, when new strategies were coming against them.

"It's a well deserved salute," said Gerard.

"They're good men."

The Chief of the Franks rode to the center of the front rank and dismounted. Gerard descended from his mount as well and stood quietly by the horses.

Commanders standing in the first row knew they would be inspected most closely and they were prepared for their leader's scrutiny.

Clovis smiled, said a few hellos, and began to stroll down the row of soldiers. As he walked he spoke to each soldier and commented on equipment or dress.

Soon he faced Dallin. He looked at the high forehead, the crooked nose and the unsuspecting eyes. This man had dared to challenge his integrity. Clovis stopped and took a long careful survey of the man. He considered his javelin, his francisca, and his short bladed scramasax. He looked at his shield and his tunic. He scrutinized his chain-mail. Then he shook his head.

"Dallin, no man here has cared so poorly for his weapons."

"My lord?" Dallin formed the question with his facial expression as well as with his words.

"Neither your sword, nor your spear, nor your ax are fit for battle!" Clovis spoke so that many of the soldiers could hear. Then to emphasize his contempt, he grabbed Dallin's francisca and threw it to the ground in disgust.

His point was made. He turned away from the soldier and made the appearance of continuing with the inspection, all the while listening for Dallin to move. As the chastised soldier stepped forward to retrieve his ax, Clovis knew. He wasn't certain if it was a sound, a shadow, or intuition, but he knew. Instantly, he grabbed his own ax and spun back toward Dallin, raising his weapon as he turned. With all the force he could muster, he brought his francisca down on the stooping soldier, burying the blade in his brain. Dallin's body, robbed of life, slumped to the ground offering only one twitch, and his blood darkened the earth where he fell.

Clovis took a deep breath looking angrily at the fallen Frank and yelled, "That's how you treated the bowl at Soissons!"

Chapter 1 *A New Chief Emerges: 486-487 CE*

All of the home guard remained silent. Some offered a sideways glance to those next to them. But none of them wished to contend with Clovis. The chief lifted his ax from Dallin's skull and wiped it clean on the new grass.

"There is nothing more to be done here today," he said, looking at the soldiers who stood nearby. None dared speak. Returning to his horse, Clovis seized the reigns from Gerard, mounted and left his men to their own thoughts.

Clovis sat on his throne, staring into space, thinking about Dallin. More than a month had passed since he had killed the man, and as he remembered the event he was both exhilarated and saddened. He was exhilarated at the authority to exercise nearly unlimited power—power over life and death—but saddened at the fear such power brought. Because of his power, he could never be sure if people were speaking honestly to him or simply trying to placate him. It was a dilemma he'd faced before and one he was certain to face again.

Gerard sat by, as he often did, serving as a resource as well as a friend. Clovis enjoyed his company and Gerard took pleasure in being with Clovis. Their time together was often lively with conversation but today they were quiet. This was time set aside for business, when Frank and Roman alike would bring grievance and proposals, accusations and requests. Today, however, few sought the judgment of Clovis. Indeed, aside from a property dispute at midday, the afternoon had been absent of activity. Their silence was broken by a guard who announced simply, "Aurelian of Soissons."

Clovis and Gerard watched a rather smallish man come before them in the distinctive garb of a Roman official: a long white toga draped over the shoulder, a garment which Clovis thought would be scratchy and unwieldy. He preferred the short tunic and leggings his people were accustomed to wearing. He rarely saw togas. They were never seen in Tournai and rarely worn elsewhere. On formal occasions a Roman might wear one, but even that was infrequent.

It was clear that the visitor was not familiar with much in the way of heavy work. His slight, bony frame poked through his tunic and his bare arms, though not flabby, were not the arms of a soldier. His face looked precise, all his features symmetrical including the scar that crossed his forehead. His face was clean-shaven and his hair was short.

Clovis leaned to one side in his throne, put one hand under his chin and the other on his hip. He gave a nod and said, "Proceed."

"Clovis of the Franks, I've come from Soissons to offer you my services."

The man spoke in Latin and Clovis responded in kind, "Your services?"

The man cocked his head, "You speak Latin?"

"I do."

"I thought there were no schools in this region."

"You think correctly. But my father understood the value of speaking the language of Rome. He acquired tutors for me."

"I see. Hmm." The man looked like he'd just learned something interesting, his gaze seeing nothing as he withdrew into his own thoughts, one eye squinting slightly.

"So I ask again: you wish to offer me your services?"

Aurelian's thoughts returned to the throne room. "Yes, my lord."

"Are you a warrior, man? Because if you are, you can be certain you'll go into battle in the first row. Otherwise you'll never see over my men's heads!" Clovis grinned at Gerard, and the two of them laughed.

"No, indeed, I'm no warrior," he said, apparently oblivious to the joke at his expense. "I'm an administrator."

"An administrator, you say? What need do I have for an administrator?"

"A great need, I believe, good Clovis." The man stood a little taller. Clovis was surprised at the directness of the reply.

"Go on." A new note of respect crept into his voice.

"I've watched you...since you defeated Syagrius. I've taken note as your lands have grown with your victories. But I've seen that you leave little or no leadership to rule in those places. In Soissons you placed guards and routed out those you thought would be troublemakers, but nothing else. No one ever approached me to ask an opinion or to seek assistance and yet I've watched over the administration of Soissons for more years than you've led your people. You may not be aware of the consequences of such a course as you've been following. It will only lead to chaos, sir. Chaos first, and contempt later. The people need more guidance than you're giving them."

"And you can give them more?"

"No, I wouldn't presume such a thing. But, with my help, *you* can."

Clovis was beginning to like this man—or, at least his forthrightness. He was proving bigger than his size alone indicated.

"What's your name again?"

"Aurelian, sir, former advisor to Syagrius."

"To Syagrius! And you wish to serve me?"

Chapter 1 *A New Chief Emerges: 486-487 CE*

"That's true."

Clovis gave a look of amazement to Gerard who shook his head in mild surprise.

"May I ask why?" Clovis asked with all sincerity.

"Good Clovis, to be an advisor and an administrator is all that I know."

"But you're a Roman. Don't you hold any loyalty for Syagrius?"

"No sir, I do not. And though he is dead, honesty compels me to say, he didn't deserve loyalty. He was a bigot and a self-serving man. He wasn't well liked, even among his own people."

"I see."

Aurelian went on, "I have a Frankish wife, sir, whom I met during my diplomatic travels to Amiens. Syagrius didn't approve. Still, I served him as best I could—so long as I held my post. One tries to do at least that much."

"At least," Clovis affirmed.

"But now I'm without a position, you see, and I'm here to offer my services to you."

Clovis arose from his chair and began to walk around Aurelian. Perhaps, he thought, an administrator could be of use. As he crossed behind the man he looked at Gerard and shaped a question with a shrug of his shoulders and a raising of his eyebrows. Gerard returned the gesture and smiled.

"Are you competent, Aurelian?"

"I studied at the Roman law school at Clermont, my lord," he said, without blinking an eye.

Clovis was not aware of the school, but the obvious pride in Aurelian's voice convinced him that the claim was one of significance.

Continuing around Aurelian, Clovis faced him. "What advice would you give me now?"

"Now, my lord?"

"Now. What needs to be done here without delay."

Aurelian blinked nervously several times and thought about his response.

"I can think of three important steps that must be taken."

Clovis completed his circuit around the Roman and re-seated himself. "And they are...?"

Aurelian decided it best to be direct. Usually directness was his chosen path, but on this occasion he hesitated. He didn't know this Frankish chief. He'd hoped he would have time to ease into advising this powerful and possibly unpredictable man, but Clovis was being direct, so Aurelian decided to respond in a like manner.

"First, though it may seem risky on the surface, it would be best to make use of the Roman government that's already in place. At your immediate command you have administrators, bankers, mints and magistrates. They're all sound. They've been functioning for years upon years effectively, centuries, in fact. It would make sense to make use of their expertise."

"You don't see them as a threat?"

"Not really, no." Aurelian was shaking his head. "They know Rome is dead. Like me, they only want to do what they were trained to do. I'm convinced they could save you a great deal of trouble. Indeed, they could serve you in many ways. For example,...were I you," the Roman crossed his arms and looked toward the ceiling, deep in thought, "I would continue to impose land taxes. The taxes aren't out of order and the people are accustomed to them. And, understand," he looked back at Clovis, "you have competent officials already prepared to collect them."

"I see." The Chief's interest was growing and he wanted to hear what else this man would say. "There's more?"

"Yes, my lord. Second, I would recommend that you move to Soissons. It's been the center of government in Belgica Secunda for quite some time. Via the Roman roads, it has easy access to the major trading towns like Reims, Amiens, Rouen and so on; and it would be easier to defend your growing territory from there."

Clovis didn't relish the thought of leaving Tournai and he could see difficulties in suggesting such a move to his people. Still, he had to admit that Aurelian's words made good sense.

"More?"

"Yes, one last thing." Aurelian looked at Gerard and then back at Clovis. His voice lowered slightly. "I'm aware that you don't worship the God of Jesus Christ as do most of the people of Gaul. Even so, you'd do well to enlist the good favor of the Church. With the Church's support the people will follow in kind."

"You're not the first to offer that advice, Aurelian. Bishop Remigius suggested the same thing to me almost five years ago. He said my rule would fare better if I were to defer to the bishops and heed their counsel. Eleutherius has recommended it as well."

"You're on good terms with Bishop Eleutherius?"

"Yes, so far as I can tell. He became bishop here the about the same time I set out to defeat Syagrius."

"He's a good start...as good as any. And since you've already had contact with Remigius, and I would guess also with Principius of Soissons...?" Clovis nodded. "Then you're well on the way."

Chapter 1 *A New Chief Emerges: 486-487 CE*

Clovis was impressed with the directness and logic of this man. "My dear Aurelian, I do believe you're correct." Clovis pursed his lips and nodded slowly, several nods. "You very well may be of help to me."

"Thank you, sir. I hope so." Aurelian bowed formally to his new ruler.

The Soissons palace that Syagrius had known so well was striking in comparison to the residence Clovis knew in Tournai. There were no rushes on a dirt floor here. Tile covered the floor, colored in blues and golden browns. The marble columns were impressive as were the baths. It was decorated with hanging plants and statues and more upholstered furniture than Clovis had ever seen. He didn't particularly like the tapestries or mosaics that Syagrius had imported from Italy. Still, the palace was spacious and comfortable and Aurelian's advice was already proving valuable. The lands ruled by Clovis were now more secure than ever and commerce had grown as Aurelian had predicted.

Every six weeks, throughout the lands that Clovis governed, the local courts or 'mallus' would convene to take care of legal matters. Only the most critical business was brought to the court in Soissons. Occasionally, though, if someone refused to abide by the decision of a mallus, a more mundane matter might come before Clovis. Often these less serious matters were the most enjoyable. Men of the countryside would bring an earthy concern about cattle breeding or a ridiculous dispute over the price of goods and Clovis found these issues refreshing diversions from his usual business.

On this day, the major item of business entailed taking steps to strengthen ties with the Church. Clovis knew it was an important step toward strengthening his reign. Aurelian, having been officially taken on as advisor, was scribbling notes as Clovis spoke. He would take care of the necessary details that emerged from his ruler's considerations.

"…and Leuilly and Coucy can go to Remigius in Reims."

"Yes, my lord."

"Where does that leave us, Aurelian?"

"Lands to the churches at Soissons, Tournai, and Reims. They're all noted and I'll implement their transfer as soon as possible."

"Good. Now, I'd like to reward some of my men." Aurelian prepared his quill for the further business. "To my officers Gerard, Adalhard and Odbert go the Roman lands to the west of Soissons.

They are to be distributed among themselves and their soldiers in a fair and equitable manner."

How convenient, thought Clovis, that the Romans left land he could use. The government lands acquired by Rome were making the move to Soissons much easier. Because there was land available to them, a large portion of the home guard was moving with Clovis rather than staying in Tournai. Gifts of land to the Churches only served to improve relations with them and there was no need to contend for the land, or displace citizens. It was simply there, on reserve, for his use as he saw fit.

Aurelian took down all the orders for land distribution and then, certain that this agenda item was secured, moved on to the final item of business for the day.

"One of the local Franks was caught robbing a Roman. The wergeld is usually 1400 denarii. 35 solidus." Frankish custom decreed that each crime was to be paid for with a wergeld, a price determined by the severity of the crime. "He refused to accept the decision of the mallus, though. The man and his victim are both here."

"Thank you, Aurelian. Bring them in."

The Roman and the Frank who were involved in the case entered the court of Clovis with several others who had witnessed the crime. Clovis listened to the Roman, who made it clear that he expected little justice in the court of a Frank. Especially as his complaint was against a Frank.

"I had just collected on a debt owed me, my lord, and was returning home when this man stopped me, knocked me down, and took my purse."

The accusation was simple enough and the witnesses confirmed the story of the crime.

Clovis turned to the Frank and asked for his story. He said nothing, and only glared at the Roman. Asked again to speak, the man still refused. Unable to hear both sides of the story, Clovis took the next step available.

"To assure a fair judgment, we will let the Gods decide your fate. We will use the 'urtheil'."

The Frank began to perspire immediately. He had hoped the judgment might be decided by combat—and he felt he had an advantage over the Roman. But Clovis had spotted the inequity of stature also, and chose this other option.

The "urtheil", the test of boiling water, was well known as a determiner of guilt, though it's use had declined since the time of Merovech. Clovis knew it was still useful, though. The accused would have his arm plunged into a vat of boiling water to retrieve a stone that rested on the bottom of the vat. Then, the arm was bound in bandages. If in three days the arm was not healed, the verdict was "guilty." If the arm healed, the accused was determined to be guilt-free. No one could remember a case in which acquittal had been the outcome, though now and then one heard stories.

The innocent, if they were of a stubborn nature, would fearfully risk the ordeal and still be found guilty. Most would confess. The guilty would usually break down at the threat of the ordeal. This case was no different.

"My lord, no, I confess! I took his money!" The Frank yelled his confession as guards began to pull him toward the fireplace. "I'm guilty! Please, I beg your forgiveness!"

Clovis was tired and it pleased him that this case was resolved quickly.

"As you're guilty of robbing a Roman, you must not only return the money..."

"Yes sir!"

"...but you must pay the wergeld of 35 solidus."

"Yes sir, but I'll need to return home, for the payment."

"Then go, but you'll return home with guards and your victim at your side."

All in agreement, the shamed Frank and the impressed Roman left to settle their account. Clovis watched them go, then looked at Aurelian.

"Anything else?"

"No, my lord. Nothing."

"Good. I'd welcome some time to rest."

Clovis stood, removed his outer tunic and took a deep breath, letting it back out quickly, expelling the tension of the day. He looked at the empty hall and spoke to his advisor.

"The days in Tournai were not filled with so many details, Aurelian. Things are changing."

Aurelian smiled and nodded. "Yes, sir, they are indeed."

Chapter 2

Princesses Survive
488 CE

Gundobad's deep set eyes tightened to slits. "I've waited a long time for this," he said. "Fourteen years. Did you really think I'd forget what you did to me?" His brother, Chilperic, gave no response.

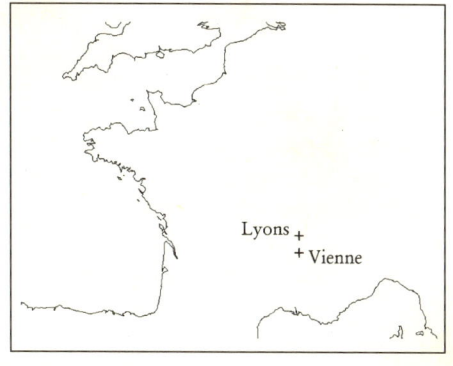

Gundobad ran his hands through his hair, remembering years of frustration. Intertwining his fingers behind his head, he stood still, reliving his past. The memory and the pain of exile was still strong. His face tightened into an expression of anger and resolve.

When King Gundevech died, leaving the kingdom of Burgundy to his four sons, Gundobad, the eldest, was in Italy, fighting alongside the Vandals. Chilperic took advantage of his elder brother's absence to declare himself the king of all Burgundy. With the help of his youngest brother, Godomar, and only half-hearted resistance from the fourth brother, Godegesil, the maneuver was easy. Gundobad returned from Italy only to be cast out by the opportunistic Chilperic.

Three years later, however, Gundobad renewed his efforts to claim what was rightly his, and this time he came with troops and threats. The prospect of a bloody war brought a compromise between the brothers that split the kingdom. By agreement, Gundobad ruled in Vienne, Chilperic in Lyons, Godegesil in Geneva, and Godomar in Valence.

The arrangement worked for years, but Gundobad never forgot his brother's treachery. His anger grew with each passing season, until he could contain it no longer. He built his army, enlisted the help of Italian troops and moved on Lyons, taking the city in a matter of days. Chilperic knew of his brother's intentions and growing strength but miscalculated both the magnitude of Gundobad's buildup and the timing of his assault. Chilperic's miscalculation brought destruction on his men as a force overwhelmingly superior in numbers swept them aside as so much dust. The walls and troops of Lyons could only delay the inevitable. Once Gundobad's army scaled the walls, they took the city easily.

Tapestries covered the stone walls of Chilperic's throne room. One depicted the bloody conclusion of a boar hunt, blood streaming from the mouth of the fallen beast, the victor standing in triumph. Another was more gentle, picturing a deer, poised at a stream, about to quench his thirst. It was a proud buck depicted, his full rack of antlers ready to meet any challenge. The tapestries had long given the throne-room a feeling of strength and adventure. Now, for Gundobad, it was a room of victory; for his brother, it was a room of defeat.

King Chilperic and his queen, Caretena, were held immobile by four of Gundobad's men. Gundobad paced before them like a wolf, never taking his eyes off his prey. Except for Caretena, all were in battle dress and it was clear that diplomacy was not the order of the day, though Gundobad feigned it for a moment. His confidence was unassailable. He was master of the moment. He stopped his pacing and focused his attention on his sister-in-law.

"Caretena...you're more beautiful than ever." He said the words mockingly as he gently touched her cheek. She was not unattractive. Her face was plain but her figure was one that could attract any man's attention. She had a full round bosom and a curvaceous waist that led to seductive, comfortable looking hips. It was clear, however, that her daughters inherited their looks from their father. Gundobad's rough knuckles felt harsh against her skin, and she turned her face away. Gundobad smiled, wickedly. "When father was alive," he turned toward Chilperic, "before you betrayed me," then back to Caretena, "it was pleasant, wasn't it? We were a family then." Caretena held no love for Gundobad and was under no illusions about the moment. She turned back toward her captor and spoke freely, her voice thick with sarcasm.

"Your father was an honorable king, Gundobad. If only you could have continued in that tradition..."

"Silence!" shouted Gundobad, his pitted face growing red. "There is no family any more! That ended when you exiled me!"

Chilperic made a futile attempt to calm his brother, "Surely, Gundo..."

"Silence!" Gundobad shouted again, even louder, as he slapped his brother. "Godomar's dead!"

The words jarred Chilperic, speeding his recovery from the backhand. He spun back to face his brother with a new intensity. "Godomar's dead?"

"He died this morning...because of you!" Gundobad stared at Chilperic with wide eyes. He leaned forward challenging a retort with his smile. There was none. "If you hadn't been so treacherous, this battle would never have happened…this battle that's killed our brother." He straightened again and took in a long deep breath. "And you must pay for his death!"

At the words, Chilperic forgot his grief. Gundobad was going to kill him. There had been little doubt to begin with, now there was not even the chance to hope. Gundobad's justification, however self-serving and false, was now made clear. Still, while there was no point in trying to avoid what must come, Chilperic felt compelled to understand what the fate of his family would be. Gundobad would rule. Godomar, a rare friend and ally, besides being his brother, was dead.

"Will you kill Godegesil too?"

"Godegesil? The fool? Do you think he's a threat?" His question dripped with disdain. Godegesil was the one person he had never feared. "Do you even believe that he's our father's son? He's incapable of trouble-making." Gundobad cocked his head as he thought about Godegesil. "But…he may be useful…" He walked to the far side of the room and looked at the tapestry of the dying boar. Then he slowly returned. "Brother, I do believe you've given me an idea. One that Godegesil will certainly appreciate." Gundobad looked up at the ceiling as he thought out loud. "If the people see that I'm willing to allow him his pitiful little castle in Geneva, maybe they'll be more willing to accept me…" He looked back at Chilperic, "No, he won't die…not yet." He smiled again, "But you are another matter."

"What about Caretena?" Chilperic was not hopeful for her fate.

"You won't have to worry about her," said Gundobad with a smile that ceased Chilperic's questions.

There was no further need to waste breath. Gundobad looked matter-of-factly at the two men who were holding Chilperic. The soldiers repositioned themselves, tightening their hold on their prisoner, as Gundobad reached for his short sword.

Chilperic was distracted by the shifting of the men and he glanced away from his brother. He heard Caretena gasp and turned to see a horrified look on her face. He followed her wild stare in time to watch the point of Gundobad's blade enter his body just below his sternum. Gundobad twisted the blade to the right and back to the left, blood pouring from Chilperic with each turn. He withdrew his sword. The guards released their grip, allowing Chilperic to fall to his knees, then finish his descent, twisting to land on his side. As he died, the expression on his face which mixed confusion, acceptance, and pain, fell into a pale, hollow, and emotionless mask.

Gundobad watched him die, then turned his attention to the grief-stricken queen.

"Even an unfaithful brother deserves a swift death, Caretena, but I have something else in mind for you." He looked at the men who held her, lifted his still blood-wet sword and with it, motioned toward the door.

The queen was escorted to the southern wall of the castle, to a well that supplied the royal residence with water. It was more than a simple hole in the ground, as most wells were. Broadly cut, nearly twelve feet across, marked by three tripods on a wide knee-high stone barrier, which also served to discourage children from getting too close to danger, the well could support the efforts of three teams of servants working simultaneously to draw copious amounts of water. No servants worked now. Gundobad stood next to the well, anticipating a carefully-planned moment. In accordance with orders that Gundobad had given earlier, a block of stone was waiting next to the well. Secured to it was a length of rope. The rock was not large enough to drag a person under water too quickly, but was large enough to cause a lengthy and tortuous struggle. With no ceremony other than a wave of his hand, Gundobad ordered the queen's execution.

The soldiers suffered the wrath of Caretena's kicking as they tied the stone to her body, lifted her up and dropped her into the well. The guards who were posted by the well could hear faint screams for nearly an hour. Then there was silence.

Sedeluba and Clotild, the daughters of the dead king, were allowed to walk along the Rhône River, north of Lyons, but only late in the day, and only after Patiens, bishop of Lyons, their guardian, determined there was no threat to them. There was reason to worry for their welfare.

Hasty arrangements were made to get the young girls to safety once news about Gundobad's strength made it clear there was a real chance that Lyons would fall. Bishop Patiens called upon trusted members of his parish to spirit the sisters away just prior to Gundobad's last offensive push. They were successful in getting the sisters out of immediate danger, though now, a reward was being offered for their capture. Large numbers of Gundobad's men were combing the countryside in search of the daughters of Chilperic. So far, Patiens had kept the whereabouts of the two princesses secret, but it was getting more difficult with each day.

While the hunt continued, Hesychius, the aging bishop of Vienne, was making every effort to build up his relationship with Gundobad.

Hesychius believed in the Trinity while Gundobad chose to follow the teachings of Arius, teachings the bishops at council had condemned as heretical. There were many, like Gundobad, who could believe in one God, but not three. Still, Gundobad was the king, and Hesychius continually sought opportunities to influence the man. Most important was the effort to stay a step ahead of the Arian king while striving to keep Sedeluba and Clotild alive.

The transition of power to Gundobad was quick and easy. With the unofficial support of both the Catholic and Arian Churches, who offered their support more out of practical necessity rather than out of spiritual wisdom, the land that Chilperic ruled came under Gundobad's authority and the mechanisms to rule both Lyons and Vienne from the throne in Vienne were soon in place. With his new territory secure, lands that now reached to the frontiers of the Franks, Gundobad regained his sense of humor and a degree of his usual good nature.

On a day when rumor suggested that Gundobad was particularly jovial, Bishop Hesychius received advice from his son, Avitus, a priest himself, that the time might be right to approach the king about the fugitive girls.

"I agree," said the bishop. He sat up in bed, covered with blankets, shivering. The room was damp and cold as always. "Now's as good a time as any…and it may be better than most." Hesychius barely got the words out before a fit of coughing overtook him. His face flinched into a maze of wrinkles. His son waited. "But you can see, my child, I'm in no condition to negotiate with Gundobad. Can you see to it?" He coughed again.

Watching his father's condition weaken, Avitus had been praying that his health would last at least until this touchy business about Sedeluba and Clotild was finished. His prayers were in vain. Though he'd come to know Gundobad quite well in recent years, never had he dealt with him on any serious level. That was to change.

"Yes, of course. I'll do what I can."

A weak wave of encouragement from his father sent the young priest on his mission. Hesychius lay back, slowly coughing his life away as Avitus departed for the court of Gundobad.

Gundobad wasn't sure he liked the look of Avitus. The priest's intelligence showed, but he looked more shrewd than his father, more worldly than a priest ought to look. That unsettled Gundobad. The fact that his advisor, Aridius, who knew how to deal with the Church, was away overseeing the assimilation of newly conquered lands only made matters worse. The priest was shown into the throne room and Gundobad greeted him with a cheerfulness which seemed shallow and half-hearted to Avitus.

"You've come at a good time, Avitus. There's nothing happening at all. In fact, it's rather boring just now. I think it's because Aridius is away. He always seems to come up with more business than anyone would believe there could possibly be. So you and I can be at our leisure today."

Avitus smiled and said only, "I'm glad." It was not difficult for him to sound sincere. He didn't like Aridius. He was convinced that Aridius was Gundobad's strength, suspecting that little was done in the court without consulting the advisor. His suspicion was accurate. If Aridius didn't spell out the details, Gundobad rarely dared to act in matters of state. Too afraid to end the relationship, Gundobad had to suffer the crafty and unappealing advisor. In truth, Gundobad did know how to rule, it was just that Aridius had persuaded him otherwise. Something in the way Gundobad spoke made Avitus wonder if the king didn't share his dislike of the man.

"So what brings you to my court?"

"Only conversation, my King." He sounded too stiff. He tried to relax and said, "Things are slow for me too." Gundobad smiled. "That's good for us both then." He encouraged Avitus to sit, pointing to a couch that rested near the throne. "Conversation seems rare these days." Avitus sat on the edge of the couch and sighed. He looked around at the hall of the king of Vienne and, now, of Lyons. The large, long room had windows down the length of one side, fireplaces on the other. Long tables ran the length of the room from Gundobad's throne to just below a balcony that jutted out over the doorway. There was no one in the room or on the balcony. Avitus offered a silent prayer of thanks.

"It's not entirely idle conversation I seek, Gundobad."

"No?" Gundobad leaned back, still looking cheerful, but assuming a slightly official posture. "What's on you mind?"

"I've received word regarding Chilperic's daughters."

Gundobad jerked forward in his throne. "You have? Where are they?"

Avitus motioned for the king to sit back. "No, no, I don't have details like that," he lied. "Only that they're alive and safe...and that they wish you no harm."

Gundobad sat back and feigned relief. "Ah! I see, no harm! Ho, such a relief!"

The sarcasm wasn't lost on Avitus, "No, it's true! They don't wish you any harm. They're afraid for their lives, though. I've been asked to seek your indulgence for them." Avitus bowed slightly.

"My indulgence? My indulgence? Priest, you know more than you're letting on." He looked sideways at Avitus who shrugged as if to say, "true". "Surely you know that I'm only protecting myself," continued Gundobad, "as any ruler would do."

"I don't doubt that, my King. But these are just girls. I know them well, as do you. I've practically grown up with them." Avitus knew he was stretching the truth, though it was fair enough to say that the girls related to the young priest more readily than to the older clergy. His father, Hesychius, considered King Chilperic a friend, having met him long before Gundobad returned to Burgundy to bring a threat of war and an eventual split in the land. "Even if their father was your enemy, you must know his children harmless."

"Do you know how many times I've heard that?" Gundobad shook his head at the priest. "I assure you Avitus, I'm only doing what's necessary. And, my friend, their capture *is* necessary!"

Reason was having little impact. Avitus resorted to emotion. "Is it necessary to kill these young women to maintain your power? Sedeluba's eighteen years old and Clotild's only sixteen!"

Gundobad's eyes glazed over as he remembered. "When they were little girls they were charming, you know. We were friends then…" He stared into space. Two nieces, innocent, willing to love their father's brother, ran to a younger Gundobad. Whatever shyness they had, brought on by the warnings of their father were quickly dissipated by a gregarious and generous presence in this new uncle. After all, Uncle Godomar and Uncle Godegesil were just fine, why not this man? Sedeluba and Clotild looked forward to Uncle Gundobad's visits, though even they were uneasy when the advisor, Aridius, was present. He was the threat.

"My King?" Avitus hesitantly broke the lengthening silence, "…Sir?"

"Yes?" Gundobad snapped back to the present, snapping at Avitus at the same time. "What is it!"

"Please Gundobad, excuse my rudeness. If I may be so bold…wouldn't exile be as effective as death—at least insofar as your power is concerned?"

Gundobad frowned at the priest. "Avitus, have you already forgotten that I returned from exile? Believe me, no exile is safe."

"Would an internal exile be possible, my lord?"

"Internal exile?"

This was the final option Avitus had discussed with his father. If this was rejected, he had no place else to go. Avitus fought to moisten his parched mouth. With difficulty he replied, "Yes, Gundobad, internal exile. You could keep an eye on the girls, without having to kill them. You could even restrict their activities."

Avitus watched Gundobad mulling over the possibilities. It was clear the king was giving his suggestion serious consideration. Avitus was grateful for that much.

"There might be something to gain here," said the king. Thinking aloud, he continued, "The people of Burgundy might appreciate it if I spared their princesses." He pursed his lips and nodded in self-affirmation. "Yes. And Godegesil could take care of them. He's always been partial to our nieces. And it would keep him busy too, the idiot." He scratched his head. "Yes, Avitus, there might be something to this idea. I could put an end to the search for the girls. That's the real annoyance." He pondered the possibilities for a moment longer and then, remembering his guest, ceased his ruminations. "But, tell me, Avitus, if I decide to go along with this idea of yours, can you make the necessary arrangements?"

"I believe I can." Avitus did his best to be sincere. Preparations were already under way. Patiens was ready to move the girls whenever word came from Vienne, and Avitus knew it. "And you can speak to your brother in Geneva?"

"If I agree," said Gundobad, slowly, making it clear with each word that he would not be prodded into action. Nor would a mere priest assume anything of him.

"Certainly, my lord," said a chastised and less aggressive Avitus.

"I'll want to be assured," said Gundobad, "that they're occupied in ways that will keep them from making any trouble."

"Perhaps they could work for the Church? I could easily arrange that." Avitus knew Gundobad was an Arian, but he risked the suggestion suspecting the King's faith was one of convenience more than one of conviction.

"If that would keep them occupied," said Gundobad, bluntly.

Avitus breathed easier. "I can see to it."

Gundobad descended into his own thoughts again and it became evident that the audience was coming to an end. Taking a deep breath, Gundobad said, "I think your suggestion has some merit, Avitus. I'll think about it and let the bishop know my decision."

"Thank you, Gundobad."

Avitus bowed respectfully and departed.

Chapter 2 *Princesses Survive: 488 CE*

Before the week was out, Gundobad sent word that he had agreed to the plan. Hesychius received the message with gratitude and prayers of thanks. Then he wasted no time in sending Avitus north to Lyons. Bishop Patiens would be anxious to hear the news.

"They don't know?" The words echoed in the church. Avitus was astounded that the girls hadn't yet learned of their parent's deaths.

"Not the details, but they suspect the worst. After all, every traveler, merchant, visitor or passing messenger brings word about it."

The strain of keeping the girls safe from Gundobad's men and from the news of their parent's deaths was visible on Patiens' face. He'd aged noticeably since Avitus saw him last. There were bags under his eyes and his shoulders were more slumped than Avitus remembered. Patiens turned and shuffled toward the altar before turning to face his young friend, "They've been asking questions. I keep telling them to wait for the truth and ignore the rumors." The bishop shook his head in fatigue. "It's been difficult and it will soon be impossible, I'm sure."

"Yes, but rest easy, Bishop, the time has come for them to learn the truth. They'll be going to Geneva soon." Patiens raised his eyebrows, a silent request for confirmation of what he hoped he'd just heard. "It's true," answered Avitus, "I've arranged an internal exile for them with Godegesil. They'll work for the Church there."

Patiens looked toward heaven, grateful that the girls would be safe and relieved that his responsibilities with them would soon be completed. He offered a silent prayer of thanks before heaving a great sigh. As he put his arm on the shoulder of his blessed messenger, the creaking of the church's front door captured his attention and he turned to look. A smile of affection bloomed on his face and in a low voice he said, "You're in luck, Avitus, here they come."

Luck? thought Avitus, not likely.

The two sisters came down the aisle looking especially lovely. Clotild wore the brighter smile, but anyone who knew the two was aware that Sedeluba could smile just as brightly with her stunning large brown eyes. Their faces were red with the blush of exertion, their hair was wind-blown, and their simple beige linen dresses were smudged with the dirt of the country, though Clotild's dress looked the worse for wear.

They'd been walking along the river, having received the Bishop's permission. Clotild tried wading, found the water too cold and slipped on the bank as she made for dry land. Returning home, they decided to offer prayers for their parents. Patiens had recommended that this small church be their only place of prayer and worship, at least until the danger was passed, so that the fewest possible people would discover their whereabouts. When they saw Avitus, they paused momentarily, amazed at seeing their favorite priest. In the next instant their excitement overran their surprise and they sprinted to embrace him, kissing him on the cheek. The gestures were repeated for Patiens, though with more respect than abandon.

"Tell us, Avitus" said Clotild, wasting no time, "how are things in Lyons?"

"Yes," said Sedeluba, "tell us, is it true that the battle's over?"

Avitus braced himself. To his simultaneous chagrin and relief, it became his burden to relate the ill news to these girls he loved. He would not take any joy in the telling but it was better that they should hear the news from him than from some stranger. "Yes, my daughters, the battle's done, long since." He paused and saw the look on the girl's faces, their unblinking eyes and lips bitten nearly to bleeding, that screamed they were waiting for the news that must follow, now that it was certain that the fighting was finished.

"The fighting ended on the day you arrived here." He paused again, hoping Divine intervention would remove this cup that had passed to him, but none came. "Clotild, Sedeluba,…" he looked at each of them tenderly as he said their names, "…your parents are dead. I'm sorry. Your Uncle Gundobad was the victor. Chilperic and Caretena died protecting your home." He allowed himself to soften the truth.

The girls stood still as they heard the report. Their eyes widened even further, their faces paled and they clasped each others hands. They had been trying to prepare for this moment. They knew their parents might die in this battle, and they'd talked about it often, in spite of Patien's encouragement to speak of other things.

Clotild threw Sedeluba's hands down and screamed "No! It's not true!" Repeating the denial she ran out of the church, tears streaming down her face. Patiens began to call out to her but Avitus stopped him. Sedeluba cried quietly, and as she did, Avitus put his arms around her. Between sobs Sedeluba asked, "What happens now?"

"I've made arrangements," said Avitus. "That's why I've come to see you." He stood back a little from the girl and lifted her face. "You'll have to help Clotild prepare. We'll be leaving soon."

Godegesil's castle stood above the shores of the great lake that supplied Geneva with water. It was not a large castle, but because of the

Chapter 2 *Princesses Survive: 488 CE*

high ground it occupied, it dominated the surroundings. Not far from there, out of sight from the castle, was St. Germain's church. It was in these two places that the daughter's of the late king of Lyons now spent their time as exiles. They lived with Godegesil, who was enjoying their company, and they worked for the poor at St. Germain's. There they fed and clothed the needy of the city, and spent time in prayer and meditation under the guiding hand of Domitianus, bishop of Geneva. Avitus visited them frequently, in accordance with Gundobad's wishes, most often as a distant and hidden observer. In the courtyard of St. Germain's, particularly when the impoverished of Geneva came for what care they might receive, there was ample opportunity to watch the sisters without drawing attention to oneself. Often the fortuitous placement of a cart, or barrels provided a shadow for the careful onlooker. Beggars, lame and whole, blind and sighted, young and old, joyous and bitter, crowded around the young women. They came seeking alms and found, not only a small offering of food or money, but also a large offering of love and kindness.

On this day Avitus felt particularly bold and drew nearer to the girls, curious to hear the conversations that filled their time. He crouched as low as he felt he could without looking obvious, and slinked up to the rear of the gathering of beggars. Turning an ear to the steps upon which the sisters did their work, he listened. Sedeluba put a bandage on one man's sore-ridden arm and then fed him. All the while the man moaned. She spoke only comfort.

"You are a child of God. That makes you worthy. You will know healing, in your heart if in no other way."

"Thank you sister," was the heartfelt reply.

Clotild was fitting a man with a cloak that she'd taken from the church's store of giveaways. She asked him of news he might have.

"News, my lady, about what?" replied the man.

"Any news at all. What goes on in the city...or out of the city? Anything."

The man shared what he had recently heard, as did many who came to Clotild. In his own conversations with her, Avitus had come to know that this was always her question. She never failed to ask for news. She learned of events in Burgundy, and, though her eyes would deaden when she heard of Gundobad, she listened carefully. Sometimes news came from other parts of Gaul which she would take in with particular relish. Occasionally she would hear news from Italy. She accepted it all, hungrily.

Sedeluba was content to say prayers with those who came to her.

Avitus watched for a long while. And as the beggars dispersed, he made his presence known. The sisters ran to him and hugged and kissed him.

One night, upon returning from their work at the church, the girls entered the dining hall of the castle to find their uncle nearly unconscious with drink. He sat in a chair with his head back, eyes closed, mumbling about Gundobad, an occasional obscenity being uttered more clearly than most all of his other words. Clotild and Sedeluba stood listening, trying to keep from laughing. It was Clotild who first broke out with one high, poorly stifled giggle. At the noise, Godegesil looked up, first with a frown on his face, then with a look of shame.

"My girls, my girls," he said, barely able to keep his eyes open, "come here and help a drunkard to his room." His nieces came to him, dragging chairs from the side of the room, and they sat down, one to each side of him. "You're good to me, you two. Good to me. Not like Gundobad, the bastard. He calls me a bastard, but he's really the bastard." Clotild looked behind Godegesil to give her sister a smile. Sedeluba returned an admonishing glare as Godegesil continued. "He shouldn't have done what he did to your parents. He didn't need to do that." This time a sharp and anxious look passed between the sisters. "What, uncle? What did he do?" asked Clotild.

"You know," he whined, "the way he killed them."

"In the battle?" Sedeluba asked.

"No, no, in the throne room! And why did he have to drown your mother. She was so kind. I hate him…I hate him!" Godegesil began to whimper and Clotild thought he was about to cry.

"Come on, then. Let's get you to bed."

The two nieces helped their uncle up and practically carried him to his room. All the while, Godegesil kept repeating, "He didn't have to drown her!"

After getting their uncle as settled as he would allow, the two went to their own room. Sedeluba began to cry uncontrollably and would not be comforted. Images of her mother struggling to breathe filled her mind. Finally, she cried out, "Oh Clotild, I miss mama and papa so much!"

Clotild's tears would not come. With a look that was as black and cold as a clear winter night, she replied, "So do I…. so do I," patting her sister's back as she spoke the words. As Sedeluba cried herself to sleep, Clotild stared silently into the growing darkness.

Chapter 3
The Bishop's Concern
490 CE

+ Chartres

For more than a month Chartres had been without a spiritual leader. Bishop Flavius was dead. The Catholic Church in Gaul was still in a precarious position. Those who followed the heretical teachings of Arius were many and widespread, in spite of the fact that the majority of the leaders of the Church had condemned such beliefs. The clergy understood how easy it was to believe in the teachings of Arius, but the heresy completely undermined the doctrine of the Trinity, and that was intolerable. Any occasion that emphasized a unified and strong Church, such as an ordination, was invaluable. Now, with Bishop Remigius of Reims presiding, Solemnus was being ordained as the thirteenth bishop of Chartres.

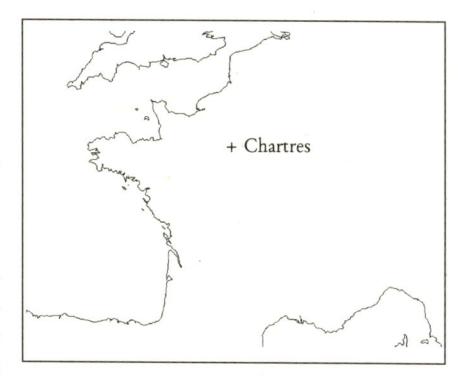

The prestigious gathering of clergy included the aging Patiens of Lyons, who was attending despite his own deteriorating health, Domitianus of Geneva, and Eleutherius of Tournai. Volusianus of Tours was also there, as was Faustus of Riez, Camilianus of Troyes, and other representatives of the Catholic Church. Avitus of Vienne was there. He was now "Bishop" Avitus, having succeeded his father, Hesychius, who had, after a long struggle, succumbed to his illness. Clovis had been invited though it surprised no one when he chose not to attend. Chartres was on the distant southern edge of the lands he ruled.

Customarily, the townspeople joined with the clergy to elect the bishop. This instance proved no different. The citizens had enthusiastically affirmed the candidate for the Bishopric. Now they collected in the Cathedral of Chartres, standing shoulder to shoulder, their bodies heating the building as they crowded forward, seeking a clear view of their new bishop. As the shuffling continued, as the temperature increased, so did the smell of people who worked hard for a living. Few noticed and fewer cared. It was an odor they'd smelled before. The younger and weaker worshippers were relegated, by a natural shoving and elbowing and cursing process to spots behind pillars or toward the back. Only when the procession of ornately costumed clergy appeared did the people grow still.

The young and handsome Solemnus entered to stand with those men whom he would, henceforth, call his peers. He basked in the gravity of the moment and looked out over the crowd which had gathered. Moved by the sight, he flexed his legs as if to affirm that he was still standing on the solid foundation of the building.

The previous night, according to tradition, Solemnus spent in prayer in the Church of St. Martin-au-Val, south of the city. From then on, Solemnus had concentrated on every single moment, not wanting to let any part of his ordination pass unremembered. The early morning walk to the Cathedral, while not solitary, seemed so; Solemnus barely remembered the presence of the other bishops who walked with him. He made his way up the hill, noticing how the trees to his right, which lined the river Eure, appeared to grow with each step he took, while the plain to his left that seemed stranded in time as the still of morning left the wheat at immovable peace.

The walk would take a quarter of an hour on a normal day, in his informal dress. Today it took nearly an hour as each step was considered and reflected upon.

Solemnus watched as the bishops arranged themselves in a semicircle before him. Remigius situated himself in the center of chancel, called Solemnus forward into the midst of the bishops, laid hands on him and spoke with a voice that reached to the most remote corners of the nave:

"O God and Father of our Lord Jesus Christ, Father of mercies and God of all consolation, author of all the ordinances of the Church. You who knows all hearts, give to this Your servant, whom You have chosen to serve, to feed Your holy flock, and to fulfill the office of high priest, Your blessing, by Your Son, our Savior, Jesus Christ, to whom with You and the Holy Ghost be glory, power and honor, world without end, amen."

A rumble of murmured "amens", brought forth from hundreds of rapt witnesses, echoed through the air.

The candidate, Solemnus, had been examined and deemed doctrinally fit. He'd been consecrated and vested with ceremony, and now Remigius readied himself to present Solemnus with the Holy Scriptures. This was the most solemn moment and the church became still. The bishop of Reims cleared his throat and lifted the book before him. "Receive the Holy Scriptures," he said, looking intently at Solemnus, "feed the flock of Christ that is now committed to your

Chapter 3 *The Bishop's Concern: 490 CE*

care, guard and defend them in His truth and be a faithful steward of His word and of His Holy Sacraments."

Solemnus bowed as he received the treasured hand-written Bible. The people in the church craned their necks further.

Remigius then presented the new bishop to the people of Chartres in his most official tone.

"Dearly beloved brethren, acclaim this man, chosen by the testimony of good works, as most worthy of the priesthood, crying out your praises together, and say: 'He is worthy!'"

The people replied, "He is worthy!" and they applauded and cheered. Solemnus bowed gracefully to the people and, after receiving the kiss of peace from the gathered clergy, the new bishop offered the Eucharist. An almost endless line of parishioners filed by Solemnus to receive the body and blood of Christ from this, their new bishop. When the lengthy Eucharist was complete, a Deacon rose, and by way of benediction, said, "Go in peace!" The ceremony was finished.

All the clergy reveled in the proceedings. The ordination rite, the Eucharist, prayers, and blessings, besides being important in this political event, were genuinely meaningful to them in a spiritual way. In these celebrations of faith there was hope, there was possibility, there was power. The Spirit was at work!

The bishops retired to a back room in the church, leaving the sound of townspeople behind. In a sparsely furnished room decorated with nothing other than a crucifix, table and three hardback chairs, they changed from their formal priestly garments to their everyday attire and readied themselves for the meal of celebration. Removing chasubles and donning more simple robes, they congratulated Solemnus, and each other, on a rite well done.

"You didn't stumble over your words at all," affirmed the elderly Patiens, patting Solemnus on the shoulder.

"And you didn't stumble over your feet!" said the jovial Faustus to Patiens, bringing laughs from everyone.

"Gentlemen," said Remigius in a mockingly admonishing tone, "let's not waste time, there's a feast waiting."

The banquet feast was spread in the hall that stood across from the church. The townspeople arrived before the bishops, which was no small feat, for the cadre of clergy wasted no time, themselves, in anticipation of the meal. The bishops forced Solemnus to lead them to their table, amid the cheers of the gathered guests. Remigius raised his hands in a signal for quiet, a direction that was only reluctantly obeyed.

"Friends," he said loudly. The commotion quieted a bit more. "Friends, congratulate your Bishop!" With that the room erupted into renewed cheering.

Toasts were offered to Solemnus, though the toast receiving the most enthusiastic response was that offered by Solemnus himself. Grinning so widely that he could have grinned no more, the new bishop raised his glass and the people quieted to listen.

"To my mother."

Nothing more needed to be said. Bernice, a slight but hardy woman, whose long suffering journey through life was very nearly legend among the populace of Chartres, was loved by all who knew her. The people roared their approval of the toast and raised their glasses. She blushed and smiled broadly at her son before casting her gaze down at the floor.

The residents of the city rejoiced in their new bishop, enjoying musicians and singers who related the history of Chartres, but enjoying most of all the feast that was spread before them. Deer, boar, and fruits from the Mediterranean graced the tables. The wine was plentiful and good. Eventually, as bellies were filled and as wine had its desired effect, the festivities quieted. Conversation supplanted oration. And at the head table, the bishops pulled their chairs into a circle, continued to enjoy the wine and, feeling philosophical because of it, considered the plight of the Church.

"The Arians are getting stronger, I think," said Domitianus of Geneva. "I'm afraid for Burgundy. Even though the faith of the people is strong, our king, Gundobad, is Arian. That doesn't help us get converts, and he doesn't show any inclination toward the faith, himself."

Volusianus of Tours joined in, "It's not any better where I serve. Not only is Alaric Arian, so are the people. Virtually all of Gaul south of the Loire is Arian!"

Volusianus had struggled with this problem in a very real way, as his colleagues well knew. He'd remained true to his Trinitarian faith in the midst of the Arian Visigoths who filled the countryside where he made his home. Too many times he'd known harrassment from the people of Alaric. His strength of devotion had long impressed the bishops. He was well respected, even by Remigius, whose respect was not easily earned.

The picture was a bleak one as, over and over again, the bishops spoke of the powerful Arians. It was the bishop of Tournai that broke stride.

"North of the Loire we struggle with the pagans."

Chapter 3 *The Bishop's Concern: 490 CE*

Glad to hear something different, the bishops focused their attention on Eleutherius of Tournai. The lanky, deep voiced Eleutherius served the Church in one of the least Christian areas. The faithful were harder to find as one approached the borders of what had been the Empire. "At least our king doesn't *hate* the Trinity. He simply ignores it." Faustus chuckled and the other bishops smiled at his minor indescretion. "Our king plunders and loots the churches and worships pagan gods," continued Eleutherius, "but he does seem to be willing to allow people the freedom to worship as they choose."

Remigius leaned forward at the words. "You mean Clovis, of course?"

"Yes," said Eleutherius.

Remigius nodded. "He's well on his way to becoming a capable ruler, if not a dangerous one."

Eleutherius again: "I agree."

"And, my brothers," Remigius addressed the entire group of clergy now, "he does, in fact, seem to be a decent man, this Clovis. He returned to me one of the silver vessels his men had looted from the church in Reims. It was ruined, but I believe his intentions were honorable."

Principius, who had traveled with Clovis when he came to Reims to deliver the broken bowl, added, "And he does seem to act with charity toward his own family…unlike what we've heard about Gundobad. From what I've seen, Clovis takes good care of his mother and his concubine."

Avitus of Vienne swallowed a large gulp of wine, his face sad at the mention of Gundobad. The other bishops made no attempt at discretion as they gazed upon Avitus, waiting for any further reaction. The history was clear, though. Politics guided the hand of Gundobad. No church, Catholic or Arian, would steer him from a path of self-interest. Nevertheless, Avitus felt compelled to offer some consolation. In spite of the image Gundobad bore in most of Gaul, his more recent conduct had been worthy of respect, even admirable.

"I have, at least," he stopped long enough to belch, "convinced Gundobad to extend limited protection to the Catholic believers in Burgundy."

"Yes," said Remigius. He smiled and remembered being a young bishop, himself. Remigius had been intimidated by a similar gatherings in his youth and he thought Avitus was handling the circumstances well.

Surveying the rest of the banquet hall, Remigius noticed, almost incidentally, that only a few of the people of Chartres were still sharing conversation. Even that subdued commotion seemed to lessen as he observed it. Some people were asleep at the tables but many had gone to their beds. Slowly, with a deep breath and with purpose in every part of his being, Remigius stood and arched his back in a long satisfying stretch. His eyes turned upward and remained so after his stretching was complete. Those bishops who had known Remigius for any length of time took notice, held their tongues, and hushed the younger priests who took in the recognizable pre-comment breaths.

After a long moment, Remigius brought his attention back to his friends, smiling at his fellow clergymen. He leaned forward, put his hands on the table and took the time to look at each one of them in the eye.

"Brothers, I have an idea I'd like you to consider." He pushed off of the table and stood to his full height again, taking on his most official air. "Among the people of Gaul there are some things of which we can be reasonably certain. For example, we can expect that those who follow the teachings of Arius won't convert to worship the Holy Trinity."

"Certainly not without the Lord's help," said Solemnus.

Remigius frowned. "That goes without saying, Solemnus." The new bishop had yet to learn that it was best not to interrupt Remigius. The frown lingered as Remigius cleared his throat. "Whatever the case," he said, "it's clear that the Arians have chosen a path that is easy and sufficient for their lazy minds. They have no reason to convert because they haven't taken the time or effort to discover how erroneous their beliefs are. Nor *will* they take the time as long as there are rulers, whom they rightly respect, who follow the same heresy." He looked around and paused for effect. "It's the rulers, the kings that we must influence if Gaul is to be rescued from this Arian threat."

"But we've tried, brother..."

Remigius waved his hand silencing Volusianus. "Yes, I know, we've tried. And we'll continue to try." Remigius cleared his throat again. "But we have to be honest and recognize that there's a very real possibility the Arian rulers won't ever change their spiritual loyalties." Remigius swathed his mouth with his tongue and took a drink of his wine before continuing. "The fact is," his voice lowered now, "we may have to do our part to remove rulers so others might stand in their place."

"Remigius!" said Avitus urgently, "some of us exist only at the favor of the kings. If they think we're plotting against them..."

Chapter 3 *The Bishop's Concern: 490 CE*

"I'm only trying to make the situation clear, Avitus. It is not my intention to make you uncomfortable." Avitus responded by pouring himself another goblet of wine and draining half of it in one long draught. Remigius didn't miss this and gave the bishop from Vienne a comforting smile before continuing. "So let's consider something else," he spoke to the whole group again, "something of which we can also be reasonably certain…that the people of Gaul, whether Arian or believers in the Trinity, will not turn to pagan gods."

The bishops murmured in agreement. Solemnus, who had remained silent since his first ill-received comment, cocked his head and squinted. He was beginning to see where Remigius was taking them. The bishop of Reims went on. "So we needn't worry about people rallying around a pagan, like Clovis. The Church in Gaul is not threatened by paganism." The bishops haltingly agreed to the obvious, uncertain of what Remigius was getting at. "But," Remigius lifted his index finger for emphasis, "what if Clovis came to believe in Christ?" Solemnus smiled, his suspicions confirmed. "If Clovis is to become a great leader, as our brother Eleutherius here suggests, wouldn't it be worth our efforts to seek his conversion?"

The bishops were suddenly intrigued.

Eleutherius spoke. "But Clovis is no more inclined to convert than the Arian leaders are. In his mind the pagan gods have given him his victories."

"I understand that," said Remigius. "But the question is: who will more likely convert to the true faith, a pagan or an Arian? I firmly believe, my brothers, that a pagan is more easily converted."

The veil of confusion was now drawn back and the bishops began to nod in enthusiastic agreement with Remigius. The portly Bishop Camilianus was the most hesitant of the group. He remembered how Bishop Aprunculus of Langres had been banished after his attempts to welcome an army of Franks into Burgundy. He didn't care to risk exile, himself, by bargaining with this Frankish chief.

"And just how are we to bring this conversion about?" he asked.

"That, my brother, is the real question," replied Remigius. "What can we do to encourage a pagan king to turn to our Lord Jesus?" He took a deep breath and slowly repeated his question, "Indeed…what can we do?"

Over Chartres the stars were shining brightly, sending their images to bounce off the few ripples that marred the river, Eure. The river ran shallow and slow, quiet and smooth. The banquet feast was over and most of the bishops were in their rooms for the night. The bishops of Reims and Vienne, however, felt the need for further discussion. Alongside the river, the only sounds to be heard were the mating calls of the insects and the soft rustle of leaves. The two churchmen walked side by side, Remigius still feeling the thrill of the day, Avitus only just beginning to recover from his overindulgence in the wine. They made their way toward a small bridge. Remigius took advantage of the privacy to offer his personal condolences to his young friend.

"I shall miss your father, Avitus. He was a fine man and servant of the Church. We shall all miss him."

"Thank you," was all the still grieving Avitus could say. His mind flitted among numerous images from the day they buried his father. The city of Vienne, showed deep and honest grief at the passing of Bishop Hesychius. The people filled the church to honor the man, whom many called the most faithful servant of the Lord in Vienne they could remember. Avitus performed his own father's funeral, striving to keep his composure as he eulogized the man. Only after his father was buried did he allowed himself to grieve.

The memories passed in a moment, though, crowded out of his mind by the more immediate and vital concern of the Church. "God is not the God of the dead, but of the living," Avitus remembered.

"I've been pondering our problem, Remigius."

"Mmm?"

"I have an idea that might be worth considering."

"Yes?"

"What if Clovis were to marry a Christian?"

"Marry a Christian? Didn't Principius say that Clovis had a family?"

"Yes, he did, but I understood him to say that Clovis had a concubine, not a wife. Even among the Franks the title 'wife' means something. I can't imagine that Clovis would marry his concubine. A concubine is nearly a slave."

"Ah," was the slow reply as Remigius considered what Avitus was suggesting. "But to encourage a Christian woman to marry a pagan? I don't care for the idea."

"Nor do I. But consider: if a Christian woman were to capture the heart of Clovis, wouldn't that increase the chances of his converting? He might consider a new faith more seriously if he were in love…and a Christian woman would surely see it as her duty to bring Clovis to the Church."

"I would hope for that much, anyway."

Chapter 3 *The Bishop's Concern: 490 CE*

Avitus could tell Remigius was still struggling with the appalling idea of encouraging the union of a Christian to a pagan.

"It is a precarious time for the Church, Father. Shouldn't we be taking risks for her?"

Remigius shook his head. "I can see the possibilities in what you propose, Avitus, but I'm afraid of what could go wrong. What if this woman, whoever she might be, marries Clovis. If he becomes a great ruler and she fails in her attempt to convert him, it could be devastating to the Church. And what of her? What if she renounced her faith?"

"I grant you, there's a risk. But the right woman could reduce that risk."

Remigius looked at Avitus, his eyes widening. "You have someone in mind, don't you?"

Avitus smiled, "I was beginning to wonder when you'd ask. Yes, I do have someone in mind."

The younger bishop paused as the two arrived at the footbridge leading to a long narrow island that ran along the entire eastern edge of the city of Chartres. He motioned to Remigius to cross first, which the elder bishop did. From the bridge Remigius could see the moss and grass that grew in the shallow waters of the Eure. A large willow tree cast a shadow on the river, blocking out the light of the stars, making the river look deceptively deep. Its darkness seemed especially treacherous, unsettling Remigius. He stopped for a moment, gazed into the murk and shivered. Then, without saying a word he moved on, continuing the conversation only after he was over the bridge.

"You have my attention, Avitus. Go on."

"Her name is Clotild. She's a princess, though not currently in the best of circumstances. Her father was Chilperic of Burgundy."

"Gundobad's brother?"

"The same. With my father, I was able to negotiate the safety of the girls after Gundobad defeated Chilperic. They're living in Geneva now with their uncle, Godegesil."

"Chilperic was Arian wasn't he?"

"Yes, he was," Avitus affirmed, "but his wife, Caretena, was a tolerant woman, and her tolerance opened many doors for us. I was a friend of the court, thanks to my father's connections, and saw the girls often. My father was one of their teachers, though I suspect they learned more from me. My age helped, I think. Anyway, the girls eventually came to believe the true faith."

"Interesting," said Remigius. He clasped his hands together, behind his back. "So, the daughters are Catholic?"

"They are indeed. In fact, even as we speak, they're involved in the work of the Church in Geneva. Domitianus works with them. In all honesty I'm surprised he hasn't thought of this. Anyway, I try to keep in touch with them, when I have the occasion to travel there."

"She's a princess," Remigius said, losing himself in thought. "Is there anything else that might recommend this woman?"

"Well, it doesn't hurt that she's beautiful, and I've found her to be strong in her faith. Her life is one of unquestionable devotion."

"It's an intriguing idea, Avitus. But the fact is, there's very little we can do about it. We can plant an idea here or there, but I can't imagine what else."

"True. We should also be prepared for the possibility that our efforts might bring disappointing results. Clotild's a spirited young woman. She may not be the least bit interested in a pagan like Clovis. And I wouldn't want to force such a relationship upon her."

"No, we can't force anything…but maybe we can encourage some things." Remigius let his voice trail off as he turned the possibilities over in his mind. Then with a quick deep breath he said, "But any hope is worth something, eh Avitus? We should trust God to guide our path."

"Yes," said Avitus, "and may God protect us all."

The two continued walking for close to half an hour, their voices silent but their heads filled with imaginings of how they, in their respective places, could promote the union of a pagan chief with a Christian princess. The wind shifted and stars began to disappear as clouds drifted overhead. A storm was approaching.

Chapter 4

The Power of Clovis Grows
490-491 CE

Nathalie screamed through hard-clenched teeth and the veins on her head bulged as the final push of a long and arduous labor brought her first child into the world. She let out a cry that could have been mistaken for a laugh; the kind that screams pain and shouts release. Clovis escaped the room hours before the birth, but his mother, Basina, remained to help. She held Nathalie in her squatting position for the last few pushes and then, baby safely on a mat, eased the mother onto her back.

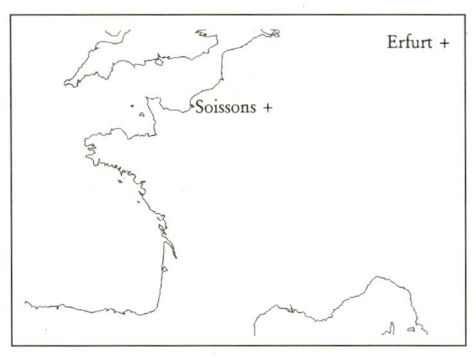

After a quick cleaning of the baby and a check for any oddities, Basina began to cry as she lifted her first grandchild to Nathalie's stomach. "A boy!" she cried, "It's a boy!"

Nathalie smiled and brought the baby to her breast. "Clovis will be pleased." Invoking the name of the Teutonic Goddess of love and beauty, she said, "Freya has blessed me."

As the baby began to suckle, Basina laid a wool blanket over them both.

Two weeks later, Basina stood on the porch, cutting wild red poppies and lavender, arranging them in a ceramic vase. She could have had a servant do the work, but this was one simple pleasure she reserved for herself. In her youth she helped her parents with the gardening often and gained a love for the earth that remained with her still. Her lips puckered as she stood back from the arrangement and considered its composition. Long fingers stroked her chin as she pondered what was missing and then, with a satisfied "ahh," she returned to the vase to make the necessary adjustments.

Nathalie, still recovering from the birthing, sat on a pillow nearby, watching while Audofleda, Basina's eldest daughter, sat quietly, arranging flowers with her mother. The younger daughters, Lantechild and Albofleda, played outside. Lantechild yelled as Albofleda, the youngest, gave a yank on her hair. Basina looked up from her work long enough to make sure no lasting damage had been done. Albofleda was already comforting her sister with apologies, ready to play again. Basina turned back to the flowers.

Clovis sat with his new son, talking nonsense, unashamed. He held Theuderic in front of him, making wide-eyed exaggerated exclamations at every facial expression he imagined the boy was attempting. The joy he took in his son was a new sensation to him, not just a good feeling, far beyond a responsibility, more like a victory. Basina looked at her son and smiled. This king has more confidence than his father had, she thought. This king knows no fear.

It was warm for May. The sun was high and the sky was a brilliant blue. A light breeze kept the day from being uncomfortably hot. The day reminded Clovis of his father. He remembered learning to ride a horse on a day like this. His father had put him on the horse and led it in a circle. Clovis recalled that he began to slip off the horse almost immediately. His father caught him, holding him off the ground, while the horse was put back into position. Then, returned to his place on the horse, the circular ride continued. Childeric laughed at his son that day, like he had when Clovis tried to lift his sword. As a boy, Clovis thought he'd never be strong enough to wield a sword so heavy. The weapon was nearly as long as he was tall. And it took both of his hands to reach around the jeweled hilt. Using all his strength he could barely raise the blade above his head. His father had laughed, watching him struggle. Now that sword lay buried with the man far to the north, in Tournai, though what it represented was still weighty for Clovis. He promised himself that, one day, he would make his father proud, and he promised himself, as he looked now at Theuderic, that he wouldn't laugh at this boy.

"Mother?" he said, softly.

"Umm?"

"Tell me how you and father met."

Basina smiled and shook her head. "You've heard it so many times! Do you really want to hear it again?"

"Please." He looked away from his mother, distracted by a bird soaring by, wings tight to its body. It began to turn earthward before a few rapid pumps of the wings lifted it again. A warbler, he thought.

While Audofleda continued to work, Basina wiped her hands on her apron and sat next to her son, on a wooden bench that stood by the work table. Nathalie shifted so that she faced them. This was a story she'd never heard. Basina patted her son's knee lovingly, and looked out into space…into the past.

Chapter 4 *The Power of Clovis Grows: 490-491 CE*

"Childeric was the wisest, strongest and most beautiful man I've ever known. He was exiled by the very people you now rule. I've told you before, Clovis, your father was the kind of man who loved women. It seemed he could never have enough of the pleasures they offered. And that's why the Franks exiled him. They were embarrassed by him." She shook her head. "I was told that he barely got away with his life. Some of his people truly wanted him killed.

"Thuringia, across the Rhine, my home, was the only place that would take him in. My husband, the king, offered your father safety and welcomed him into his court—a decision he came to regret."

She smiled and tilted her head.

"Childeric was too much a leader to be done in by his weakness for women. His friends knew it well. Before your father was run out of Tournai, he went to his friend, Wiomad," she looked at her son, "the father of your friend, Gerard, and they devised a plan that would return Childeric to power." She relaxed into her memories and as she did, she brushed a loose strand of hair behind her ear, then cocked her head and gave a poignant look as she remembered someone long forgotten by most of the Franks. "Bertolle too. He was a part of it. Do you remember him?"

Clovis nodded his head, as if he did remember, though, he could remember the man in name only, familiar from the stories his father told. Clovis was barely walking when Bertolle died.

"Their signal was a gold coin, split in two. Childeric kept one half, and Wiomad the other. When it was safe for Childeric to return to Tournai, Wiomad's half of the coin would serve as notice that the time had come. It took years.

"In the meantime, the Franks chose the Roman, Aegidius, to rule. Syagrius was his son, you know," Basina directed the information to Nathalie, then paused and smoothed her apron, thinking about how glad she was that the man who hated her husband and son more than anyone was now dead. She'd lived with that threat for too long. "Eventually, your father conquered Aegidius." She looked at her son and broke into a sheepish smile. "But that's not what you asked about, is it?"

Clovis smiled and patted his mother's hand.

"No, mother, it's not."

Basina blushed. "I'm sorry. Your father came to Thuringia and stayed there for four years. It was a wonderful time! It was a difficult time. While he was there, I came to love him and he began to love me. Had anyone discovered it, we would have been killed. My husband,

Basinus, was not as wise or as strong as your father, but he was, without a doubt, more unforgiving than any man I have ever known.

"So we spent the better part of those years finding brief moments here and there, becoming well-versed on the hiding places of the castle. There were more than even the builders could have known, if that's possible. And we became experts in quiet love-making. It was both wonderful and terribly risky.

"Then, one day, your father received one half of a gold coin…Bertolle brought it…a message that his people wanted him back. Wiomad had worked in the most deceitful and ingenious ways to cause the Franks to be discontent with Aegidius.

"And that was the end. The man I loved was leaving and there was nothing I could do that would stop him. So I let him go. I watched him ride away."

"But you went after him," Clovis said, like a child repeating the end of a story before the teller could say the words, as if to confirm that the ending was still the same.

"Yes, dear. I couldn't stand it. I was afraid I'd go mad. So I decided to follow him. One day, I left under the pretense of a pleasure ride, saying that I'd return in no more than an hour. It wasn't a good ploy. A better story would have given me more time, but I only wanted to leave.

"I left everything behind and rode as fast as my horse would take me until I caught up with Childeric. He asked me why I'd followed him and I said, "I only know that you're strong and that I've come to live with you." It sounds silly, I know, but it's true. Later I warned him that if I ever found anyone better or stronger, I'd desert him too." Basina's smile was mischievous.

"My reason was good enough for him. He loved me. And though he knew that he would win only anger and hatred from Thuringia, he agreed we should be together."

Basina beamed as she told the story. Her eyes glistened with the pain and joy that memories bring and Clovis smiled at her. He was sorry that she had been widowed.

"I'm strong too, mother."

"That's true, my son." She stroked his hair.

Clovis handed his son to her. "And what father ruled will seem tiny compared to what I will rule someday." As he spoke he rose to his full height and looked beyond where his sisters played, out over the landscape. "With every victory I'm stronger. I'll reign over more than father ever imagined!"

Chapter 4 *The Power of Clovis Grows: 490-491 CE*

"You *are* a strong warrior, Clovis. But remember…remember, you must be wise too." Basina sounded protective.

"I am wise."

"Yes, I know."

"And I'm beautiful too, aren't I?"

"Are you asking me or telling me?" she inquired, smiling,

Clovis turned back to his mother wearing a look of fierce determination that reminded Basina of her beloved Childeric. He looked into his mother's eyes and, slowly, beginning with his own eyes, he allowed a smile to grow on his face.

"I'm asking, mother."

Basina's heart melted and she embraced her only son.

"Yes, my son, you are beautiful…and wise and strong! My dear son!"

Clovis returned the hug and then kissed his mother before taking Theuderic and lifting the child up before him.

"Mother, do I look happy?"

"What?"

"Do I look happy?"

Basina looked at Nathalie and rolled her eyes.

"Yes, Clovis, you look happy."

"Good! Because I *am* happy!"

Nathalie's soft smile revealed her pleasure at having given Clovis joy. Brought to the side of the Chief of the Franks as a concubine after the defeat of her people, she knew there was little chance she would ever be a wife to Clovis. But in the little more than a year since she'd been in Soissons, Nathalie had discovered that she loved the man. Basina could see it, though no one else had guessed.

Clovis cuddled Theuderic and looked tenderly at his woman. "Nathalie…," he shook his head and looked at his firstborn again, "…I still think he looks like me."

Basina and Nathalie both laughed. They'd been through this a dozen times since Theuderic had been born. Albofleda and Lantechild both thought Theuderic looked like Nathalie. Basina thought he looked like his grandfather, Childeric. Nathalie stayed diplomatically neutral. But Clovis insisted that his son looked like him and the others good-naturedly gave in.

"Look how long his hair is! He's already looking like a chief!"

"He'll grow up to be a handsome chief," said Basina. Her immeasurable pride in her son and grandchild poured from her heart.

Clovis looked up at his mother and then back into his son's tiny squinting face. "Yes," he said slowly, "he *will* grow up, won't he? He'll rule in my place one day. And then perhaps he'll have a son, and his son, another." He took on a more intense look, and said to Theuderic, "I hope your sons…and their sons…will remember me."

Basina and Nathalie exchanged looks of a shared understanding, and they knew this man, this strong chieftain, realized he was also a mere mortal, bearing all the normal fears of men.

"They will," Basina said, "If you give them something to remember…they'll remember." The sound of her voice caused Clovis to turn toward his mother. In her face he saw the pain of old memories.

"The threat of Thuringia is one I don't intend to live with," said Clovis as he sat back in his throne.

The casual comment jarred Aurelian. His outward appearance remained calm, but all his senses were instantly focused on Clovis. Years of service to Syagrius had taught Aurelian to pursue information first, before any effort was made to challenge or convince. The years had also taught him that frequently the most valuable information came in ways other than words. He looked carefully at Clovis, checking for any subtle signals that might be coming from the man. Clovis sat quietly musing as Aurelian examined him.

"Sir?" he said, hoping for more insight.

"Thuringia, I said. They're a threat we can no longer ignore."

One of Aurelian's primary functions as advisor to Clovis was to be an objective voice. Clovis trusted his advisor to speak honestly when he disagreed with his chief, but Aurelian knew that there were times when his job was simply to help Clovis think things out on his own. He decided that this was one of those times.

"Because of the rumors?" he asked.

Aurelian, Clovis and everyone was talking about a skirmish that had taken place near Tournai. With every telling the stories became more and more gruesome. The most recent version Aurelian had heard said that a group of Franks had been slaughtered, the men and children by the sword, but only after they'd been forced to watch as the women had their arms tied to the necks of horses and were then dragged through brambles and trampled as the horses were lashed to flight. Their houses had been burned. It seemed a purely malicious attack. No goods were taken, only destroyed. Some were saying that Basinus, the king of Thuringia had led the strike, though there was no proof of that. For all anyone knew it could have been one of the several bands of robbers that roamed the countryside around Tournai.

Chapter 4 *The Power of Clovis Grows: 490-491* CE

Clovis crossed his legs and began to pat his raised knee rapidly. The fidget was one nervous habit Aurelian had learned well. It said that Clovis was not sure of himself.

"Yes, because of the rumors. But I don't trust the Thuringians in any case. I've been thinking of this for a while."

"Why don't you trust them?"

"History, mostly. My mother was their queen, you know." Aurelian did know. "She left her throne for my father, and I'm afraid they've carried a bitter taste in their mouths about it ever since." Clovis raised his eyebrows and shrugged. "I'm not surprised, though. After all, they gave my father refuge, and what did he do for thanks? He stole their queen."

"Ah," was all Aurelian said. He was more comfortable now, convinced that Clovis was only toying with the idea.

"Our other frontiers are secure," continued Clovis. "With Gundobad in Italy, fighting against Theodoric, we don't have to concern ourselves with Burgundy."

"No," affirmed Aurelian. "And Alaric is there too, fighting *with* Theodoric."

"The south is not a worry then. How about west?"

"The Armoricans? They don't seem to be interested in anyone but themselves. We are, however, beginning to see some increased trade there."

"Any need to worry about them?"

"Not that I can see."

Suddenly Aurelian was uneasy again. This was not toying at all. This was a pretense hunt. Recently, Clovis had captured the island city of Paris, though not without difficulty. The strong willed and popular Christian woman, Genevieve, in rallying the poor of the city, had caused no small delay as the Franks tried to take the city. Christians had gathered with her to defend their home against the pagans. Those who lived outside of Paris, on the banks of the Seine, moved onto the island, throwing up barricades on the bridges behind them. For the most part they were without weapons, but they held the advantage of position. Ultimately, however, in the strangest victory Clovis had ever known, Paris succumbed. One day the siege was on and the next, he and his men were offered the city. There were no signs of a siege beyond the barricades. Leaders that met with Clovis intimated that not only had Genevieve rallied people to resist the Franks, she had also encouraged them to surrender in peace. Clovis didn't care how it came about, as long as Paris fell to him.

Other cities, too, had come under his reign. His reputation and power was growing as was his hunger. He ruled more than his father had ever dreamed of ruling and now his thoughts were turning to the east. Clovis was trying to increase the size of his realm and Aurelian knew in his heart that his king was already contemplating the arrangements necessary to put this campaign into motion.

His concerns were interrupted by the arrival of a messenger who handed him a dispatch. The secretary took it and read silently, the look on his face becoming one of bewilderment.

"What is it?" asked Clovis.

Aurelian dropped the message to his side and looked at Clovis. The disbelief on his face was echoed in his words, "Zeno is dead!"

Clovis was not especially moved. He'd had no contact with the Emperor. But he saw the dismay in Aurelian's face. Aurelian had served the Empire long and faithfully. He could not help but react with shock, even though the Empire had long since faded from prominence in the life of Gaul.

Aurelian called to mind an earlier time when the Empire had ruled everything, been everything, at least to him. He swallowed hard and breathed the shallow quivering breaths that precede sobs. Clovis was surprised at the show of emotion from this usually stolid man and offered what sympathy he could.

"We'll send our condolences, of course."

Aurelian clenched his fists, took a deep breath, let it out and then another, blinking back tears as he forced his attention back to the present. He gave Clovis a nod of agreement and made a mental note of the need to send a letter.

Clovis was in need of Aurelian's insights and composure but, it was clear that, for the moment, they were lost. He had no intention of dwelling on the fate of the Empire but could see that Aurelian could do nothing else. Heaving a frustrated sigh he said, "No more business today, Aurelian."

The secretary sniffed and said, "As you wish, sir."

It didn't take long for Aurelian to regain his composure. A great blanket of curiosity soon comforted him when it was learned, through subsequent reports, that Zeno had been succeeded by a domestic who had served in his court. Anastasius was his name, chosen by Zeno's widow, who gave him her hand in marriage as well. It rapidly became clear that the Emperor in Constantinople would have even

Chapter 4 *The Power of Clovis Grows: 490-491* CE

less influence in Gaul than previously. The distance to Gaul, along with the diminishing importance to the Empire of this outlying land, would cause Anastasius to direct his energies elsewhere. The affairs of the Franks soon returned to the center of Aurelian's thoughts.

Meeting with Clovis about the decision to attack the Thuringians convinced Aurelian that his ruler's mind was made up. The Franks were going into battle. Aurelian wasted no time in securing an alliance with the court of Chief Siegbert, who ruled the Franks in nearby Cologne. They had felt the sting of Thuringia before, paying the price of assisting Childeric when he'd departed with Queen Basina.

Four weeks sufficed for the call to arms to be issued, the weapons and supplies to be procured, the army to gather and the journey to be made, bringing the Franks east, by way of Cologne, to the banks of the river, Gera, near the city of Erfurt, ready for war.

The Thuringians were distant cousins to the Franks and it would have surprised no one that the two armies looked alike. Standing ready to defend their land, they wore the same style of armor and carried the same kinds of weapons as the Franks. Clovis wondered if he was about to engage his own family as he looked out at the defensive forces of Thuringia. Were the children of his mother's brothers here?

Gerard stood with his chief, quiet as he tried to assess the strength of this enemy.

"They're outnumbered," said Clovis.

In fact, the only major difference between the two armies was that of size. Clovis and Siegbert were willing allies now, side by side, claiming the only advantage that either army knew: numbers. Now, with Siegbert and Clovis joined in common purpose, the army of the Franks swelled to 15,000, far larger than Thuringia's.

The day was warm, hazy, heavy with humidity, which, everyone knew, would make for a short battle. Before the fighting began the men were already soaked with sweat. Even in their peak condition they would not last long. Numbers became all the more important on such a day. Heartbeats quickened as the armies scrutinized one another, a terror began to grow among the men of Thuringia even as confidence grew among the Franks.

Axes and javelins flew at one another and in moments the ranks of the opposing armies met. The thrown weapons were removed from turf and flesh for use against their previous owners and close combat ensued. Following the yells of charging men, the sound of muscle and bone being hewn joined with grunts and groans as the music of the field. Only the screams, which never lasted long, rose above the thrashing of battle. Driven by vengeance, the Thuringians fought with more anger than Clovis had ever known from an enemy.

Over the years, conflicting reports came to Tournai from across the Rhine, some suggesting that Basinus, the cuckolded king, had died, others saying he was still in power. Clovis wondered if he was here, an angry and aged king, infuriated that this offspring of the vile Childeric would dare to insult him further with battle.

The armies of Clovis poured around the Thuringians, nearly surrounding them in the initial onslaught. The defenders found themselves back to back, facing outward as they fought for their lives, no longer imagining that victory was a possibility. The Franks pressed in, completing their encirclement of the enemy, soon reaching the point where the outer ranks of Thuringians were the only warriors with room to fight. Those inside could only watch until the men in front of them fell into a growing pool of Thuringian blood.

In less than an hour the battle was done. What few Thuringians survived were taken and bound, soon to become slaves. King Basinus was never found.

A severely beaten Thuringia was added to the lands ruled by Clovis. Siegbert shared the glory and willingly agreed to assist in the administrative tasks. Tribute was to be paid and equally shared. Thuringia would know the protection that the Franks could offer in time of invasion, though few expected any real help would ever be seen. Greater warning of invading forces would be the true reward of claiming these lands, and though the spoils were to be shared, Clovis knew that increased lands meant increased power. For the time being, that was enough.

Chapter 5

A Seed is Planted
492 CE

The country home was surrounded by beehives that provided honey for a goodly number of the nearby villages. The hum of the insects was the song of the land, constant and relaxing, soothing and sustaining. Separating the hives from the residence was an herb garden dominated by lavender, of which the bees seemed particularly fond. The house itself was extravagant. Columned halls and mosaic tile floors complemented the sculptures and landscape murals that decorated it. No less than eight fireplaces kept the rooms warm in winter and the extensive walking paths provided a pleasant setting for evening strolls in the more temperate seasons. Bishop Remigius made the four day journey, heading south from Reims, arriving several days before Avitus, bringing his cousin wine, blessings from Reims and thanks for the use of his home. His cousin was more than happy to offer his residence to the bishops. With a business trip before him, their presence assured that his servants wouldn't be taking advantage of him in his absence. He was off to Marseilles for a shipment of olive oil, which he expected would contribute substantially to his coffers once it was sold to clients in the south.

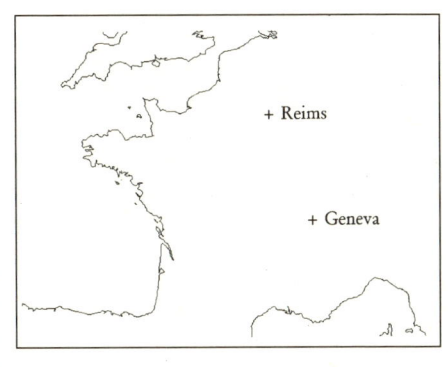

Remigius was glad to oversee the estate, but more delighted to return to the country. Reims flourished now under the good favor of Clovis. New lands were granted to the Church and Remigius found Clovis to be especially accommodating. He was more tolerant of the Church than the bishop had expected and his willingness to indulge his people was making him a popular ruler. And yet, even with such hopeful circumstances, the recent weeks had been trying ones for Remigius. It seemed as though the more he tried to put things into order, the more chaotic they became. The indiscretions of a young priest from Épernay were causing an uproar; the efforts to build new churches north of Reims were consuming a great deal of time, and that, combined with the normal demands on a bishop, gave him little time to be at peace. He welcomed these few days away and they prepared him for the business that lay ahead. By the time Avitus arrived, Remigius was refreshed and ready for his guest.

It was an indelicate arrival. Avitus caught the heel of his boot as he stepped off the carriage and fell to the ground in front of Remigius. Assisted by the young carriage driver, the elder bishop helped lift his colleague off the ground.

"It's so good to see you again," said Remigius, "even in this condition." He brushed the dirt off his friend's cloak and then embraced him warmly. Avitus and Remigius had become fast friends through meetings and correspondence over the past two years. Avitus was beginning to see his host more as a peer and less as a mentor.

Straightening his cloak, Avitus countered with, "You're so easy to impress, Remi!"

The bishops laughed and turned toward the house as servants arrived to stable the horses and unload the luggage that had come with Avitus from Vienne.

"You're early," said Remigius.

"I thought we could use the extra time. There's so much to talk about."

"Yes, but first, I think dinner would be good for us both. Interested?"

"More than interested! Traveling does amazing things for an appetite."

"Then, let's not waste time!" They entered the house, Remigius giving instructions that dinner should be served immediately.

As they dined they spoke of Burgundy and Gundobad; Clovis and Soissons; and the emerging power, Theodoric in Ravenna. But mostly they spoke of what all clergy were speaking of: the Arian weed that was threatening to choke the true Church. The heresy of Arius was surviving with greater tenacity than any of the Catholic bishops would have thought, and it was becoming more than a slight bother to Church.

That the teachings of Arius should be so strong a century and a half after they were condemned by the leaders of the Church, appalled them both. The Church was doing well enough in Burgundy, all things being considered. King Gundobad was busy with the affairs of state and didn't have time to champion the Arians, but his implicit support of the Arian Church, made evident by his participation in Arian worship, was enough to convince Avitus that the Catholic Church was threatened there. Not surprisingly, the people of Burgundy were following their king.

Chapter 5 *A Seed is Planted: 492 CE*

In Reims things were better. The respect Remigius commanded was serving him well. His concern, though, was more for Gaul at large than for his own region, and it was a profound concern.

"This battle with the Arians is too important to lose!" he said.

"I agree," said Avitus through a mouthful of duckling mixed with wine. "But what can we do?" He swallowed. "We're lucky to maintain our freedom to worship at all with so many Arian rulers around us."

"True," said Remigius, "But freedom of worship hasn't been our problem; not with Clovis on the throne."

"Has anyone tried to convert him?"

"Oh, he and I have talked about our Lord Christ, but he doesn't show much interest." The bishop of Reims sighed. "Still, he does allow the people to worship as they wish. And, since he conquered Syagrius, he's actually been courting the good favor of the Church. His counselor, Aurelian helps on that score." He squinted at Avitus, "I'd even say that, without trying to, Clovis not only allows freedom of worship, he encourages it. I'm grateful for that."

It wasn't much, Remigius knew. He tried to make it sound more significant that it actually was…and failed.

"Remigius, I recall our discussion in Chartres about Clovis. Isn't it time to do more than talk about the possibility of his union with a Christian?" He punctuated his question by popping a grape in his mouth and biting down.

Remigius took a mouthful of wine and held it a long time before swallowing. "Yes, I believe so," he said at last.

Both bishops were afraid to go further. They tried to turn their attention to the meal, but Remigius and Avitus both knew that this first step demanded a second. They sipped their wine nervously as they contemplated what they were about to do.

"If Clovis sees Clotild, he'll want her enough," said Avitus.

Remigius looked slyly at his friend.

"Do I catch a hint of lust in your voice?"

Avitus smiled at Remigius and said, "If you saw her, my friend, and didn't feel something, I'd say that you were losing your gifts of discernment. She is a glorious woman!"

Avitus remembered his last visit to Geneva when this idea first occured to him. The sisters served the needy as always. That day, for some reason, he imagined a providential one, he looked at the women in a new way. Sedeluba looked unapproachable yet welcoming, accessible as a servant, no more. No effort was taken on her part to lure or charm, only to love and serve. Her dress was functional, her manner purposeful, her heart open.

By contrast, while her clothes were identical, Clotild was, in fact, alluring, able to spark the hopes of lonely men. They gravitated toward her more casual demeanor, which was sensual and infectious. She and her sister both looked like their father, but Clotild's features were more striking. Her lips were fuller and redder, her cheek bones higher, her nose more elegant, more delicate than her sister's. Sedeluba's eyes could not be rivaled for sheer beauty, but they didn't cry out to see more, like Clotild's did. Her faith was not lacking, thought Avitus, but Clotild would require a man before long.

"I hope I'll get the chance to meet her," said Remigius, serious again.

Avitus didn't miss the change in mood, and it sobered him somewhat. "Emissaries of Clovis are often in Burgundy. They come to Geneva. I could start there by mentioning the princess. If I choose my company well, maybe Clovis will hear about her."

"Perhaps so. And while you're at that, I could suggest to him, somehow, that his power might be enhanced by a well arranged marriage. It's not much, but it's a beginning." They both knew there was little more they could do. They looked at one another and sighed in unison.

"So be it, then," said Avitus. The words were barely out of his mouth before he gave a huge yawn. "Ah me, I've had too much wine...if that's possible." He chuckled. "Do you think we could continue this tomorrow?"

Remigius laughed and pushed himself away from the table. "Drinking or talking?"

Avitus chuckled again. "I meant talking."

"Of course," said Remigius. "Perhaps our dreams will show us our next step."

For Remigius the chance to meet with Clovis came with blessed swiftness. No more than a week had passed since his meeting with Avitus, and Remigius was back in his residence barely a day when word came that Clovis was in Reims and would be paying his respects to the bishop.

Clovis was ushered into the Bishop's chambers and was about to be announced, and would have been, had Clovis not put his hand over the attendant's mouth. What he saw captivated him. Looking across the room, he saw Remigius at the window sill, feeding sparrows. They came to him, first looking up at him, then pecking the bits of bread that he held in his fingers. Clovis watched for a long time, impressed

Chapter 5 *A Seed is Planted: 492 CE*

by the bishop's gentleness. He leaned to one side to get a better view, and the birds, startled by the movement, darted away from the window sill. Remigius called to them and then, suspecting the reason for their flight, turned his head. Clovis bowed deeply.

"Ah, Clovis! Welcome!"

Clovis smiled at the greeting. He liked the bishop. Remigius was a man of power who didn't seek to conquer him. The kingdom Remigius defended was of another realm and, as bishop, he wielded his worldly authority with integrity. Clovis respected that.

Remigius came back from the sill, and embraced Clovis, wondering if there was a reasonable hope that this man would, one day, call Christ his Lord. He gestured to a seat and the two men made themselves comfortable.

"I'm sorry. I didn't mean to frighten the birds. I've never seen anyone feed them like that. How do you do it?"

"Oh that?" said Remigius. "That's nothing. They just come to me for food. It's really nothing." He looked embarrassed. "How are you?"

"I'm well, Bishop."

"I understand you've won Thuringia."

"Yes. My land is increasing and my strength with it."

Remigius nodded. Silence followed, a silence which made him uncomfortable. He'd made the decision to introduce a new and sensitive subject to Clovis. How to raise it was the problem. It would have been easier if Clovis had been summoned. This chance meeting was too sudden, too soon. Still, he didn't want to waste the opportunity.

"What brings you to Reims?"

"A land dispute involving one of my commanders. A silly thing, really, but it pays to keep commanders happy."

"I'm glad that circumstances brought us together again."

"As am I, Bishop."

The two of them enjoyed beer and cakes and conversation, building upon an already firm relationship. Finally, Remigius, known as an orator and surprised by his own inability to introduce his own agenda, decided to force it.

"Clovis," he said, massaging the palm of his hand, "Do you have time for a walk? There are some things I'd like to show you. Things you should see when you visit this city."

"I can make the time, certainly." Clovis reached for another cake.

"First, though, let me ask you…" Remigius stood and walked to the window. A sparrow flew to the sill, looked Remigius up and down, and then seeing there was no food, departed. The bishop smiled briefly in acknowledgment to the bird and then continued, "are you happy with the way things are going for you?" With his back to Clovis he winced at his own words.

"Bishop?"

"I mean…" Remigius gave up, "…never mind. Why don't we walk?"

A leisurely stroll brought the men to the memorial of Jovin, and a boldly sculpted marble sarcophagus depicting a warrior on horseback slaying a lion.

"Have you heard of Jovin?" Remigius asked.

"No."

"He governed here, lived here and, as you can see, is buried here. He was a champion for Reims; a great soldier, not unlike yourself. Of course, Rome doesn't impress us as they once did."

"I suppose not," said Clovis as he looked at the figure on the coffin.

Remigius made another attempt: "Have you considered the threats that face you from the other rulers in Gaul?"

Clovis was surprised by the question but Remigius was so intent in the asking that he felt he should give an answer. "Of course I have," he said. "I think about it constantly."

The men walked on further coming to a striking mosaic of two gladiators doing battle. The men were both nude, both wielding swords, only one holding a shield.

"Is this how Romans fight?" Clovis chuckled as he spoke, "because if it is, it's no wonder Rome is impotent!"

Remigius laughed with his guest before returning to his question.

"Do you do anything about it?"

"About what?"

"About the other rulers in Gaul."

"Remigius, you know the answer to your own question. The emissaries I send out go to secure the relationships. Even now. And my army is strong in case diplomacy fails us. Why are you asking me this?"

Remigius frowned.

"It's occurred to me that you might consider getting married."

"What?"

"Please, listen. It's important to me, to the Church, that you stay in power. You're good for the Church and anything I can do to insure your position will be, it seems to me, effort well spent.

"If you took a wife from one of the surrounding lands, I thought it might gain you an ally. Have you thought about that at all?"

Chapter 5 *A Seed is Planted: 492 CE*

"Remigius, I have a woman, a good woman." He thought of Nathalie. She wasn't his wife, but she was loyal. That counted for something.

"I know. I just thought a marriage might serve you."

"I let my soldiers serve me."

"Of course," was all Remigius could say. He knew that there would be little to gain by pushing further. The seed had been planted. Perhaps Avitus would do the watering.

Gundobad and Godegesil, brothers and kings, were on good terms with the Catholic Church, even though they, themselves, remained Arian. While Avitus spent most of his days near the court of Gundobad, it was not at all unusual to see his face in the court of Godegesil, either. And on this day, in the city of Geneva, where Godegesil ruled, Avitus made an appearance.

"It's a day of business, Bishop," said Godegesil as he climbed into his throne. "But you're welcome to stay, if that's your wish."

"I thank you, Godegesil. I would like to stay for awhile. I've only just arrived in Geneva and I'd welcome a chance to relax."

The bishop sat by quietly as Godegesil moved through the day's business. Most of it was rather routine, none of it controversial. News from various parts of the Empire and greetings from rulers that accompanied trade agreements or gifts of conciliation filled the better part of the day.

Avitus was content to listen. There was always something to be learned, politics from other lands, hints of intrigue, scales of exchange. Typically, though, mundane matters filled the docket, so when emissaries of Clovis were announced, he couldn't believe his ears. Making his way into the city, climbing the familiar narrow cobbled roads, Avitus had fully expected he would wait for days, weeks or conceivably months before coming across men who were loyal to Clovis. He wondered how he would stand in the court of Godegesil day after day without arousing suspicion. Now, less than half a day into his stay, that question needed no answer. Here they were, men from Soissons. Avitus wondered if this was an encouragement from God.

"Luillaume and Baldewin from the court of Clovis, king of Soissons," announced the secretary.

The men were shown in and came to stand before Godegesil. They were still in the dusty clothes of their journey, their hair was windblown and their faces shone red with exhilaration.

"Greetings, King Godegesil, from Clovis of Soissons, Chief of the Franks, and from us, your servants, I, being Luillaume, and this," he directed attention to his companion, "being Baldewin." Both men bowed deeply.

"Greetings to you and to your chief," returned Godegesil, a slight nod and a raised hand offered in exchange for the bows. "I trust you've had a fair journey?"

"Yes, thank you, sir, we have," answered the one who was called Baldewin.

"What business do you bring?"

Avitus wasn't the least bit interested in their business but watched the men closely, nonetheless. If, by their words and demeanor they revealed enough about themselves; their greeds, lusts, ambitions or loyalties, he might better discover how to approach them.

The men weren't particularly distinctive. Both were average in height and appearance for Franks. And they were clearly versed in their tasks as emissaries, stating their business, but no more. Eventually Avitus concluded that he would have to approach these two blindly. Nothing they said gave him any useful information. Even so, he was confident that these men, like all men, would be attracted to anything that might serve their own interests.

Before long, Avitus perceived that the business with the men from Soissons was drawing to a close. He rose to take his leave. Godegesil noticed the move and raised a hand to bring discussion to a halt.

"You leave us, Bishop?"

At Godegesil's words everyone, including the two men from Soissons, turned to look at Avitus. He felt himself blushing.

"My apologies, king Godegesil. I didn't intend to disrupt your business. The travel's taking its toll. If you would excuse me, I need to rest."

"Of course, Avitus. Rest well."

With short but gracious bows the two said farewell. Godegesil turned back to the business of the moment and Avitus made his way into the streets of Geneva. He positioned himself close to the residence of the king and waited for the Franks.

He waited and was able to enjoy the sight of three young women passing by, before Luillaume and Baldewin exited the castle. By their confident stride Avitus concluded the Franks had been in Geneva before. They walked to a nearby inn, one that Avitus, himself, frequented when he visited the city. The bishop followed them inside.

The low beamed ceiling flickered with the light from candles that rested on the tables and upon a long mantle that circled the inside

Chapter 5 *A Seed is Planted: 492 CE*

wall of the inn. To the left of the entrance was the kitchen, to the right, a large fireplace. A constant low murmur filled the place as patrons conversed.

Luillaume and Baldewin sat in the center of the room, ordering meat and wine. Their business had gone well and they were in high spirits.

Good, thought Avitus, but before he could think any more, a familiar voice called to him.

"Ah, Father Avitus! Back in town! Come, sit! Where is Father Domitianus today?" The portly proprietor recognized his regular customer and wiped clean a seat for him.

Avitus smiled and accepted the hospitality saying, "Away on business I believe." In truth, though, he had no idea where the bishop of Geneva was.

"A quiet meal for you then," said the innkeeper.

"I welcome it."

The proprietor brought venison, fresh fruit, and bread, cheese and a bottle of red wine to the Bishop's table. Avitus ate with satisfaction while always watching the two Franks who talked and laughed in the center of the room.

One of them reached out to pat the behind of a passing waitress, bringing more laughter. But the men were only a little obnoxious, and those seated around them enjoyed their jovial mood and harmless antics.

Later in the evening, long after Avitus had finished his meal, the two men finally concluded theirs. They called to the waitress, who was quite familiar to them by now, and they paid for their meal, including a generous gratuity. Making their way out, they passed by the bishop and nodded to him respectfully. While nodding in return, Avitus spoke.

"Excuse me, gentlemen. Could you spare a moment?"

The two paused, surprised at the request.

"Just a brief word," assured Avitus.

"I suppose we have a moment or two," said one of the men. They remained standing.

"You're Franks." It was not a question.

"Yes, Bishop, we are that. I'm Luillaume, and this is Baldewin."

"From the court of Clovis?"

"Yes," said Baldewin, sounding suspicious, "how did you know?"

"I'm Avitus, bishop of Vienne. I was in the court of Godegesil today when you arrived."

"Of course," said Luillaume, "I remember you now. I thought you looked familiar. You said you needed rest. I thought you meant a nap rather than a drink."

"Rest takes many shapes, my friend." Avitus smiled and the Franks smiled in agreement. "I'd be interested in knowing more about you and your king. Do you have time?"

"It would be an honor my good Bishop," said Baldewin, "but it's late and we're returning to Soissons in the morning."

"I won't keep you long, I promise." Feeling that more incentive was going to be needed he added, "And, if you haven't had your fill, perhaps I could offer you the enticement of some more wine?"

"Certainly we must honor the promise of a bishop," said Luillaume to Baldewin. "Surely we can stay for a moment."

Baldewin acquiesced and the bishop encouraged them to take the two chairs that were opposite him. More wine was ordered and poured.

"Good. I'm glad you can stay for a while. Through my talks with other bishops in Gaul, I've come to learn something of Clovis. He intrigues me and I'd like to learn more. What's he like?"

"What's there to tell that isn't already known?" asked Baldewin. "Clovis is the greatest warrior in Gaul. He defeated the Roman, Syagrius, and only a fool would challenge him."

Avitus smiled. "Your loyalty will certainly never be in question, my friend. And I've heard what you say, from others. But tell me, is he a good king?"

"As good as they come," said Luillaume. "There's not one better as far as I know. And you must know that even the Church supports him."

Avitus chose his words carefully now, "I know that Remigius and Eleutherius speak highly of him, but the Church seeks a heavenly authority, my friends...a kingdom that God rules."

At this, the Franks were silent. Avitus feared that he'd made a mistake in not simply agreeing with them. Even though the Church could not openly support a pagan, the bishop asked himself, what harm could it have done to have agreed with these men. Especially when what they said was true. Now he suspected time was short, so he became more direct.

"Has he taken a queen?"

"A queen?" asked Baldewin. "He has a woman, if that's what you mean."

"I've heard as much, but a woman is not necessarily a queen. A queen strengthens a king—or at least, a good queen does." Avitus gulped down the last of his glass and poured another, saying, "He must be looking for a queen. A man as wise as Clovis."

Luillaume and Baldewin were uncertain. This idea had never occurred to them.

"I suppose so..." said Luillaume, noncommittally.

"Yes, I'm sure he is," said Avitus. "Yes," he said again, adding emphasis to his conclusion. The Franks looked at him, silent. "It's a hard search, finding a queen," continued the bishop. "After all, she must be more than of proper lineage. She, must be strong and wise, charming and fair. Why, I tell you, I've heard of kings holding contests to find their queens. Indeed, in the Holy Scriptures, Esther became queen to King Ahasuerus because she won a beauty contest. Some kings even offer rewards to the one who finds the right woman to be queen. Does your King Clovis hold contests?"

The two Franks looked at each other and shrugged their shoulders.

"Because, if he is, I wonder if anyone has called Clotild to his attention."

"Clotild?" the two asked in unison.

"Clotild. You don't know her? Oh, ah, perhaps I should hold my tongue." Avitus feigned fear.

"No, no, please continue," Luillaume asked, his interest growing.

"No," said Avitus, as he looked at the people occupying the other tables in the inn, "perhaps it's not a good idea to talk about it."

Baldewin lowered his own voice, "You're afraid, Bishop. Why?"

Avitus leaned forward.

"You really don't know about Clotild, do you?"

The Franks shook their heads.

"I suppose I should expect that. She's been exiled since her father was killed—since she was little more than a girl." He looked around the room again. "But I really should hold my tongue!"

"Bishop, don't be afraid of us. We're leaving tomorrow, and we don't have any desire to harm you. You've aroused our curiosity. Don't stop now."

Avitus looked at the two, seeing men who recognized an opportunity when it came their way. The ploy, as simple as it was, had worked. Don't be too willing, now, he silently warned himself.

"There's no point. She doesn't really exist."

"What? Doesn't exist? Bishop, have you been telling us lies?"

"No, no, she doesn't exist because King Gundobad in Vienne doesn't wish her to exist. He killed her parents and wished to kill her too. But an internal exile was arranged for her and her sister on the condition that their lives be kept private."

"So this Clotild does exist!"

"Oh yes, and she's all I described: fair and charming, strong and wise, and before Gundobad killed her father, she was a princess too. Now the only people who ever see her are the beggars who come to the church of St. Germain, here in Geneva. But I talk too much...too much wine." Avitus tried to sound disgusted with himself.

"Not at all," said Baldewin, "you've done us a favor by not teasing us."

"Don't let others know that you are aware of Clotild. It could be dangerous."

"No, Father, we won't betray you."

Avitus hoped they were telling the truth. If the story of this night ever got to Gundobad's ears, there was no telling what his reaction might be.

"But you say that Clotild is here, in Geneva?" Luillaume asked.

"Yes, indeed! The two sisters have served the Church here since their exile and they'll serve here for years to come, I suspect. I've come to know them, and I assure you, I don't know of any women who are more worthy of their royal blood."

The Franks turned toward one another with looks of disbelief and wonder on their faces. Avitus didn't miss it.

"Oh, it's true, my friends. I wouldn't lie to you, but you mustn't tell anyone that I told you." The bishop pretended fear again.

"No, no, of course not," assured Luillaume. He put his hand on the Bishop's shoulder in a show of confidence.

The Franks had come upon more than they had bargained for when they'd agreed to sit with the bishop. Luillaume looked excited. Baldewin, the careful one, was looking anxious to leave. Avitus decided to offer them a way out.

"I've kept you too long," he said. "The wine...it makes me talk. Please, go. I've kept you longer than I should have. And have a safe journey home," he said with especial sincerity.

Baldewin immediately looked relieved. "Thank you, good Bishop. May we carry your greetings to Clovis?"

"Yes, please do...from Avitus, bishop of Vienne."

The Franks rose and shook the Bishop's hand and made their way out of the inn.

Avitus watched them as they stooped to pass under the door post and stepped out into the Geneva night. In a low voice, he said, "Carry not only my greetings, friends, but gossip too!"

CHAPTER 6
A PROPOSAL
493 CE

Baldewin stood with Luillaume in the great hall of the palace in Soissons, relating to Clovis the details of their encounter with the bishop of Vienne.

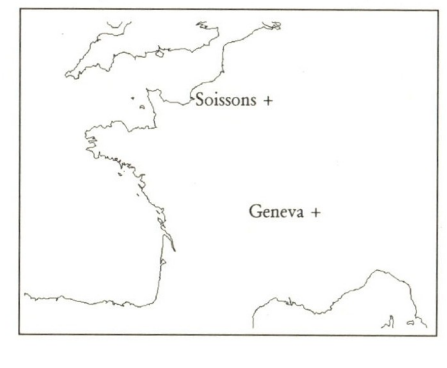

"Avitus was drunk, you say?" Clovis was amused that the rumors about Avitus enjoying his wine overmuch seemed to be based in fact.

Baldewin shrugged. "I couldn't say for sure, but like I said, he did have several glasses of wine while we sat with him."

"And he seemed quite familiar with his glass," Luillaume added, a smile crossing his face.

Clovis laughed. "I see," he said. He stepped down from his throne and walked to the window, allowing his curiosity to direct his thoughts. "And only beggars can visit this woman...Clotild?"

"That's what he told us. The only people who ever spend any time with her are those who come to the church for help...aside from her uncle, Godegesil and the bishops who serve the church, that is."

Clovis sucked at a tooth and tapped his index finger on the frame of the window. Since Remigius had suggested marriage as a political tool, his mother and Bishop Principius had mentioned marriage as well, with similar motives. Basina had the interest one would expect of a mother, but also knew that a good queen was an asset to a ruler. Principius shared his brother's concern. Clovis wondered if the emergence of this woman, Clotild, was an omen. With a blink he returned his attention to the two men who waited before his throne.

"Well done, my friends. You've served me well and you have my thanks."

A quick wave informed the men that their report was finished. The two bowed respectfully and departed.

Near the entrance to the hall, a small alcove held the documents and materials which regularly came into service as Clovis tended to the affairs of governing. There, on a chair against the wall, Aurelian had been sitting quietly, listening to the reports of Baldewin and Luillaume. Now with the emissaries gone, he pursed his lips, stood deliberately, crossed his arms, and walked slowly over the stone floor toward Clovis.

"You're intrigued by this, aren't you?"

"Yes, Aurelian, I am." Clovis was back at his throne now and sat in it comfortably. Aurelian came to lean against the throne's high back. Both men stared out over the empty hall. "I was about to ask you what you thought of it."

Aurelian pursed his lips even harder and took in a long, slow nasal breath before speaking.

"Well, my lord, when Chilperic ruled in Burgundy, it was said that he had two fair daughters. I never saw them or heard more than the claim that they existed. I must say, though, I'm surprised they survived when Gundobad defeated their father."

"So am I. Still, I'm inclined to trust the word of Avitus. Even the word of a drunken Avitus." He paused, raised his eyebrows and smiled. "Especially the word of a drunken Avitus! Perhaps that's most trustworthy of all!"

Aurelian gave a sharp smile that faded quickly as he posed his next question.

"Has Avitus proven himself to be trustworthy?"

"Oh, I don't really know. Remigius trusts him and confides in him. That should lend Avitus some credibility. I'm willing to trust him enough to want to learn more about this woman."

"Certainly, my lord."

Aurelian had remained non-committal on the question of marriage. Clovis appreciated his silence on the subject. Aurelian was valuable to him; objective and careful; able to see possibilities, both good and bad; and smart enough to know when to mind his own business. His marriage was a solid one but he didn't insist that everyone's relationships must be the same.

Clovis could imagine natural advantages in a well-planned marriage, though not to somone like Clotild. If only her father was still alive and ruling. Still, he wanted more information about Clotild. He stood and left the room in contemplative silence, leaving his secretary to reflect alone.

It was only two days later that Clovis shook Aurelian's world by leaping back to the discussion of Clotild with the simple declaration: "I want you to find out what this woman is like."

"My lord?" Aurelian stepped away from the throne and leaned his ear toward Clovis, uncertain that he'd heard correctly. He was still thinking of a conflict between two tradesmen who had only just exited.

"I said, I want you to find out what she's like. This Clotild."

Chapter 6 A Proposal: 493 CE

"Sir?" The secretary struggled to catch up with what his king was thinking.

"I've decided we should consider the advantages of marriage and this seems a good place to start."

Aurelian was in full stride now, the tradesmen forgotten. "You want to do this now?" He asked calmly.

"Yes, now. I want you to go to Geneva and meet her."

Aurelian's face squeezed into an expression of pain and he said, "There must be men who are more qualified for this than I!"

"But I trust *you*, my friend," said Clovis sincerely. "You know what marriage is about, and if I'm going to take action on someone's opinion besides my own, I need it to be yours."

"Gerard. What about Gerard? He's been married. He could go."

"His wife died years ago, Aurelian. You're married now. And besides, I need him here. You don't need to worry about business. We can survive without you, for a little while at least."

Normally that thought would have hurt Aurelian but he was too busy trying to wriggle his way out of this assignment to worry about it. "But you've heard that only the beggars are allowed to see her."

"Yes, I did. That's why you'll need a disguise."

Aurelian looked at Clovis and saw the resolution on his face. He lowered his head in resignation and said, "Yes, of course, sir…a disguise."

Within a week, Aurelian was making final preparations to be on his way. His analysis of the situation, or "predicament" as he described it to Idena, his wife, convinced him that the prudent course of action would include gaining from Clovis the permission to act on his behalf, to speak, as he explained to his ruler, with the voice of Clovis, to make decisions based on his assessment of whatever situations might arise.

On this issue the judgment of Clovis was favorable.

"You have my every confidence, Aurelian," he said.

"I will do everything in my power to honor and deserve your trust."

A ring of pledge was given to Aurelian, which he could offer to Clotild in the event that circumstances called for a promise of commitment.

Aurelian looked at the stretch of road before looking back at his wife, who stood with Clovis and Basina on the porch of the Soissons palace. A final wave and he began.

His departure left the residence quiet. Clovis knew that little work would be accomplished in his advisor's absence. That knowledge proved more disconcerting when, before the week was out, a remarkable letter arrived in Soissons. From Theodoric, the king of Italy, the letter requested the hand of Audofleda, the sister of Clovis. No urgency was expressed in the letter, which was good, for Clovis had no idea how to respond. Instantly, however, the wait for Aurelian's return became an anxious one.

The cold day surprised no one in Geneva. It was still early spring. The winds were more insistent than usual, though, driving people indoors. Sedeluba and her sister, Clotild sat inside the gates of St. Germain's Church receiving those beggars who sought alms in spite of the chill.

Needs differ among beggars and the sisters found themselves, at various times, washing a dirty man's feet, feeding a hungry woman, comforting a mother and her sick child or giving clothes to particularly needy beggars. The poor and the sick huddled close around the young women in a semi-circle, nearly three bodies deep, a strategy that provided a welcome windbreak for those on the inside of the circle.

In the crowd, one man took his time, apparently unable to manage more than a slow shuffle. As a space appeared in front of him, he hobbled into it. His hunched back added to his already disconcerting appearance as he was unshaven and was wearing dirty and tattered clothes. But few noticed, for among the poor of Geneva he didn't look out of place.

His eyes, however, were more attentive than the others and his ear was turned toward the two charitable sisters listening intently for the clue that would tell him which of the women was Clotild. He was getting very close to having to ask their names outright when one turned to the other and said, "So many people!"

"More every day," said the other, sighing.

Then the watchful beggar got what he needed.

"We just do what we can, Clotild."

"I know," said Clotild as the man focused his attention on her. "But it never seems to be enough, does it?"

There was no mistaking that the two were sisters, but Clotild was more beautiful. Her hair caressed her smooth cheekbones and covered her ears before twisting into a loose braid that reached half way down her back. Her full lips parted in a warm smile to reveal her remarkably straight teeth. The broad hips and full breasts that she had inherited from her mother were not hidden by her clothes and the hands that were folded in front of her were strong.

Chapter 6 *A Proposal: 493 CE*

The attentive beggar limped forward, now in the front rank of the crowd, watching the richness of the woman, a wealth of spirit which could not be hid by any work, however humble. Soon he inched forward to look into the kind and compassionate face of the young Clotild. He knew in his heart that he would be inviting this woman into a new life.

Clotild sat him down next to her. She reached for a bowl that sat between the two women and placed it before her on the ground. She knelt at the feet of the beggar and withdrew a wash rag from the bowl, wringing it to nearly dry. It was too cold for a good washing. As she began to rub the man's feet with the cloth, he bent toward her so he could whisper to her without being heard by the others.

"My lady, Clotild, I'm no beggar—but please, hear me out. I mean no harm."

Often the beggars would whisper to her, sometimes with blessings, sometimes with thanks, sometimes with proposals for support if she would become a private nurse, occasionally with invitations to bed. She had learned to respond with equanimity, ready to show gratitude when it was called for, strength when it was needed, but loathe to show either indignation or shock when it was expected. Experience taught her that those who would suggest the impossible typically knew they would reap no harvest from their poorly sown ideas. This man's urgency was different. For the moment, she decided to pretend that nothing unusual was happening. She continued washing the man's feet, struggling to keep her eyes downcast.

"Go on," she said calmly.

"My name is Aurelian. I'm in the service of Clovis of the Franks. I've come here from Soissons. He sent me, in this disguise, because we learned that only beggars were allowed to see you."

Aurelian reached into his cloak and brought out a gold ring with a fine garnet stone. He held it so none could see it except Clotild, and she stifled a gasp when she saw how exceptional it was.

Aurelian continued, "My king has heard of your beauty and your wisdom." Clotild showed a look of amazement that Aurelian didn't miss. "Oh yes! You shouldn't look surprised. Even in Soissons we've heard of you. And he wishes to make you his queen." Aurelian, completely taken with Clotild, never even considered that Clovis might object to the assumption he was making. "This ring is his pledge of faith to you."

There was silence for a long moment as Clotild examined the ring while trying to look as though she was drying the beggar's feet. She was reeling inside. She had dreamed of a different life, but never had a possibility such as this dared cross her mind. Here was a chance to escape Geneva. Now, even now, a glimmer of hope grew that she might have revenge on Gundobad. Her thoughts were interrupted by Aurelian.

"Is there an answer I can take back?"

Clotild shook her head and suppressed, with only minor success, her luminous smile.

"Tell me your name again."

"Aurelian, my lady."

"Aurelian, is he a good man?"

"I can tell you I find him honorable and fair, a good ruler."

Clotild rested her hand on Aurelian's shoulder, closed her eyes and said a silent prayer. Could this actually be happening? Should she trust this stranger? But it was happening. God had sent this man to her, she reasoned, and she could not turn her back on what God might choose to do with her life. She blinked in amazement, and a smile returned to her face.

"Take this message: Clotild rejoices at the prospect of being his queen!"

She reached into her pocket and withdrew a single gold coin, a solidus, and handed it to Aurelian.

"For your journey back. Perhaps it will speed you along your way. Tell your king, if this is truly his intention, that he must seek my hand from my uncle, Gundobad, in Vienne. But, my kind messenger, tell him to hurry. My Uncle's advisor, Aridius, has been in Constantinople on business. He'll return soon, and I can assure you, he won't approve of this match. So, please, tell him to make haste."

"You have my promise."

From her finger, Clotild withdrew her own ring and placed it in Aurelian's hand. "Here's my sign of good faith. Now, go."

"I leave right away," said Aurelian, already standing to his full height.

"May God be with you!" said Clotild, and he was gone.

Another beggar stood in Aurelian's place, astonished at seeing what appeared to be the healing of the hunchback. Clotild looked at the sickly and hopeful man, and compassion filled her heart.

Clotild was everything the rumors had suggested and more. She was beautiful and intelligent. But more importantly, and to the amazement of Aurelian, she was willing to be the queen of Clovis. Her warning that time was short was urgent enough that Aurelian decided to make the journey back to Soissons as rapidly as possible.

Chapter 6 A Proposal: 493 CE

Taking no time to change out of his disguise, he departed Geneva, heading for Soissons. In hopes of saving a little time, he chose to go by way of the less well traveled northern road, a more rugged journey, avoiding the longer route through Vienne that the Roman road afforded. He was glad to steer clear of Gundobad's stronghold.

Arriving at the Saone river, near Chalon, Aurelian could see there were still hills to climb. Thus far, the travel had been invigorating and generally solitary. Now he was glad to see the Roman road aiming north. The ever present merchants were on the road along with messengers, the occasional pilgrim, and even a small contingent of Roman soldiers, a rare sight these days.

Aurelian nestled in a grove of trees and enjoyed the distant pulse of the river, surging as the breeze allowed the water's whisper to come to him. He waited until the Romans were well along their way. Though he knew how to deal with Romans he also knew that Romans heading into Gaul would not be a jovial group. There was no reason to risk challenge from them. Once they were far passed, Aurelian stood, stretched and took a deep breath readying himself for the next leg of his journey. He made for the river, toward a wide, shallow run, to cross and join the road.

His abrupt entry onto the way startled a young man who was traveling alone. Coming from the trees, Aurelian strode onto the route just behind the man, who, upon hearing the sound of Aurelian's footfalls, spun around to face whatever danger might be present. He was barely more than a boy and his wariness, along with the fact that the boy had only one arm, made Aurelian think he might be a good and safe traveling companion.

"Sir?" said the lad, turning his armless side away from Aurelian, raising his walking stick in front of him, and coming to his toes, readied for a sprint.

"I'm just a traveler, boy. I'm no threat to you."

The boy stayed turned, his stick ready. The tone of Aurelian's voice was assuring enough, though, for him to settle back on his feet.

"I have no money, if that's what you want."

"Boy, a Roman guard just passed ahead of you. Do you think I'm going to risk my neck for whatever pittance you might have?"

The stick was lowered, though no ground was given.

"I'm walking the same way as you and neither of us will get very far this way."

The boy backed away slowly, offering Aurelian the opportunity to pass. Aurelian nodded and walked past him.

It took only three steps before the youth came to walk alongside Aurelian.

"My name is Stephanus," he said. "I'm on my way to Paris."

Aurelian raised his eyebrows. "That's a good journey."

"There is a great saint in Paris, by the name of Genevieve. I'm told she heals people."

Aurelian suppressed a frown, never believing that Genevieve could replace an arm.

"It appears we'll be on the same road for a while," he said.

"Perhaps we could go there together," said Stephanus.

"I appreciate your invitation, but I'm on my way to Soissons. I have business there."

Even as he said it, he thought it sounded too haughty for a beggar. Quickly he added, "I have family there."

"I have no family, and no one will give a one-armed man work. That's why I beg."

As the miles and days became memories, the men began to know one another, talking about people who were rich and about those far off, cloudy days that all people remember, when things were better. Aurelian enjoyed his disguise more now than ever. He invented a past for himself and played the role perfectly. He had been a merchant and had lost his fortune during the plundering that followed a battle near his home village. Now he was trying to rebuild his life. Aurelian enjoyed the stories he concocted but no more than Stephanus did. They shared the tales of their scars and Aurelian surpassed his own expectations as he pointed to the scar on his forehead and described how a woman had hit him with a bottle one night as he had sought to violate her.

"She was pretty, but not willing."

Stephanus laughed. "Isn't that always the way?"

Aurelian suddenly thought of Idena, whom he had never violated, "No, it isn't."

Touching his one hand to his own forehead, insisting that a small mark was a scar, Stephanus confessed his wound was of a less dramatic origin.

"A horse kicked me when I was a little boy."

The time together passed quickly, the weather was cooperating, bringing clear skies and light winds. Stephanus decided to change his plans so he could continue on with Aurelian as far as Troyes. "It doesn't matter if I take one road over the other," he said. "Paris isn't going to move."

The days, one after another, shared a similar character as the walking proceeded and the conversation continued. Each man learned

Chapter 6 *A Proposal: 493 CE*

what the other would share, but neither offered much of substance; tales, mostly, which both suspected were all grand lies, but enjoyable anyway. By the time they set up camp on the last day they would spend together, the two knew they might have been friends had they lived in the same place. Expecting to say their farewells in the morning, light conversation and grateful compliments led them into sleep.

Upon awakening the next morning Aurelian discovered he had slept alone. Stephanus was gone, along with Aurelian's wallet which bore the money that Clotild had put in his care. Aurelian's hand shot to his pocket, checking for the ring she'd given him and he breathed a sigh of relief when he found that blessed gift to be safe. His anger burned, he kicked at the cold ashes of the fire, wishing Stephanus was there to kick, but there was little to do now, other than continue on his way. So he did. He quickened his pace now, feeling an urgency growing within him as he remembered Clotild's encouragement for haste. He swore at the absent Stephanus the whole morning.

Clovis could see Aurelian was tired. The secretary, turned secret-envoy, stood at a sloppy attention as he related the story of his intrigue and misfortune. He closed with the presentation of Clotild's ring.

"Rest assured, Aurelian, I'll replace the money." He took pity on his friend and offered him a chair.

"I'd better stand, sir," said Aurelian. "If I sit I'll fall asleep."

Clovis accepted his friend's refusal and said, "I spent a lot of time thinking, while you were gone, Aurelian, about the benefits of getting married...about what Remigius said." Also, he admitted silently to himself, about Theodoric's proposal regarding Audofleda. "I'm convinced that it would be wise to marry. If this Clotild is all you say, Aurelian, then we must trust her warning and not waste time."

"Oh, my lord, she's all I say and more. And I'm convinced that she was honest in her concern for haste."

"I don't doubt it. Of course we'll want to send an appropriate message to Gundobad about all this."

Aurelian nodded his agreement.

"But before we do that, I have news as well."

"Yes?"

"I received a letter from Theodoric while you were gone. He's seeking Audofleda's hand in marriage!"

"Your sister?...Theodoric of Italy...the Ostrogoth?"

"Yes, can you believe it? I'm not the only one, it seems, who's thinking of marriage and politics."

"Things are not so secure in Italy, unless something's changed while I've been away."

"No, nothing's changed," replied Clovis, "yet. But Theodoric will rule soon. That's my guess."

Aurelian began to sway slightly as fatigue overtook him. His eyes started to roll up into his head despite his efforts. Seeing his friend's exhaustion, Clovis was merciful. He rose from his throne and came to his secretary, turning him toward the door.

"The letter to Gundobad can wait, Aurelian. Go. Sleep."

Chapter 7
An Alliance Is Formed
493 CE

Clovis sat on a stone bench in the garden of the palace, tearing apart a piece of bread. He placed the crumbs beside him, then tried not to move. Since that day when he'd witnessed the bishop of Reims feeding the trusting sparrows in the window of his residence, Clovis had secretly endeavored to duplicate the feat. The winter had postponed his project, but now, with the warmth of spring, he was trying again.

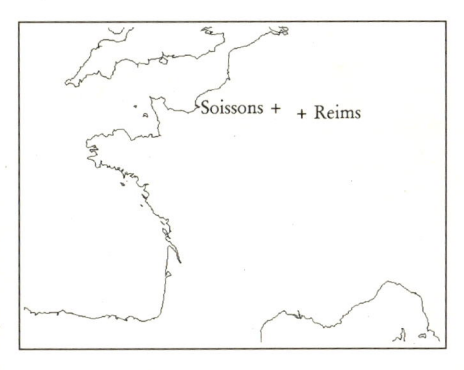

As he sat, the chirping of the birds brought back a moment in his childhood. On a warm day with the softest of breezes, very much like this one, he was recovering from a hard day at play, lying against the southern wall of the stable, enjoying the warmth of the sun. In that moment of rest, a small sky-blue butterfly found a perch on his hand. In his fatigue he had not moved and the butterfly had stayed, pumping its wings slowly, regularly, like a beating heart. The memory made him smile.

A sparrow flew to the edge of the bench and looked at Clovis, then at the crumbs and then back at Clovis. He saw the bird out of the corner of his eye and he didn't dare turn to look. The sparrow made one hop in the direction of the crumbs before the sound of footsteps frightened it into flight.

"My lord?" said a cautious Aurelian, coming into the glade.

Clovis was sorry his efforts were interrupted but it was with only the mildest frustration that he said, "Yes, Aurelian, what is it?"

"We've just received some news I think you should hear."

"Yes?"

"It's about Theodoric and recent happenings in Italy. Considering your thoughts about giving Audofleda to Theodoric in marriage, the news especially concerns me."

Clovis let out a deep breath, focusing on the world of power once again. He shifted his weight on the bench, turning to face Aurelian fully. "Go on, then, what concerns you?"

"Theodoric now rules in Italy."

"Yes? Well, as I said, it was only a matter of time. We both knew that." Aurelian bobbed his head in assent. "How did it finally happen?"

"That's what concerns me. Theodoric used Bishop John of Ravenna to trap Odoacer."

"But there was a siege…"

"Please, hear me, my lord."

"Yes, of course." Clovis could hear the unusually high degree of agitation in his secretary's raised voice. His scarred forehead was red and furrowed. Aurelian was usually self-contained. Clovis knew it was time to listen. "Please," he said, gesturing for Aurelian to sit and carry on.

Aurelian hesitated, looked at the bench and shook his head in mute denial of the invitation. He turned away from Clovis, recollecting his thoughts, then he turned back.

"The siege became too much for Odoacer and he negotiated for a surrender. Theodoric convinced Bishop John of Ravenna to arrange a peace accord between the two leaders, which would have Theodoric and Odoacer sharing power in Italy. Apparently a banquet was planned in celebration of the truce. Theodoric arrived with his men, and he killed Odoacer with his own hands."

"So Theodoric wins," said Clovis, calmly, as he turned over in his mind the impact this would have on him.

"Yes, because of his treachery."

"Does that bother you, Aurelian? It's not the first time we've seen treachery."

"No, it's not. And it probably won't be the last. I simply don't want you to be the object of such deceit, and I would caution you about Audofleda's wedding. I'm aware of the political advantages of marriages between ruling families, but, in this instance, I don't trust the groom." Concentrating on the situation, and unaware of the bread crumbs he crushed, Aurelian sat next to his king. Clovis allowed it. "I know you're thinking seriously about permitting the marriage," said Aurelian, "I just thought you should know what's happened. And," he looked at Clovis, "if you grant Audofleda's hand, don't attend the wedding."

"I'm grateful for your concern, Aurelian. I'll consider what you've said."

Aurelian recognized that Clovis had ended the conversation. He returned to his more formal self, stood and asked to be excused, receiving his king's dismissal. He walked deliberately back toward the palace, bread crumbs falling from his cloak, leaving his ruler to his thoughts.

Chapter 7 *An Alliance Is Formed: 493 CE*

Clovis knew Aurelian's concerns were legitimate. But the political issues that bothered Aurelian didn't bother him. As long as Theodoric was talking about marriage with Audofleda, the political threat was minimal. What bothered Clovis most about Theodoric was what he was hearing from the priests. Their condemnations of Theodoric's Arian faith were unanimous and without compromise. Clovis was just beginning to feel that his ties to the Church in Gaul were solidifying, and he didn't want to jeopardize that. The Arian Church was not so powerful here as it was in other parts of Gaul, and there was little doubt as to how Remigius and his fellow bishops would react to this marriage. Above all these concerns, Clovis worried about his sister's welfare.

He brushed what remained of the crumbs off the bench and then off his hands. He offered a look of resignation to unseen birds and rose from his place. There was work waiting in other quarters.

Remigius especially enjoyed the writings of Augustine and had undertaken to re-read them. With the scarcity of books, Remigius was one of the few people in Gaul who had such an opportunity. Now, though, his eyes needed rest. Leaving the writings at his desk, he went to the window to be with his birds. The sparrows nesting in view of the window had learned that when the bishop sat there, food often followed. Remigius perched himself on the sill and within minutes, a sparrow was on his finger, eating crumbs from his other hand.

"There you are," said the bishop, softly. "My, you're hungry today. Let's let the others have some."

He continued, oblivious to the fact that Clovis had entered the room.

Only three days had elapsed since Aurelian had interrupted Clovis during a similar moment. Now the King of the Franks was in Reims seeking counsel, but unable to disturb the bishop. Clovis was silent as Remigius chattered with the birds that hopped around the crumbs on the sill. Soon the crumbs were gone and the birds departed. Remigius said his farewells as they climbed into the sky. Then, turning back toward the room, he jumped at the sight of his visitor.

"Oh my! Clovis! You startled me!"

"I'm sorry, Father. I didn't mean to. I was enjoying the birds."

"Ah, yes, my birds." He looked back at the window, with kindness in his eyes, "They must please God." Then he said, "Come, have a seat." He pointed to a new padded bench that sat next to the desk.

"Thank you." Clovis seated himself, finding the bench as comfortable as it looked.

"I'm glad to see you, Clovis, but I wasn't expecting a visit. What brings you to Reims?" The bishop seated himself at the desk.

"I have a religious matter I'd like to discuss with you."

"A religious matter!" Remigius could barely believe his ears. A political matter in relation to the Church he could well imagine, but this was not expected. "I'm curious at the thought. After all, you and I worship different Gods, don't we?" Remigius cocked his head and looked quizzically at Clovis, "Or has that changed?"

"No, Remigius, my Gods are not your Gods." Clovis was clearly out of his element, and the bishop could see his discomfort.

"A religious matter. Well. Please, then, go on." The bishop sat back, folded his hands and placed them in his lap.

Clovis cleared his throat and swallowed with difficulty. He had not considered how he might begin, and now that the moment was here, he wasn't sure what to say. He rubbed his eyes, stroked his mustache and stared at the floor.

"I think this is a religious concern," he said, uncertainly.

"Well, whether it is or isn't, I'll try to be of help." Remigius spoke sincerely, trying to reassure this powerful but obviously uncomfortable man.

"Theodoric in Italy has asked for my sister's hand in marriage." He looked up at the bishop, "Audofleda's hand."

"Interesting," mused Remigius. Not surprising, he admitted to himself, but indeed interesting that alliances were being established so soon, so far away. He'd met Audofleda only once in passing. She was certainly old enough to marry, he thought. "You're concerned about the proposal?"

"Yes…"

"Can you tell me why?"

Clovis stood and began to pace slowly, his stride made timid by concern for his sister.

"First, history teaches me that I should not trust this man. He lies to his emperor, and he killed Odoacer under the pretense of a peaceful meeting."

"Yes, I've heard. But those sound like reasons you should trust him."

"Bishop?"

"Yes, of course! You should trust him to be a king. You should trust him to act in ways that will further his own position and power. These alliances happen all the time, Clovis. You know that."

Chapter 7 *An Alliance Is Formed: 493 CE*

Clovis shrugged.

Remigius continued. "Has anyone commended Audofleda to him?"

"No, not to my knowledge."

"Then it's my guess that he's making this proposal only to secure an alliance with you. You can trust him to be self-serving. And I'm sure, Clovis, he expects the same from you."

"We Franks have always taken mates among ourselves, Remigius. Usually, that is." Clovis thought about Aurelian's wife, Idena. She'd married outside of her Frankish tribe, and there were growing numbers doing the same. "Now my sister's being asked to become the wife of an Ostrogoth."

"Clovis, even your own father stole another chief's queen. Have you forgotten that already?"

Clovis frowned and said, in a voice that clearly stated he would not be treated flippantly, "No, Bishop, I've not forgotten."

"No, of course not," said Remigius in a repentant tone.

Clovis looked away from the bishop and his eyes darted back and forth, looking at nothing in particular. Slowly he returned his gaze to Remigius and said, quietly, "At least the Thuringians worshipped the same Gods as we did."

"Ah!" said Remigius. "So, here lies the religious issue!"

Clovis looked at Remigius, admonishing him with his glare. "This is not a puzzle to solve!" he said. Taking his eyes off of the bishop, only after making his frustration clear, Clovis sat down and chewed on his mustache. Remigius waited.

"You've said that Theodoric is a heretic…an Arian. I've heard you rail against the Arians. You've used Theodoric as an example." He sighed. The conflict between the Arians and the Catholics made no sense to Clovis at all, but he did understand angry words. More than a few were coming from the Catholic Church. Until now, he was glad to let the Christians handle their own struggles. Now he feared their difficulties were becoming his own. "My sister believes like I do, Bishop. To you, we're pagans."

"But Clovis…" Remigius tried to protest.

"No, Remigius. I've heard you say the word. Pagan. It means nothing to me. I only worship the Gods my parents worshipped. And it may be that Arians and Pagans are equally horrible in your eyes. That doesn't bother me either. I know what I am and you can believe what you wish. But, Remigius, I don't know anything about these Arians, and I'm afraid for my sister. Are the Arians really as dangerous as you say?"

Remigius knew how much importance the Franks placed on the family, and yet he was surprised by the deep concern Clovis was displaying. It impressed him. If only more people in power felt so much passion about their kindred, he thought.

Theologically, Remigius considered both Pagans and Arians to be infidels. On that count, Clovis was right, but the bishop knew what the political consequences could be if he alienated Clovis. The true Church needed Clovis as an ally. That he would ponder the religious issue at all, let alone bring it to a bishop, was impressive. Remigius decided that integrity deserved honesty. He pushed away from the desk and went to his guest.

"My friend, our Lord Christ was once accused of trying to overthrow his king. To this charge he responded that his kingdom was not of this world. There are two great realms, you see. The realm of the world and the realm of the Spirit. Our teacher, Augustine," he waved at the papers on his desk, "called them the 'City of Man' and the 'City of God'. Theodoric wants to grow in power in the City of Man, so he seeks your sister's hand. It has little to do with the realm of the Spirit.

"I would never encourage a believer in the faith to marry a pagan…or an Arian. They are one and the same in my mind." He thought he saw Clovis flinch. "But, I can see little harm in one infidel marrying another…except that they tend to bring infidel children into the world."

"Then I don't need to fear for my sister in this marriage?"

"Clovis," Remigius sat on the bench next to him, "I want you to know that I'm honored by your honesty and your confidence. I hope I return the compliment with my own candor. I don't think you need to worry about Audofleda's safety, if that's what you mean. Certainly no more than anyone fears for his sister when she enters into marriage. As far as matters of faith are concerned, it is later that you must fear for her…at the time of judgment."

Clovis didn't understand all the spiritual concerns. They confused him. He remained uneasy about Theodoric's ties to Arianism but he wasn't certain why. Still, he *could* understand political motives and as he came to believe that Theodoric's intentions were purely strategic, the less he feared for his sister.

"But, understand," continued Remigius, "if Audofleda does marry Theodoric, their marriage won't be blessed by the Church—that is, not unless they convert."

Chapter 7 *An Alliance Is Formed: 493 CE*

"I understand."

Remigius was excited that Clovis had approached him about this marriage. The Frank hadn't suggested anything about the possibility that he, himself might marry, and the bishop dared go no further. He had to wait on Clovis. But he couldn't help feeling hopeful.

Clovis stood to leave.

"Thank you for your time, Remigius. You've given me a great deal to think about."

The bishop rose to see Clovis out. "May God be with you and with your sister."

Uncertain as to how he should respond, Clovis nodded and said, "Thank you," then made his exit.

Within two months Audofleda was in Italy, Theodoric's queen, and a new alliance was formed.

Chapter 8

The Betrothal
493 CE

Chalon +
+ Geneva
Vienne +

Gundobad's secretary, Aridius, was in Italy on a mission to Theodoric, leaving the more mundane affairs of state, the workings of day to day government, which weren't going as smoothly as usual, to an irritated king. Too many decisions are related to too many other decisions, thought Gundobad. Too many incompetents in the world, all bringing their problems to me.

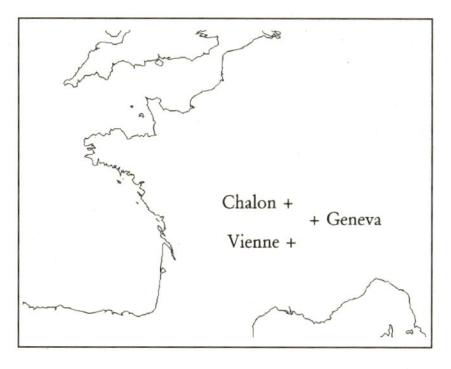

A young messenger, unfortunate enough to arrive late in the day, bore the brunt of the royal anger.

"Speak!" The sharpness in Gundobad's voice made the messenger, and the guard who had announced him, cringe.

"I bring correspondence from Clovis, ruler of the Franks in the region of Belgica Secunda, sir," said the boy.

"Go on." Gundobad sat back to listen and looked at the messenger, offering nothing like comfort.

Clearing his throat, the runner began to recite the memorized message, a copy of which he held in his hand.

"Most wonderful King Gundobad, ruler of all Burgundy. It has become known to us that there is a woman in your kingdom who is desirable and charming. A woman of wisdom and beauty and stature. Clovis of the Franks deeply desires to be joined to her in marriage. You will no doubt see the benefits of this marriage and the alliance it will create. The benefits are so profound that there is no choice for us but to demand that you immediately allow Clovis the hand of Clotild, your niece, the daughter of Chilperic. Please choose a place where we may come for the betrothal. Signed, Aurelian, secretary for Clovis, Chief of the Franks."

"He demands?" The frown on Gundobad's face deepened. To no one he asked, "How did he learn about her?" He considered the puzzle for a moment. "It must have been my imbecile brother!"

The messenger nervously cleared his throat again and gave Gundobad a look of petition.

"What?"

"There is more to the message, sir."

Gundobad rubbed his face and his lips tightened.

"Continue."

"Clovis wishes it to be understood that if you do not comply, he will prepare to come with an army of Franks to meet you."

It was more than Gundobad could take. Flushed with anger, he bellowed, "Let him come, whenever he wants! I'm prepared to go against him with my own army!" Then, thinking better of it, and calming a bit, he looked at the quivering messenger before him and said in a lower tone of voice, "There will be no response just now. Remain with us for a few days. I assure you, you'll be returning with an answer."

The messenger relaxed somewhat and remembered to hand Gundobad the written message. As soon as the boy was gone, Gundobad summoned an attendant and said, simply, "Bring Godegesil to me!"

Ten days later, Godegesil found himself in Gundobad's court, shaking with anger at the accusations his brother had leveled against him.

"You called me away from Geneva for this?" He screamed the question. "I have no idea how word of Clotild got to the Franks!"

"How else could it have got out?"

"I don't know! It could have been the Church. She serves the Church. Maybe that was where word got out…or the poor, she works with the poor. Who's to say that one of those people didn't pass word on about her? It could have been anyone, damn it! A chance encounter, even idle conversation with one of the emissaries of Clovis could spread word of Clotild everywhere." Godegesil was not about to be saddled with this offense.

Gundobad looked at his brother with disdain. He knew Godegesil was telling the truth, but he wished otherwise. It didn't matter much. The fact was, Clotild's whereabouts had become common knowledge. Gundobad shook his head in resignation.

"Clovis wants to take her as his queen and in all honesty, I can't think of any reasons to deny his…request." He let out a sigh. "We already trade with him. An alliance couldn't hurt that. And the Franks are valiant warriors. We don't need them for an enemy." Gundobad let go of his anger, swallowed and said in a more relaxed voice, "But I don't like the audacity of this Clovis." He paused and scratched his head. Godegesil was mute. Gundobad looked at him and asked, "Do

Chapter 8 *The Betrothal: 493 CE*

you think the Church will allow this marriage? A Christian woman with a pagan man?"

Godegesil, more at ease now, slouched in a chair. "I don't have any idea."

"We should talk with the bishop," Gundobad concluded. "He might decide the question for us. If the Church denies the wedding, so shall we." He nodded at his decision, convinced it was the best course, all the while wishing Aridius had never gone to Italy.

Bishop Avitus, in his full priestly garb, stood with the elderly Sylvester, bishop of Chalon-sur-Saône. From the chancel, Avitus looked out over the people who filled the small chapel, and wished Patiens could have seen this. Nearly two years had passed since the kindly bishop of Lyons had died. Avitus imagined that he would have taken great joy in this occasion. Franks and Burgundians had come together in the fortress city of Chalon-sur-Saône to witness the betrothal of Clovis, King of the Franks, to the Burgundian princess, Clotild.

On one side of the chancel, Godegesil waited for his niece, Clotild. She was still in preparation and had yet to enter the church. On the other side stood Clovis, tapping his fingers against his thigh. He was clothed in his battle dress, with mail and shield, though he had foregone his helmet. He had bathed for the betrothal and his clean blond hair was braided and lay on his back. Aurelian stood with him, as did Gerard.

"It shouldn't be long now, my friend," said Gerard as he watched his king fidgeting.

"No, I expect not," was the stilted reply.

A murmur in the rear of the church confirmed the prediction, and all eyes turned toward the door as Clotild entered on the arm of her uncle, Gundobad. He too, was in battle dress, weapons bright, clothes new, clean and colorful, looking as proud as he could, making full use of this opportunity to be seen by his people. Here, as he patted his niece's hand, they witnessed him as more than simply a king or conqueror, but also as someone capable of sentiment.

To Gundobad's surprise the Church granted its approval to the ceremony, so he decided to make the most of the occasion; a formal betrothal, stating the intention Clovis and Clotild to marry. Clovis would now be family. The choice between making an ally or an adversary seemed clear. Burgundy would be stronger. He hoped Aridius would concur.

Clotild walked down the aisle, staring straight ahead, struggling to contain her hatred toward Gundobad. This was the first time they'd been together since Clotild and Sedeluba had been orphaned. The stories of their parent's executions were told over and over again in Burgundy, each version more gruesome than the last. From a quick thrust of a sword to being flayed, Clotild's father died for her more times than she would have thought possible. Her mother as well, being drowned, raped, tortured and gibbeted. She blamed Gundobad for each death as if the stories were all true. Walking next to him, she was barely able to retain her sense of composure. Behind her came Sedeluba, her sister, more serene, yet still unforgiving toward this murderer.

Clotild wore a gold necklace, set with garnet stones, and a bright yellow dress, accented with red trim, held in place with a simple gold brooch. The ring Clovis had sent to her by way of Aurelian, graced her hand. Her hair was pinned up and her bearing was stately. As she drew near, she allowed a more confident gaze to rest on Clovis. The Frank thought he saw her eyes widen slightly when she looked upon him—or maybe he hoped he saw it. He was certain, though, that her mood improved considerably when, at the end of the aisle, she separated from Gundobad.

Clovis leaned toward Aurelian and whispered, "You weren't lying. She's truly beautiful."

Aurelian grinned and said, "Indeed she is." He took pleasure as he watched her now, remembering her kindness, the touch of her warm wet hands on his dusty feet, the brilliant smile she gifted him with that day. She glanced at him now and, though her smile was more restrained, it clearly spilled from the same font as had the earlier smile.

Clovis, Clotild and Bishop Avitus converged in front of the altar for the betrothal. Around them, their family and friends gathered. Sedeluba, and Lantechild, the sister of Clovis who had made the journey at her brother's request, joined Aurelian, Gerard, Gundobad and Godegesil. Crowding in behind them were a large group of Frankish and Burgundian soldiers who, while interested in the betrothal, were more anxious to join in the celebration that would follow the ceremony.

"It is a time of joy as you are betrothed," said Avitus, loudly, quieting the crowd.

Clovis and Clotild looked carefully at each other. Clotild was as impressed with Clovis as he was with her. He looked strong and respectable. His eyes revealed intelligence and integrity, something she

Chapter 8 The Betrothal: 493 CE

was not accustomed to seeing in rulers. There was no treachery or guile in his face. It made Clovis all the more handsome.

"Your families join you..." said Avitus, glancing at the honored guests surrounding Clovis and Clotild, "and the Church celebrates with you." He wondered how many people understood the importance of this event. He imagined that, in Reims, Remigius was celebrating.

Avitus concluded his part in the ceremony by inviting Bishop Sylvester to come forward and offer a prayer of blessing, a prayer which the old bishop wheezed and which few people heard.

Clovis nodded his acknowledgment to the bishops and to the prayer, and then, at Sylvester's prompting, turned to Clotild.

"In the fashion of my family and tribe, I state my intention to take you as my wife, with my people as witnesses." He pivoted slightly and tipped his head toward his attendants. He then held out a solidus to Avitus. The coin was a familiar symbol to the Franks, saying that a bride had been purchased.

Avitus accepted the symbol graciously, even though he found the gestured somewhat distasteful, and passed the coin to Gundobad. Then he encouraged Clotild to make her response. Avitus had tried to assure Clotild that betrothal to an infidel might actually be part of God's Divine plan. She had accepted the idea and seemed more than willing to go through with the ceremony. He only hoped her resolve would not fade before the two were actually wed. Even at this moment, Avitus held his breath, fearing that a last minute hesitation might have crept into Clotild's mind. He didn't have to hold his breath long.

"And I make my pledge," she said, "to be wed to you in the name of my Lord, Jesus Christ."

Upon a benediction, barely gasped by Sylvester, the crowd cheered, and the church emptied as people made their way to the feast awaiting them in the square opposite the church.

Tables were filled with extravagant dishes, prepared by the proud people of Chalon. There was more than enough food for the guests, though by the end of the day, the wine supply would be exhausted.

At the head table, Gundobad, Godegesil, and Clovis sat together, Clotild being certain that her betrothed was between her and her uncles. Aurelian sat at the end of the same table watching and listening closely, unable to lose himself in the festivities. Light conversation, especially when enhanced with wine, often revealed useful information. Aurelian didn't want to miss anything. He paid close attention to everything and noticed the profound coldness that issued from Clotild whenever Gundobad addressed her in any way. It was a bitter cold, which he doubted would ever thaw.

As the day drew to a close, new friends said their good-byes. Franks prepared to return to their homes in Belgica and Clovis spoke his farewell to Clotild.

"I return to Soissons to prepare for the wedding." He wondered if his mother had already begun. "In the meantime, I've selected some of my men to accompany you on your journey. They'll keep you safe."

"As you wish," said Clotild.

"Can I offer you anything more?" asked Clovis.

"Not unless you can make the time go by more swiftly." Clotild smiled broadly. Clovis blushed at what he took to be a compliment. "Hurry, if there's any way that you can!"

"I shall." He bowed and walked away. He was charmed by his bride-to-be, and hopes for a joyous wedding were already filling his head.

Clotild stood still, watching Clovis depart. She tried to imagine the depth of change her life was to know. Her musings so captivated her that she was oblivious to her sister who came to stand by her side. She jumped when Sedeluba spoke, though she never took her eyes off the departing Clovis.

"I believe you'll be happy with him."

"Yes,...I think you're right," Clotild replied, recovering from the start. There was a long silence during which she shifted her gaze from Clovis to her sister. "But I'll miss you."

Sedeluba looked tenderly at her sister. "And I you." She embraced Clotild in a way that mingled love and sadness. Slowly breaking from the embrace, they looked at one another, each wanting to secure an enduring mental image of the other. Sedeluba ended the moment. Her look of grief gave way to a remarkable smile. "I have betrothed myself too," she said.

Clotild's eyes narrowed slightly and she frowned, not understanding.

"What?"

"Yes, yes!" Sedeluba laughed at the expression on Clotild's face. "I've promised myself to the most wonderful and glorious husband of all...our Lord, Jesus."

It took only a moment for the statement to register with Clotild.

"You've given yourself to the Church?" She stood back from her sister and looked at her. "But...when did you decide? How did you decide?"

Chapter 8 *The Betrothal: 493 CE*

"I spent long hours discussing it with Father Domitianus and Father Avitus. I've prayed and prayed and only in the last week have I felt my prayers answered."

"Oh, you'll be happy! You're made for this!" Clotild hugged Sedeluba with a joyful embrace. "Where will you be?" she asked, breaking from the hug. A quick glance showed Clotild that Clovis was out of eyeshot, permitting her, at last, to turn away and walk with her sister back to their lodgings.

Sedeluba took here sister's hand. "For the time being I'll stay with the sisters in Geneva."

Clotild sighed in relief. "Then we'll have time to talk," she said, though they both knew that once they returned to Geneva, Clotild's time would be consumed in preparation for her journey to Soissons.

It was Sedeluba's turn to sigh. She slowed to a stop as her eyes misted over. She squeezed Clotild's hand and said, "I'm lonely already."

―――◆―――

Vienne was a welcomed sight. The city walls stood firm, offering the assurance that all was still well in Burgundy. The visit to Italy had been a successful one, but tiring. New ties had been established with Theodoric, now the undisputed ruler in Ravenna. It had not been easy. The fact that only two and a half years before, Gundobad had stood with Odoacer against Theodoric, had complicated the task. But a new tone had been set and Aridius felt good about what he'd accomplished. And now, Aridius could see the walls of Vienne. Here was home, here was family, but most important, here was power. It would be a pleasure to resume his place in the court of Gundobad.

His role of emissary to the court of Theodoric, King of Italy, had afforded him a sense of authority, but not of power. Carrying greetings and gifts, and establishing and strengthening alliances were all necessary tasks, but they were little more than the inevitable by-products of being about the affairs of state. He'd done enough soldiering in his day to know that force was not the same as power. Real power, Aridius had decided, was to be found in local affairs. It was in the local sphere of influence that one could have immediate impact. It was within the confines of a city that the results of coercion could be seen. It was among a finite number of people that threats had life. It was with Gundobad that manipulation brought the most amusement. He was pleased to be home.

Before Aridius could shed clothes that were still smelling of travel, he was called before his king. He left his belongings in the care of a passing guard and made his way into the throne room where Gundobad, anxious to talk with his secretary and advisor, welcomed him enthusiastically.

"See," said Gundobad with a wave of his hand at nothing in particular, "we were able to survive in your absence."

Aridius smiled at what he knew was good-natured jesting. "I never doubted that you would," he responded.

Gundobad invited Aridius to sit, an invitation which the secretary readily accepted. His endurance was fading now. While glad to sit, Aridius was not ready to chat. He waited for Gundobad's lead.

"So, the time with Theodoric—did it go well?"

"Indeed it did. Our alliance with Theodoric is secured. I believe any wounds from our past battles have been healed."

"Don't believe it, Aridius. Theodoric is smarter than that. Our past provides more than one handy excuse for him, whenever he needs it."

"Yes, you're right, of course."

"Still," said Gundobad, good naturedly, "you've done a good job and I want to hear about it—but later." He raised his eyebrows and pointed toward a table stocked with food, silently encouraging Aridius to help himself. Aridius shook his head. Gundobad shrugged and said, "Tell me, then, the rest of your journey…was it pleasant?"

Aridius thought about the sights he'd seen. The images brought to mind rejuvenated him for a moment. "More than pleasant. Ravenna's a striking city. Since Theodoric took the throne, there's been a great swell of activity. I saw a play there, a Greek play, by Euripides—very entertaining. We should bring the plays back to Burgundy. It's been so long since we've seen them. I'm certain they'd be well received.

"The artists are producing wonderful mosaics there. The most amazing I've ever seen and you and I have seen some fine ones." Gundobad listened with interest. "They've begun construction on a new cathedral for the Arian's. From what little I saw, I expect it will be spectacular!"

"Aridius! I didn't know you valued such things."

"We all have our gentler sides," replied the secretary. "If you'll allow me to say so, my lord, we have nothing so grand in Burgundy." Aridius half stifled a yawn, his fatigue apparent. "I must apologize. I'm tired from the journey."

"Not at all. I understand. But indulge me. Before you go, I have news that may make nearly as big of an impression upon you as did your fair Ravenna." Aridius showed his curiosity with a single raised eyebrow, enough to encourage Gundobad to continue. "I've just re-

Chapter 8 *The Betrothal: 493 CE*

turned from Chalon…" Gundobad said, but before he could speak another word, Aridius interrupted:

"You're not going to suggest that poor little Chalon is a treasure like Ravenna!"

Gundobad laughed.

"No, not at all. No, it was there that we betrothed my niece, Clotild, to Clovis, of the Franks."

Aridius dropped his smile instantly and leaned forward in his chair. He felt his toes and fingertips tingle, his face got hot, and suddenly he was no longer tired nor the least bit lighthearted.

"What did you say?"

"Clotild and Clovis are going to be wed."

Aridius came to his feet.

"But we put Clotild and Sedeluba in Geneva to avoid something like this! How did it happen?"

Gundobad was surprised at his advisor's reaction to the news and it irritated him.

"It *has* happened, Aridius. And with my blessing! That's all you need to know. Nothing can change it!"

Aridius spotted his King's agitation and took a moment to regain his calm. He silently admonished himself for losing control of the situation. Fatigue was no excuse. He knew how Gundobad would react to his challenge—not so much in anger as in defense. This was a time for reason, not contention.

"My King, do you recall why we placed the restrictions of internal exile on your nieces?"

"Because Avitus and his father negotiated an…"

"That's not what I mean. I mean, do you remember that we placed those restrictions on them because we feared that one of them might seek revenge on you for the death of their parents. What if Clotild uses her position as the wife of Clovis against you?"

Gundobad shifted uneasily in his throne. He frowned and looked away from Aridius.

"The deed is done, Aridius. We can't undo it. Even now, I expect that Clotild is preparing to leave for Soissons. She's being escorted by 200 Franks, as well. What can we do?"

"You must stop this wedding if you can!" Aridius sounded desperate. "Perhaps we can come up with some excuse that would make the wedding unwise. Maybe we can dissuade Clovis, somehow."

"I can't imagine how. Clotild's a desirable woman. Can you think of any reason why he wouldn't want to marry her? Besides,…"

Gundobad's whole body sagged as he sense he had failed miserably, "there's no time."

Aridius frowned and shook his head, staring at the floor as he considered the options. "An accident then—or better yet…" Aridius looked up at Gundobad, smiling, "You said 200 men are escorting her?"

"Yes."

The advisor's smile widened. "Consider this: what if the Franks were to inflict a grievous wound against Burgundy and as we defended ourselves the princess was unfortunately and accidentally killed? That would end the possibility of the marriage and it might even bring apologies from Clovis for the indiscretions of his men."

"Yes, perhaps," said Gundobad, slowly.

"Yes…of course."

Gundobad was suddenly more insecure than he had been in weeks. He didn't like the feeling. Neither did he like the fact that Aridius was clearly more accomplished in these matters than he. Worst of all, Aridius was right. Submitting, he asked, "How do you suggest we proceed?"

"I'll send a message to Godegesil, with your permission of course, directing him to stall the entourage. Hopefully that will give you enough time to gather troops to engage the Franks. I hasten to add, we must be sure that none of them escape. If word gets back to Clovis that we were the aggressors, he'll surely retaliate."

Gundobad, though at a loss for alternatives, felt uneasy about the scheme. He was beginning to believe his life was actually threatened by Clotild's freedom and surprised he hadn't considered it before. If this plan didn't work, there was a great deal to lose.

"Are there no better alternatives, Aridius?" Gundobad was leaning forward, his elbows on his knees, his hands clasped before his mouth. He bit his thumbnail.

"No," was the simple and irrefutable reply.

Gundobad sighed in resignation.

"No, I suppose not. Go then, and get your message off to Godegesil. I hope he has enough brains to stall them without betraying our deceit."

Aridius was already backing toward the door, less desperate and more confident now. "I'll prepare a messenger immediately. I pray, for our sakes, that we're not too late."

Chapter 8 *The Betrothal: 493 CE*

In the dim and damp hall of the Geneva castle, a breathless messenger stood at attention. Godegesil looked in amazement at him, astonished at what had just emerged from the young man's mouth.

"Delay them?"

"Yes, my lord, King Gundobad asks that you delay Clotild and the Franks who are escorting her. You're to keep them in Geneva as long as you can."

"Was there any reason given for this?"

"None, sir."

"And your king told you this?"

"Not the king, sir. His advisor, Aridius, gave me the message."

"Ah. So Aridius has returned."

"Yes sir."

"That explains it," said Godegesil. He quietly added, "He's worse than Gundobad." Godegesil had never liked Aridius. The advisor showed him no respect whatsoever, though he feigned it, a mocking gesture that was tinged with just enough sarcasm to betray the contempt he truly felt for Godegesil. Knowing that Aridius had his hand in this, the ruler of Geneva decided how he would respond.

"But you're too late. They left this morning. You must hurry back with the news! There's no time to lose!"

The messenger stumbled as he was turning to leave. Godegesil noticed his fatigue and he nearly commanded the young man to wait. Then he thought better of it. The messenger's fatigue would slow his return.

As the young man departed, Godegesil said, quietly, "Indeed, there is no time to lose." With the boy gone, he called for yet another messenger.

——◆——

Normally the Roman roads afforded the most rapid travel between the major cities of Gaul. But Clotild and her traveling party, chose the same route Aurelian had used several weeks before. Striking out from Geneva they traveled the local roads through the cultivated hills of Burgundy, aiming toward Chalon and avoiding the longer route that took the Roman road to Vienne before turning north. Once at Chalon, they could rejoin the Roman roads and make good time north through Troyes and Reims and on to Soissons.

The Franks charged with accompanying Clotild were escorting her just beyond the hill country when a messenger arrived with news for the princess. Gerard, leader of the escort, rode with the messenger to Clotild's wagon. She stood in the wagon as they arrived.

"My lady," said the messenger, "Godegesil wishes to inform you that Aridius has returned to Vienne and wants to stop your marriage to Clovis. He pursues you even now."

Clotild closed her eyes for a moment and opened them again as she took in a calming breath. Would she never be free of Gundobad? Would he always be a torment to her? She thanked the messenger and dismissed him.

Once the rider had turned back toward Geneva, she said to Gerard, "I was afraid this might happen." She watched the messenger's form shrink in the distance as he headed back toward Geneva.

Gerard was convinced that this was not a time to contemplate, but a time to act. After as long a moment as he could allow, he said, "We could make better time, if I may suggest it, if you would travel on horseback. Can you ride?"

"I've only ridden once," she replied.

"If you could ride, you'd be doing much to assure your safety. We could continue on with your belongings and possibly still outrun Gundobad's men."

"Are you sure?" Clotild asked.

"About saving time?" Gerard nodded his head confidently. "Yes, I'm sure."

"Then I'll ride," she said.

Gerard didn't waste a moment in readying a mount for the princess. He was more concerned than he let on about their chances of escaping from Burgundy without a battle.

"I'll send a dozen of my men with you." In his most comforting tone he added, "Clovis will be surprised to see you so soon!"

Clotild smiled. She was under no illusions about their situation, either. Aridius would not easily submit to defeat and Gundobad would heed any suggestion of his secretary. There would be an army coming.

"Thank you, commander. Clovis was right. You serve me well."

"It's my privilege," he said as he bowed graciously.

Clotild acknowledged Gerard's bow, lightly jumped off the wagon that had carried her from Geneva, and, barely needing Gerard's help, mounted the horse.

The exhausted messenger bearing the news of Clotild's departure met Gundobad's troops at Chambery as they advanced toward Geneva. He was nearly dead with fatigue. He was brought to Aridius who had some difficulty getting the message from him.

Chapter 8 *The Betrothal: 493 CE*

"What are you trying to say, boy?"

"Too late...gone...wedding."

Eventually Aridius deciphered what the messenger was saying and decided they would have the best chance of overtaking Clotild's escort if they reversed their own direction and took the Roman roads back through Vienne, then north through Lyons and on to Chalon. The reversal was executed immediately, and a race for the border of Burgundy commenced.

"Mother, I think we're about done."

It was more wishful thinking than assessment. Clovis was beginning to tire of the preparations for his wedding. In the grand hall of the palace the decorations were already up. Sweeping lengths of brightly colored fabric, gathered at regular intervals, surrounded the room. Blue, white, yellow, green, and red, they made the room sing with color. Flowers were just coming in, despite Basina's concern that it was too early for them, and their fragrance brightened the hall further. The room was more festive than ever. It was enough, thought Clovis, though his mother didn't seem to concur.

Basina continued with her efforts, directing workers who were busy adjusting a canopy above a door so that it met with her approval. Without taking her eyes off the workers she said, "No, no, my child. So many more details..." She frowned, knowing that the final touches would not be complete until the moment of the ceremony itself, if then. "But, yes," she said, turning to her son, "the bulk of the work is done."

"I'm going to leave you to the details, then."

"Where are you going?" Basina asked.

"To meet Clotild."

Basina smiled tenderly at her son. "Take my regards to her." She touched her son's face, gently. "Things are in order here, and every bride needs to know she's welcomed. Go to her."

Basina looked at her strong and handsome son and thought, how much he looks like his father! She smiled again, and as Clovis kissed her cheek, she thought what she already believed: Clotild is truly a fortunate young woman.

The boundaries within Gaul were not clearly established at every point, but it was generally accepted that the border between Burgundy and the land of the Franks wove part of its way north from

Avallon to just south of the city of Troyes. Clotild and twelve Frankish horsemen stood on that part of the border, atop a slight ridge, feeling the exhilaration of having run and won a great race. Clotild had surprised the men, and even herself, with how well she'd handled her horse. That alone had saved half a day's time.

As she looked back over the ground they'd just covered, her homeland, Clotild thought of her mother and father. She remembered the look on their faces as they rushed her and her sister into hiding. It was the last time she saw them. Her jaw muscles tightened.

Adalhard, leader of this smaller band of Franks noticed and asked, "Is something wrong, my lady?"

"No," said Clotild, curtly. She took in a deep breath and pushed it out roughly. "But there is something I would ask of you."

"My lady?"

Clotild remained in thought a moment longer, making certain of her decision.

"Yes," she said, "take half of your men, and rejoin your commander. He may need your help." Adalhard was not displeased at this command and nodded his approval. If there was to be fighting, he didn't want to miss it. "With any luck," continued Clotild, "they'll be ahead of my uncle's men. Help them if they need it. But if they don't, and if you're not in any danger, I want you to leave my uncle a gift."

"A gift?"

"Yes." Clotild smiled so coldly she frightened Adalhard. "Leave him a gift of twelve leagues of land, laid waste. Cause whatever ruin you can." Then Clotild spoke to herself, or perhaps to her parents, but all the Franks heard her, "I want my uncle Gundobad to know that I no longer claim loyalty to him or to Burgundy. And I thank God that vengeance for the lives of my parents has begun!"

"As you wish. If the Gods allow it, it shall be done."

Clotild blinked at the reference to "the gods" but recovered quickly, saying, "Thank you. The rest of us will go on."

The men divided and encouragements were offered as each group went their separate and opposite ways.

Clotild, and the six who rode with her, had traveled less than a day's journey when they saw horsemen approaching from the north. It soon became apparent that it was Clovis who was riding toward them, and the Franks let out a shout of triumph when they recognized their leader's form, his braid flying behind him as he rode.

Chapter 8 *The Betrothal: 493 CE*

Seeing the small group of riders Clovis arrived only slightly comforted by the sight of Clotild. Before offering any sort of welcome he demanded, "The others! Where are the others?"

Quick assurances were offered, though no one was certain their companions were safe.

"You were forewarned?"

"A runner from Godegesil got word to us."

"Godegesil…" Clovis was both comforted and angered by the story. "Gundobad…" he continued to assess the situation. "Gundobad went back on his word? He'll pay for such treachery!"

Clovis took the reigns of his horse and turned back toward Burgundy.

"Sir!" said one of the men, "we have the lady with us."

Clovis paused and looked between his soldiers to see Clotild. He turned again toward Burgundy, then back again. He relaxed his grip on the reigns and stroked his mustache.

"The light's fading. We'll wait until morning." With even that much of a plan, Clovis was able to relax enough to properly welcome his betrothed.

He kissed Clotild's hand. "I'm sorry, I thought you were still…"

"No." Clotild shook her head. "There's no need to apologize. You were worried. I'm glad to be in your care at last, and your men have been good guardians. I only hope no harm has to come to the others."

Clovis looked toward Burgundy once again and said, "Whatever circumstances they're in, they can deal with them. They're strong…good in battle."

The Franks lit a campfire and settled in for the night, sharing the details of the race for the border.

"We never saw anyone to challenge us," said one of the men.

"But we weren't waiting for anyone either," said another.

"The first man continued, "And the princess was incredible. I've never seen a woman ride like her!"

"Oh?" said Clovis, as he looked at Clotild.

She smiled and looked down into the flames, glad that it was dark enough so no one could see her blushing. She was also glad that no one seemed to notice she was shifting her weight as she sat, trying to ease the pain of a sore rump.

Clotild's riding skill especially impressed Clovis and he found himself being increasingly taken with her.

"I look forward to the ride home, even more than I thought I would," he said.

It was mid-morning of the next day, as Clovis, Clotild and their companions rode back toward Burgundy, that the rest of the escort, unscathed and refreshed from a day of pillaging, came into view.

Four days later, as Clotild was seeing her first distant glimpse of Soissons, Gundobad, in Vienne, received word of the failed attempt to stop her. Aridius made a particular point to mention the land that had been brought to ruin.

"They must have known we were trying to stop them," said Gundobad. "There's no other reason to wreak havoc on the land. They were trying to slow our pursuit, that's all."

"No, my King. You're wrong."

Gundobad looked hard at Aridius. "What do you mean?"

"Even if they did know you were trying to stop them, this was not simply a response to that. There was too much damage. Whole vineyards were trampled and burned, homes destroyed, churches. The animals were all killed, though very few people died—only those who put up too much of a fight it seems." He pointed a finger at Gundobad. "This is the first payment on a debt of vengeance. If I were you, I'd pray that Clotild never repays this debt in full."

Chapter 9
A New Bride
493-494 CE

The noise from the gathering crowd made Principius sigh, rise from his chair, walk across the room and close the door.

"Thank you," said Remigius. The bishop of Reims sat facing the groom, Clovis, who had agreed to this consultation with the bishops as one condition he must meet to receive the Church's blessing on his marriage. The other conditions were to be revealed now. "As I was saying, Clovis, you must know how delighted we are for you. This is truly a joyous occasion. And, as you can hear," Remigius tipped his head toward the door, "all Soissons shares in that joy."

Clovis did his best to be dignified. He had no idea his wedding day would bring such anticipation. With just enough firmness to betray his case of nerves, he said, "To be wed to Clotild is a great honor."

"Yes...indeed," said Principius, who was still standing by the door. He didn't miss the tension in the groom's voice but he was wise enough not to take advantage of it, and he knew better than to make light of it. "You're gracious to say so." Principius walked around Clovis, looking at Remigius as he passed behind the Frank, "But, Clovis, before the wedding, there's one thing we need to make clear, and that's the matter of how your children will be raised. After all, Clovis, can there be a more effective way to assure dedication to the Church than to begin one along that path in infancy?"

"You may remember, Clovis," Remigius said, his aging voice crackling with phlegm, causing him to clear his throat with a hack and a swallow before going on, "when we spoke of your sister's marriage to Theodoric, I suggested that there might be some specific concerns if a Christian was to marry a non-believer." Clovis nodded his head. "This business about children is one of those concerns."

Remigius took a long breath and put on a comforting smile. He knew if Clovis accepted this condition, even if he refused to convert, the Church would be sure to have a loyal king in the future.

"I see," said Clovis. He didn't want to agree to anything that he might regret later. He forced himself to put his thoughts of the wedding aside. "I take it, then, that you seek my pledge regarding the children?"

"An agreement, yes," said Principius.

Clovis knew better than to go on without specifics.

"To the effect that…?"

"To the effect that you will agree to raise whatever children you have by Clotild under the guidance and authority of the Church." With that said, Principius sat next to his brother to wait.

The silence that followed was so deafening that Remigius and Principius almost flinched. The constant sound of the gathering congregation, evaporated as they concentrated upon Clovis, sitting motionless, staring back at the two bishops.

What the bishops were asking seemed to be nearly inconsequential. That thought made Clovis nervous. He pondered the proposal looking for hidden consequences. As he considered the situation, he maintained a grave look that made his questioners shift in their seats. But Clovis could find no hidden traps—no reason to refuse. He took in a long, deep breath and gave the bishops a look of resolve.

"I agree. The children Clotild gives to me will be taught in the ways of your…of her Church."

The bishops let out their breath simultaneously. Clovis had given them a long, tense moment. They had surmised, correctly, that he would agree to this condition. While Clovis held little interest in the spiritual matters of the Church, they knew he was concerned with how the Church could benefit his position as ruler. It appeared that marriage would enhance his power. The agreement was almost a certainty, but Remigius and Principius both breathed easier now.

The necessary tools for formalizing the agreement were on hand, and once the pledge was made, witnessed and signed, Clovis returned his thoughts to the wedding.

"Shall we go?" he asked, more confident now. The bishops assented and, together, the three of them rose and went to the door which opened into the crowded nave of the church.

Clotild entered from the back of the church, causing the crowd to hush. And, with admiring gasps and whispers, the people quietly expressed their approval of the bride's beauty. With the help of her own servants, Basina had prepared the princess for this moment.

The queen-to-be wore a white tunic with a sash of olive green. The tunic reached to the floor and its sleeves would have hidden her hands had they been at her side, but because she held flowers before her, a

Chapter 9 *A New Bride: 493-494 CE*

view was allowed of her hands and wrists. They were well adorned with rings and bracelets, all silver, sparkling like dew on grass, set with garnets and opals. Around her neck, Clotild wore a simple necklace which intermingled coins with beads. Her hair was pinned up as it had been at their betrothal and was decorated with rhinestones.

Basina walked beside her wearing a green tunic, trimmed with gold. She looked as proud as she would have, had she been able to attend her daughter Audofleda's wedding to Theodoric. Basina wanted to savor the moment and had to grab the arm of the nervous Clotild who was very nearly ready to run down the aisle. The two processed slowly, deliberately, giving all those present a chance to appreciate them.

The church was filled with Franks from the tribe of Clovis and with other citizens of Soissons. Standing in a place of honor, near the front of the church, were the guards who had escorted Clotild out of Burgundy. They looked particularly proud as they watched Clotild move toward them. She was here because of them. They felt as much a part of the day as anyone present.

Just as Clotild completed her walk there was a murmur off to her right. She looked to see her groom enter. No more than a score of steps later, he stood by her side, smiling at the woman who was to be his wife. He thought she looked even more beautiful than she had at their betrothal.

Principius took his place in front of them, flanked by the bishop of Reims. Looking first at Clotild and Clovis, then at the crowd, Principius began.

"The Lord be with you!"

"And also with you," replied the people.

Standing next to Aurelian, Gerard tried to comprehend the ceremony. It was strange to him. Principius spoke of the ways of marriage, ways all too conciliatory for his taste, and Gerard felt confusion and discomfort, imagining that most of the soldiers were sharing the same uncertainties. He looked over his shoulder at the congregation, a mix of the citizen's of Soissons and the soldiers of Clovis. It was clear who was familiar with the ways of this Christian Church. There was, on their faces, a look of understanding and eager anticipation. Those unfamiliar with what these Christians did looked as though they were asking the same question Gerard asked himself: What will the Gods do today? Is this ceremony an offense?

Remigius, imposing in his gold trimmed chasuble and beaded robe, appeared comfortable in the moment. He showed no indication of fear. That helped Gerard. He'd learned that Remigius was a man of insight, a man whose opinions were respected by many, including Clovis. Remigius has never shown a desire to undermine the authority of Clovis, thought Gerard, quite to the contrary, he's offered support and counsel. Now he's relaxed and apparently enjoying the wedding. Perhaps there's no reason to worry. After all, Gerard reasoned, our chief is taking a wife, he's not changing the world.

He looked back at Clovis and Clotild, who seemed to be as happy as two people could be, and he became eager for the wedding feast. Celebration was a ritual he understood.

The first friends Clotild made in Soissons were Basina and Lantechild, Basina's second daughter. While Clovis dealt with the business of being a ruler, these two helped to sustain the new queen. Basina served as Clotild's guide, as she tried to make her way through the customs and culture of the Franks.

"It's not so different in Burgundy," reflected Clotild as Basina told her about the work of the court.

"No, I suspect not," returned Basina. "All rulers fight the same battles. In fact, I think all men fight the same battles over and over again."

"What do you mean?"

"They're always trying to prove themselves. They can be great men, but there's always an insecure side to them."

Clotild thought of Gundobad and Godegesil and knew it was true for them. "I like Aurelian," she said, certain that it was the contrast between him and Aridius that made him so likable.

"He serves your husband well. And he's more secure than most men I've known. But then, servants are almost always more self assured than rulers. They have fewer enemies."

Clotild understood and nodded knowingly. She understood, too, that her role as the wife of Clovis had just taken on a deeper definition. She would be strength and confidence for him, a servant even as she was his bride.

Lantechild, almost the same age as the new queen, became Clotild's closest friend and keeper of romantic secrets. She was pretty, Clotild thought, much like her mother, but with the same high forehead as Clovis. She was looking forward to her own wedding, an event as yet uncertain since she had no love and no man had sought her hand. Still, there was time, mused Clotild, and she resolved to keep her eyes open for any possibilities of romance she might direct into Lantechild's path.

Chapter 9 *A New Bride: 493-494* CE

Usually the secrets they shared were Lantechild's secrets, dealing with people Clotild was just beginning to know: Luillaume, who was in love with a servant girl in the palace; Idena, Aurelian's charming but inconspicuous wife, who, she suspected, was drinking too much, "She's just so quiet!"; various guards; and distant rulers, their stories obtained by rumor, mostly. Occasionally she spoke of her brother, his love for Clotild, his passion for his people, his concern for his son, Theuderic.

In this new and foreign land, Clotild cherished the friendships, grateful to be accepted into the family. She adjusted to marriage no more rapidly than any bride. In fact, it took her longer than most. Not only did she have to adjust to her new husband, a kind but demanding man, she also had to deal with the stress of living among a new people. Here she knew no one and, though all the people of Soissons knew who she was, the wife of Clovis, none knew her heart or her character.

Nathalie, by whom Clovis already had a son, was regularly present in the court. Clovis assured Clotild that there was no reason to be concerned with his former concubine. "You're my wife. And she's in Tournai, after all."

The words were small comfort to Clotild. For, though Nathalie had indeed removed herself from the palace, at the request of Clovis, she visited often. Clovis had insisted Theuderic remain with him, causing Nathalie to take whatever opportunity she could to see her son. With every visit, Clotild felt threatened. Even in her absence, the mother of her husband's first-born was constantly present in Theuderic. He would forever be the first child, the heir. Nathalie, as well, was a challenge. Clovis continued to have feelings for her, Clotild could tell. Still, she mused, he has feelings for me too. I am here. She is not. Thus, she built up her confidence between Nathalie's visits.

Late one afternoon, during a loud spring thunderstorm, Nathalie entered the palace, dripping wet, just as Basina and Clotild, who had been walking together, happened to pass through the front hall. They stopped and stood in silence, staring at Nathalie. In the uncomfortable moment, understanding that Clotild did not need to face Nathalie any longer than was absolutely necessary, Basina took charge.

"Look at you, you're soaked! Come," she said as she rushed Nathalie off, "we'll get you some dry clothes."

In the quiet that followed, Clotild's cloud of anxiety descended again and she sought out her husband.

Basina took the opportunity to visit with Nathalie herself, giving Clotild time, she hoped, to gain her composure.

"She doesn't like me," said Nathalie, toweling off her head.

"Clotild? Of course she doesn't," was Basina's reply. "But then, she doesn't know you, does she?"

"He married her! What was wrong with me?"

"Nothing my dear, nothing." Basina stroked Nathalie's cheek. "He cherishes you. You gave him his little boy."

Nathalie smiled, knowing that Basina spoke truth and could do nothing other than try to comfort her. Clovis had married and that would not change. She was under his care, but she felt alone. Perhaps there would be another man, someday, somehow..." she let her imaginings fade.

Upon discovering from a servant that his mother was in the palace, Theuderic took it upon himself to say his own hellos, running into the room and shouting "Mother!" before jumping onto her lap. As mother and son visited, Basina excused herself to find Clovis.

Clotild stood by quietly as her mother-in-law entered the throne room.

Basina knew that by now, Clovis was well aware he had a visitor, She decided to announce the news, anyway.

"Nathalie is here."

Before she could say another word, Theuderic ran into the room, zig-zagging around his grandmother and shouted his own announcement, "Mama's here! Mama's here!" and he leapt into his father's lap.

Basina waited only a moment and then asked, "Should I send her in?"

"In a moment, mother," he said as he tried to get a handle on his son. "I'll send for her."

With that, Basina returned to share what little time she could with the mother of her first grandchild.

Theuderic wore the features of his father, the same nose and eyes, and as Clotild watched him she could already see some of his father's mannerisms. Some of the swagger was there. Already he was willing to accept challenges.

He didn't appear to notice Clotild but snuggled up to his father in a most affectionate way. Clovis gave his son a hug and then Theuderic pulled away from him so he could look his father square in the face.

"Father, are you brave?"

"Yes, Theuderic," said Clovis, adding a chuckle, "I am brave."

"Mama says that brave people die young."

Clovis looked at Clotild who returned a look of tenderness. Theuderic's innocence softened her mood.

Chapter 9 *A New Bride: 493-494* CE

The boy followed his father's eyes and saw the Queen's expression. He didn't know Clotild well yet. And though he held no personal animosity toward her, he had come to know that his own mother did. He frowned.

Clovis saw the grimace and tried to regain his son's attention by saying, "Oh, did she say that?"

"Yes, father, she did. Will you die because you're brave?" He reached up and began to play with the pin that held up his father's cloak.

"Theuderic, everyone will die someday."

The boy frowned in thought. "Even if they're not brave?" he asked.

"Yes, my son, brave or not, we will all die. Even the Gods will die."

Clotild hadn't learned much about the gods that Clovis worshipped, other than what Avitus had taught her. Her sense was that his gods were, at best, interesting. Certainly, she thought, they couldn't be any match for the one true God. Now, with the subject out in the open, she listened intently.

Theuderic stopped playing with the pin and looked up at his father. With what was very nearly horror in his voice he asked, "Even Odin?"

"Yes, Theuderic, even Odin. You remember the stories, don't you? One day the giants will face the Gods of Asgard and the Gods will die. But they'll be brave and heroic as they fall. They won't be defeated." Rolling thunder echoed through the sound of the rain. "Hear that, Theuderic! Odin and Thor are at work, even now, preparing for the battle!"

"But they'll die?"

"Yes, but they'll die heroes. Don't you want to be a hero?"

"Yes, father."

"That's good!" said Clovis and he mussed his son's hair.

At that moment a servant appeared, announcing that supper was ready. Theuderic, more interested in food than in the fate of the Gods, jumped from his father's lap and ran past the servant, out of the room. Clovis watched him the whole way, smiling.

Clotild kept still until Theuderic was out of the room. She could barely believe what she had heard her husband say and she could hold her astonishment in no longer.

"That was terrible what you told your son!" she said. Her voice came out in a high pitched squeak.

Clovis was taken by surprise and turned to his wife with a look of confusion on his face.

"What do you mean, terrible?"

"Terrible! You gave the child no hope."

"Hope? What do you mean?"

"It's bad enough for Theuderic to learn that his father is going to die. But if even his gods die, how can he have hope?"

"Do you really think Theuderic cares about hope?"

"Hope's important!"

"Of course it is." Clovis was frustrated at the question and didn't really want to argue about it. "I gave him hope, Clotild. There's hope to be a hero, to deny defeat, to join the Gods in the last struggle. That's hope."

"Gods! Clovis, the gods you worship are nothing!" She surprised herself with her own boldness.

"Nothing?" Clovis became defensive. The Gods of Asgard had provided great joy for Clovis in his youth as he had listened to the stories of their bravery. His father, Childeric, had told him the stories of Odin and Tyr, Balder and Thor. They were wonderful stories of adventure and heroism. Now, recalling his pledge to the Church, he wondered if the stories he told his children might not be more important than he first thought. There were no priests in his religion like there were in Clotild's. But, to the mind of Clovis, his father, heroic in so many ways, seemed very nearly one of the Gods himself. The Gods had yet to desert him and Clovis was disturbed that Clotild would attack them. "Nothing, you say? The Gods have given me victory after victory. And as long as I please them with my courage, I continue in victory." He raised his voice as he spoke. "I believe the Gods have favored me!"

"Favored you?" Clotild felt the need to push her case now that she had begun. "They offer you nothing but death. You, yourself, said that they're doomed to defeat! What kind of victory is that?"

Clovis let his wife speak her mind.

"My God is eternal. And he offers victory even over death, if we submit to Him."

"Victory in submission?" Clovis said, incredulous. He could make no sense out of the idea of victory through submission. An impossible concept! "Nonsense!"

Clotild had said too much, and though she had a great deal to learn about Clovis, she understood her new husband well enough to know it was time to be quiet. Strength and heroism were the divine attributes he knew. Surrender and submission were concepts he wasn't ready to comprehend. She knew she wouldn't convince him of anything this way and she decided to drop her challenge for the present. She smiled and stroked her husband's arm and conceded the skirmish.

Chapter 9 A New Bride: 493-494 CE

"This time, I'll be the one to submit," she said.

"This time?" Clovis was frowning.

Smiling, Clotild stood and coyly brushed her husband's hair back from his brow.

"Yes," she said, "this time."

She said the words with such playfulness that the mustache of Clovis twitched almost imperceptibly as he gave a slight smile. "Mmm. I see," he said. "This has been just one battle in the war?"

Clotild cocked her head and squinted dramatically.

"Yes, I suppose you could say that."

"I see..." he said slowly, giving a knowing look and a good-natured smirk. "Well then, let's eat," he said as he stood. "Battle always makes me hungry."

"What about Nathalie?" asked Clotild, regretting the question as soon as it had escaped her lips. She didn't wish to be an ally of the woman.

"Ah, yes." He raised his eyebrows, remembering. Clotild was warmed in the thought that Clovis might actually have forgotten about the visitor. "You go on, Clotild. I really must see her." He patted her bottom softly and, after giving her husband an equally soft kiss, Clotild went to supper.

As their carriage rolled along on its way to Paris, Clovis and Clotild watched the workers laboring over their crops. It was harvest time and the fields were active. Peasants swept across the land, transforming lush fields of gold into brown vacant patches of ground.

The procession, which included forty horsemen, followed the course of the river Aisne, traveling east as far as Compiegne where the river flowed into the Oise. They turned to the southwest and continued to follow the river, eventually departing from the river road, traveling due south, into forestland. Shortly after entering the forest, they stopped to enjoy the spectacle of a woodsman felling a tree.

"It's for the new church in Chantilly," he told them, ceasing his work long enough to wipe his brow. He was proud of his efforts and it came through in his voice. "God grew this to be the main beam," he said, patting the tree in honest appreciation of the miracle it was.

The Franks rested long enough to watch the man at his work, his strokes of the ax impressively consistent and strong. The tree fell with a crackling as loud as any thunder Clovis had ever heard.

After the tree was down, Clotild gave the man a gift of 20 solidis for the church. At the gesture, Clovis smirked and shook his head.

He didn't really care whether Clotild supported the Church or not. Indeed, he continued to give lands to the Church, himself. But he enjoyed the mischief of aggravating his wife now and then. Clotild ignored him.

The view of plenty changed considerably as Paris neared. North of the city swamplands dominated the landscape. It was only when the Seine was reached that dwellings appeared again, and then only a few. Paris was growing but the population was spilling off the island city onto the southern bank of the river, land less prone to flooding.

Crossing the bridge onto the island, it was evident that little or no attempt had been made to rid the streets of refuse and the smell of rotting food scraps and human waste permeated the air. This was Clotild's first visit to Paris and Clovis had the entourage go around the inside of the wall, starting with the east side of the island. They saw people in tatters, begging as the carriage passed by. The families were pale and gaunt from malnutrition. Rye bread and ale were their staples. They would eat what vegetables they could get; turnips, carrots and onions, but in winter no vegetables at all were to be found. What food they had would go into a cauldron that was rarely emptied. Broth was added to its contents daily. Occasionally someone would catch a rabbit or a boar and that addition would be a special treat. But with trade on the decline, something Clovis was trying to remedy, the local markets offered less and less, and conditions for the poor were gradually worsening.

Clovis noticed the poverty when the city had so willingly fallen to him. He suspected one reason for the surrender had been the hope of something better. Since then he'd done what he could to encourage commerce in the area. There was no reason why this city shouldn't be thriving, he thought. It disturbed him that things looked even worse than they did three years before.

A sudden yelp from Clotild caused Clovis to order their caravan to a stop. He tried to follow Clotild's gaze, but at first, all he saw was the same crowd of poor people he'd been pondering. Clotild looked out upon blind people carrying walking sticks; beggars sick and coughing, holding sores; people shaking with palsy; and invalids struggling with makeshift crutches. All, with silent respect and notable politeness, were gathering around the singular figure of a woman who was in her later years, perhaps her seventies, dressed very much like those who surrounded her. She was washing the wounds of the people and blessing those who came to her. Genevieve.

Clotild watched with nostalgic longing. It seemed as if a lifetime had passed since she had shared in the same work in Geneva.

Chapter 9 *A New Bride: 493-494 CE*

Clovis, too, watched intently. He was struck by the immense respect being granted to this old woman. He'd seen honor expressed for the aged before, but not like that offered to Genevieve. There was hope in the faces of the crowd that spoke of a trust he rarely saw conferred.

The people were gathered together in the shade of the wall which protected the city. The church named Saint Étienne shared the wall with the city, adding her bulk to the defense of Paris.

Clovis thought back to his own campaign against Paris and remembered how effective those defenses had been. It had been an unusually tedious siege, he recalled. He found it difficult to believe that these poor citizens could have defended the city so effectively. But now, as he looked at the faces of the people as they stood here around Genevieve, he understood the kind of power loyalty can bring.

It was several minutes before the woman looked up and saw them through a break in the crowd. She stood to her full height, which was considerable, and asked that a path be cleared so she might go to the street. With nothing less than reverence, the people obliged her. As she passed, the gaze of the people followed her, turning nearly a hundred pair of eyes toward the carriage, the old woman's destination.

She came to a standstill before the carriage, looking into the face of Clovis. Her eyes were large with self-aware innocence set in wisdom-grown wrinkles. She smiled even as her lips parted to speak.

"It's been a long time, Clovis."

"Hello, Genevieve."

Clotild was surprised that her husband knew this woman and her mouth opened slowly at the thought. Clovis and Genevieve both noticed and grinned at her astonishment.

"You know each other?" Clotild asked.

"Yes, my dear, many years ago he came here to fight. I stood with my people then," she gestured again to the poor behind her, "but when we met, I could see his father in him." A further look of wonder came to Clotild's face. "Oh yes, I knew him too. And while your husband is not baptized, I knew when I met him that God has plans for him. He was meant to rule here."

Clotild crowded her husband aside as she listened to Genevieve.

"My husband has business he must attend to," she said, "but I would like to stay with you for a while and work with you...if you'll permit it."

Genevieve looked into the eager eyes of Clotild.

"If your husband will allow it, I would consider your help a gift from God and the blessed Virgin."

Clovis felt no need to disagree, especially since he knew Clotild's mind was made up. He helped her down from the carriage, but with his usual caution, insisted that two of his men accompany her.

Clotild gave Clovis a quick hug before he left to address his business on the south bank of the river. Then she walked with Genevieve toward the people who awaited them, their soldier escort walking behind.

Genevieve's look was austere. Her graying hair was cropped short and she wore a plain dress adorned with a single piece of jewelry; a simple medallion on a chain, a bronze coin with a cross engraved upon it. Clotild noticed it immediately.

"An interesting necklace," she said.

"It was a gift," said Genevieve, holding the medallion tenderly. "Father Germain of Auxerre gave it to me when I was seven. He was traveling through the countryside, on his way to Briton, preaching against the heresy of Pelagius. He told me that I would give myself to God's work. And later, in memory of my consecration, he gave me the necklace as a gift."

"It's lovely."

"Thank you. But it doesn't feed the people. Come, there's work to be done." She picked up her pace. Clotild, and the soldiers following, found themselves running to catch up.

The pain and pleasure of charitable work consume time rapidly and the crowds were diminishing along with the sunlight when Clovis returned, business done, to collect his queen. She smiled and waved when she saw the carriage and he had to admit to himself that she looked radiant. He stepped down from the carriage and watched her work. He'd never seen her so glowing, so full of joy. It seemed to be coursing through her body; it appeared to wash over her face, a face that now beamed; it flowed around her entire bearing, bringing out a disarming smile, enlightened and visionary eyes, and arms reaching to the entire world that she might embrace it—reaching with such abandon that Clovis didn't, for a moment, doubt that she might actually be able to reach so far and so wide. And suddenly, strikingly, ecstatically, Clovis understood the loyalty that Aurelian carried for this woman, for this was how he had seen her first in that Geneva churchyard so many months before. He hadn't been exaggerating after all. In the guise of a beggar, this was what Aurelian had seen!

As the last person seeking help bowed in thanks and backed away, Clotild stood, her work for the day complete. She ran to her husband who was now walking toward her. She enfolded him lovingly in her arms.

Chapter 9 *A New Bride: 493-494* CE

"I haven't felt so full-since I left Geneva!" she said. "This has been wonderful!"

Genevieve followed Clotild, strolling slowly, arriving just as the two concluded their welcoming embrace.

"You've made my wife happy, Genevieve. I thank you."

The old woman shook her head.

"There's no need to thank me. Thank our God in heaven. Clotild's been a great help." Genevieve rubbed Clotild's arm as she spoke. "She's given of herself and has generously offered a gift of money as well."

"I approve, of course," said Clovis.

"But more," continued Genevieve, "she's told me about you...most of which I knew. For instance, you're still not a believer in our Lord Jesus."

"No, I'm not."

"But you're not an Arian or a Pelagian either." The tone of her voice made Clovis glad that he was neither. "She told me something of where you've been and what you've done since I saw you last. I believe your father would have been proud. But because of what I've learned, I would ask something of you."

Clovis enjoyed thinking that his father would have been proud of him. His feelings toward Genevieve warmed.

"Please then, go on."

"You hold prisoners, I understand, from your encounter with the Thuringians."

"I do." Clovis looked at Clotild and frowned. Clotild looked at Genevieve with adoration.

"I ask that you release them."

"Genevieve," said Clovis, his jaw tightening, "I will not."

"That is what I ask," said Genevieve, resolute.

"Genevieve," began Clovis again, more slowly this time, wishing to be accurate, "recently, Remigius of Reims told me that there are two cities, one of the Gods and another of the world. You, it appears, serve the city of the Gods. Please, allow me to act out my worldly affairs as I see fit."

"My good Clovis, I wouldn't presume to order you. I merely make my request. The bishop, Remigius, is correct, of course. But the two cities are not without relations. Just as you are here in Paris for business related to Soissons, I am in this worldly city on business relating to God's city. I'm only asking that you release the prisoners so that they may return to their families. There's no other worldly motive."

Not prepared to argue with the woman and seeing the consternation on Clotild's previously radiant face, Clovis hesitated. After all, he thought, terms have been arranged with the Thuringians. Everything's been settled there. Perhaps there is no advantage in keeping the men. But this woman...and Clotild's face...

"All I can offer, Genevieve, is to say that I'll consider your request." His tone was conciliatory.

Clotild beamed once again and Genevieve smiled warmly.

"Then I will accept that offering with thanks," she said.

Genevieve bade farewell to her new acquaintance, assuring a tearful Clotild that they would meet again. Clovis and his queen boarded the carriage and the two waved a further farewell as they departed.

The caravan was barely off the island when Clotild said, "She's the most saintly woman I've ever known!"

Clovis, impressed with Genevieve as well, though for different reasons, said, "I've never met a woman so shrewd in her ability to manipulate...save my own mother. You have to respect her for that, if for nothing else."

"She doesn't manipulate!" said Clotild, horrified at her husband's words. "She's a woman of faith!" Clotild's defensiveness was far more than was necessary.

"I don't deny her faith," said Clovis stroking Clotild's knee. "I'm only saying that her years have certainly taught her how to accomplish her goals."

"God grants her success because of her faith."

"Perhaps, Clotild, perhaps. Or maybe her successes give her faith."

"Mmmm," was all Clotild could say. She decided to enjoy the peace of her heart, rather than to contend with her husband. She smiled weakly and rested her head on his shoulder. Clovis leaned his head so that it rested on Clotild's thick hair, and he was pleased she was happy.

For weeks, the memory of the encounter with Genevieve brought a blush to Clotild's cheeks that made her even more appealing to Clovis. After long deliberations with Aurelian, Clovis decided to release his prisoners. The act thrilled Clotild and she became more peaceful, more loving than ever. Now, as Clovis looked at her, dusk brought a further softness to his already beautiful queen. Backlit by the fading light from the window, a halo appeared around her head as the last rays of the day's sunshine struck the loose strands of hair that floated free from the bulk of her long tresses.

Chapter 9 A New Bride: 493-494 CE

He could see her smiling as she moved toward him. She swayed as she walked, folded her arms over her stomach, and kissed him without saying a word. Clovis recognized the signs. She was, in her own playful way, hiding something.

"Are you going to tell me, Clotild?" he said in his most unassuming voice.

She smiled more broadly but remained silent.

"Tell me, wife! Don't waste my time because you know you'll tell me everything in a moment." His voice didn't betray the slightest bit of anger; only the full recognition of the game.

"I like to see you wonder," she said, spitefully.

Clovis began to move toward his wife.

"Tell me, Clotild, or I'll tickle you!" He lunged at her.

"No, Clovis, please!" she backed away unfolding her arms so she could fend off his attack.

He moved a little faster and she screamed and broke into a run. It was half-hearted at best. She stayed within the room and in seconds she was screaming in glee, lying on the floor with Clovis straddled atop her, tickling her, saying, "Tell me, tell me!"

She gave a gasp, the loudest scream yet, and, laughing between words, said, "I'll tell you, I'll tell you!"

Clovis laughed with her and stopped the tickling long enough for Clotild to catch her breath and inform him that she was going to bear him a child.

Chapter 10
Ingomer
494 CE

The baby fussed as his mother and father argued.
"You promised that the children would be raised in the care of the church!"

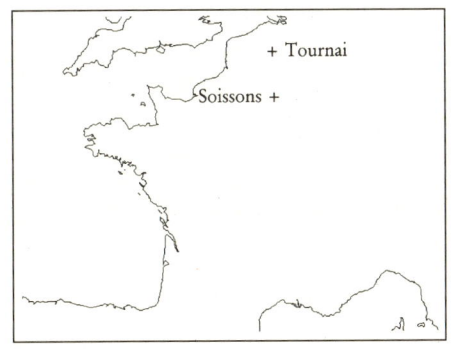

Clotild was adamant, but too tired to make a display of her insistence.

"But I made no agreement about this, this…"

"Baptism."

"Yes, baptism. I made no agreement about that."

The baby whimpered and Clovis looked at him, lying next to Clotild. They'd named him Ingomer. Clovis didn't like the idea of this boy, his son, going through this strange ritual. The rituals of his people were meaningful enough, but this ritual of baptism, that his son might be visited by some spirit, this frightened him.

"Clovis," Clotild made an extra effort to sound especially sincere, "the baptism is a part of raising our children in the Church…a necessary part!"

"*Why* is it necessary?"

The birthing of her son had been difficult and Clotild had yet to get up from her bed, but she was unwilling to lose this battle for the baptism. She fought to raise herself, shifting her weight and coming to one elbow. The effort was exhausting. She took a shallow breath, and before she dropped back onto her pillow, she said, weakly, but clearly, "It is."

She thought about the gods Clovis worshipped, still convinced that they were nothing more than stories with which you occupy little children. They had no power. Their names had no power. She could believe nothing else. Her son would be baptized into the Church.

Clovis saw his wife's fatigue and didn't want to tire her, but his struggle with this idea of baptism continued.

"I made no agreement to this rite, Clotild," he tried to be tender, "and I don't intend to consent to it now."

"I've already begun to make arrangements," said Clotild. "I sent word to Bishop Eleutherius in Tournai. That's where the baptism will be." Clovis didn't miss the resolve in her voice. She went on. "And you did consent to it, whether you acknowledge it or not, when we were married." Bothered by her firmness the baby began to whimper again and Clotild shushed him softly.

Clovis turned away from Clotild and briskly paced the room several times before he dared to speak again. He was angry that his wife had made these plans without consulting him, though as he paced his anger faded. He tried to remember exactly what he'd agreed to on their wedding day. He could recall nothing about this baptism. What kind of power did it carry? What would it do to his son? It was clear to him that Clotild was immovable on the issue. Still, he needed to understand.

When he had calmed and his pacing was over, he asked, "Why Tournai?"

"I asked your mother about it," said Clotild softly. Her eyes were closed. "She suggested it would be a good thing for you to share this with your people there."

Clovis pursed his lips in frustration and began to weigh the advantages and disadvantages of this baptism. A conscious effort set his fears aside for a moment and he considered how a show of solidarity with the Church might be of value. He pulled a chair to where his wife lay, sat down and began to stroke her hand.

"I did agree that the children would be raised in the Church. I do remember." He drew in a long breath before asking, "Does the Church see this baptism as necessary?"

Clotild saw his mind was changing. She wasn't surprised. Of the virtues Clovis could claim, fairness was near the top of the list. He wasn't above reconsidering his decisions. She opened her eyes to look at him.

"Yes, my love. It's necessary for the soul of our son." She stroked Ingomer's brow and the child frowned and yawned.

"Is that what the Church says, or what you say?" Clovis lowered his head to receive the answer.

"It's what we both say." Clotild grasped her husband's hand softly, trying to ease his anxiety.

Clovis lifted his face to look at Clotild. "Then we'll baptize him in Tournai, as you say."

Clotild's muscles relaxed with her husband's statement, nearly causing her to collapse with relief. She looked at him and smiled with such tranquillity that Clovis could not help smiling back.

Chapter 10 *Ingomer: 494 CE*

"You knew I would give in, didn't you?"

"No." She laid her head back on the pillow and let out a long satisfied breath, "But I knew you had to."

"When will this Baptism happen?" Clovis asked.

"I gave Eleutherius the date of one week from Sunday."

"Are there preparations to be made?"

"Some. But there's time. Basina said she'd help."

"Mother?" Clovis raised his eyebrows.

"Yes. I was surprised too. She doesn't understand what difference it all makes, but she could see it was important to me. And I suspect she's glad to do anything that will show off her new grandson." They both looked at their child, now sound asleep.

Clovis chuckled quietly, "That much I can believe!"

Clotild, let her hand slip from the hand of Clovis and she closed her eyes again.

"I'm tired, Clovis. Let me sleep awhile."

"Yes, of course, sleep."

Clovis kissed his wife, lifted Ingomer from the bed and then made his way out of the bedchamber. Before he was through the door, Clotild was asleep.

———

The day of the baptism was cold and blustery. Whirlwinds were betrayed by the leaves they had captured; leaves that eventually broke free to be blown across the steps of the only Catholic Christian Church in Tournai. It was on those steps that Clovis stood proudly before the people of the city. The small courtyard that stretched out from the porch of the church was swarming with people who were constantly shifting to make room for yet another spectator.

One concession that had been offered to Clovis was that the baptism would be held on the steps of the church. That way the members of his tribe who still lived in Tournai could witness the event. The small church was not able to accommodate the many warriors who were glad for any chance to celebrate with their chief.

Basina stood on one side of her Chieftain son and Clotild stood on the other. Clotild wore a white tunic and held a restless Ingomer, who was likewise dressed in white; a baptismal robe made by Lantechild especially for the occasion. Clotild brushed a fly from the garment and smiled at the thought of Lantechild. Only Basina, Clovis and herself attended Ingomer to this Christening, aside from a few guards. Clotild knew she would enjoy sharing the details of the day to those who stayed behind, Lantechild and Albofleda among them.

In the front of the crowd, Clovis saw Nathalie with his son, Theuderic. He nodded to them and smiled, then turned his focus to the baptism.

With winter coming quickly, he had no desire to prolong this event. He looked at Bishop Eleutherius and encouraged him to begin with the ceremony.

Having asked the appropriate questions of Clovis and Clotild, and having sprinkled Ingomer's head with the holy water of baptism, Eleutherius, bishop of Tournai, pronounced:

"Ingomer, son of Clovis, I baptize you in the name of the Father, the Son and the Holy Ghost. Amen."

A final blessing was offered and, though not many of the Franks understood what had taken place, a hesitant cheer rose from the rather tentative crowd. In the same moment that the cheer went up, Basina leaned toward her newly baptized grandson to offer a grandmotherly kiss. She stopped suddenly and spoke in a grave tone. The commotion of the crowd drowned out her words but Clovis and Clotild could tell that something was wrong.

"What did you say, mother?"

Basina took Ingomer from Clotild and repeated herself loudly, "I said, something's wrong with your son! Come! Quickly!"

Clutching Ingomer to her, Basina ran into the throng of people and grabbed Nathalie explaining as they ran, that they needed the use of her home. Clovis and Clotild followed close behind. Basina spoke with such gravity that Nathalie didn't waste any time asking why, but, dragging Theuderic beside her, led the way. Her urgency opened up a path before her in the crowd that, to a casual observer, appeared impassable. They covered the short distance to her home in an interminable moment.

Once inside, Basina laid the gasping baby on a table and tried to comfort him. Gradually he quieted somewhat but he refused to take Clotild's breast. Eventually, the baby fell into a fitful sleep assuring the worried onlookers enough so that, in turn, each took a few hours sleep.

The house was dark, lit only by the fire. Nathalie came to sit beside Clotild as her vigil continued.

"Are you going to be all right?"

"I think so," said Clotild, keeping her gaze on her child.

"I could…"

"No. Nothing, thank you."

In spite of the moment, Clotild didn't want kindness from Nathalie. The two women sat quietly for half an hour.

Chapter 10 *Ingomer: 494 CE*

"You love him, don't you?" Nathalie broke the silence.

"What?"

"You love him. Clovis. Don't you?"

"Yes, I do."

"So do I."

Clotild looked down and sighed. It was a conversation she knew had to occur sometime or another. "I know," she said. Things were quiet again.

"Do you think he loves you?" Nathalie continued.

"I'm sure of it...Do you think he loves you?"

"I don't know. I thought he did...once."

Clotild felt the pain in the woman's heart even through her concern for Ingomer. It was not hard to feel for this woman. "I think he still cares for you."

Nathalie's chin quivered and she put her hand on Clotild's back, rubbing back and forth gently. There was no need to discuss things further. The two knew where they stood. After a moment she broke the silence once more.

"I hope Ingomer will be well."

Clotild's voice cracked into a stifled sob and she was barely able to utter the words, "Thank you."

Nathalie held Clotild as she cried away as much of the fear and tension as she could. She held her until the crying stopped and then asked, "Will you be all right?" Clotild nodded. Nathalie rubbed her back one more time. "If you need anything...." Clotild nodded again. Nathalie rose, put another log on the fire and retired.

By the next morning Ingomer had settled down and his color was good enough that they decided to make the trip back to Soissons.

The journey would take a full two and one-half days and they began as soon as they were able. The roads were generally good and the traveling was as comfortable as could be hoped for. Even so, Ingomer's condition worsened. Less than two hours out of Tournai his color began a slow shift from slightly pink to ashen gray.

Basina's concern grew with each passing league and she tried, with increasing ineptness, to hide her worry. Her attempts at cheer, causing her to issue forth with nervous laughter and banal stories, only upset Clotild all the more.

Clovis spent most of the journey in silence, staring at the sickly child. He noticed how, even in sickness, the child was attractive...like his mother, he thought. He glanced up at her weary and worried face. Even now, she was beautiful. It was oddly comforting to him. But his comfort did not last long, for with every turn of the carriage wheels, Ingomer's condition deteriorated. He became listless and didn't respond to any efforts to comfort him. Soon, the child dropped into a sleep that was so deep Clovis, Clotild and Basina weren't sure if they should be concerned or relieved.

"He must be exhausted, poor dear. He's been fussing so," said Basina.

"Yes, I'm sure that's what it is," said Clotild as she stroked her baby's brow. Clovis remained silent.

They arrived at the residence and without wasting a moment, Clotild, holding her son close to her, descended from the carriage, entered the house and took him to her bed-chamber. Lantechild and Albofleda, ready to welcome them, were surprised by Clotild rushing past without any acknowledgment of their presence.

Ingomer was, once again, in his baptismal robe. All his other garments had become soiled during the trip. Rather than changing him out of the robe, Clotild decided to let him sleep. She put him down and gently stroked his frowning face. Feeling a chill, she went to the fireplace to start a fire. As the kindling lit, she turned back to her son and gasped. He had turned a deep shade of blue and the only movement he made was a slight twitching of his feet.

"Clovis!" she cried, "Basina!"

She stood still and screamed their names again, all the while staring at her son, trying to reach to him but unable to move. Before her husband, his sisters, and their mother arrived, the baby had stopped moving. Ingomer was dead.

Basina chose the burial site and Clovis made preparations for a traditional Frankish burial. Clotild offered no argument. She only wanted to be left alone.

On the day following Ingomer's death, Clovis, Clotild, Basina, her daughters, and Aurelian gathered on a hillside east of Soissons. Gerard, representing the home guard, stood with them as well. Though the ground was beginning to freeze, a hole had been dug sufficiently deep for a burial.

Ingomer lay to the side of the grave, wrapped in a cloak of his father's, one with sturdy material and a finely crafted silver buckle. Clovis and Clotild stood over him, Clovis supporting his wife with one arm and tapping his free hand against his thigh. Basina stepped forward, knelt next to the corpse, and tucked some coins inside the cloak.

"In case there is expense on his journey to Valhalla," she said ceremoniously, directing her words to her son.

Chapter 10 *Ingomer: 494 CE*

Aurelian then stepped forward carrying a small pot in which he had placed dried fruit and meat.

"Food," he said. He took care to set the pot down gently beside the swaddled body.

Then, Clovis, released Clotild to his mother's care and stepped forward himself. From his own cloak, he pulled out a small scramasax that, in spite of its petite size, was too large for the infant. He rested it across Ingomer's body. The hilt was nearly larger than the baby's head and the blade curved down the entire length of the small form, coming to a point a hand's breadth past Ingomer's toes.

"To fight the giants with," he said, more to the quiet form of Ingomer than to anyone else.

Surrounded with his provisions, his weapon, and with his kingly cloak, Ingomer was laid to rest, his head facing toward the rising sun. Gerard and Luillaume held the corners of the blanket upon which Ingomer lay and lowered him into the earth. Soil broke away from under the feet of the men and fell into the hole.

The sound of dirt falling on Ingomer's body, transported Clovis back to his father's burial. He remembered his mother taking off her own jewelry and casting it into the grave, fearing that the hundreds of gold and silver coins already in the grave would not be enough for the journey to Valhalla. The sound of the jewels hitting the body were very much the same as this.

Childeric's tomb had included 300 gold bees and a crystal orb, not to mention the head of his favorite horse. Basina had not cried that day. Neither had the young Clovis. But today, Basina did cry as she embraced the shaken and shaking Clotild. Clovis looked at the two of them and noticed that his wife was not crying. Instead, as Basina wept on her shoulder, Clotild murmured steadily. Clovis drew closer, and he could hear. She was saying prayers for their dead son's soul.

A pall hung over the palace. Clotild had no children—no joy to fall back upon—only emptiness. She roamed the halls of the residence alone. The passageways seemed dark and lifeless to her now; not the same halls she had walked so often. What had once seemed a bright and inspiring house was now somehow more foreboding than inviting, more confining than she remembered it to be.

Nearly three weeks after Ingomer's burial, Clovis watched a motionless Clotild as she stared into space, her eyes red and swollen. His compassion had run low and his anger would remain buried no longer. Next to him sat a tinted glass vase, blue, that his sister, Lantechild, had given to him as a wedding present. It was one of the finer examples of the craft, and had made the journey all the way from Greece. Clovis grabbed it and threw it across the room where it smashed into countless pieces. Clotild's eyes, now filled with surprise, turned upon him.

"Why did you do that?" she asked.

"Because I can't strike your damn God! That's why!"

"What?"

"Because of your great God," he said mockingly, "our son is dead!"

"Clovis!" Clotild said, in horror.

"He killed him! Your God…your Almighty God…who hears and answers prayers. He's killed our son! If Ingomer had been dedicated in the name of my Gods he would have lived! But you had him baptized in your God's name and he died. My Gods are angry and your God…your God is a murderer!"

As Clovis erupted he allowed the possibility to creep into his mind that if his Gods were angry they might have killed Ingomer. But he dismissed the idea so quickly that it was almost as if the thought had never been there.

Clotild received his fury and tears began to stream down her cheeks. She clenched her fists, trying to stop herself from shaking.

Clovis looked at her and said, "It's tearing you apart and there's nothing I can do!" More than anything he wanted Clotild to get on with her life. He knew death well and had accepted the loss of his son readily. But his wife's pain hurt him more than he'd imagined it could.

Clotild, still staring into space said, "At least he was baptized!" She shook her head and a tear dropped onto her hand. She wiped it on her leg. "I don't grieve for Ingomer." Her trembling voice rose gradually to a cry that sounded as if she was trying to convince herself of the truth. "God has taken our son to be with Him. Ingomer is with angels in heaven! I'm only grieving for myself now."

She broke into sobs, her fists clenched against her bowed head. Clovis, having no more words to offer, watched Clotild in silence. And then, unable to imagine anything that might comfort her, he turned in frustration, leaving her to cry alone.

Chapter II

Armorica
496-497 CE

Little more was said about the effects of baptism after that day when Clovis walked out on Clotild. On those rare occasions when the subject did arise, it served only to anger him and sadden her. But now it was necessary to mention it again. A year and a half after Ingomer's death, Clotild gave birth to another son, Chlodomer. Clotild would not allow her son to remain unbaptized. No reasoning on the part of her husband could sway her, no murmuring among the Franks who worked in the royal residence could tempt her to reconsider and no pleadings of Nathalie could move her.

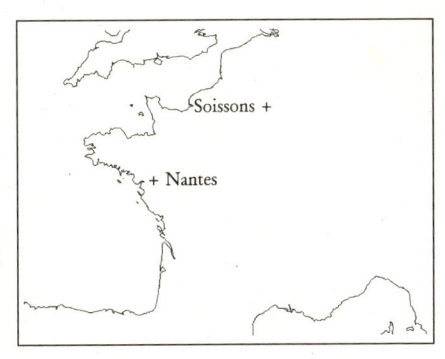

Since Ingomer's death, Nathalie and Clotild had become as close as their respective positions and histories would allow. The distance between them was still significant, though they no longer viewed one another as competitors for the affections of Clovis. Nathalie's love for Clovis was an honest one which Clotild could not fault. Nathalie had come to accept the fact of lost love and had even joined herself to another man. Nathalie's concern offered to the grieving mother had helped Clotild through some difficult moments. For all Nathalie might represent, Clotild learned she held no malice toward children and no disdain for those who grieve.

Nathalie's own superstitious fears compelled her to try changing Clotild's mind about the baptism, but her efforts were to no avail. The rite would be performed. Clotild had decided.

Clovis was not in a mood to argue. Far to the west, relations with the Armoricans were deteriorating. There had been recent border skirmishes near Le Mans and several Franks had lost their lives during journeys undertaken to expand trade with Rowland, the ruler of Armorica. Slaves who had revolted against their Armorican overlords, now lived as robber bands known as the Bagaudae. More than a few Frankish tradesmen had crossed paths with them and paid with their blood.

Adding to the difficulty, the borders between the two peoples were poorly defined. Skirmishes all along the borders were becoming more frequent. Attempts by Clovis to protect his people from the robbers were met with angry protests by the Armoricans. Gerard traveled with a sizable force to establish a Frankish presence, a measure to protect innocent traders, but the Armoricans would not allow armed Frankish soldiers to freely roam their land. Nor would they take the necessary measures to safeguard the Frankish traders. Tempers were growing hotter with each incident, and every day Clovis felt increasing pressure to make a decision, either to engage the Armoricans or to withdraw from relations with western Gaul altogether. Arguing about a baptism was not his primary concern—especially since he knew Clotild would not change her mind.

With reluctance, Clovis allowed Chlodomer to be baptized by Principius of Soissons. Clotild looked tenderly upon her new son as he was Christened. Clovis requested a small private baptism, a request that Clotild gladly agreed to, and throughout the ceremony, witnessed only by Basina, her two daughters and Aurelian, Clovis stood stoically by his wife, worried that he'd made a poor decision. Chlodomer cried.

To everyone's horror, within minutes of the baptism, Chlodomer began to choke between sobs. Very soon, it was clear that he was more distressed than a healthy baby ought to be. When Chlodomer quit crying and began to shake, everyone worried that baptism would, once again, take an innocent child's life. Principius, though he tried to assure the family, also feared for the baby.

"So! Another child dies at the hand of your God!" shouted Clovis. The Bishop's efforts notwithstanding, anger surged out of control in Clovis.

Joining with Principius in defense of her God, Clotild didn't hesitate to say, "He won't die!" though she was not certain in her heart that her words would prove true. "I'll pray to God that he be spared," she added.

"Your God will kill him—like he did Ingomer!" said Clovis, derision in his voice.

Principius finally succeeded in diffusing the situation by diverting attention back to the more immediate concern, "Please, the child!" And for a moment, anyway, the argument ended.

The baby showed no signs of improvment over the course of the next week. And with each passing day of Chlodomer's illness, the tension in the palace mounted. Clovis's hatred for Clotild's God grew, but he couldn't find the words to sufficiently express his loathing.

Chapter 11 *Armorica: 496-497* CE

The pressures from the west grew as did his anger, until one day, it became too much for him. Spurred by his rage, and glad to have a reason to escape Soissons, he decided to confront the Armoricans.

His ability to talk with any civility to his wife was nearly gone. For days they fought whenever they spoke. So it was with simple, quiet words that Clovis informed her of his plans. As Clotild tried to feed her fitful son, Clovis came and stood in the doorway of the bedroom.

"I'm needed elsewhere," he said softly. Clotild looked up at him, trying unsuccessfully to hide the surprise in her face. "I'm going against the Armoricans."

"When?" asked Clotild.

"I'll be leaving tonight."

He paused awkwardly, wanting to embrace his wife, who needed him now, as he well knew. He leaned toward her but his new son gave a loud cry at the same instant, distracting him enough from his wife's need that his own anger burned again. He looked at Chlodomer, muttered, "Enough!" and then walked out of the room without offering a good-bye.

Clotild pulled her son closer and cried.

"O God most high, why must I suffer the pain of watching my babies die. Have I displeased you in some way? Has my marriage to a non-believer brought this judgment upon me? Father Avitus told me our union would be acceptable to you as long as I tried to turn the heart of my husband toward your Son, Jesus. But perhaps I haven't tried hard enough.

"Heavenly Father, must it be our babies who receive your wrath? Are *they* not acceptable to you?

"I don't know these kinds of things, my Lord. I only know that I love you and I love my husband and I love our baby.

"Please, Almighty God, spare our child. Grant him his life and ask what you will of your servant."

Clotild was on her knees gazing out of the window of her bedchamber, seeing nothing except what was in her heart. Before her prayer was complete, she began to sob as the sounds of Chlodomer whimpering and of Basina trying to comfort him came to her from the next room. Basina had taken charge of the baby so Clotild could sleep. But prayer came before sleep. Once her prayer was finished, Clotild dropped her head into her hands and cried, knowing that she had done all she could for her son. She cried until she was too weak to hold herself up. Then she slumped to the floor and cried until she slept. Chlodomer continued to whimper a few minutes more and then, not because of, but rather, in spite of Basina's cooing, quieted, falling into a deep sleep.

Clotild awoke early the next morning, bewildered as to why she was on the floor. Her confusion lasted only for a moment, then she remembered. She also remembered that her husband had gone to battle though she needed him now more than ever. In the morning's stillness she felt his absence deeply. The silence surrounding her was especially deep and she become alarmed at how profound and complete it was. She picked herself up off the floor and prepared herself for the worst as she went to find her son.

Just outside the door of her room she saw Basina asleep in a chair, her head lolling to one side and Chlodomer sound asleep on her ample and comfortable lap. Clotild breathed a sigh of relief when she saw him. She reached to him and softly stroked his brow.

Chlodomer frowned, opened his eyes and screamed such a great and terrible scream that Basina jerked to consciousness. She nearly sent the baby tumbling to the floor, catching him even as Clotild made a grab. Basina cradled the boy and, once he was safe, tried to shake off the grogginess of her night's sleep. Then, realizing that the baby was in need, she looked to Clotild, whose face was filled with worry.

"What are you waiting for, my dear?"

"What?"

"What are you waiting for?"

"What do you mean," Clotild said beginning to cry again. "Is my baby going to die?"

"Going to die? Certainly not! Or at least, he won't if you'll feed him." Basina's eyes widened as she smiled broadly. "My dear, your baby is hungry!"

"Hungry?...Hungry?" Clotild's sobs slowly evolved into a giggle, then into laughs of relief and then into more tears as she reached for her baby and slipped her gown off her shoulder. She held Chlodomer to her breast and he eagerly and hungrily suckled.

Two weeks later, as Chlodomer continued to gain strength in Soissons, Clovis stood with his men before the island city of Nantes.

Chapter 11 *Armorica: 496-497 CE*

"By now they have the message," said Clovis to Gerard. He noticed, for the first time, flecks of gray around his friend's temples. It suited him, Clovis thought.

"Without a doubt," affirmed Gerard, "but I wonder if this siege will bring a victory. They've been more difficult than any people I've warred with since your father ruled."

"Even the Alemanni?"

"I never fought against them, but they may be the one exception." Gerard remembered the stories his father told of Attila and how the Alemanni had fought beside the Hun. Even now the thought of facing the Alemanni frightened him.

Both men stood looking at the city they besieged. It was Paris all over again, an island stronghold that would not fall easily. A cold and penetrating wind was blowing and the sunlight was little relief. As they looked on, they shifted their weight from one foot to the other to keep their circulation going.

"The siege will work, Gerard. They always have."

Gerard nodded his head…and wondered.

Inside the walls of Nantes, a visiting priest, Maxentius, had gained the ear of Rowland, the ruler of the Armoricans. That was a rare enough occurrence for anyone, but especially during the time of a siege. Maxentius had proven himself to the king by not wasting his time. His efforts gained him an audience whenever he requested one.

"You've been under siege for two months now," said Maxentius. "Your people are nearly ready to give up the fight. The cold hasn't helped, and they've begged me to ask you to do something."

Maxentius knew it was Clovis that laid siege outside the city. And he knew that Remigius and other bishops were quietly supporting Clovis as he grew in power. In principle, Maxentius agreed with what Remigius was doing. But Rowland *was* a Christian, and he had protected Maxentius throughout this siege. That counted for something.

Normally, Maxentius spent his time in the monastery of Liguge near Poitiers. There, he was under Visigothic rule. He was in Nantes visiting old friends when the siege began. Now he was involved, like it or not, and it appeared that Rowland was fighting a losing battle. Maxentius offered himself as an agent for seeking terms that might resolve the situation.

"Yes," Rowland said, "yes, something has to be done. I knew we could last out the winter, but that's nearly over. I doubt we can last much longer. Still, I'm not going to send a priest out as my negotiator. I'll go myself, first."

Immediately Maxentius took issue with his protector.

"Too dangerous," he said, shaking his head vigorously. "A meeting must be arranged. Until then, a leader should stay in the background, ready to rally his men if it becomes necessary. Clovis respects the Church...for her power if not for her truths. I'm certain I could arrange the meeting. They won't harm me."

Rowland was uneasy with the approach but he had to admit that Maxentius made sense.

"Are you certain they won't harm you?" he asked.

"As certain as I can be, my lord. But I must leave the final decision with God."

The priest could see Rowland was giving his idea serious consideration. He wasn't, however, given to snap decisions, except when absolutely necessary. Later that morning Rowland consulted with his advisors who agreed that it was premature for Rowland, himself, to venture forth. They discussed the options well into the day, the result being that, as night began to fall, Maxentius was granted leave to meet with the Franks.

"Every night! Every night! They strike and escape with no casualties of their own. It has to stop!" Clovis was perplexed. He knew the siege would be a long one. The river protecting the city assured it. Boats were both supplying the city and transporting soldiers. But the attacks under cover of darkness were becoming the greatest irritation for the Franks. Four men had died and one was fighting for his life against a deep wound to his side.

Efforts to build a naval force were under way in Paris, and a navy might stop these attacks, thought Clovis, but there was no sense in pondering such a tactic. There were no boats available. Not yet. For now he only wanted to stop the Armoricans from crossing the river for their nighttime strikes. His thoughts were interrupted by the cry of a sentry.

"Ho—look!"

The sentry was on high ground taking advantage of the light cast by a nearly full moon. His outstretched arm pointed toward the northern edge of the city. All eyes followed its direction.

Just outside the walls of Nantes there was a single figure carrying a torch in each hand. Wearing a white tunic it appeared brighter than the moon. The figure entered a boat and crossed the river. Gaining land the form began to move straight toward the camp of Clovis. The eeriness of the scene began to unsettle some of the Franks, and in order to calm them down, Clovis sent a unit of riders out to see who this was.

In moments they covered the ground from the camp to the torch bearer. Gerard, who led the group, called out.

"Halt! Who approaches and for what purpose?"

"I would see Clovis, ruler of the Franks," said the figure.

"Your name! Or you'll see no one," said Gerard.

"I would see Clovis, ruler of the Franks," the man repeated.

Gerard was not inclined to put up with tricks. He raised his sword preparing to strike this strange character down.

"I play no games, man. Tell me your name or die!"

The brightly lit face turned upward and eyes filled with wisdom and confidence, void of fear, stared into the eyes of Gerard. Gerard looked back at the visitor and sensed that there was a purpose in this man that should not be hindered. Slowly he lowered his sword. And with only the slightest hint of pleading in his voice he said,

"My King will demand a name, sir."

"Maxentius…a priest."

Gerard gave one nod of his head, turned his men about. The priest soon stood in front of the tent that served as quarters for Clovis. The king was waiting, and when he learned that Maxentius served the Church, he allowed two thoughts to pass through his mind. On one hand, he wondered how anyone could believe in a child-hating God like the God of Christ. On the other hand, he thought the far-reaching arms of the Church might be of considerable assistance as he sought to bring this siege to an end.

"A servant of the Church? Then I welcome you, Maxentius." Clovis took a long look at his visitor. He was a peaceful man, that was certain. Clovis had known other priests who served the Church only to reap her benefits and power, but he saw no such motive in this man.

"Thank you, Clovis," said Maxentius, "We have need to talk."

"Then come." Clovis gestured to the opening of his tent. "At least we'll have the appearance of privacy here." He directed a glance at Gerard, acknowledging the fact that secrets came easily enough through tent walls while, at the same time, giving him permission to listen in on this particular conversation.

Clovis offered Maxentius a seat on one of the many cushions that covered the floor of his tent and seated himself against a large bundle of cushions that rested near the middle. Once settled, Maxentius got directly to business.

"I come to suggest, and arrange, a meeting between you and your adversary, Rowland."

"A meeting?"

"Yes. A meeting. To end the siege."

"Maxentius," Clovis pulled one knee up and rested his elbow on it, and stroked his chin "I'm sure your motives are pure, but why would I want a meeting to end this siege? We're very capable of staying here as long as it takes to conquer these Armoricans. Why should we settle for anything less?"

Maxentius knew that he must not betray too much information. If there was any point in this meeting, it depended on the two leaders meeting on relatively equal ground.

"Sir, with the supply of water that the Loire brings to Nantes, they can withstand a siege of nearly interminable length. My opinion is that we've arrived at a stalemate, and I've convinced Rowland that it serves no one to continue this confrontation. God permitting, I hope to convince you of the same thing."

"Is Rowland willing to negotiate?"

"That I cannot say. He is willing to meet and that might suggest something. But I leave the conclusions to you."

"Also, Maxentius, how can we be sure the meeting will be safe?"

"There is a location where a meeting could take place. It would be in full view of both armies and accessible to both. If either side sees an act of treachery, they can respond. I've seen the place and I can promise it will offer every chance for a safe meeting. Still, you would have to trust my word."

Clovis only uttered, "I see." He thought about bishop John in Ravenna who had negotiated the peace between Odoacer and Theodoric, only to bring Odoacer to his death. His eyes narrowed. Maxentius continued.

"Rowland has no desire to conquer you. He only wishes to protect his land and his people. I believe he can be trusted to meet with you in good faith."

Clovis nodded. He stood, took in a deep breath and walked to the door of his tent and called out, "Gerard!"

Gerard appeared instantly, "Sir?"

"What's your judgment?"

Gerard looked at Maxentius, still moved by the priest, unsure of what he should say in front of him. Clovis spotted the concern in Gerard's hesitation.

"Speak freely, Gerard."

"We could lay siege longer, and I believe we're having an impact, otherwise, why would this priest be here? Still, I wonder if it's worth the effort. It's cold and the men would rather fight than wait. They would rather go home to their families. If there's a way to conclude the siege, I say let's put an end to it."

"Thank you, Gerard. I'd like to see this siege end as well." Clovis then turned back to Maxentius. "But not without some recompense. Not only have we lost time in the siege, but we've lost good men because the Armoricans have been unwilling to protect our tradesmen from the robber bands." Clovis stood and took in a deep breath and held it for a moment before going on. "Yes, Maxentius. I'll meet with Rowland. There are some things we must come to terms on, though. And I will continue this siege if I must." He looked Maxentius in the eye as he spoke this final warning.

"As you wish," said the priest, looking back at Clovis with equal resolve. "I'll inform him, and, if he agrees, I'll send you word as to the time and place." Maxentius stood to leave.

"Good," said Clovis. "My men will escort you back to the river." The priest assented, though there was no need. Maxentius led the Frankish escort as they returned to where they had first met. Gerard was more courteous this time as he saw the priest onto a skiff that waited at river's edge to return the visitor to the city.

Surprising himself, Maxentius convinced Rowland of the logic of being submissive to the demands of the Frankish king. It seemed clear to the priest that even if Clovis demanded that he, a Frankish chief, be accepted as ruler of the Armoricans, little would change. It would mean little more than an administrative note. A tribute would have to be paid of course. But day to day, the presence of the Franks would barely be felt.

Rowland had been surprisingly receptive to these ideas. Clearly he was tired, but, so said the storytellers of Nantes, that had made little difference in the past. Rowland was renowned for his judgment under pressure. Perhaps, thought Maxentius, in this set of circumstances, Rowland simply understood that compromise was the better choice.

With new hope in the outcome of a meeting between the two kings, Maxentius made the necessary arrangements for the conference. A message was sent to Clovis with the details, and as the messenger departed, Maxentius prayed out loud, "May your will be done, O God."

Across a broad valley, northeast of Nantes, on the banks of the Erdre as it flowed toward the Loire, two large armies assembled, one facing the other. Each had been carefully instructed as to what was about to happen. Both armies knew that this gathering was for negotiations, not for battle. Reasons for attacking had been spelled out in detail. The commanders of the troops knew what signals to watch for, what activities were to be expected and what movement was to be considered a threat. By mutual agreement, Clovis had withdrawn from Nantes, allowing Rowland's army to assemble without danger of attack.

The first suggestions of spring were appearing in the valley, and amongst the greens, browns and yellows that carpeted the valley of the river Erdre, both armies watched a single form move. According to plan, Maxentius approached the place in the valley, half-way between the armies, where the two rulers had agreed to meet. Once in place, he unfurled a red flag and waved it first to the Armoricans who responded with their own banner, and then to the Franks who returned the same sign.

At that signal, four horsemen came forward, two from each side of the valley. From the Franks came Clovis accompanied by Gerard. They were armed, prepared for treachery. This had been agreed upon by both rulers. They knew better than to be foolhardy. Rowland and his aide, rode from the opposite side of the valley.

The armies looked on as the two pairs of riders drew together. They were only yards from Maxentius when they finally brought their mounts to a halt. Simultaneously, Clovis and Rowland dismounted, leaving their aides, to watch their horses, making the last few yards to Maxentius on foot.

Maxentius was the first to speak, "There's work to be done," he said with authority, "and I leave you to it." Then he took a position just out of earshot of the rulers.

The two rulers stood quietly assessing one another, each noticing the other's weapons, build and bearing. It was Rowland who spoke first.

"It's been a difficult siege."

"Yes, for both sides, it appears," replied Clovis, not ashamed to honor another warrior.

The two men offered a nod of respect to the other and sat on the logs that had been rolled into place for this meeting. They both shifted their weight as they sat, getting comfortable.

"Maxentius believes there's a path that may bring an end to it," began Rowland.

Chapter 11 *Armorica: 496-497 CE*

"He might be right in that. But that depends upon us, doesn't it?"

"Indeed," said Rowland.

Clovis went on, "I bring terms that will end the siege, if you accept them."

Inwardly, Rowland was struggling. Maxentius had given sound advice: be flexible. But Rowland's emotions were telling him that he could not give in to every demand of the Franks. And the arrogance of Clovis didn't help.

"I have terms too, Clovis. I hope our concerns are compatible. But, go on...what are your terms?"

"There are only three, Rowland. First, from now on, I will be considered ruler of the Armoricans, and I will demand the allegiance of the people of Armorica. Second, trade in Armorica must go on unhindered. That means that the trade routes must be protected against the Bagaudae. And third, a tribute will be paid to me as your ruler in an amount that will be decided upon once trade is secured." Clovis looked carefully at Rowland to see any indication as to how he might be hearing the demands. But he saw none. "That is all," he said.

Rowland fought to keep his anger contained. Now was not the time to lose control. Now was a time to choose words carefully as he tried to wed his demands with those of Clovis. Pride would only bring on destruction. He began slowly.

"My terms are these: first, trade must be carried on in the usual channels, Armoricans doing the stocking, buying and accounting. I don't want my people to be out of work. I want them to have something to say about their own livelihoods. Second, I will still rule," he said this with particular force, "as your governor. My administrators will be your administrators. Policy will come to me so that I may implement your wishes. And third, you'll come to our aid against the Visigoths who have, on occasion attacked our southern border. And you'll assist us against other attacking armies as well."

Clovis couldn't help but respect the man. He would have given the same response had the roles been reversed, but he suspected he would not have been quite so diplomatic.

"A reciprocal agreement is appropriate. As I protect you and come to your aid, I can expect you to come to my aid as well."

"Of course."

Troops on either side of the valley watched as their rulers continued their talk. Eventually the rival leaders stood and walked to their respective companions who remained with the horses. A host of imagined conversations took place in the minds of the warriors while, in actual fact, Clovis and Rowland were simply conferring with their aides, making sure no business had been left undone. Heads nodded, heads shook, soldiers continued to wonder and soon, the leaders returned to face one another again.

"Your terms are acceptable, Clovis, if the siege is lifted now."

"Agreed. However, a small contingent of my men will remain here with you, as emissaries, while our terms are put into action. They can serve as our immediate lines of communication. At least until other arrangements are made."

"Acceptable."

"Can you guarantee my men's safety?"

"Yes, you have my word," said Rowland.

The short encounter convinced Clovis that Rowland was an honorable man. He considered the man's word to be sufficient.

"You can expect to see my men departing tomorrow."

"And we will look forward to serving you as our ruler." The words barely made it out of Rowland's throat. Still, in spite of his ambivalence, he extended his hand to Clovis. The new ruler of Armorica accepted it and the negotiations were final.

The men parted, and soldiers, who had held their breath in concern for their rulers, breathed again. It was with a sense of both victory and loss that the soldiers watched their rulers shake hands. They could go home now, and that pleased them. But they were warriors, and there was disappointment too, for there would be no battle today.

A similar sense of victory and loss was felt by the leaders. Clovis had gained at least a provisional claim to Armorica, while having left his siege incomplete. Rowland had survived the siege of the Franks, but relinquished his rule in ending it.

As the kings rode back to their men, Maxentius stayed in his place and said a prayer of thanks.

Throughout the three months that Clovis faced the Armoricans he heard little from Soissons. News rarely made its way from Soissons to Armorica, except by way of the traders, and they were few in the winter season. One interesting piece of news he received was that the bishop of Tours, Volusianus, had been banished from his city by the Visigoth, King Alaric. Volusianus had made the mistake of showing sympathy to Frankish causes. Clotild would be upset by this news, Clovis was certain. She revered St. Martin of Tours and respected the bishop of that city more than the bishops of many other cities.

Chapter 11 *Armorica: 496-497 CE*

Regarding Chlodomer, Clovis heard very little. In a communication from Aurelian, which was concerned mostly with business, the secretary included what was barely more than a passing comment, stating that the child was still alive.

Clovis missed his bride and his concern for his son had not lessened. It was a particularly anxious Clovis who entered Soissons at the head of his men, receiving the welcome of his people. Well warned of the returning army, the Franks of Soissons, along with a good many of the Romans who still remained, lined the streets singing songs and clapping their hands. Clovis and Gerard rode side by side.

"A fitting welcome I think," said Gerard.

Clovis gave a grateful nod. He was glad to be home, not only victorious, but also knowing that there were only a few Franks who would grieve this war.

The men gradually dispersed, joining their waiting families, heading for their own homes. The riders continued on together, ending their journey at the stables which waited behind the palace. The horses were left in the care of servants and Clovis embraced Gerard sending him to his own home with grateful thanks. Then, alone, he turned to the palace, worried that no one from his family had been on the streets of Soissons to welcome him.

He climbed the steps to a back entrance and received the welcome of a robust and smiling Clotild who waited at the door.

"I have missed you!" she said, throwing her arms around her man's neck. "I have missed you so!" She squeezed him tightly and began to cry.

Clovis closed his eyes and held her close.

"Chlodomer?" he asked, after a long moment.

Clotild broke her embrace and smiled through her tears. "Come see." She took her husband's hand and led him into the palace. In the kitchen Basina stood, holding a laughing baby which she offered to Clovis.

He took Chlodomer, kissed Basina, listened to his wife's news and grinned foolishly as he held his drooling son.

The story of Clotild's prayer for Chlodomer and the child's almost instantaneous recovery impressed Clovis, especially when Basina confirmed it. Prayers of thanks might be in order, thought Clovis, but he was not yet convinced that Clotild's God was worthy of his worship and adoration. For now, he was grateful he had a healthy son and a happy queen.

Chapter 12

Tranquillinus
500 CE

Clovis was often reminded how glad he was that he'd accepted Aurelian's offer to serve as his secretary and adviser. The nuances of diplomacy and the motivations of rulers had become clear to Clovis under the capable and subtle tutelage of Aurelian, a relationship that now spanned more than a dozen years. With endless patience, Aurelian encouraged Clovis to understand how routine matters impacted on the whole of his rule. On this particular day the effort was not necessary as business began on a pleasant and interesting note.

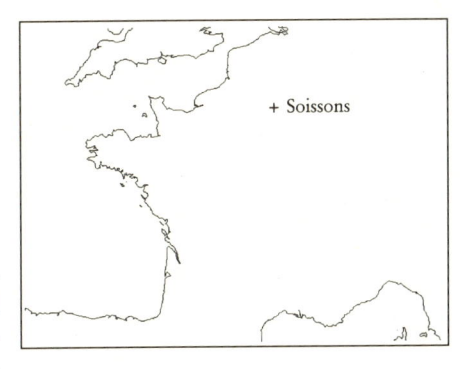

"The nobleman Arnoul, Count of Reims seeks to release one of his slaves," said Aurelian.

Though slaves continued to be valuable in terms of commerce, the freeing of slaves was becoming a familiar sight. Since the Church had begun to discourage slavery, especially when the buying and selling of slaves caused the breakup of families, more were being freed.

The procedure was one that Arnoul, a nobleman, had been through before. Waiting to come before Clovis, he knew what to expect. He and his slave would come before the throne and he, as owner, would announced his intention to free the slave. Then, the slave would offer a coin; whatever he had. Arnoul, rather than taking the coin, would bat it from the hand of the slave signaling that he was willing to make the deal without price being attached to it. Then documents were drawn up for the slave, evidence of his freedom. Aurelian motioned for Arnoul and his slave to come stand before the king.

Clovis rather liked the freeing of slaves. As a conqueror, he had enslaved more than a few men. But, in spite of that, slaves were no less human to Clovis. They were merely victims of war. And it pleased him to watch the way they received their freedom. Those who had only recently been brought into slavery often displayed their still burning anger; while those who had grown up in servitude, knowing nothing more, were very often frightened by the prospect of liberty. All were excited.

This man was somewhere in between those two extremes. He was glad to be ridding himself of his status as slave, the whole idea was appalling to him. He was not especially angry. On the other hand, neither was he afraid. Clovis looked closely at him, noting his intelligent eyes, and his proud bearing. This man will adjust well, he thought.

The coin was batted from the slave's hand and it fell, echoing throughout the hall as it landed on the floor. Aurelian then went about drawing up the necessary documents, offering Clovis and Arnoul a brief moment for conversation. "Freeing another slave, Arnoul? I see you here more than anyone."

"I'm just trying to abide by what the Church wishes, sir. Remigius can be very persuasive."

"He can be that," said Clovis. "And, tell me, how is Leonard? Well, I hope."

"Indeed he is, too much trouble for his mother, I think, though he was courteous enough to send his best wishes to you."

As Aurelian stepped forward, his papers ready, Clovis added, "Take my greetings to him."

"I will."

The former slave who had remained still and silent until now, came forward to make his mark on the documents. He was a Visigoth who'd been captured as a boy during a skirmish near Le Mans. He was still young and full of promise. Once his mark was made, Aurelian handed the pen to Arnoul, who signed the papers without hesitation. Then, having said their thanks and farewells, two free men walked out of the room.

"Arnoul's a good man. Too religious for my blood, but a good man," said Clovis. "How long since Leonard was baptized?"

"Three years, I seem to recall."

"He's a good boy." Clovis reminisced for a moment about Arnoul's son. Arnoul had asked Clovis to be godfather to the boy, hoping that his business dealings with the king had been pleasant enough to court his favor. Clovis had accepted Arnoul's invitation, less frightened by the ceremony since Chlodomer had survived his own baptism. He remembered the struggle Principius went through at the thought of a non-believer being a godparent. It had all worked out, finally, and Clovis acquired a godson. They rarely saw one another, but on infrequent occasions Clovis would hear how Leonard was doing.

An eruptive belch brought Clovis back to the present. "What's next, Aurelian?" he said, half laughing at his burp, wiping his mouth on

Chapter 12 *Tranquillinus: 500 CE*

his sleeve in an attempt to rid himself of the sour taste the belch had brought with it.

"Next, my lord, Theodoric, King of the Ostrogoths, sends a message and a gift."

Prompted by a wave from Aurelian, a young man dressed in the brightly colored formal attire of the Ostrogoths, gold trimmed tunic with a braided cord belt, stepped forward to deliver the message.

"The court of Theodoric, King of Italy and the Ostrogoths, sends greetings to you, Clovis, King of the Franks in Soissons." Time and repetition had, at last, made Clovis comfortable, with the title, 'King'. "Theodoric your servant,..." Clovis immediately recognized the diplomatic form and just as quickly denied it any credence, "...and Audofleda, your sister, are well and hope to see you soon. Until then, may your strength and reign increase. Accept, if you will, a gift: Tranquillinus, a physician."

The messenger stepped aside as an older man moved forward. He was a tall, lanky man with fluid movements. He clasped his hands in front of him and looked directly at the king with professional attentiveness. His gray hair and slightly slumped shoulders gave evidence of his years. He was well into his fifties, perhaps even sixty, Clovis guessed, but fit, agile and alert. The man bowed formally.

"My lord," was all he said.

Clovis leaned forward in his chair. "A physician?" Tranquillinus bowed formally again. "And where's home for you, physician?"

"My name is Tranquillinus, my lord, if you please." Clovis was surprised at the man's haughtiness. "I come from Adrianople, near the city of Constantine, where, for twenty years, I belonged to the finest guild of physicians there is."

"Then you are a fine physician?"

Tranquillinus bowed formally yet again.

"I should like to think so, sir, though 'fine' is dependent on the health of the patient, isn't it?"

Clovis looked intently at the ceremonious figure. "I suppose you're correct."

"Indeed I am. After all, a dying man is not likely to call me a fine physician—even though I am! Oh," he continued, now paying no attention to Clovis, who sat waiting, wondering about this man, "I suspect there are those scarce few who can spot good technique through the veil of failure. But they are rare, I know. Why, only once in my career have I..."

"Tranquillinus! It's enough! Thank you!" Clovis grinned in amusement. "We're happy to receive your services. And I'm certain that you will be consulted as soon as the need arises."

The physician bowed lowly.

Aurelian interjected, "In a moment someone will show you to your quarters."

Tranquillinus bowed once again and moved back a step. The messenger came forward to fill the spot that Tranquillinus had vacated, and concluded his message.

"May you enjoy and use this gift, and through your pleasure, bless our king, and your friend, Theodoric."

Clovis smiled and said, "Please carry our thanks back to your king. He will hear of our good pleasure very soon."

"Thank you, my lord."

The messenger was shown out, as was the physician. Aurelian directed a soldier who was standing in attendance to see that Tranquillinus was made comfortable in a room on the southern end of the palace. Then he returned to Clovis. The king was chuckling.

"He's a foolish old fellow, eh, Aurelian?"

"Foolish, perhaps, but I suspect he's a good physician. I've heard of the guild he mentioned. It is, supposedly, a fine one."

"Mmm," hummed Clovis. "What do you think it means?"

"Sir?"

"The gift. What does it mean? Why is Theodoric doing this? Should I be wary?"

"No," Aurelian replied quickly, "I don't believe there's a need for concern here. Theodoric may be powerful, but he's not powerful enough to consider attacking you. He's too far away and has trouble enough in Italy."

"That's what I'd be inclined to say. And I'm not thinking of attack. I was thinking more that this might be a ploy to soften me for some diplomatic move. There must be some reason for him to send me such a gift."

"My guess is that it's nothing more than a friendly gesture, my Lord. He sees that you're increasing your strength. I suspect he's simply protecting himself against that day when you're powerful enough to attack him. This is merely an extension of the effort that began when he married your sister."

Clovis was incredulous. "Could he really be so concerned?"

"Remember, my lord," said Aurelian, "not only have you defeated Syagrius, a Roman; a feat worthy of respect in and of itself, but

Chapter 12 *Tranquillinus: 500 CE*

Burgundy's King Gundobad, Clotild's Uncle, has opposed Theodoric. How can he trust him? In Theodoric's mind you could join with Gundobad and cross into Italy from Burgundy. No, the more I consider it, the more I believe that he's making a friendly and intelligent gesture…and you wouldn't harm yourself by offering a generous gift in return."

Clovis smiled in amazement.

"Am I so worthy of respect?"

"It would appear so," answered Aurelian.

Clovis didn't hear him. A vision of the world passed through his mind and he saw the lands and rulers and armies all eyeing him, the King of the Franks. He enjoyed the image.

"It's true," he said, "I am a warrior to be respected. Why shouldn't other rulers take me seriously?"

"Yes, indeed," replied Aurelian.

Clovis blinked several times, shaking off his thoughts of grandeur and then looked at his advisor.

"How do you think I should respond, Aurelian?"

"As I was saying, a generous response might be in order."

"Yes. I believe you're right. Let it be done. Select an appropriate gift, Aurelian. You're better than I am with these things."

"As you wish." The secretary turned halfway toward the door. "With your permission, then…?" he said. Clovis nodded and waved him on. Without another word Aurelian departed to fulfill his task.

Clovis watched him leave, thinking about all that was happening. He was now a power to be reckoned with. He frowned and put his hand on his stomach. It had been hurting for more than a day, and the pain was becoming an annoyance. "It will pass," he told himself, and he stood to leave. "There are things to be done…things to be done." As he turned from the throne, he belched again, flinching at the smell of bile and cringing at the sour taste in his mouth.

Clovis lay in his bed with the worst stomach pains he'd ever known. On his side with his knees pulled up to his chest, he worried that his illness might be seen as weakness. Clotild sat next to him, stroking his arm. Tranquillinus stood at the foot of the bed, stoically observant.

"Help me, physician!"

The physician bowed deeply, "Tranquillinus, if you please, my lord."

"Yes," Clovis said with irritation in his voice, "all right. Tranquillinus."

"We all have need of a physician at one time or another during the course of our lives," said Tranquillinus. Then he became silent again and looked at Clovis. He looked at him closely, taking everything in. After a time of being surveyed, without any explanation as to why this examination was proceeding so, Clovis became uncomfortable.

"Why are you staring at me?"

"To discern your illness, my good King. Hippocrates teaches us that sight is a most excellent tool for determining a prognosis."

"And do you see what's wrong with me?"

Tranquillinus walked around the bed one more time and then backed away from it to sit on a nearby chair.

"That would be a diagnosis, but yes, my lord, I do. I believe that you've fallen victim to your own wealth and power."

Clovis made no effort to hide his anger and he commanded, "What do you mean, physician?"

Tranquillinus, understanding the anger, but keeping his own perspective, rose from his chair and bowed deeply.

"Tranquillinus, if you please, my…"

"Yes! Tranquillinus! Explain yourself!"

"I only meant, my lord, that the life of a king is rather opulent compared to that of most human beings. You can see it in a king's lodgings, his dress, the company he keeps and the places he travels. But it's made most clear in the diet he consumes."

"Diet?"

"Truly." He sat down again. "I learned from your mother, who is a charming woman, by the way…most gracious…" A glaze came over the physician's eyes and he sat motionless, smiling.

"Tranquillinus!" said Clovis, after a long silence.

"Yes! Um-hmm, yes!" sputtered Tranquillinus as he looked up, "Yes, now, what was I saying?"

"Diet," said Clotild, softly, trying to help Tranquillinus and calm her husband in the same moment.

"Oh yes. As I was saying, my lord, I learned from your mother that you eat hard-boiled eggs and old hard cheese. Neither are good for you, my lord. Please eat fresh cheese. Stick to meats, especially pork, though older pork, not the young meat. Eat vegetables, beer and sauces of wine and honey. I'll make a list for you if you wish."

"Will it help the pain?"

"I believe so, if you follow the recommendations. Getting enough sleep and taking walks wouldn't hurt you either."

"Then I'll do as you say, Tranquillinus. We'll see if you're as fine a physician as you seem to think you are."

Chapter 12 *Tranquillinus: 500 CE*

"Yes, my lord." Tranquillinus arose and bowed once more to Clovis.

"And Tranquillinus…"

"Yes, my lord?"

"Your bowing gets tiresome. If you're going to be my physician, I'll need to trust you. I cannot trust someone who bows like you do. Please…no more."

Tranquillinus began to bow, a long-standing habit, and looked confused as he stopped himself.

"I will…do my best," he said, slowly.

"Thank you. That's all."

Tranquillinus bowed and then shook his head in a self reproving way, made more obvious by the self admonitions he mumbled as he left.

Clotild smiled at the old physician's efforts. She stroked her husband's brow and said, "I'm beginning to believe that you're in capable hands."

"Let's hope so!" said Clovis and he curled into a tighter ball and moaned.

Chapter 13
Gundobad Is Challenged
500 CE

It was, for the greater part, a time of peace. While there had been some harsh words exchanged between the Franks and the Visigoths, mostly over the banishment of Bishop Volusianus from Tours, they were not of major consequence. The border with the Visigoths was reasonably quiet. Tribute from the Armoricans had been decided upon in an amount acceptable to both parties. All the administrative mechanisms were in place. To the northeast, the Thuringians, though still feeling the humiliation of their defeat at the hands of Clovis, were keeping their anger contained. After nine years, Frankish rule was proving less oppressive than many Thuringians had, at first, expected.

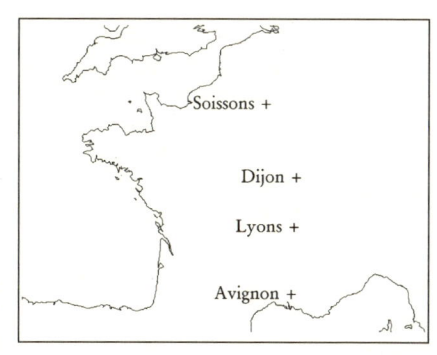

Clovis, fully recovered from his stomach ailment, continued to strengthen his rule by granting more land to the Church and to his own people. Fortunately, Rome had acquired sizable tracts of land in Gaul, and there was yet a great deal of it to parcel out.

Clotild continued to voice her beliefs. She told stories of Jesus to Chlodomer, often in the presence of her husband. Clovis bore it well, fully aware that Clotild still hoped for his conversion. Most of the stories passed over him like fleeting clouds, making little or no difference. On occasion, though, he would listen in his own private way, curious about this Jesus who could calm storms but would let innocent children die.

Lantechild proved a challenging listener, posing questions and eagerly asking for more stories when Clotild thought it was time to stop.

"How can that be, three gods in one?"

"It's as God intended," Clotild replied, hoping the answer would be meaningful to Lantechild who was already attracted to what the Arians were teaching. She told what stories she knew and offered what answers she had, and trusted God to work in Lantechild's heart.

The time was nearing for another child to be welcomed into the family and on an uncomfortably hot summer day, Clotild was glad to be quiet. She played on the floor with Chlodomer, building towers from sticks. Between the heat and her pregnancy, it was all she could manage. Clovis entered and stood solemnly, surveying the scene.

Clotild looked up at him and said, "Come here. Sit and play with your son." She patted the floor next to her. She could tell that her husband had something on his mind. Clovis accepted the invitation.

For a moment he watched his son attempt to build his tower higher only to see it collapse under the weight of another stick. Chlodomer's mother and father laughed at his look of dismay and, with comforting words, encouraged him to begin again. As he rebuilt, Clotild looked hard at her husband, concerned by his furrowed brow. "What is it?"

"I've just received a message from your uncle, Godegesil."

"Oh? Is he well? Does he say anything about my sister?" Messages were rare from Clotild's family and she was curious about the contents of this one.

"He's well. But he said nothing about Sedeluba."

"It's Chrona, now. Remember?"

"Yes, Chrona. I forgot." Since entering the religious order, Clotild's sister had taken the name "Chrona" and Clovis was not yet used to the change. "No, nothing of Chrona, but his message does speak at some length of your uncle, Gundobad."

"Oh?" said Clotild, her tone instantly cold.

"Yes. And that's what bothers me."

"Isn't he well?" she asked, with mocking concern.

"He's fine for now."

"For now?"

Clovis shifted his weight and looked at his wife. "Godegesil is planning to attack Gundobad."

Clotild looked interested, but said nothing.

"The two have been at odds it seems…"

"As always," Clotild interjected. "Ever since I can remember, they've been fighting. Gundobad's always won. He's older, stronger. I'm surprised that it's taken this long for Godegesil to rise up against him." She frowned and picked up a stick that Chlodomer had dropped, "He'll lose though."

"Perhaps not."

"Why do you say that?" she said, looking up from her son.

"He's asked if I'll help him in a plot against Gundobad. He says that he'll pay me tribute if I help him. Whether he kills Gundobad or just runs him out of the country, he'll pay me tribute. The two of us together could defeat Gundobad, I'm certain of that."

Chapter 13 *Gundobad Is Challenged: 500 CE*

Clotild leaned back and stretched her legs, her bulging belly nearly blocking her feet from view. She considered what her husband was saying. She thought about her parents; how Gundobad had killed them; how he would have killed her, had the bishops not interceded on her behalf. Her hatred for Gundobad still burned.

"I would welcome such news," she said, relishing the thought.

Clovis watched Chlodomer tumble another stick building. The absence of any hesitation of Clotild's part, while he'd expected none, helped him make his choice. He leaned over and kissed his wife before rising to leave.

A return message was prepared for Godegesil that read, simply, "Call on me when you need me." Aurelian made the necessary arrangements for its conveyance and it was sent to Geneva.

A reply would not be long in coming.

Gundobad knew that most of his subjects didn't understand or care about the struggle going on between the Christians who called themselves "Catholic" and those who called themselves "Arian." They simply needed to know that their God was preparing a place for them; a place less trying—more joyous than the world they already knew. But those in positions of power looked at it differently, and tensions were running high as the different Churches protected and promoted their own views.

Gundobad began to see the destructive tendencies of that tension, and how the people of Burgundy, turning in increasing numbers to the Catholic Church, were becoming more and more dissatisfied with the leadership of an Arian king—*his* leadership—and he decided to take measures to resolve the disputes.

In Lyons, in the fall of the year, Gundobad, King of Burgundy, called together a council of church officials in an attempt to bring about a reconciliation between the Arian and the Catholic Churches. At the suggestion of Avitus of Vienne and Bishop Stephen of Lyons, Gundobad agreed to open the meeting on the feast of Saint Justus. There were still people living who remembered their elder's tales of Justus who had served Lyons as bishop over a century before. The story of Justus leaving his position as bishop in an act of conscience continued to inspire the people of Lyons. The feast of Saint Justus would be an appropriate time for the conference.

The religious and political differences between the bishops were considerable, more significant than Gundobad had imagined. His understanding of their concerns was limited, aside from the obvious struggle for power. He understood clearly enough, though, that of the bishops he questioned, few expected much to be accomplished.

On neutral ground, coming together in the royal residence rather than in either the Arian or Catholic churches, the bishops began with small talk, including a discussion of the commissioning of plans for a new palace at the Vatican, which many of the bishops thought unnecessary. But foremost in the minds of the Catholic bishops was the recent and questionable ascent of Symmachus to the position of Pope.

"The Cardinals made their choice," said Avitus, "and Symmachus succeeded our revered Pope Anastasius II in an appropriate way!"

"No," said a dissenting bishop. "Laurentius should have been Pope!"

The discussion gained momentum and emotion but remained civil. Gundobad thought the deliberation was, for the most part, pointless.

It was the Arian bishops who brought substance to the meeting, taking the initiative to discuss the nature of God's work in the world, espousing their own doctrines in opposition to the Trinitarian formula that others had devised. Discussion became clamor as the initial day of the meeting progressed.

Early in the afternoon of the first full day of the gathering, Gundobad was called out of the conference to receive a message. He had asked not to be disturbed but the message was rightly deemed important enough to interrupt the meeting. Clovis was preparing to attack. The Franks were already on the move. Fed up with what he could only perceive as bickering, Gundobad returned to the proceedings determined to force the discussion onto something meaningful.

He entered the hall and marched to the center of the room. "Your attention!" he said, not willing to be denied. It took only a moment for those present to turn their focus toward their host. The bishops gazed upon Gundobad with curiosity and distaste. Such interruptions were not familiar to them. Gundobad didn't wait for silence. "You who call yourselves bishops and Priests of the Christian faith! You who call yourselves Catholic—you rant and rave over what you call heresy and then you support a pagan ruler! If you truly profess the Christian religion, why do you support an infidel? Why don't you restrain the King of the Franks instead of encouraging him?" He took a moment to look at each of them, eye to eye, making no effort to hide his challenge.

"Clovis has declared war on me! He marches into Burgundy even as you sit here and argue whether or not your God has three faces or one!"

Chapter 13 *Gundobad Is Challenged: 500 CE*

Avitus felt compelled to speak, "My King, we're ignorant of this. We don't have any way of knowing the motives or intentions of Clovis. How could we?"

Gundobad was angered at the lack of response.

"Only Avitus speaks? Only you? And even at that you offer no help. Perhaps you want to have a pagan ruling all of Gaul!"

Avitus tried to reason with the king. "Gundobad, kingdoms sometimes fall because rulers have forsaken the law of God. Perhaps if you were to join in the true faith and live by the law of God you'd rule in peace."

Gundobad was incensed that Avitus would use this dilemma to advance the authority of his Church. Gundobad had chosen his faith, with serious consideration and no bishop was going to judge him. Not now. Not ever. "I do acknowledge the law of God!" he said, "But three Gods I will not admit!"

Gundobad grabbed his cloak and looked around at the faces of the bishops one more time, seeking any indication of assistance, and saw none. Even the Arian bishops were more concerned with their lofty musings than with his immediate problem. He sneered in disgust and stormed out of the hall.

Bishop Aeonius of Arles broke the long silence that followed.

"Brothers, this is only the first day of our gathering. There is so much more to discuss. Perhaps we should labor to discuss things in a more Christian spirit."

Agreement on the point was without exception and once again the guardians of the faith took up the subject of the nature of God.

Aridius learned from one of his many paid informers; one who worked as a legitimate trader, that Clovis and his men, armed for war, had advanced beyond Troyes. There was no doubt that their direction was leading them into Burgundy. They were moving toward Dijon.

On Gundobad's instructions, Aridius, ignorant of Godegesil's treachery, sent a conciliatory message to Geneva, aimed at smoothing over recent conflicts, and asking for aid in the impending battle with Clovis. There was little doubt in their minds that Godegesil would respond to the plea. Therefore it was suggested in the message that he meet Gundobad's troops at Dijon, so that there, together, they could stop Clovis once and for all.

A full three days after Gundobad learned of the advance of Clovis, the Franks made camp just outside of Dijon. Now they waited for Gundobad's forces. Clovis expected Godegesil to arrive soon, as well.

There was ample time to survey the land around Dijon before Gundobad arrived. The terrain was only slightly hilly to the east of Dijon, much less so than to the west, and, aside from the fields that followed the course of the river, the entire area was blanketed with trees. Clovis positioned his Franks so Godegesil, whom he expected would arrive from the east, could easily join their ranks. If they were delayed, Clovis reasoned, they could still join the fray without interference from his men.

To the south, a clear view of the Ouche River valley assured Clovis that he would have sufficient warning of Gundobad's approach. To the rear was forest.

The day was comfortably cool and a light drizzle was falling when Gundobad's troops moved into the valley and across the river. Clovis readied his men as they watched the mass of warriors approaching. Upon seeing the position of the Franks, Gundobad stopped to make camp, organize his command post, and situate the supplies that would not be carried into battle. Then, as a single unit, the Burgundians marched on the Franks.

Gundobad surveyed his opponents as best he could. Marching uphill it was difficult to get a clear view of the numbers he was facing. The drizzle further impaired his assessment of the Franks. Clovis commanded a large army, but it didn't appear insurmountable. "They placed themselves well," he thought out loud. Then more quietly, "You make us march uphill, Clovis. Well done."

Seeing the large expanse to the east he commented to Aridius, who stood beside him, "Look! Room for Godegesil. I wonder if Clovis knows?"

Aridius frowned.

"If he does, he must have very good spies."

"Hmmm," was Gundobad's reply, "Whatever the case, Godegesil must be close."

"Closer than you might have guessed," said Aridius. He raised his arm to point.

Gundobad looked to see the leading soldiers of Godegesil coming into view.

"Your timing could not be better," Gundobad said to his distant brother. As he spoke the words he tried to pick out his form at the head of his men. "Now we'll rout this Frankish cur!"

Chapter 13 *Gundobad Is Challenged: 500 CE*

With new vigor, Gundobad encouraged his men into battle, pointing to their brothers from Geneva who had come to join them in victory. He was confident now; eager to be ruthless.

The men shouted and whistled, waving their swords when they saw Godegesil's men. Then they grew silent. It appeared that Godegesil was about to encounter the Franks alone. Gundobad watched the scene quietly. Puzzlement slowly turned to disbelief as Gundobad and his men saw no axes flying, no blades flashing, heard no soldiers yelling. The ranks closed and the Franks of Clovis, along with the Burgundians of Godegesil turned to face the suddenly inadequate forces of Gundobad.

"Betrayal! We've been betrayed!" Gundobad shouted. His anger exploded into rage and, screaming at the top of his lungs he cried, "Death to Godegesil!" He repeated the words, leading his men in a chant, "Death to Godegesil! Death to Godegesil!" and he ordered his army forward.

The battle was joined. The initial blizzard of franciscas and lances was met on both sides by raised shields and unintentionally butted heads as men dodged the weapons. The men of Clovis and Godegesil had the advantage of the high ground and their weapons flew farther. Few of Gundobad's men could throw their missles uphill with any effect. Grunts and screams were followed by the fierce yells of war as weapons were pried from soil and bone to be used again. Then, with the proximity that made flung weapons useless, the men fought hand to hand, swinging axes and wielding swords.

It was the terrain that determined the battle. Gundobad's men fought well, but they were off balance, fighting both aggressors and gravity. Combatants knocked down by the blow of an ax fell backward and were set upon before they had a chance to rise—dead before they could utter a cry for help.

Not long into the clash, Gundobad knew he was defeated. The battle was quickly coming to a disastrous end. His troops, diminished by heavy casualties, were being pushed back by the far greater numbers they faced. Gundobad forgot about Clovis.

"I'll kill you for this, Godegesil" he growled at his unseen brother. Looking for him in the mass of soldiers he repeated, "I will kill you!"

Aridius knew time was growing short.

"We must flee, my King."

"Yes," said Gundobad thickly, "What?"

"To the south. We can regroup to the south. But we must run, now, or we'll join the dead!"

Gundobad, stunned by the events of the last hour, nodded his head and allowed Aridius to order the retreat.

The Burgundians withdrew, anxious to get clear of the ruthless Franks. Regrouping in Lyons, they stood again to face Clovis, still outnumbered. The Franks attacked, bringing more heavy losses upon them. Gundobad was forced to retreat past Vienne in an attempt to steer the Franks clear of his capitol. To the relief of both Gundobad and Aridius, the ploy worked. The armies of Godegesil and Clovis followed the retreating armies.

Gundobad's troops made a final stand in Valence only to be defeated again. Leaving weapons and provisions behind, Gundobad, Aridius and a small remainder of troops fled from Burgundy to Avignon, to the protection of the Visigoths.

A full month beyond the victory at Dijon, Godegesil was on the throne in Vienne, ruling what had once belonged to Gundobad. Clovis had granted him a small contingent of troops in an effort to quell any resistance which might come from the people of Vienne as they adjusted to their new ruler. Now, however, looking up at the walled city of Avignon, the King of the Franks meant to deal with Gundobad. The thought never left his mind that he might avenge the murder of Clotild's parents, but vengeance or no vengeance, Gundobad was too formidable of an enemy to ignore. The rage of a humiliated king did not die easily and Clovis didn't like the idea of leaving such an enemy alive, able to retaliate. Gundobad was inside the imposing walls that Clovis now faced. There was no option but to lay siege.

He made the necessary plans with Gerard.

"Only a small force will be required on the north side of the city," said Gerard. "The Rhône will thwart any escapes there."

"I agree," returned Clovis. "A ring around the southern part of Avignon should be simple enough. How long do you think it will take?"

"There's no way to tell, but the siege can be under way within twenty-four hours, I should think."

Clovis nodded. "Let's get on with it then."

The demand for Gundobad was conveyed to the Visigoths, and the siege began.

"You will lose this siege, Gundobad," Aridius said matter-of-factly. He chewed and sucked on a piece of dried meat looking out over the

Chapter 13 *Gundobad Is Challenged: 500 CE*

campfires of the Franks. "The people here won't let Avignon fall for a foreign king."

"Then do I surrender without a fight? You and I are the only ones left from our court, Aridius. Even our families are left behind." He thought of his sons, Sigismond and Godomar. Both were old enough to fight and had stayed in Vienne to defend the city. Gundobad had no way of knowing if they were dead or alive. "Do we give up without a struggle?"

Gundobad understood the options. Surrender or be taken by force. Neither choice pleased him. He remembered how his men were scattered before the Franks at their last confrontation near Valence. Only a very few of his soldiers were with him now...not enough to do battle. He turned to his advisor with a pleading look.

"Help me, Aridius!"

"Be calm, my lord. There is another way. Or at least there *may* be another way."

Gundobad quivered at the hopeful thought that there might be an unforeseen option. He raised his fingers to his mouth and asked a question that he prayed would have a satisfactory answer.

"How so, Aridius?"

His advisor gestured to a bench. The two sat down.

"If I can speak with Clovis..." said Aridius.

"Are you serious?" Gundobad could hardly believe his ears. But Aridius didn't answer. He was lost in the formulation of his plan.

"Yes, perhaps he can be softened. I think he would hear me...yes, I think he would."

Gundobad quieted now, recognizing what he had seen before. Aridius was at work. There was no wisdom in trying to discuss things with him now. Better to let him do what he did best: scheme.

Aridius thought out loud, "I couldn't come to him as myself. Perhaps as a resident of Avignon. He's never seen me. No,...I could be a deserter. Yes, I could appear as a deserter who came with you from the battle. Maybe I could convince him to leave you here—exiled—but under tribute to him. That way he doesn't incur the cost of the siege, but you're no longer a problem and he gains income from you as well."

Gundobad had been interested at first but now appeared defeated. "A tribute!" he said, "I would rather puke than pay tribute to that bastard!" He stood and went to the battlement, looking out at the Franks encampment. "Besides, with what, my friend, would I pay such a tribute? I left everything but my skin in Vienne!"

"I'm sorry, my lord," Aridius was sympathetic, "but money is not our immediate concern. Promises can gain time, and that's what we need. Where we'll find tribute is the least of our problems. What we need is a way to make this Frank lift the siege or we'll both meet the ax."

"Yes," said Gundobad, encouraged by his friend's cool head, "perhaps we can buy some time if nothing else." He looked his advisor in the eye. "You are truly my friend, Aridius. I leave it to you."

A man clad in the clothes of a Burgundian stepped into the light of the campfire. As Franks jumped to their feet, clasping their swords, the man fell to his knees, bowed his neck and placed his hands on the ground. It was risky, Aridius knew, but less risky than dealing with one Frankish guard out in the dark. That was too uncertain. A larger group would be less threatened by one man.

"I come seeking your favor," said the kneeling figure, "Please hear me."

The Franks surrounded the man. A quick order was given to make sure no other Burgundians were hiding in the shadows.

"There's no one else," said Aridius.

"Quiet you!" said a Frank who then reached in and slapped his prisoner's head. "You'll talk. But not until you're told!"

Aridius had been unwilling to take the risk of entering the main camp. There was danger enough in reaching this point. He had gone as far as he had dared, and was proud of how deeply he had penetrated the defenses of Clovis.

Assurances shouted from the dark eased the tension and soon Aridius was lifted to his feet and roughly led back into the dark, toward another circle of fires—the main camp. One soldier ran ahead to alert Gerard, who was awaiting the prisoner and his captors when they arrived.

Without a word, Gerard looked the prisoner over and then led the group toward a fire that burned before the largest tent in camp. Seating himself in front of the tent, Gerard motioned to a log which sat on the opposite side of the fire. The prisoner was shoved into place and for a long while Gerard simply looked at his face.

"Who are you?"

"My name's Averic."

"How have you come to be with us, Averic?"

"By my own will, sir. I've deserted my King."

Chapter 13 *Gundobad Is Challenged: 500 CE*

Gerard raised an eyebrow and looked at the slight figure before him.

"Deserted? Why? You're not a soldier, that much I can see."

"I was in charge of King Gundobad's personal gear." The man bowed his head in mock shame. "I'm not proud of what I've done, sir, but I had to do something. Gundobad is beaten and he won't be able to survive a siege."

"No?" asked Gerard.

"Oh, I'm sure the town could survive," said the prisoner, hastily backtracking, "but Gundobad won't. He's going mad. He talks of battle and yet he has only a handful of men. He has no way to return to power and yet he plans attacks. The soldiers are unwilling to commit suicide and so Gundobad threatens them with execution. I have a family in Vienne, my lord. I want to see them again."

Gerard was not particularly moved. Deserters were not worthy of respect, nor could they be trusted. Gerard would have killed any of his own men who had deserted. This man was no better.

"Why did you come here? You could have avoided us altogether and returned to your home."

"I considered that, my lord. In the long run, I feared for my life. If your king is to rule my homeland, which seems likely, I would rather serve him than die at his hand."

Not an unusual occurrence, thought Gerard. He'd seen it often enough when Clovis had defeated others. The defeated often wished to become one with the victors.

"I see," he said.

The questioning continued, Gerard seeking information regarding the situation inside Avignon. There was little of use. At last, Gerard placed the Burgundian under guard and told him that if his words proved to be true he would be welcomed among the Franks. Gerard was under no illusions though. He made certain that Averic was watched for a while longer, just in case. Then, the matter settled as far as he was concerned, Gerard waved the deserter and his guards away.

In the days to come, Aridius, alias Averic, had a great deal to do. He had to worm his way into the good graces of the Franks and impress them, not only with his knowledge of Gundobad's situation, but also with the sincerity of his desertion. He wanted to provide enough information to catch the attention of Clovis, enough to be summoned, but not so much that he would be seen only as a malcontent or an eccentric. It was a fine balance, but Aridius went about his work with confidence. He knew his own capabilities and that he needed to speak personally with the king.

His first step, before he could hope to see Clovis, was to befriend his captors. It was not terribly difficult. When it was necessary, Aridius could be a charming man. His quick wit and well honed story-telling abilities served him more than adequately. Soon he knew, by name, the men who were guarding him and he had learned a considerable amount of information about each of them: where they lived when not warring, what kinds of families they had, who was the best warrior.

As he pursued his plan to gain the confidence of his captors, four days passed. He had yet to meet with Clovis and he was growing anxious. His chance came on the fifth day. Gerard was walking among the men, giving encouragement as the siege continued. When Aridius saw him approach, he began talking to one of his guards about how he had been with Gundobad from the beginning and knew him almost as well as his own family did. His voice rose as Gerard came close.

"Yes, I was with Gundobad in Italy and also when he returned to Burgundy to kill the king and Queen of Lyons. Of course," Averic added, "that was before my king went mad."

The method was sufficient. Later that day, almost in passing, Gerard told Clovis about this man and his claims. Clovis asked to see him.

"I've already interrogated him," said Gerard. "What he knows isn't of much help to us."

"But he knows Gundobad," said Clovis. Not only was he hoping for help in the siege, but suddenly he was interested in the possibility of learning more about the death of Clotild's father.

"Yes, my lord, but what good is that if Gundobad's losing his mind?"

"Who said Gundobad's losing his mind?"

"That was the prisoner's opinion. I didn't think it would change our plan of siege, so I never mentioned it."

"No, it probably wouldn't have changed anything, Gerard. Still, I'd like to see this prisoner. Bring him."

Aridius stood before the long-haired king and looked at him with respect. He could see the strength of Clovis in his bearing, the intelligence in his eyes. Aridius quickly discerned that this king could be cruel and ruthless if the situation demanded it. He would not underestimate him.

Chapter 13 *Gundobad Is Challenged: 500 CE*

Clovis trusted Gerard and didn't waste any time with questions about Avignon. Rather, it was history he desired.

"I'm told that you've been with Gundobad for a long time."

"Since before he claimed Chilperic's throne, my lord."

"Did you help him claim that throne?"

Aridius knew that he had to be careful. But he was prepared. He had planned this moment in detail.

"I was there. And if I may say so, sir, aside from the current circumstances it was the only time that I desired to leave Gundobad's service."

"Why's that?"

"My lord, I understand that kings do what kings must do, even against their own kin. But against his brother, Gundobad was more than cruel."

Again, Aridius walked a fine line. He wanted to be in the good favor of Clovis but he didn't want to encouraged him to kill Gundobad.

"I've heard that he is a vile man," said Clovis.

"On occasion. He's capable of ruling well. I've seen it. The truth is, though, a good number of his people may take pleasure in his downfall."

"Perhaps it will please them more to have his head."

"You may be right. Though I'm not altogether certain of that. I'm not sure the prize is worth the cost."

"What do you mean?"

"If I may be so bold, sir," Aridius lowered his head momentarily, "it seems to me that Gundobad's head will not matter much to the people of Burgundy since he is now defeated. If a new king is what they desire, that's what they have. What happens to the old king would seem to be of little consequence. And further, if I may say so, his head on his shoulders might be more valuable to you than his head on a stake."

Clovis looked hard at Averic. He didn't like the idea of letting Gundobad survive this campaign. He knew Godegesil wouldn't care for it. His eyes narrowed.

Under the penetrating eye of Clovis, Aridius felt himself beginning to sweat. "Forgive me, my lord, I speak too much."

"No," said Clovis, "I want to hear more. How can your mad king be of use to me?"

"My lord, this battle is won. The victory is yours. What good does it do you to lay waste to a kingdom that could be profitable? Your men ravage the countryside for supplies to fill their stomachs—land that could be serviceable. And, in addition, why gain the price of one head that pays its tribute with a single bloody payment when you could exact tribute from a live Gundobad and profit every year?"

Clovis was thoughtful. This siege would likely be a prolonged one. Neither he nor his men needed that. And it was true, in the course of feeding his troops the surrounding lands were being ruined.

"You still feel some loyalty to the man, don't you?" asked Clovis.

"I've served him for many years," was the simple reply. Clovis appreciated the honesty.

"Your words make sense, Averic. We shall see. I may follow your advice."

Averic was removed, once again placed in the care of guards and returned to the camp that had been his home during the past week. Clovis waited for him to be gone and then called for Gerard so they might consider what Averic had proposed.

Slowly, word came to Aridius hinting that his efforts had proven worthwhile. He learned, after another two days, that messengers had gone into Avignon, and a deal had been struck with an eager Gundobad. He'd paid his first tribute willingly and agreed to further payments. Clovis was satisfied with the agreement, so said the rumors, and the Franks would soon be leaving for home.

Aridius smiled at the news but wondered how Gundobad had acquired the funds for the tribute. His king had yet to run out of tricks. Sometimes he wondered why Gundobad relied on him so much. The king was not without talent.

When word of their imminent departure spread among the Franks, their mood lightened instantly. With the news came the rumor that it was the prisoner, Averic, who had provided the critical information, helping to bring about this welcomed state of affairs. Suddenly Averic became a popular conversation and dinner partner.

"You'll like Soissons," said the guard who brought Averic his food this night, "It is a good place, with good people."

"You sound as if you think I'll be coming home with you."

"Won't you?"

"I have family in Burgundy." It was a lie Aridius told easily. "I'll stay there."

"Bring them along," was the simple response.

"I'll be celebrating all the way home," said another guard, now feeling his wine.

"I don't intend to stop even after I arrive," said a third.

Chapter 13 *Gundobad Is Challenged: 500 CE*

The men laughed and Aridius celebrated with the Franks throughout the night. In the morning he helped them prepare for their departure. And when the Franks moved north, back through the marshes, Aridius traveled with them.

On the second day of the journey, as the Franks moved into a landscape spotted with cornfields, it was noticed that Averic was missing. It was generally assumed he was only momentarily lost among the host of soldiers who were making their way home, but he was not seen again.

Three days after the Franks had lifted their siege of Avignon, a lone figure trudged up a dusty road to the fortress city. Gates opened to him and Aridius returned to his place at the side of his king, Gundobad. Now the real work was to begin.

Chapter 14

The Church Grows in Strength
500 CE

As servants refilled glasses with wine, Clovis and Godegesil sat back, stomachs full, celebrating their victory. The throne room in Vienne was filled with the best of Gundobad's stores, laid open to the conquerors, prepared for the new king. Godegesil could hardly believe he had won out over his brother. Never before had he known this feeling: exultant in righteous victory, smug in power, satisfied in life, his side free of the thorn named, Gundobad. He swallowed a gulp of wine and grinned expansively as he looked around his new residence and upon the soldiers who celebrated with him. Even with his victory, though, he knew there was work yet to be done.

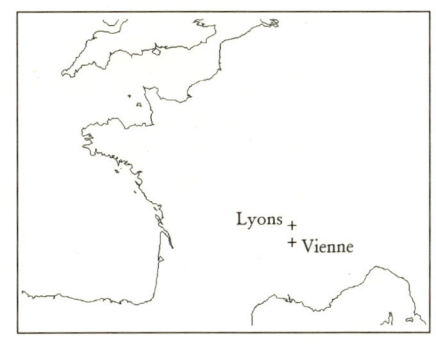

"Of course, it will take some time before the people of Burgundy accept me wholeheartedly."

"Oh yes," said Clovis. "Sometimes people are grateful to be rid of a bad leader, but rarely does change set well with them. Sometimes it takes a show of force to insure their loyalty."

"I hope that won't be necessary."

"And I agree," said Clovis. "At least, for the time being, you're secure. I'm leaving you 5,000 men."

"5000? That's more than two Roman legions!"

"Most of them are your people anyway." Clovis was glad Godegesil was impressed, but the truth of it was, many were men of rural Gaul and Burgundy who joined the army as it marched toward Avignon. "A few are my men, no more than a few hundred. They'll serve you well, but with any luck, you won't need them."

Godegesil smiled, nodded, and swallowed all in the same instant. He was happy to have the additional troops.

"I just wish I could have finished Gundobad," continued Clovis.

"Do you think I need to worry about him now?" Godegesil looked anxious.

Clovis opened his mouth to speak, only to hesitate at the sound of a soft, deep rumble in the castle. He watched as the wine in his goblet rippled into a tiny, windswept lake. Waves moved under his feet—too subtle to see, but too obvious to ignore. Dizziness nearly overcame him and the blood drained from his face. He grabbed for the edge of the table, looked at Godegesil and was surprised to see that he didn't seem the least bit concerned.

"Don't let it bother you, Clovis," Godegesil chuckled at his guest's anxiety. "These quakes happen here now and then. There's nothing to worry about." The motion ceased as he spoke.

Clovis shook his head nervously.

"You're not convinced, are you?" Godegesil asked in jest, toying with his ally's uneasiness. Clovis tried to maintain his dignity.

"A quake?"

"That was a small one."

"I've heard of them, but this is the first time I've felt one. Are the Gods angry?"

"Oh my no, Clovis. If God was angry there wouldn't be a stone standing here." Clovis looked around, still skittish. "That was only a belch."

Clovis intended to be under way as soon as possible, and decided that to leave now would be prudent.

"Soissons will wonder how our campaign went, Godegesil. I'll be on my way."

"You have my gratitude, Clovis," said Godegesil, "May your journeys be safe…and without quakes." He smiled at his cleverness before adding with all sincerity, "And please, carry my greetings to Clotild. She's a treasure and I miss her."

Clovis accepted the compliment for his bride, glad to turn his thoughts toward his departure.

"I'll carry your good wishes along with the news of our victory. Clotild will be glad to hear from you."

Clovis stood slowly, making certain the ground would support him, then, comforted in the floor's solidity, spoke again to his co-conspirator, "I've heard that Christian bishops are in conference at Lyons. With your permission, I'd like to stop on my way back and see them."

"Of course, feel free. The conference is over, I believe, but those bishops always linger, just like guilt!" He laughed as he waved Clovis on his way. "There are quakes there too!" He laughed again. Then was alone, to deal with the people of Burgundy, the people of Gundobad.

Chapter 14 *The Church Grows in Strength: 500 CE*

The shouting in the chamber held everyone's attention. No one noticed Clovis enter. He came in with Gerard, quietly seating himself next to a kindly looking bishop. Few heads turned and none wondered why these new guests were among them. The bishops were watching one of the more heated arguments that had resulted since the beginning of the well-meant but ill-fated conference between the Catholic and Arian leaders.

Clovis leaned toward the elderly bishop on the bench next to him and asked, "What's the shouting about, Father?"

The bishop, having never met Clovis and not certain who his questioner was, responded courteously nonetheless.

"Our meeting is falling to pieces, I'm afraid."

"Oh?"

"Actually, the conference has been over for weeks. Officially. But these," he swept his arm across the scene, "have decided to stay and debate matters of faith. There's not much else to do, I suppose. That's why I'm still here." He chuckled.

"I see," said Clovis, enjoying the moment of anonymity. He looked around the room at the faces of the clerics.

"That man over there," said the bishop as he pointed with a crooked finger toward an elderly man whose face was turning redder by the second, "is Sylvester. A good Trinitarian but a little emotional."

Remembering Sylvester from his betrothal he asked, "He's from Chalon-sur-Saône, isn't he?"

The bishop raised his eyebrows and looked more closely at Clovis.

"Why yes, he *is* from Chalon. How would you know that? You're not a bishop, incognito, are you?"

"No, father!" Clovis laughed. "I've had business in the area before, that's all."

"Well, as I was saying, Sylvester is a good Trinitarian, only much too emotional. He's arguing with that man," the bishop nodded to a man across the room, "the one pointing and yelling there—who is Bonifacius of Vienne. He's an Arian and there is no convincing the Arians of the truth. I don't know why Sylvester's even trying. It's frustrating to say the least."

"You, then, are a Trinitarian, I presume."

"Yes, of course…oh, forgive me. I should have introduced myself. I'm Victurius, bishop of Grenoble."

"Burgundian?"

"Yes," said Victurius, "most of us here are. And under the rule of an Arian!" He shook his head. "I simply don't comprehend how the Arians can so easily reject the obvious truth! I just can't understand it. No." He shook his head again in frustration. Then he turned and looked at Clovis. "And who are you, my son? You're not Burgundian, are you?"

"No, Victurius, I'm Clovis, ruler of the Franks in Soissons. I've come to listen, and learn what I can from the bishops."

Victurius barely heard the end of the sentence before he rose to his feet and, waving his arms frantically, fought to gain a hearing.

"Brothers! Brothers! Hear me a moment, I beg you! Hear me!"

The room quieted somewhat, though a great deal of mumbling remained over the issue under discussion. In a moment, though, Victurius had the floor.

"Brothers, hear me. The essence and nature of our Lord are issues of importance, it's true. But a more immediate issue is at hand. As you know, Clovis of the Franks has defeated Gundobad. My brothers, this Clovis is with us now. This great warrior and leader has come to learn from us what he can, or so he's told me." He winked at Clovis who sat, confused, uncertain as to what Victurius was trying to do. "But I think *we* can learn from him. He will have great influence in what path is opened up in matters of faith. Speak, Clovis, tell us where you stand!"

Clovis was stunned at the presumptuousness of Victurius, but his face revealed nothing of it. He leaned over to Gerard and whispered in his ear.

"What do they expect me to say?"

"We don't answer to these Christians," said Gerard.

It was true. Clovis owed these men nothing. He rose slowly and straightened his tunic. All eyes were on him. He looked coldly at Victurius and then began.

"My friends, I don't hold anyone in contempt for the religion or gods they choose to follow. I am, in your eyes, a pagan. My Gods are not your gods. But I rule over many Christians. And whether they believe in three gods or one is of no concern to me."

At that moment, his eyes met those of an anxious Bishop Avitus. This was the man who had helped save Clotild's life when Gundobad sought to kill her. The lines on his face betrayed more than his years. They showed the toll the experiences of those years had taken. Clovis remembered his wife's anger toward Gundobad and the religion he claimed. He understood something of what Avitus had risked in order to save the young princess and, later, to be so bold as to betroth her to Clovis in front of Gundobad, himself. Suddenly he felt shame at leaving Gundobad still alive. He realized he had an opportunity to do something that would please not only his wife, but also the bishops who had become nothing less than his allies. Hadn't Remigius said, stay on good terms with the Church? A moment's thought convinced him that he had little to lose.

"However," he continued, "there can be only one king in a land. And, it seems that there can be only one king for the Church. So I choose to support that King, Jesus, who is worshipped by you who claim three gods."

The bishops were shocked into silence. But only for seconds. Then an outburst of cheers came from the Catholic bishops and shouts of anger and disbelief came from the Arians. Gerard sat amazed and silent, his mouth hanging open at the proclamation of his king.

"Then you are a Christian?" shouted Victurius above the din.

"No, I told you, my Gods are not your Gods," said Clovis.

"Not a Christian?" mumbled some of the bishops. Confusion over how a pagan could support the Church began a new debate.

"Those not for you are against you," challenged the Arians.

"Those not against you are for you," returned the Catholics in a predictable exchange.

Soon the Arians rose as a group and left. The remaining bishops could only express to one another their amazement; what good fortune this was for the Church!

Clovis made his way through the bishops, back to Gerard and out the door.

"Clovis," whispered Gerard at his first opportunity, "you haven't forgotten our Gods have you?" He was still amazed at what he'd heard.

"Not you too, Gerard? Why does everyone care what I believe! No, of course not! It was a favor to my wife," said Clovis, and he laughed.

"To your wife?" Gerard shook his head, even more amazed, though a moment before he wouldn't have imagined it possible. "You mean that you upset this conference as a favor to your wife?"

Clovis laughed, "Well, I suppose you could say that, but I wanted to support Avitus. And, Gerard," he patted his friend on the shoulder, "in the end, this may serve us. This was a greater opportunity than I'd expected." Clovis stopped his retreat from the Bishop's meeting, his hand still on Gerard's shoulder, and stared out into space. He wondered if the Catholic Church would emerge victorious over the Arians. What would it mean? It was a gamble to put his lot in with them, he knew. How might it benefit him, if and when they did prevail? How might he suffer if they did not? He looked back at his friend. "This is an interesting time, Gerard, an interesting time."

Chapter 15
Gundobad Returns
502 CE

In the twenty-first year of the reign of Clovis, in the second year after the defeat of Gundobad, the exiled king refused to pay the tribute he'd promised to the King of the Franks. What money he had was being used to finance an army.

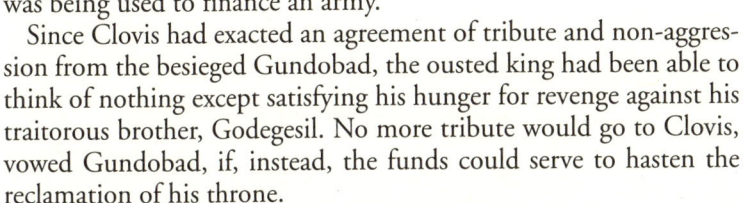

Since Clovis had exacted an agreement of tribute and non-aggression from the besieged Gundobad, the ousted king had been able to think of nothing except satisfying his hunger for revenge against his traitorous brother, Godegesil. No more tribute would go to Clovis, vowed Gundobad, if, instead, the funds could serve to hasten the reclamation of his throne.

Gundobad met with his Visigothic protector, Alaric. A meeting was hastily arranged in Avignon as Alaric returned from Italy. The young Visigoth was nearing his thirtieth year now, no longer requiring advice in the ways of kings. His preference was to meet in private with Gundobad, to deny the presence and whisper of Aridius. An insecure Gundobad did his best to convince Alaric that, as far as neighboring countries were concerned, an ally was better than an adversary.

"After all, your people have given me refuge," said Gundobad. "You certainly can't expect Godegesil to offer you his friendship."

"No," replied Alaric. The logic was clear to anyone who knew the two brothers, and Alaric did. He looked at Gundobad as he considered the situation. Gundobad was a better choice for king than Godegesil. Burgundy bordered his lands. Clovis was worry enough for Alaric without adding an enemy on the eastern frontier.

"You'll have aid and troops, Gundobad. I look forward to returning my friend and ally to his proper place in Vienne."

Gundobad smiled and bowed graciously to Alaric. He dared to think there might actually be a chance to see the inner courts of Vienne again.

To Gundobad's surprise, on the basis of written correspondence alone, Theodoric of Italy offered his assistance too. Gundobad couldn't help but shake his head in wonder. "Enemies aren't bound to be enemies forever, eh, Aridius?"

"It would appear not," his advisor replied, though he understood Theodoric's reasoning.

Italy's northern border had nearly been violated as Clovis had driven south to Avignon. And though Theodoric had gained some security in marrying the sister of Clovis, he couldn't afford to let his brother-in-law approach that close again. If Godegesil stayed in power, Clovis was as good as on his borders. It was not acceptable. Gundobad must regain his throne. In that way Burgundy would serve as a buffer between Italy and the Franks. It was the prudence of a seasoned leader, however, that made Theodoric insist on an assurance from Gundobad that this campaign was aimed at Godegesil alone, and not at Clovis, a minor concession for Gundobad. His anger at Clovis could burn another day.

A number of soldiers, scattered after the consecutive defeats Gundobad suffered, rallied with the news that Alaric and Theodoric were coming to their leader's aid. Though their loyalty might well be questioned, Gundobad was not in a position to reject willing warriors, so they were extended a warm welcome. The day finally came when the preparations for war were deemed sufficient and Gundobad moved against Godegesil. With 7000 troops at his command, Gundobad marched a week to arrive before the gates of Vienne.

Spies had informed Godegesil of Gundobad's intention and the week of Gundobad's advance was spent in preparation for battle or, more likely, for a siege. Now, from the castle walls, Godegesil looked out on his brother's forces and saw he had the advantage over Gundobad. A simple message from Gundobad demanded he surrender the city. In an even more direct reply, Godegesil refused.

"I'd have done the same," said Gundobad to Aridius when the refusal was received. He looked out at his army, less than a quarter of the number that had once fought for him, and said, "Our troops are something short of overwhelming."

"Shall I begin preparations for a siege?" asked Aridius, knowing full well his King's mind.

"Yes, let's get it under way. I expect it will be a long one." Gundobad knew his own city and had always been confident that a siege would succeed only with great difficulty. Still, he had to do this. He had no intention of giving in.

Gundobad did have two things in his favor. First, though Godegesil had been warned of his advance, Gundobad knew there had not been time for his brother to gather enough supplies for a protracted siege.

Chapter 15 *Gundobad Returns: 502 CE*

Second, Gundobad knew his brother was a weak and frightened man. Often, his decisions stemmed from desperation rather than from reason, and Gundobad knew that Godegesil would do whatever he thought was necessary to maintain his power, even if what was necessary proved rash or dangerous.

After nearly four weeks under siege, Godegesil was informed that the city's supplies, while not seriously depleted, were running low more rapidly than was advised. Reports told him that there were only enough provisions for the men who were defending the city. Therefore it was decided that, in order to withstand a longer siege, the people not critical to the defense of the city would be expelled.

Citizens of Vienne were separated into categories based on their value to the defense and functioning of the city. Soldiers were included without question. Few others were allowed to stay. Women and children had little say in the matter and, along with the frail and elderly, were put outside the city walls. The priests weren't included in the calculations and were allowed to stay with their churches. As the first light of dawn appeared, nearly two thirds of the city's common people were cast out of their homes, out of their town, out of their protective fortress.

Among those expelled was a Jew named Hanoch. Being Jewish, Hanoch had few friends in Vienne. Rarely did Jews move this far north. Hanoch's father had come here escaping the irrational prejudice that was becoming all too common in the south. Hanoch could remember the hopes his father had held as they began a new life in Vienne, and life had been reasonably good. Trained as an engineer, Hanoch proved himself an asset to the city. For over ten years he'd been charged with the maintenance of the aqueduct that provided water to Vienne. The work was strenuous, making Hanoch a strong and imposing man. It was not in his nature to fight, but few doubted that he could defend himself, if circumstances called for it. So, he was left alone. Now Hanoch was cast out, and he was furious. He sought out his former king.

The morning sun was above the horizon now and Gundobad was well into a planning discussion with Aridius. They both welcomed a break. Hanoch was familiar to Gundobad and it comforted him to see one of his citizens, even as it angered him to see such a deep look of shock and dismay in the man's eyes.

"Yes, Hanoch, I remember you, the keeper of the aqueduct. You say you can help us?"

"Yes, my King. I still call you 'my King' because the one who sits in your throne has no right to the title. He's incompetent and indifferent to the people. Yes, I can be of service. And if you'll hear me out, I believe you'll judge me to be an honest man."

"I've no reason to believe otherwise, Hanoch. I remember your work. Go on. How can you help end this siege? And, more importantly, why would you want to try? If we fail and Godegesil learns you've been helping me, it will cost you your life."

Hanoch was weary. He was outraged that Godegesil would cast him, or anyone else, out of the city and he wasn't in the mood for questions. His life had been filled with people interrogating him. He was continually defending himself; proving that his presence was an acceptable risk. Jews faced it always. He pursed his lips and fought to control his anger. His wife came to his side and wrapped her hands around his arm, resting her head on his shoulder, trying to calm her husband. His fists clenched, showing the power in his forearms and his barrel chest heaved as he took three deep breaths before speaking.

"My lord, I've served our city for well over ten years now, making certain that the people of Vienne had water. I've worked hard and I've always dealt fairly with you and the people of the town. And now your brother, that worthless excuse for a ruler, if you will forgive me, has cast me and my family out of our home. That is why I wish to help you. To depose that incompetent fool and to bring sanity back to our city. Is that reason enough?"

There was no doubting the man's sincerity. Even Aridius was impressed by Hanoch's passion.

"Yes, Hanoch, that's enough," said the king, a comforting note in his voice. "How will you help? Will you carry a sword or an ax?" Hanoch gave him a distasteful look. "Or perhaps you're here as an informer. Is that it? Can you tell us where their weaknesses are?"

Gundobad cocked his head, hopefully. He avoided looking at Aridius who, he was certain, had considered this long before he had.

"Better. I can take you to their only weakness—a fatal weakness!" Hanoch's eyes narrowed. "And once we're there, I can lead you into the city!"

Gundobad was dumbfounded.

"Fatal weakness? Hanoch, we both know how strong that fortress is. Where is this Achilles heel?"

"King Gundobad, isn't it obvious to you? The aqueduct! I can lead you to the vents of the aqueduct—and they're not guarded!"

"What?"

Chapter 15 *Gundobad Returns: 502 CE*

Gundobad knew the vents but he couldn't imagine that they stood unguarded. Was Godegesil that incompetent?

"The truth, my lord, I swear it. I walked by the vents on two successive evenings just before I and my family were commanded to leave. At one time, the lower vents were used to release the overflow. But, you may remember, new vents were constructed to the east when another reservoir was added. Those vents are guarded. The old vents were blocked because wolves and bears had been entering the city through them. Remember?" Gundobad nodded his affirmation. "It appears the vents are forgotten already. They're unguarded, and I can take you there."

For a long moment Gundobad sat in silence. The possibilities were too astonishing to grasp.

He whispered in amazement, "Unguarded! Did you hear, Aridius? Unguarded!"

Aridius was already shaping a plan of attack. "Night-time would be best, of course," he said, mostly to himself, but loud enough so Gundobad and his new soldier could hear.

"Certainly at night!" agreed Hanoch. His excitement grew as his idea gained acceptance. It was beginning to appear that he might get his wish to bring disaster to Godegesil.

"How many could pass through the vents at a time?" asked Aridius.

"Not many. Two at most," Hanoch said. Then he hastened to add, "But there is a large area on the inside of the vent that's in shadows. That's unguarded as well."

Aridius digested the additional information and after a long moment, turned toward Gundobad.

"My lord, I believe we might be able to bring this siege to a close, if our friend's information is accurate."

"You can depend on it," interjected the Jew.

"You have a plan?" asked Gundobad, already knowing the answer. Aridius smiled and nodded. "Of course."

"Then, my friend, let's get on with it. I've been away from my throne for too long."

In the dark of a moonless spring night, a long line of warriors stood, swords ready, anxious to gain entry into the walled city of Vienne.

Through the trees along the river, Hanoch had led Gundobad's soldiers to where they now waited. Two of the strongest soldiers stood with the vengeful engineer beneath the aqueduct. Large boulders blocked the old vents.

"Start there," said Hanoch, pointing to the far side of the vent.

As quietly as they were able, using their weapons as tools, the soldiers began to wrench the stones away from the vents. The grinding sound that resulted shouted that there were intruders, or at least it seemed so to the breathless invaders, but the noise brought no response from the other side of the vent. A short wait in silence and then, carefully, the two soldiers continued with their work. In less than an hour the vents were clear and Vienne lay waiting…vulnerable.

Gundobad sat gazing at the front gates of the city, listening intently to the late night noises. His soldiers had been given explicit instructions. Silence was to be maintained until the command came to charge the front gate. Simple enough, thought Gundobad, but the timing had to be precise. He knew that if the men charged too soon, Godegesil's troops would be alerted, their readiness increased, their senses sharpened by fear, and the attack from the inside would likely be thwarted. If they charged too late, the surprise of the small group of soldiers sneaking into the city by way of the aqueduct vents would be little more than an inconvenience. Gundobad knew they must charge when Godegesil's men were most distracted. Then they would have a chance. By now, he figured, Hanoch should be inside the city.

As he listened, Gundobad tried to imagine what was happening on the other side of the walls that stood between him and his throne. His men were obeying orders, staying quiet as death. The low sound of the river, gently running, oblivious to the quietly unfolding assault, was punctuated by the hoot of an owl. The sounds of the night crowded forward, as Gundobad listened and he wondered if the noise would drown out what he knew he must hear. Then, from inside the walls of Vienne, a muffled commotion, brought on by what could only be the surprise attack, came to his ears. Instantly he shouted the charge. 2000 soldiers, some Burgundian, some belonging to Theodoric and some to Alaric, ran shouting toward the gates of the city. The noise they raised caused the defenders a moment's confusion; just enough so that a small band of Gundobad's men who had entered Vienne through the vents were able to break away from battle inside and make their way to the main portal of the city. They killed the few guards still there, and opened Vienne to her attackers. Within seconds, half of Gundobad's men had flooded through the gates and fierce fighting filled the courtyard, spilling into the streets of the city. The other half of Gundobad's men held back, Gundobad with them.

Chapter 15 *Gundobad Returns: 502 CE*

Godegesil was asleep when the attack began, though since the siege had been imposed he'd not been sleeping well at all. For too long he'd been under his brother's power and he couldn't help but worry that Gundobad might succeed in this assault. He knew what his fate would be if his brother ever sat on the throne again. The clamor of the surprise attack awoke him with its earliest sounds. Before he was out of his bed he knew that something was seriously wrong. He threw on a tunic and, grabbing his sword, ran out of his room.

Once in the streets, he found one of his soldiers, wide-eyed and running. Godegesil grabbed his arm, bringing him to a restless halt.

"Report!"

"The main gate, my lord! Breached!"

"Has anyone gone to rouse the other men?"

"I'm on my way now," said the soldier, frantically pulling away from his king's grasp to continue on his mission.

Assured that reinforcements were coming, Godegesil set off for the town gate and battle.

He rounded the corner of a building and found himself looking down the street at a sickening sight. His men had broken ranks and were fighting in confusion. There was no leader to direct their efforts and some soldiers were looking for ways of escape.

The invaders, on the other hand, encouraged by the confusion and hesitancy of the defenders, fought with growing enthusiasm. Godegesil recognized Hanoch, armor clad, swinging a long-sword, pushing back a line of men with no help from others. The man's fierceness inspired the rest of the invaders to follow his example. Defenders began to break and run.

"No!" shouted Godegesil, "Help comes!" He ran into the heart of the fighting.

There was still a chance that the attackers would be defeated if the soldiers of Clovis, few though they were, joined the battle. In the two years since Godegesil took Gundobad's throne, a small force of Franks, a gesture offered in recognition of their new alliance, regularly stayed in Vienne. Unfortunately fate quartered them far from where the battle now raged. Godegesil was certain they were coming and would arrive soon. In the meantime, he fought to rally his own men.

He ran to the highest place in the courtyard, on steps that led to the watchtowers. From his position he could see the battle spread out before him and all in the courtyard could see him. He yelled a rallying cry and fought with more skill than he knew he possessed.

The effort did not go unrewarded. His men took heart and drew together with renewed strength. But it was too late. Before reinforcements arrived, before the tide completely turned, Gundobad, himself, led the second half of his invading forces into the widened breech. He entered upon his horse, his confidence building as Godegesil's troops were swept away before him like so much dust.

Godegesil looked straight into his brother's face. Gundobad returned the gaze, sneering before he mouthed the word, "traitor". Disregarding the rest of the battle, Gundobad rode toward his brother.

Godegesil knew better than to face Gundobad. He bolted through the fighting, twice narrowly escaping the sword. He ran into the streets, just moments before Gundobad's horse broke free from the chaotic battle.

The only place he could hope to find safety was in the Church. The closest was St. Paul's where Bishop Bonifacius led the Arian Christians of Vienne. The bishop was inside, awakened by the battle, lighting candles in prayer when Godegesil burst open the church doors.

"Hide me!" cried a panting and desperate Godegesil.

"What?" The bishop spun around at the plea.

"Hide me! Gundobad's broken into the city!"

"Rest easy, my son." The bishop lifted his hands in a gesture of comfort, as if he was trying to quiet a group of children. "He won't violate the Church. He has too much respect for that."

Gundobad was clear of the battle more quickly than Godegesil imagined possible. His horse was fast and agile, making the sharp turn onto the street where St. Paul's lay, in time to allow Gundobad a glimpse of his brother as he slipped into the Arian Church. His anger at his traitorous sibling outweighed his regard for the Church and he showed no hesitation as he burst into St. Paul's, sword in hand, just as Bishop Bonifacius finished his comforting words to Godegesil.

Godegesil looked up in horror.

"No!" he shouted.

The bishop turned to face his former king. "Gundobad, you would dare to violate the house of God?"

Gundobad, burning with a rage that had festered since his brother's betrayal, didn't say a word. His lips peeled into a hateful smile and he advanced toward Godegesil.

Bonifacius stepped in front of Gundobad in an effort to protect Godegesil, who was backed up all the way to the altar of the church. He looked into the venom-filled eyes of the pursuer and shivered at the depth of the man's hatred.

"Gundobad! Not here!"

Chapter 15 *Gundobad Returns: 502 CE*

Distracted by the protective move of the bishop, Gundobad stopped. He looked at his brother, quivering in fear, and at the resolute Priest before him. A memory of the conference of bishops flashed in his mind. He remembered their unwillingness to act against Clovis as he moved against Burgundy. Arian and Catholic, alike, had failed him. He searched his heart for any reverence he might still hold for the Church and found only emptiness. There was no deference; no fear.

With one hand he thrust his sword into the gut of the bishop, grabbing the man's shoulder with his other hand. And when he had turned his weapon once, he withdrew it and shoved the dying Bonifacius aside.

Godegesil pressed himself even harder against the altar. Wide eyed, he looked at the slain bishop and then back at his brother. In a pleading voice, Godegesil uttered his last word,

"Please,..."

"Traitor!" shouted Gundobad. And with a single thrust, he pinned Godegesil to the altar with his sword. Then he lifted his ax from his belt and hacked off his brother's head.

"Traitor!" he yelled again. This time an echo from within the church returned to him as if it had come from the church itself, "Traitor!"

The Franks Clovis had ordered to remain in Vienne, never made the battle. The soldier who had been sent to retrieve them ignored the order he'd been given and fled for his life. It was later that the noise of others fleeing awoke the Franks. Before they could raise their swords to fight it was clear to them that surrender was the only option. In a moment the Franks were surrounded, disarmed, and locked in towers that had been built to defend the city.

Gundobad learned of the men belonging to Clovis, and decided not to risk further war with the King of the Franks. Without delay he had the soldiers sent, in chains, to Toulouse; exiled to the territory of the Visigoths, hoping that Clovis would appreciate the fact that he had spared his men's lives. Alaric, seeing the transfer of men as a declaration of victory for his ally, proudly accepted the prisoners.

Others who had conspired with Godegesil were tortured and executed. Hanoch received special privileges for his part in the siege. His family gained a prominence that few Jews had ever known in Gaul. It was only after Gundobad was certain that such post-battle details were addressed that he turned to the concerns of the city.

While in power, Godegesil had directed his efforts to the defense of the city, forgetting entirely the basic needs of the people. In less than two years, the trade income had fallen, taxes had risen and the people of the town were struggling to maintain their previous standard of living. Gundobad could see how much work needed to be done, but the people didn't trust the throne. Not now. Not even with Gundobad upon it.

Gundobad did what he could for the short term by lowering taxes to a previous rate and by easing the trade regulations. Then, taking a risk, he drew on the towns reserves to help feed the people of Vienne. The gesture did not go unappreciated, and before long one could hear shouts of support aimed at the castle saying, "Praise be to God, our king has returned! Our king has returned!"

Aridius stepped back from the work of governing, giving Gundobad room to maneuver. He'd never seen him so self-assured. Capable to do the work of a king, and more secure than ever, Gundobad ruled, and Aridius contented himself with a lesser role. Still trusted as an advisor, but needed in a different capacity, he accepted an assignment to rebuild the defensive structures that had been damaged in the war, towers and gates, certainly, but most particularly the aqueduct vents. He set about his business, glad, for the time being, to let Gundobad reign.

It would take a full day for the water to run from one container of the clypsedra to the other. The large stone cylinder now stood empty. As it filled, it would raise, at a nearly imperceptible rate, a small wooden platform, upon which stood the carved image of a man dressed in brightly colored clothes. Fixed to the inside of the cylinder was a ruler, etched with markings that corresponded to the hours of the day. The figure's outstretched arm pointed to markings telling the passage of time. The gift pleased Gundobad.

Another gift, a sundial, was more familiar to him, but no less pleasing. He looked with growing interest at the clocks and his face broke into a smile of delight.

"Remarkable!" he whispered. He looked at the young man before him, the messenger who had just presented the gift from Theodoric. Gundobad felt an increasing sense of strength and relief. His relationship with Theodoric was growing. He was feeling more confident in his own power, less concerned about Clovis. "Read the message again," he ordered.

Chapter 15 *Gundobad Returns: 502 CE*

"Yes, my lord." The boy, clearly well educated, lifted the message before his face and read: "Cassiodorus, secretary to Theodoric, King of Italy; to most revered Gundobad, King of all Burgundy. Greetings and salutations. It is with respect and honor that, on behalf of our king, Theodoric, I send this gift you have requested. Have now in your country what you have seen in Rome. It is right that we should send you gifts, because of our new relationship as allies.

"It is said that under you, Burgundy praises the discoveries of the ancients; and through you, she lays aside her barbarous nature. May Burgundy now arrange her daily actions by the movements of God's great lights. The order of life passes in confusion if we are unaware of the division of time. Men are like beasts, if they only know the passage of time by the pangs of hunger. Certainty is undoubtedly meant to be entwined with human actions. May peace be with you and your subjects."

The lad looked up at Gundobad once he completed the reading.

Gundobad stepped from his throne and walked around the water clock that stood a full five feet tall. He smiled, shook his head in astonishment and said, "It is most remarkable!"

The strain from the war with Godegesil eventually dissolved. Gundobad's schedule relaxed enough that he was able to think on the events of the last two years. One day, in the course of his reflections, he felt the need to summon Bishop Avitus. The bishop was glad to oblige, arriving in time for supper.

Greetings were exchanged between the two as if no conflict had occurred. In fact, thought Avitus, the throne rooms looked as though nothing unusual had transpired. There was one difference, however, that Avitus could not avoid noticing. There was no Aridius present. In the past, the secretary and advisor would be absent from these sorts of meetings only if he was out of the country. In those times, conferences with the king were rare. And since the day when the Church arranged for Clotild's betrothal, Gundobad had proven uneasy when faced with officials of the Church. Normally, he would insist that Aridius be present. Avitus knew Aridius was still in the city, and that knowledge made him particularly attentive.

The two were brought wine and bread and they tried to make themselves comfortable. It was not easy. All the while, as more food arrived, silence held reign when conversation would normally predominate. Avitus was aware of the difficulty Gundobad was having in his efforts to be nonchalant. The bishop tried to ease the mood.

"The people seem happy, having you back in the throne."

"Oh?" Gundobad remained stiff.

"Many have mentioned how pleased they are that you've relaxed the laws your brother forced upon us."

Gundobad eased a little and smiled.

"Good. Good. I intend to do even more. Many of the laws—even some of the ones I, myself, instituted—are in need of change. And, as it seems feasible, I'll be changing them too."

Avitus could see that this brought Gundobad pleasure.

"That will, no doubt, meet with the people's approval."

Gundobad grunted noncommittally and stood. Avitus frowned as he watched the king start to pace. Gundobad paused at one point and gulped down his wine. Then he took a deep breath, turned and looked directly at Avitus."

"I killed my own brother, Avitus…" Gundobad was abrupt but the bishop didn't appear surprised or concerned, "…my own brother!"

"Yes. I'm aware of that."

"It was necessary, Father." He paused. Avitus didn't respond.

"I killed Bishop Bonifacius too." The tension in Gundobad's voice was increasing.

"I know."

"He was the bishop of the Arian Church. My Church."

"Yes, I know." Avitus saw no need for more commentary.

Gundobad tried to go on, but wasn't certain how to proceed.

"I can't…I don't think it wise to call myself an Arian anymore. Don't you agree?" The King's expression was pained.

"I can understand why you'd think so. But what are you suggesting?" Avitus barely dared to admit his suspicions. Gundobad confirmed them, however, with his next words.

"Tell me about your Triune God again. And about how Jesus was God, while God was God."

Avitus couldn't disguise his astonishment. He nearly choked on his wine, set it down and leaned forward. "You're thinking of converting!" he said.

Gundobad continued, nearly oblivious to the Bishop's reaction. "So many of my people are Arian though."

Avitus thought he sounded defeated.

"My dear Gundobad," the bishop was sympathetic, "people should follow kings. Kings should never follow people. People need leaders. That goes in religion as well as in war."

"Yes, perhaps you're right."

"So you *are* considering converting?"

Chapter 15 *Gundobad Returns: 502 CE*

"Considering it, that's all," said Gundobad. The admission visibly relieved him and it seemed as though a great weight had been removed from his shoulders. He sat back with a willingness in his eyes that touched Avitus.

"Then, my King," said the bishop, "let's talk."

Chapter 16

Shifting Winds
502 CE

Chlodomer, now six, pretended to be the king while his five-year-old sister, Clotild, named after her mother, willingly played the part of the queen. Four-year-old Childebert had to settle for playing the prince. The baby, Chlothar, not a part of the game, cooed and gurgled in the wooden crib that stood against the wall. Clovis sat with Clotild near a window that opened out onto a view of the city north of the palace. The sky was hazy, what flowers were visible looked wilted and people were moving slowly.

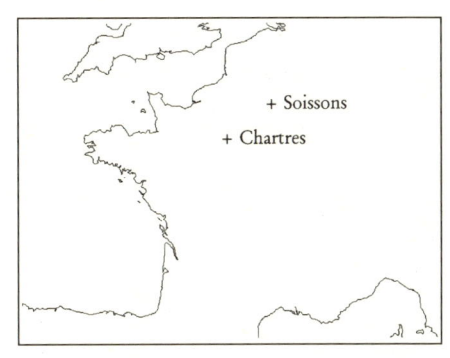

It was unusually warm, even for one of the closing days of spring. Most everyone was predicting a brutal summer. When the wind gusted, its whisper ran through the grass, its caress rustling the leaves, but in recent days that was infrequent. Today only the laughter of the children came to the ear of Clovis. It was refreshing in its own way.

Increasingly, Clovis appreciated these times of peace. The children certainly created a great deal of chaos, but in spite of it, his enjoyment in being with them grew daily. He knew the glory of victory, and his heart beat more rapidly when he remembered his triumphs. But he also knew the profound grief of life lost. He'd felt it too many times, had watched life end more times than he cared to recall, had introduced eager death to innumerable warriors who would have gladly done the same for him.

Chlodomer got up from his play and came to rest his hands on his father's knee.

"Mama and I took a walk around the whole city."

"Did you?" asked Clovis.

"Yes, and I was very good. She said so." He looked to his mother for her confirmation, smiling when she nodded her agreement.

"Well, you are a good boy, aren't you?" said Clovis.

"Yes," was the simple and honest reply.

Clovis smiled at his son and at Clotild. He rubbed Chlodomer's head and started to tell his son that he would be a good ruler one day, but stopped when a servant appeared in the doorway.

"What is it?" asked Clovis.

"A messenger, sir."

"I'll see him here."

The servant departed to be replaced by a young soldier, new to the palace guard.

"Étienne, isn't it?"

"Yes, sir."

"What message is this?"

"Sir…" The soldier looked at Clotild and the children and hesitated. Recommended by Baldewin, Étienne was capable and proving himself competent. His uncertainty in this moment, however, grew from the prudence borne by inexperience. There was no paranoia or mistrust, only a lack of precedence, for his news was not happy or usual.

"It's all right," said Clotild, recognizing the look. She'd seen the ambivalence before, in other men. Sometimes it meant bad news, sometimes good. She'd quit trying to guess which. "Chlodomer and I have work to do, don't we?"

She picked up little Chlothar from the crib and turned and tickled Chlodomer. He laughed and ran out of the room squealing, "I'll beat you, I'll beat you!" not knowing, or even caring, where they were going. The other children raced out in pursuit.

When they were gone, Clovis looked back at the soldier.

"Sir," the soldier began, "Gundobad has retaken Vienne. Godegesil is dead, and our men serving there have been exiled to Alaric."

Clovis leaned back in his chair, rubbed his eyes and sighed deeply. "Damn!" He spit the word from his mouth. "I should have killed him when I hand the chance!" He shook his head. "Damn!" He looked back at the soldier. "How did you come by this?"

"One of our men was released by Alaric to inform us of the situation."

"Then there's no doubt?"

"None, sir."

Clovis stood and arched his back deeply, groaning as he stretched.

"Gundobad's command! Well, I suppose our first business is with Alaric. Gundobad will have to wait."

Now, but for the characteristic tapping of his fingers, Clovis stood dead still, thinking. Alaric had been almost as much of a problem to him as the Armoricans had been. For years there had been border conflicts. It was getting tiresome.

Chapter 16 *Shifting Winds: 502 CE*

Remigius made the journey from Reims to see Principius, though it was not merely a social call. Long ago, Remigius learned that regular visits to the churches in the region of Belgica secured his own position of authority. It was an added pleasure that such business brought him now and then to see his brother. A brief stay in Soissons, then he would go to Chartres by way of Paris, then perhaps as far as Tours, before visiting Orléans, and then returning to Reims. The more churches seen, the better.

His visit with his brother was now complete, a satisfying visit, as always, and before continuing on from Soissons, Remigius stopped to pay his respects to the king and queen. To do otherwise would be rude. He was always careful to avoid the risk of insult. On this particular day, however, Remigius arrived in the court of Clovis, more anxious than usual, for he had some remarkable news. The kind of information he rarely got to share.

"You especially, Clotild, might find this interesting," he said, receiving a glass of wine from a servant.

"Tell me, Father," said Clotild.

"You know that Gundobad rules again in Burgundy?" asked Remigius, fully expecting that she did know.

Clotild lowered her gaze to the floor, saying nothing. Clovis spoke for her.

"Yes, Bishop, for more than a month now. Because of my incompetence, Clotild's uncle continues to kill her family. Her uncle Godegesil was the price of Gundobad's latest venture."

"Yes, of course." Remigius looked tenderly and apologetically at the queen. "I should have been more gentle. I beg your forgiveness." He took a gulp of wine, quietly reproving himself.

"We've sent a diplomat to Alaric to undo a part of Gundobad's work," said Clovis. "He's exiled some of my men to Toulouse. When my messenger arrives, though, I expect Alaric to release them."

"I'm glad to hear it," said Remigius sincerely. He hoped his sympathy would ease the tension in the room. "I hope they'll be returned soon."

"Thank you Father," said Clovis, his mood lightening only slightly.

"And," said Remigius, "what I have to tell you may yet be an encouragement to you, Clotild." The queen wiped a tear from her cheek and raised her head to look at him, in hopes his prediction would prove correct. He went on in the most matter-of-fact way. "Gundobad has been meeting with Avitus, and the good bishop recently sent word suggesting Gundobad may be ready to convert to the true faith.

We can't be certain yet, but there's hope. He's holding back, afraid of what his people will say.

"Avitus has only spoken to him once, actually, but think of it! A Catholic believer in Gundobad would mean gaining the support of another whole kingdom! And yet, I suppose I shouldn't presume too much."

Clotild's bitterness did not fade in the least, nor would it ever. Still, she was intrigued by the possibility of her uncle converting. She allowed herself to wonder if such a conversion would have any impact on her husband's view of the faith, but held her silence.

Remigius pushed ahead, "Of course, he's already regaining the favor of his own people. He's begun to change laws, so says Avitus, giving the people more power and freedom. And the bishop tells me he's winning back some of his popularity. Not only that. His son, Sigismond, is now betrothed to Theodoric's daughter."

Remigius could see this news further unsettled Clovis. The King was becoming more and more absorbed in his own thoughts. There seemed little to be gained by carrying on. Remigius found a convenient place to stop and concluded his visit.

"I must be under way if I'm going to make my next appointment," he said, "I move more slowly these days."

Clovis saw the bishop out, strolling along at his guest's pace, saying almost nothing, remaining deep in thought. He offered Remigius a warm, and yet somewhat detached farewell, and then watched as the bishop boarded the carriage that would take him, next, to Paris.

As the entourage departed, Clovis called for a servant, who arrived just as the bishop's carriage disappeared in the hazy distance.

"Find Aurelian. Send him to Gerard's house."

"Yes, sir." The servant ran back up the stairs aiming first toward the study, where Aurelian would most likely be found.

More slowly, Clovis descended the steps of the palace and went directly to Gerard's home.

A surprised Gerard met Clovis at the door. Since Clovis had come to Soissons, Gerard had not known him to casually visit the people of the city—not even his friends. It wasn't a matter of Clovis being unwilling to associate with his subordinates. It was simply that due to the pressures of governing, time was at a premium. Others were typically summoned into his presence.

Gerard warmly welcomed him and took pains to make him comfortable. He pulled up a hard straight chair, the only kind of chair he

Chapter 16 *Shifting Winds: 502 CE*

owned, from the corner of the room and invited Clovis to sit. He poured wine into a goblet from an orange terra cotta pitcher that rested on a table by the fireplace and pushed it into his friend's hand. A good fire burned but Gerard added a log to it anyway. Rattled by the appearance of his chief, Gerard fussed only because he didn't know what else to do.

"Please, Gerard, relax. We need to talk and I wanted to meet as soon as possible. That's all. Don't make this something it isn't." His voice was tired but his tone was reassuring.

"Of course," said Gerard. He sat down and assumed the well practiced posture of a soldier awaiting his orders. Clovis looked long at his friend's posture, well aware that Gerard would be vigilant always. He was a consummate soldier.

Occasionally, Clovis wondered why Gerard never took another woman after his young wife, Ileswintha, died of the fever. Once, after a night of drinking, Gerard tried to explain, able to say only that his commander had died. They'd laughed about it then, but Clovis believed the truth of it, that Gerard had lived to do her bidding and now, no orders were being issued.

"Aurelian is on his way. We'll wait for him."

"I see," replied Gerard. "You won't have to wait long."

Clovis turned to look out the door, where Gerard's attention was focused, just in time to see Aurelian come over the threshold, dressed in ceremonial garb. He was now the Count of Melun. Clovis had, at last, decided how to suitably reward his secretary for his loyalty. Aurelian's pride showed daily, as he insisted on wearing the official dress that did honor to his office and to his town.

The town of Melun, southeast of Paris, had been neglected in many ways by Clovis, and by Rome before him. Making Aurelian Count of that town was good for both the secretary and Melun. Aurelian was already making changes in the life of the people there. Though being a count was demanding in its own way, Aurelian found he could remain in service to the king, for aside from occasional ceremonial visits, his work on behalf of Melun was easily done at a distance. Gerard and Clovis rose together to greet their friend and Gerard showed the secretary to another of the chairs.

"I spoke with Remigius today," began Clovis. "He related information to me that I found…that changes some things. It seemed wise, based on what I've learned, to reconsider our plan to retaliate against Gundobad." Clovis took a deep breath and said, "I've decided against it."

Aurelian and Gerard looked at each other and then back at Clovis. The plans had only recently been completed and were already being implemented.

"Without discussion?" said Aurelian. "What about the exiles? What about Clotild?" he asked in a demanding tone.

Clovis frowned at his secretary.

"Yes, without discussion." He paused to make sure Aurelian understood how he felt about the challenge. "Without *any* discussion."

Aurelian understood immediately. "My apologies, sir. I hurried here and it was a shock to hear your words without having time to prepare for them. So many preparations have been made. Please forgive me."

Clovis relaxed somewhat and continued.

"Though I don't like the idea, it's becoming increasingly clear that Gundobad will go on being a force in the life of Gaul. His son, Sigismond, is marrying into Theodoric's family, and that complicates things further." Clovis narrowed his eyes as he thought about Gundobad. "Damn I hate this idea! But we will not attack."

Aurelian broke in, with a less challenging tone, "He refuses to pay the tribute we'd agreed upon."

"I'll release him from the tribute," answered Clovis.

"We could defeat him, my lord," said a supportive Gerard.

"Yes, Gerard, I believe we could, but there's more than meets the eye here. Suffice it to say that Gundobad is luckier than he will ever know. There will be no battle."

Clovis nodded in a way that added emphasis to the finality of his words, then he continued with enough haste that his friends didn't have a chance to say anything further.

"Gerard, you'll need to inform our soldiers. I know they've been gathering for weeks. Make whatever explanation you wish, I imagine no excuse will please them."

"And you, Aurelian," the king went on with barely a breath, "you'll need to compose a letter to Gundobad, releasing him from his tribute and taking steps toward forging an alliance. Don't make it too conciliatory."

Clovis stopped and looked upon his silent friends. He appreciated their position and was grateful for their trust.

"I know this is odd," he said. "Thank you for serving me so well." With a tilt of his head, the king offered only the suggestion of a bow, then, insisting that he'd show himself out, departed,

Aurelian was still for only a moment, then he lightly slapped his hands on his knees, took a deep breath, and said, "Then there's work to be done."

Chapter 16 *Shifting Winds: 502 CE*

He rose, smiled courteously at Gerard, and turned to leave.

Gerard walked him to the door and stood there a long time, watching him walk with his own confident brand of purposefulness. When Aurelian was out of sight, Gerard retreated back into the comfort of his home. As year added on to year, he found that it was taking longer and longer for him to build lust for battle. He realized he was not as unhappy about the canceled call to arms as his men would be. He looked at the few rooms that he called home and the awareness washed over him that these particular walls gave him more comfort than his sword ever had.

With her uncle back in power and no hope for vengeance, Clotild buried her anger. It still lived in her, a well hidden but continual prayer that God's love would not supercede God's vengeance. She believed she would see retribution, one day. But for now, she trusted God and hid her obsession in an intentionally busy life.

Genevieve's example in Paris was sufficient inspiration to cause her to make a similar effort for the unfortunate in Soissons. When the daily demands of her own children were met, she would turn to the needs of the poor. Other servants of the Lord, young sisters in the faith, would join her on the steps of St. Paul's church. Very much as she had in Geneva, she prayed with the people, sometimes fed them, and, when necessary, cleaned their wounds.

The people of the city thought her involvement a remarkable thing, and the Queen's reputation grew with each passing week. Nothing kept her from the steps of the Church. There she was oblivious to all else, concerned only with those who came seeking her help.

On the longest day of the year Clotild was at the Church, doing what fed her soul, when the hermit with the sad smile arrived before her. That was how she would remember him: the hermit with the sad smile. He was not afflicted by hunger. His fat cheeks were a healthy pink, uncharacteristic of the beggars who frequented the steps of the church. Neither was he sick nor wounded. His stride was strong and the way he carried his few belongings betrayed no frailty. His clothes were well worn, but certainly not in tatters, and at first, Clotild wondered why this man was here. Then she noticed his expression. It was devoid of joy. The man grinned with this mouth, but his eyes showed only anguish. The sadness Clotild saw communicated a want deeper than the material world could meet.

She put her hand on his shoulder and asked, "What is your need, my brother?"

"Please," he said, pleading, "a prayer. I only want to be loved by God. I pray in my hermitage, but...my prayers are not sufficient."

Tears filled Clotild's eyes at the sadness in his voice. She reached to hold the man, pulling his head to her breast as she began to pray.

"Dear God, love this child of yours. Forgive whatever sins he might carry and bless him now." The hermit began to cry. Clotild held him more tightly and continued praying, her words of less consequence than the miracle of a prayerful heart which conveyed truth and comfort to the man's wounded soul.

She held him for a long moment after finishing her prayer, then whispered, "Don't leave." Reaching into her pocket she pulled out two solidi, placed them in the hermit's hands, and added, "God be with you."

He looked at the money, a considerable sum, placed it in his pocket without saying a word, and reached into his own bundle of belongings. He drew out a blue piece of cloth, nearly as long as Clotild was tall and half again as wide. Woven into it was a design of lilies; three large white flowers filled the field of sky blue. He handed it to Clotild and said,

"For your husband. May it, and God, protect him."

Clotild accepted it graciously and wondered if this hermit might not be an angel. But she remembered the sadness in his plea and discounted the thought. She frowned almost imperceptibly as she tried to understand. She knelt to place the gift on the ground beside her and when she turned back, the hermit was gone. A sickly woman stood in his place. Clotild looked at her and asked, "What is your need, my sister?"

Bishop Solemnus of Chartres was confident in his knowledge of the faith and of his position in the Church, but he was nervous about this task, nonetheless. Upon receiving the assignment from Remigius to instruct Clovis in the faith, he'd instantly wavered. Since his ordination he'd served as catechist for innumerable people who were seeking entry into the ranks of the believers, but never had he instructed a king. This was altogether new, and knowing how Remigius felt about the role Clovis was playing in the life of the Church, Solemnus didn't dare fall short of success.

By informing Clovis of Gundobad's conversion, Remigius had caused Clovis to reconsider the political advantages that came with membership in the Church. Clovis saw Gundobad's power increase in ways that astounded him. And with that example before him, he asked Remigius to arrange for religious instruction. Solemnus was selected, not only because of his reputation as a teacher, but also because he had no significant political ties with the king. Remigius hoped that fact would keep Solemnus objective.

Remigius made it clear to Solemnus that Clovis had not claimed the faith. The teaching tools for incoming Christians, prepared by the revered Augustine, were not to be used in this case. Rather, these were to be simply informational sessions. Clovis would ask questions and Solemnus would answer them. Now was not the time for indoctrination. Solemnus kept all this in mind as he watched the King's carriage roll up the road toward the south entrance of the church.

As they arrived at the cathedral Solemnus said, "Greetings in the name of the Lord!" thinking as he said the words that he sounded too enthusiastic. "Welcome to Chartres!"

Clovis stepped down from the carriage, stretched his back and looked at his surroundings. From this spot, the highest ground in the city, he could see wheat fields in the distance. He looked long, appreciating the sight. Turning to offer his arm to Clotild, he helped her down from the carriage and only then addressed the bishop with a simple, "Thank you, Father."

"I look forward to our meetings," said Solemnus, "I hope I can answer your questions regarding the Church and our Lord." Clovis was uncomfortable with the Bishop's willingness to announce the purpose of the visit so openly. The king glanced around to see who was within earshot. Solemnus didn't notice. He ushered the two travelers into the shelter of the church, talking nervously the whole time. "It's something of a new assignment for me, but I'm sure things will go along fine. And we'll get to that soon enough. But first, I think you, my lady, may be interested to learn about another visit." He looked at Clotild who, tired from the journey, had difficulty returning more than a look of mild curiosity.

"A friend of mine," said Solemnus, "Bishop Domitianus, serves our Lord in Geneva..."

"Yes," said Clotild, her interest growing, "I know him. Is he here?"

"Yes, he is. And I understand your sister, Chrona, serves the Church there too?"

Clotild jerked to attention at the mention of her sister, forgetting her fatigue.

"Yes, Father, she does."

Solemnus smiled when he saw the look of intrigue on Clotild's face. "Then you'll be pleased to know that your sister is here in Chartres," he said.

Clotild took a step backward and her mouth fell open.

"Here? Now?" she exclaimed.

"Yes!" laughed Solemnus. "She's here with a group on pilgrimage from Geneva, on their way to the Basilica of St. Martin's in Tours. Bishop Domitianus is with them."

No sooner were the Bishop's words out of his mouth than a door opened behind him and Chrona appeared. During their time apart, Chrona had gained weight and it showed in her face. Clotild noticed it immediately and thought it suited her. She was nowhere near obese, but her cheeks were rounder than before, free of wrinkles. The two sisters ran to each other, embraced, laughed, cried, and embraced again.

"My ladies," said Solemnus, "if you wish to talk in private while the king and I converse, please, Chrona, feel free to return to your room. We'll be in the chapel."

The women quickly agreed and departed, Chrona showing the way. Then, turning to Clovis, Solemnus saw that he was smiling at his wife's good fortune. Solemnus was comforted by the grin and with renewed confidence said, "Shall we go?"

The two men went to a small chapel that stood off the nave of the church. It was dimly lit and offered the meager comfort of a single wooden bench where they seated themselves. The altar was graced with a simple Crucifix and nothing more. Clovis took in the austere surroundings and, focusing on the Cross, wasted no time in asking his first question.

"Tell me, Solemnus, is your God a powerful God?"

Solemnus, sighed at the question and sat back on the bench. If all the inquiries were like this one, the time with Clovis would be quite comfortable indeed.

"Yes," he said, "He's the maker of heaven and earth, all things."

"But is he powerful?"

"I would have thought the Creation itself would suggest that, but yes, God is powerful. He thwarted a great leader, the Pharaoh, in Egypt…in order to rescue his people. The Philistines were defeated and so were the Assyrians and Babylonians. Yes. He's a powerful God."

Clovis continued looking at the Crucifix.

"Is he more powerful than my Gods?"

This was more complicated. Solemnus didn't want to offend the warrior king, nor did he want to be less than honest with him. He took a moment to consider his response and thought it best to stay simple.

"I believe so."

"What does he do?"

"Forgive me, Clovis, what do you mean?"

"How does he demonstrate his power?"

"Oh, I see." Solemnus crossed his legs. He took in a long slow breath and let it out past puffed cheeks and pursed lips. Another long breath and then he spoke: "God is the maker of all things, as I've said. And our Lord will judge us in the end. All things and all people are subject to God."

"Father," Clovis looked away from the Crucifix and at Solemnus, "my Gods don't wait to judge. Their justice is swift. Why does your God wait?"

Solemnus began to see that this encounter would be more complicated than he'd expected. He shifted his weight and pondered his answer. Clovis was waiting.

Arm in arm, Clotild and Chrona made their way to the house in which Chrona had stayed the previous night. Very nearly skipping, as they often did in their childhood, they made their way down from the hill of the church, through a winding street that ended beside the river, and to the front of the residence. Still holding hands they sat on a bench before the house.

"You look wonderful, Clotild! Are you well?"

Chrona stroked her sister's arm.

"So much has happened since I saw you last," Clotild replied. She shook her head slowly, unable to take her eyes off of Chrona, still amazed that they were really together again.

"Then tell me, how do you find your husband?" said Chrona in her most lascivious voice.

Clotild giggled in a way that reminded them both of their youth. "You're so curious!" she said.

"I only want to know if you're happy," said Chrona with false indignation.

Clotild warmed in the knowledge that Chrona was still the sister she remembered. "Yes," she said, "I'm happy. My husband's strong and powerful. He's good to his soldiers and to his family. But," she sighed, "he still doesn't believe."

"Could that be changing now?" With a look of hopeful curiosity, Chrona tilted her head back toward the church.

"I wish I knew," said Clotild. "He's not always easy to understand."

Clotild pondered the enigma of her husband. He allowed her to believe as she wished. For that matter, he afforded the same luxury to everyone he ruled. Aside from his anger at God for Ingomer's loss, he held no animosity toward the Church. For some reason, though, he still chose to adhere to the impotent faith of his ancestors. She couldn't understand why he was so blind to the love of God. Still, she was firm and unending in her efforts to share her faith with him and to pray for him.

Chrona saw her sister's concern and said the only thing she could think of that might comfort her.

"I'm sure you do what you can, Clotild. You must leave the rest to God."

"Yes," agreed Clotild, "I suppose you're right." She sighed again, more heavily this time, and for a long moment the two kept silent. Finally the eternal concerns were wrestled into their place and more worldly matters came back to their minds.

"Is he good to you?" asked Chrona.

"Oh, he's been wonderful! We only fight about our beliefs…because of Ingomer, I'm sure." Her eyes misted up for just an instant. "His sister is very near to being baptized, though. Perhaps that will…" she drifted off into what she worried were false hopes. "The children are baptized, of course…except Theuderic."

"I'd love to see the children!" Chrona said, "Though I doubt I'll ever get the chance." Clotild nodded sadly.

"His family has been good to me," continued Clotild, trying to be more jovial, "especially his mother. And you know," Clotild's face shone with childlike glee and she took Chrona's hands into her own, "I think she's being romanced by our physician. It's such fun to watch them. He's very proper; always bowing and apologizing," she mimicked the bow that Tranquillinus had perfected, "and she's so blunt! I wonder if anything will ever come of it." Clotild smiled and shook her head at the possibility. "But now tell me, Chrona, how have you been?"

"I serve our Lord. What more could I want? We're building a hospital at the church. Father Domitianus works very hard on it. It's nearly done, which means my work is about to begin."

Chrona was sincere in her enthusiasm and Clotild turned and curled one leg up under her in order to face her sister as the history of their years apart was unveiled. They spent the day telling stories that would never be recounted in song or around campfires before a battle, stories about the poor and the young, the weak and hurting souls who filled both their worlds.

Chapter 16 *Shifting Winds: 502 CE*

"Bernard? He's still there?" asked Clotild, a nostalgic smile coming to her face as she remembered the man with no feet who was a regular visitor to the sisters at St. Germain's.

"Always. He asks about you, too."

Clotild cocked her head, curious at the thought.

"What do you tell him?"

"I tell him that you are a queen." Clotild blushed but said nothing. Chrona grinned at her sister's discomfort and continued, "He says that he always thought you were."

The sisters laughed and both shook their heads just as their mother used to do.

Finally, with the sun slipping behind nearby rooftops, Chrona reluctantly called a stop to their time together. "I'm leaving early in the morning," she said, "I must sleep and you must get back to your husband." It saddened them both to say farewell, but their spirits were filled, for it had been a joyous day. Chrona accompanied her sister to the front of the church and kissed her good-bye. As Clotild turned away she prayed God's blessing upon her sister, her husband, and herself.

Inside, she found Clovis quiet and unwilling to talk. Solemnus seemed polite but not enthusiastic. "There's much to consider," was all Clovis said.

Chapter 17

Alaric
502 CE

The summer heat was unrelenting in the southern city of Toulouse. The assault of oppressive temperatures was in its fifth week, and cruel, heavy humidity added to the discomfort that was causing Visigothic tempers to shorten and flare. Alaric was as irritable as anyone, and his temper did not improve as he considered the growing strength of Clovis. The threat Alaric perceived persuaded him to forgo a trip to the Mediterranean, further darkening his already sullen mood.

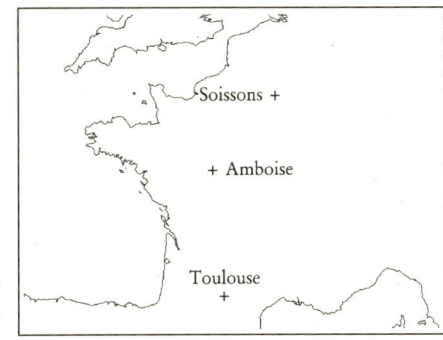

"We're next," he stated bluntly, causing his secretary, Marcus, to look up at him.

Alaric sat drumming his fingers on the throne. In manhood he had none of the charm of his youth. His nose was large, as big as a horse's ass, so said his enemies, his eyes were still set inordinately wide, and his hair was beginning to thin, which only made his oversized ears more visible.

"Sir?" Marcus had no idea what Alaric was talking about.

"Next! We're next! Clovis must be preparing to attack us."

"Why do you say that?"

Alaric shook his head in frustration. "I don't know. When he conquered Syagrius, that brought him to our northern boundary. He's made terms with the Armoricans to the west. He's attacked Gundobad to the east. His own relatives are to the north. He has no need to fight there. He has no need to fight anywhere…except here. We're on his only vulnerable border. And we accepted Franks as prisoners from Gundobad! Damn! We're next. I'm sure of it! How could I have been so stupid!" In frustration he kicked out at the air.

"But the prisoners have been returned. And any move against us would threaten Theodoric. Clovis would think twice before attacking us," said Marcus.

"Perhaps," moaned Alaric as he closed his eyes, "Perhaps." But he was not comforted.

Marcus tried to assure his king. "You're Theodoric's son-in-law! Surely that would offer some security." He hoped it would anyway.

The recent marriage of Alaric to Theodoric's daughter was entirely a matter of politics. He had to believe the relationship would offer some protection.

Alaric sighed and said, "I doubt if Theodoric will get involved in any conflict unless it directly threatens him." He began to shake his head. "He won't be a deterrent. Clovis can come against us at will." He drummed his fingers some more and then slapped the arm of the throne soundly. "We'll have to arrange a meeting with him!"

Marcus frowned. "We have been meeting with the Franks, you know." Marcus had been struggling for months, trying to come to an agreement over the border that the Visigoths shared with the Franks. "I grant you, progress has been slow, but…"

"That's not what I mean!" snapped Alaric. "This is too important for delegations. I have to meet with Clovis myself, in person. We must convince him…I must convince him, of the necessity for a peace pact between us." Alaric was nodding while keeping his gaze cast downward. "Yes, a conference—a peace conference between the two of us." He looked up at Marcus, "Arrange it. The sooner the better."

"As you wish," Marcus answered. He knew that there was no point in arguing. It all seemed premature to him, but he had seen this look on his King's face before. He left Alaric, drawing up the proposal in his mind even before he was out of the room.

Having heard the Visigoth's proposal for a conference, Clovis asked Aurelian, "What's the point of a meeting with Alaric? Are the negotiations going so poorly that he fears war? Or are the negotiators just not doing their job?"

"From what I hear, sir, our delegation is doing fine." Aurelian gave a conciliatory shrug. "Oh, it's slow as usual—all the details, you know. But I don't think this proposal comes from any concern over the border talks." The secretary was confused. The sudden proposal of a meeting had taken him by surprise and he was trying to make sense of it. "Nor can I imagine that Alaric's afraid of war." Then a thought occurred to him and a look of astonishment crossed his face, "Unless…"

"Unless what?"

"Unless Alaric thinks you're planning an invasion!"

"That's nonsense! We don't have any plans to make war with him!"

"No, my lord, we don't…not yet anyway."

Clovis smiled at the suggestion and finished Aurelian's thought, "And Alaric has no way of knowing."

Chapter 17 *Alaric: 502 CE*

"Exactly!" affirmed Aurelian.

"Could it be a trap?"

Aurelian puckered as he thought. "No," he said, "I don't believe we need to worry about that. The terms of the meeting seem reasonable." He looked at the dispatch again, "He's picked an island in the Loire for the conference...near Amboise. It's on one of the stretches of recognized border between us. It should be safe enough."

"I agree," said Clovis. "Is there any reason why we shouldn't accept his invitation?"

"Not that I can see," replied a pensive Aurelian. "In fact, when this is over it may finally settle the border disputes once and for all."

For a few moments, Clovis pondered the decision. It was silent in the room as Aurelian watched Clovis ruminate. He'd learned to trust his ruler's judgments, primarily because, unlike his previous employer, Syagrius, Clovis was not afraid to ask for others' opinions. The path seemed clear to Aurelian. There appeared to be something to gain by meeting with Alaric, and very little to lose. Still, he was curious about the Visigoth's motive. At last, Clovis spoke, his decision made:

"I'll meet with him."

The date scheduled for the conference afforded enough time to make the necessary plans and still enjoy a leisurely ride to Amboise. Pleading from Clotild finally caused Clovis to relent, granting her request to be included in the entourage. The truth be known, Clovis was glad to have her along. Lately, they'd had very few hours together. Seeing to the business of his growing kingdom had consumed most of his time. And there would be more business when Clovis met with Alaric. This was a perfect opportunity for Clovis to share a few days with his wife. The children were left in the capable hands of their grandmother Basina, who was, though no such arrangements had been made, under the willing and watchful eye of the physician, Tranquillinus. Aurelian, who was making the journey with them, was charged with all the details of the trip so that the king and queen could be free to enjoy one another's company.

They rode first to Paris, taking time to visit Genevieve. She continued in her ministry to the poor and the long held burden was taking its toll on her. She looked thin and haggard, and her appearance worried Clotild.

"You should eat more, Genevieve," she told her, "You're wasting away!"

"How can I have a full stomach when my children go hungry?" Genevieve replied. She smiled and touched Clotild's face with her fingertips. "My dear, I'm warmed by your concern for me. But you know that helping my people is what feeds me. This is what nourishes me."

Genevieve wished for no more talk of herself. At her insistence the conversation turned to other news. In the few minutes they had together, Genevieve told Clotild about the continuing struggles of the poor in Paris, sounding more discouraged with each detail of the people's poverty.

"The more I do, the more people there are, the more children, the more empty stomachs!"

"You can't meet every need," assured Clotild. "Our Lord told us we would always have the poor."

Genevieve waved away the painful truth as if it were a bee on the attack. "No," was all she could utter on the subject.

What money Clotild had, she offered to Genevieve. And Clovis promised he would send more when he returned to Soissons, but with a glance at the poverty that surrounded them, they could see that, whatever the sum, it would not be enough.

Clotild, trying to lighten the conversation, related the story of her sister's visit, including as many details as time would allow, much to Genevieve's pleasure. Genevieve asked about the poor of Soissons and Clotild told her of the hermit with the sad smile. Genevieve gave a knowing nod. Then, almost before it had begun, their visit was over, and they said their farewells.

Though the visit pleased Clotild, she could not rid herself of concern for Genevieve nor of the striking contrast between their two lives. For several hours she rode in silence, reflecting on the path the Lord had chosen for her.

Taking the Roman road that headed south out of Paris, it was only after they had passed Orléans that Clotild broke her silence and commented on the most scenic segment of the ride. Passing along the Loire past Blois on the way to Amboise she marveled at the beauty. From a high spot in the road they could look across a carpet of lush trees and see the Loire winding through the forest. The river glimmered aquamarine, reflecting a cloudless sky.

"So peaceful!" said Clotild.

"Yes," replied Clovis, relieved that Clotild was speaking again, "maybe it's a good omen."

Chapter 17 *Alaric: 502 CE*

The king and queen watched the passing scenes of men felling trees, bee keepers tending the hives, and a boy with his clappers scaring the birds away from vineyards that lined the road.

Soon the travelers entered the borderlands. Soldiers were more a part of the scenery with each passing league. Clovis could see Visigothic troops on the other side of the river. But their movements were routine, as far as he could tell, and didn't give cause for worry. Clotild, on the other hand, not being schooled in the ways of war, felt threatened the entire time the soldiers were in view.

On the evening before the conference was to be held, Clovis, Clotild, and their escort arrived, welcomed into the camp Gerard had set up in advance. It was situated directly across from the city of Amboise, which could be seen on the high bank opposite the camp. The Isle of St. John had been chosen for the meeting. It lay low in the river between the Franks and Amboise, quietly massaged by the Loire. From either bank of the river it could be viewed in its entirety. No trap would be laid there.

Tents stood in a semi-circle around the main campfire, all facing the river. Food was being prepared and a hearty greeting met the king and his queen. The soldiers rose as the entourage pulled in, taking provisions and belongings from the wagons to convey them to where their ruler would reside over the next few days.

Once their belongings were unloaded and a warm meal was in their stomachs, Clovis left Clotild in order to meet with Gerard and Aurelian, to discuss the details of the next day's parley. Gerard assured his friends that the final matters had been settled as to how and when the conference would begin. A meeting with Marcus, secretary to Alaric, held earlier in the day, had resolved those issues.

As Clovis listened, he peered across the river. He could make out the campfires of the Visigoths just east of the city of Amboise. Somewhere over there, Clovis thought, Alaric stands. He wondered if Alaric returned his gaze.

The commotion of soldiers getting up to relieve themselves gave rise to the same need in Clovis, and so his day began. Stepping out of his tent he shivered in the morning chill. He urinated on the roots of a nearby oak tree, then he groaned and stretched out the kinks in his back. Standing still for a moment, he enjoyed the chatter of birds, the caws of ravens and the distant crow of a rooster, before returning to his tent. Once inside he looked at Clotild, still peaceful in her slumber. What little he had heard of angels made him wonder if this was what they looked like. There was nothing in her countenance but peace. No remorse or regret, no anxiety or cunning. Only peace. He gently and reluctantly shook her awake.

"It's morning," he whispered.

Clotild moaned softly, rolled over and looked into her husband's face and smiled her acquiescence to the beginning of another day.

A light breakfast of bread and fruit was waiting when the king and queen emerged from their tent. Clovis was not especially hungry, only able to nibble at piece of bread.

Afterwards, Clotild braided his hair, parting it down the middle of his head. She said nothing of the gray hairs which were infiltrating his locks. When she was done, Clovis returned to his tent to don his brightest, most regal tunic. The blue and red trim on the sleeves and collar of the white shirt lent him an air of formality that pleased him. He tied the shirt at the waist with a leather belt.

Aurelian prepared to accompany him, as did a contingent of four soldiers he'd chosen with Gerard's help. The number of escorts had been previously agreed upon, and care was taken to select soldiers that would fight ably, if the need arose. Aurelian also recognized the need for men who could be dignified, even diplomatic if that was demanded. The latter was a requirement somewhat harder to satisfy among the men. At last, however, he had them.

Gerard was charged with the care of Clotild and would stay with her in camp. Though no traps were expected, there was always the possibility of treachery. Gerard was ready, just in case.

Six Franks climbed aboard a small boat that launched into the waters of the Loire. At almost the same instant, another boat, also bearing six men, entered the current of the river from the opposite shore.

Alaric's preparations were meticulous. As host of the meeting, he'd done everything in his power to make the occasion a pleasant one, hoping to charm Clovis into an agreement. The previous day, Alaric's men had rafted to the island an array of tables, chairs, tents and cooking gear; making ready for a time of feasting as well as for the business of peacemaking.

Having a shorter trip to the island, Alaric and his men arrived several minutes before Clovis. He quickly disembarked and, taking two of his attendants along, went to the northern side of the island in time to see the Franks land. Still too far away to call out, Alaric continued his approach, watching as Clovis offered a hand to Aurelian who was struggling to get out of the small boat. Never having spent much time in a boat, Aurelian, was uncertain of his footing. He lost his balance and, unable to reach his King's hand, fell over backwards into the river, rising from the waves just as Alaric spoke his welcome.

"Greetings, Clovis!"

Clovis turned, leaving Aurelian to regain what dignity he could, already regretting this indelicate start, and smiled the most confident smile he could manage as he faced his host.

"And greetings to you! I presume I'm addressing Alaric?"

"You presume correctly," said Alaric as he bowed. "And if you'll secure your boat…" he looked at Aurelian and grinned with good humor, "…and your men, I'll lead you to our meeting place. A feast is waiting."

At the invitation, and remembering Theodoric's treachery toward Odoacer, Aurelian came quickly to the side of his king, still dripping wet, and whispered, "My lord."

Clovis gave the most subtle nod, acknowledging the need for caution, and then said to Alaric, "I'm honored."

"I'm attended by only two men," said Alaric, as he looked at the soldiers with Clovis, "because the others are preparing for your arrival." He pointed toward them, only about a hundred yards away and accomplished, in the same act, a gesture of trust and a warning of caution against taking advantage of his small welcoming party.

A few minutes later, the Franks and Visigoths, now properly introduced, stood before tables filled with duck, venison, sausage, bread, cheese and wine.

"My breakfast was small, Alaric. This is a tempting table."

"Please, enjoy," was all the invitation anyone needed. Clovis lifted a roast duck, but waited to take his first bite until the eagerness of the Visigoths convinced him that the food was not only safe, but desirable as well. The precaution didn't escape Alaric's notice, nor did it surprise him.

The food was good and they ate well into the afternoon, with great energy, but drinking moderately, keeping an eye on each other while putting on the appearance of congeniality. They avoided talk of borders, armies or nations, speaking, rather, of the food, the hunt, the river, and those who cannot boat, a discussion that brought color to Aurelian's cheeks and laughter to the gathering. Once sated, Alaric and Clovis took a walk—once around the island—to settle their stomachs before sitting down to talk about peace.

Setting out down the shoreline, Clovis cast a cautious eye toward the southern bank of the river, observing the troops Alaric had brought with him. He was encouraged to see that Alaric's soldiers numbered only what might be expected for an occasion such as this: enough to do battle if necessary, but not enough to deny the hope of negotiations. There was nothing to suggest treachery, and Clovis began to enjoy the stroll.

"It's a good land, Gaul, isn't it?" asked Alaric, having noticed the scrutiny of Clovis.

"A rich land," affirmed Clovis.

"Richer, now that Rome is gone!" Alaric laughed a single, "ha!"

"I like to think so," returned Clovis, remembering the fallen Syagrius, offered up for the sacrifice by Alaric, the boy king, "though we both played a part in that."

"You more than I," Alaric tried to sound conciliatory.

As the walk led the two around the island, on to the northern side, Alaric took his own investigative look at the troops Clovis had gathered. He too was encouraged and relieved.

"It appears we'll be able to do our work, eh, Alaric?"

"It appears so to us both."

They continued on in a silence broken only by the sound of the river. The walk concluded with the men seating themselves in the shade of a tent, lounging comfortably on the chairs and cushions Alaric had provided. The secretaries sat next to their respective leaders as the negotiations began.

Clovis did not waste time.

"You've asked for this meeting to shape a peace agreement."

"Yes," Alaric affirmed.

"Are you fearing an attack from me?"

Alaric sat upright. He'd expected Clovis to be forthright, but not quite this bold. Alaric had heard that Clovis was adept at matters of state. He had expected more tact. Even Marcus tensed at the words.

"Your reputation as a diplomat precedes you, Clovis. Would you ask such a direct question at the outset?"

"My good Alaric, I only want to arrive at an agreement as quickly as you do. There's no point in wasting each other's time. Either you fear an attack from me, so you seek peace, or you fear attack from others, so you seek alliance. I only want to know what's expected of me and what's hoped for by you."

Alaric was still off-balance. He'd not been expecting this. Aurelian's guess had been correct that directness would work to his King's advantage. As he watched Alaric's face redden, he was glad that he'd advised Clovis to take such a direct route.

"I fear attack from no one!"

Chapter 17 *Alaric: 502 CE*

Feeling unsure of himself, Alaric chose to take a conservative approach. At least, he thought, that might give me some time to sort things out...time to determine how much I should betray to this Frank...time to consider how much I should offer.

"No, certainly not," said Clovis.

"It's only that every border skirmish we have hurts both our peoples," said Alaric. "We should do what we can to better their lot."

So, thought Clovis, we will dawdle in negotiations!

The talks could have gone on much longer than they did, but the avenue Alaric chose to follow completely convinced Clovis that there was no reason for Alaric to call this conference other than the fear of unprovoked attack from the Franks. It was that particular fear that gave rise to this conference, not border disputes, not the need of alliance to ward off other enemies, but fear of the Franks, and nothing more. That determination on the part of Clovis helped shorten the talks. Clovis knew how to proceed and Alaric seemed glad to follow any course that promised a signed peace pact.

They proceeded to negotiate throughout the day, through the night and into the next day. There were boundaries to agree upon, words to clarify and documents to be drawn up. Aurelian and his counterpart, Marcus, were kept busy and enjoyed a guarded camaraderie as they worked in their similar roles.

Before two full days had passed; days filled with more detail than drama, more punctuation than declaration, more questions from Aurelian and Marcus than squabbles between Alaric and Clovis, a pact was agreed upon, drawn up and signed. The Franks bid farewell to the Visigoths, and the Visigoths to the Franks, and the two groups parted company.

Sitting quietly in the back of the boat until they were out of ear shot, Aurelian spoke, "Alaric's afraid of you, you know."

"Yes," said Clovis, "I knew that early yesterday."

"If he's afraid of you, I wouldn't trust him. If he ever becomes more afraid of someone else, he'll drop this agreement without a second thought."

"I know. I never trust a weak ruler."

"I wouldn't call him weak, my lord. A poor leader, perhaps. But not weak. He has armies and alliances enough. Even though you're Theodoric's brother-in-law, don't forget, Alaric is his son-in-law. I'd keep a close eye on him."

Marcus watched the boat containing Clovis and his company as it moved toward the north bank of the Loire.

"I don't know if he'll honor the pact, my lord."

"What makes you say that?" asked Alaric, his gaze not shifting from the departing Franks.

"He knows...he knows that you fear him."

"I don't fear him!"

"No, sir, of course not." Marcus retreated, "I meant that he knows this pact is for protection rather than for friendship."

Alaric didn't disagree. He knew Marcus was right.

"Many agreements are motivated in the same way."

"True," said Marcus. "But I'd watch him, just the same."

"He won't attack us! He'll honor the agreement."

Alaric sounded like he was trying to convince himself. In truth, he wasn't sure that he believed his own words. At least for now he was safe...at least for a while. He watched the boat bearing Clovis reach the opposite bank and he wondered how long it would be before the King of the Franks would return.

Chapter 18

The Alemanni
504 CE

Heading south, past the city of Cambrai, the messenger took a long look at the activity in and around the town. There were people going about their business at the marketplace and the road was crowded with merchants. Trade appeared more vital here than it had in many other places along the messenger's path. He went on, riding toward Soissons, as the sun dipped behind the trees.

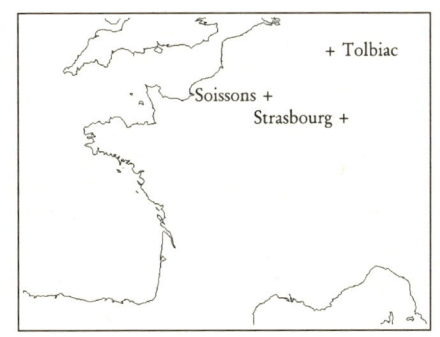

There was still snow alongside the road. An early spring had melted most of what had fallen, but a particularly wet winter dropped enough snow that dirty slush still remained in shaded places.

Wearied by the long journey from Cologne, but knowing that his destination was near, the messenger took a deep breath and decided not to rest on this night. He continued riding, startling an occasional nocturnal animal, arriving in Soissons just as the first light of dawn was casting its ruby glow on the horizon.

He found the residence of Clovis, a distinctive Roman building, and made his way, through guards and officials, to the presence of the king, himself. There, in spite of his exhaustion, the messenger began a spirited recitation of the news with which he'd been charged to bring.

"Slow down, young man!" said Clovis. "It's too early for such a quick story. Take a breath…" Clovis took a breath with the messenger and slowed the pace of his own speech, "…begin again." Clovis leaned forward in his throne, prepared now to listen.

"Yes sir," said the young messenger, trying now to regain his composure after being censured by the king. He returned to the beginning of his tale. "Your kinsman, Siegbert, sends me. He's under attack and needs your help. The Alemanni have begun to invade."

"The Alemanni?" Clovis raised an eyebrow. Over the years, Gerard had mentioned the Alemanni more than once. They had a formidable reputation, and the possibility that they might now be a threat unsettled Clovis.

"As I left Cologne, they were moving toward us." The young man paused as he recalled the frantic preparations that were underway as he left his home. "Luckily we were warned early by our spies and we we're preparing for them, but king Siegbert believes this is only the beginning. He thinks that Cologne is simply the door to Gaul. He doesn't think the Alemanni will stop with us. Will you help?"

Clovis didn't miss the all too obvious hint. He knew he couldn't risk a challenge from the east. He was glad he'd met with Alaric. With his southern border reasonably secure, at least for the time being, he felt comfortable saying. "Yes, tell Sigismond we'll help."

The young man turned to leave, but Clovis could see the fatigue in his determined eyes.

"Wait," he said, "you'll stay here for the night. Your message won't be delayed enough to matter. You'll outdistance us well enough tomorrow."

"Yes sir," said the messenger. He was close to collapsing and with the prospect of rest, he very nearly fell where he stood. Clovis called for a servant to lead the young man to sleeping quarters where the messenger dropped asleep before the servant closed the door.

"You're going to war again," said Clotild. Clovis paused and looked at his wife. "I can tell, you know. It's in your eyes."

Clovis flashed a smile. He knew there was no point in trying to trick Clotild. He'd stopped trying long ago. He shrugged in acknowledgment of the truth and returned to his thoughts of the Alemanni and the coming battle. Clotild's sense of his moods was unfailing. The mood for battle was one she'd come to recognize too clearly. She didn't like it, but she'd learned to live with it.

"I have a gift for you, then," she said, hoping to draw her husband away from his concerns, if only for a moment. Clovis allowed himself to be distracted and looked up at his wife. "Stay here," she said, exiting with a spring in her step that seemed more lively than usual. She was gone only a moment, then Clovis saw her peek around the corner of the doorway. She stepped out slowly, using her body to hide the gift.

"Show me," said Clovis. "What is it?" He thought Clotild was especially beautiful when she was being coy.

"I hope you don't mind," she said, "I've done some work on your shield."

Clovis was cautious, trying to determine whether he should be angry or not. He was protective of his battle gear, and normally, Clotild would never touch it. That was as it should be. Curious, he spoke tentatively, "Yes?"

"A hermit gave some material to me," she said sheepishly, "he said it would protect you." She didn't want to appear superstitious. She pulled out the shield. "I hope you like it."

Clovis watched as Clotild brought his shield into view. Once it had been dirty and worn. It had served him long and well, but now it was transformed. The once aged and dull shield was now bright and distinctive. The blue cloth with the woven patterns of lilies had been sewn around the shield and it looked for the first time in its existence, like the shield of a king.

He stood and took the shield from his wife and looked at it closely. "I do like it!" his voice carried a tone of honest admiration. He lifted it up to check its weight and balance, turning it to see it in different light.

"The hermit said it will protect you," Clotild repeated.

"And I'm certain it will," said Clovis, though he knew the decoration wouldn't last long against a swordsman. He set the shield against the wall so they could both stand back and admire it. He put his arm around the waist of his smiling queen and silently wondered if such a distinctive shield would make him a better target on the battlefield.

Since the messenger had disappeared from sight, having hastened ahead of the Franks to tell Siegbert that help was on the way, five days had passed. It would be another eight days before Clovis and his men would reach Cologne. Word had gone out to the Franks and more were joining in the march to Cologne each day.

Clovis, riding at the head of the troops, keeping a steady but relaxed pace, turned to Gerard, who rode next to him.

"What do you think our chances are against the Alemanni?"

Gerard was silent for a moment. For once in his life he was not confident that victory was theirs. In the distant past the Alemanni had been no more than an odd assortment of plunderers, but time had brought them together into a nation. Rome had felt the sting of their army on more than one occasion.

"They have a reputation for being brave in battle…even fierce," said Gerard, "Daniel Dremrud, their king, has never been defeated, I'm told."

"But can *we* defeat him?" Clovis asked. He was impressed at the way Gerard studied potential enemies. He couldn't remember a time when he'd asked Gerard a question about the military strengths or strategies of an adversary that his friend hadn't answered with certitude. As he listened to him now, though, he was concerned by Gerard's hesitancy.

"Anyone can be defeated..." Gerard pursed his lips and inhaled deeply through his nose, "Yes, anyone, even Daniel Dremrud and his Alemanni."

"I remember my father saying that Daniel's father was a great king from Britain," Clovis mused.

"Yes. It's true. Daniel's father fought the Saxons while your father sheltered them. But he didn't have any connection with the Alemanni. I don't know how Daniel became their king. Some wedding alliance I suppose. But ever since his reign began, the Alemanni have been warring."

"I'll be curious to see him," said Clovis. Then, almost as if he was persuading himself, he added, "Our army's strong. Our chances are as good as they could be."

Gerard nodded slowly, uncertainly, and they rode on.

On the morning of their eleventh day out, scouts informed Clovis that the troops of the Alemanni were nearing Cologne, having already crossed the Rhine. Clovis decided to approach from the south, going to Trier and then turning north. Messages were dispatched to Siegbert detailing the plans. They would converge southwest of Cologne.

Late on the day before battle, Siegbert, who had brought his armies wide to the west around the approaching Alemanni, joined Clovis on the southwestern edge of the Plain of Tolbiac. The officers and kings conferred as the troops settled in for a night of fitful pre-battle sleep.

"The Alemanni will arrive soon," briefed Clovis, "and they are, by now, aware of our strength. We've captured several Alemanni scouts. We can assume we've missed others and that reports are getting back to Daniel Dremrud." Clovis tipped his head toward his cousin, "Siegbert and I are confident we can prevail tomorrow." Even as he said it, Clovis hoped he sounded convincing. He shot a glance at Gerard, who kept his gaze downward.

Sentries were set, and though no one expected any activity before morning, few Franks slept soundly.

As the morning light grew, Siegbert and Clovis watched a long line of Alemanni soldiers appear on the opposite side of the plain. Low clouds hung in the sky and the air smelled like snow. The call to

Chapter 18 *The Alemanni: 504 CE*

battle was sounded and the Franks moved forward, readying their franciscas for flight. They marched down a slight grade toward the northeast to meet the Alemanni head-on. They walked in a tight group and Clovis and Siegbert watched from the rise.

Clovis noted the cold day, confident that his men were capable of fighting an extended battle. But as he watched the enemy troops advancing, he knew that the Alemanni would not fall easily to defeat. They marched together, clearly a well trained army.

As warriors arrived within throwing distance, Clovis and Siegbert could see axes and lances being launched. Then, very quickly, the field became chaotic with battle, only the flying braids of hair distinguishing the Franks from their enemy. Men on both sides of the conflict bled too soon. Yells of challenge were soon overtaken by moans of the dying.

It was not long into the battle that Clovis caught movement out of the corner of his eye. He turned and saw, to his horror, another line of Alemanni forming to his right.

"Damn!" he said, with horror in his voice.

Siegbert turned away from the battle to see what Clovis saw…what the scouts had failed to see.

"No!" was all that Siegbert could utter. All the Franks were in battle with none in reserve. And now these additional Alemanni were flanking them.

The Franks would need all the help they could get and since there were no other reserves, Clovis and Siegbert dug their heels into the ribs of their mounts and made for the battle. Having some idea where their commanders had entered the fray, the two leaders parted to get warnings to them as quickly as possible. Clovis could see Gerard near the southern end of the battle but Chloderic, Siegbert's son and commander, was considerably further to the west. The reserves of the Alemanni would reach the battle near Clovis first. He arrived just in time to warn his men. He shouted and pointed toward the new threat as he rode toward Gerard. Clovis reached his friend and jumped from his horse just as the Alemanni swept into the battle like a huge wave. So fast was their engagement that almost as soon as they attacked, they were past where Clovis stood. His shield served him well and he emerged from the assault unscathed. A glance at his shield surprised him as it too had suffered no damage. But the onslaught exacted a devastating price elsewhere. Many of the newer recruits, who had joined the Franks on their journey eastward, fled for their lives.

Clovis watched as the Alemanni drove further and further into the battle that was quickly shaping into a rout. In the distance on a small rise in the plain, Clovis could see Siegbert. He was off his horse too, fighting valiantly, but new enemies arose with each one that Siegbert cut down.

"My Gods have left me," said Clovis out loud, his voice echoing the disbelief he felt. "My Gods have abandoned me! This is Ragnarok!" Stories his father told him of Ragnarok, the Day of Doom, flashed in his mind. This would be a day to mourn. Clovis shook his head and tears came to his eyes, as he watched the battle worsen. Then, for reasons he couldn't explain, he remembered what Solemnus had told him about the power of Clotild's God—how this God had defeated the Philistines and the Assyrians. And then he recalled the odd farewell Aurelian had offered to him as he prepared for this campaign. "My King," he'd said, with real concern in his voice, "If the need arises, don't be afraid to pray." Aurelian had never offered such advice before. Clovis was aware that his secretary held to the same religion Clotild did, but never before had it come forth in their dealings. The farewell had surprised and unsettled him.

Clovis was taught as a child: "Brave men can live well anywhere, cowards dread all things." In an instant he decided it might actually be a brave act to pray. He would not be afraid of it and he accepted it as his last resort.

He looked up at the clouds, wondering if his words would penetrate them, and prayed, "Lord Jesus, whom Clotild says to be God, grant your aid to me now. I make a vow that if you will give me this victory, I will believe in you and be baptized in your name. My own Gods have abandoned me. Rescue me!"

He looked back to the battle, instantly ashamed at what now felt like weakness, cowardice, but wondering, nonetheless, if something might result. In the mass of men he picked out Siegbert again, just in time to see a thrown ax take him down as it struck him in the foot. Surely, thought Clovis, the battle's over. No sooner had the thought crossed his mind than a man appeared on the hill next to where Siegbert lay. His elaborate battle dress showed that he was more than a mere foot-soldier. In the brief instants during which events were unfolding, Clovis thought, "So, that's Daniel!"

The Alemanni king raised his own ax to finish the job of killing Siegbert, but he never brought it down. For, at that same moment, one of Siegbert's men pierced Daniel's heart with a well aimed thrust of his lance. The King's last scream cut through the noise of the battle, and many of the nearby Alemanni turned their attention in time to see Daniel, their king, fall dead.

Chapter 18 *The Alemanni: 504 CE*

The next seconds brought a turn in the battle that Clovis could not have hoped for a moment before. The collective gasp of the Alemanni allowed the Franks to regroup and brace for the next round of battle. Men lifted up their comrades, and soldiers, who a moment earlier had been ready to fall, now regained their balance. Siegbert pulled himself up with the help of one of his men to show that he still lived. Inspired by the sight, his men began to fight with new energy.

Without their own king, the Alemanni commanders hesitated and that hesitation brought fear to the hearts of their soldiers. It was the critical moment. From then on they fought in retreat and soon they were on the run, with Clovis leading the Franks after them.

Six weeks of skirmishes along the Rhine assured that the Alemanni were in full retreat. Near Strasbourg, the defeated army crossed the river, running south, hoping for Theodoric's protection. Before long Clovis decided to end the pursuit and camped his troops outside of Strasbourg, with the intention of returning home. He ordered a small number of scouts to continue on, to make sure that the Alemanni weren't regrouping for another attack. While they waited for the scouts to return, he encouraged the men to celebrate their victory. They obeyed willingly, enjoying the wine and the most succulent pork they'd ever tasted. Soon, the days spent waiting for the final scouting parties became weeks, and just as the weeks became enough to encompass a month, the scouting party returned, bringing with them a messenger from the court of Theodoric.

His voice was clear as he spoke, "Theodoric congratulates you on your victory over the Alemanni."

Clovis put up a hand and the messenger stopped. With wonder in his voice, Clovis said to Gerard, "He knows already!"

"Runners must have gone to him directly from the battle," said Gerard.

Clovis shook his head in amazement. "No, I think maybe Theodoric knew about this from the beginning." He motioned for the messenger to continue.

"Theodoric says his wars have been the most profitable that have ended in moderation and he advises you to pursue the fleeing Alemanni no further."

Clovis and Gerard looked at each other, surprised that Theodoric would try to exercise his influence this far north. Clovis waved the messenger to a halt again. He turned to the leader of the scouts.

"How did you find the Alemanni?"

"They won't be fighting again soon, sir. They're running for cover. I've seen nothing that would make me think they're regrouping to fight."

Clovis accepted the report and summarily dismissed the advice of Theodoric. It was irrelevant. They would go no further, and, indeed, would soon be going home. Once again, he encouraged the waiting messenger to continue.

"And lastly," said the envoy, "Theodoric says that a gift is coming to you in Soissons from your sister, his queen. When you return, you'll find a harper has arrived. May your journeys be safe." His message complete, the messenger stood back and awaited what response might follow.

"A musician will be a welcomed addition to the court, eh Gerard?" said Clovis.

"Perhaps he can play songs of your victory against Daniel!"

Clovis laughed and invited the messenger to share a meal with the men before beginning his journey back to Italy.

After his own repast, Gerard stood and rubbed his buttocks. "The men should be preparing to leave," he said. "Perhaps I should get them started."

"Before you do,..." said Clovis.

"Yes?"

"I need one more thing. I must find a Christian—a man of wisdom—someone who will instruct me on the way home." Gerard wasn't sure how to respond and he remained silent, his confusion evident. Clovis tried to explain by saying, "I made a pledge, Gerard." His captain and friend bowed in acknowledgment, ever respectful.

Gerard entered Strasbourg that same afternoon and, after making inquiries at the Cathedral, came to stand before Bishop Vedastus of Toul, who had been meeting with the bishop of Strasbourg.

"Yes, my son," said Vedastus upon hearing the request, "I would be honored to accompany and teach your king." He'd heard a great deal about Clovis, and was excited to meet him. Gerard, pleased at his own luck, was courteous as he led the bishop of Toul out of Strasbourg, on toward the camp of his king.

It was nearly dusk when they arrived. The temperatures were beginning to drop and Vedastus pulled his cloak more closely around him as Gerard introduced him to his leader.

"I'm most grateful, Father, that you've agreed to join us." Clovis reached out a hand to the bishop.

Chapter 18 *The Alemanni: 504 CE*

"The pleasure is mine, sir," replied Vedastus as he took the hand and shook it. "I'm certain that I'll enjoy the journey, and I expect we'll find much to talk about." He bobbed his head up and down as he said the words.

Clovis nodded at the compliment and said, "Yes, Father, indeed. There's much to discuss."

Chapter 19

Baptism
504-505 CE

As they watched the embers of campfires pulse and fade, Clovis and Vedastus talked. Vedastus was enjoying his evening conversations with the king. There was no need to defend the faith now, only explain it.

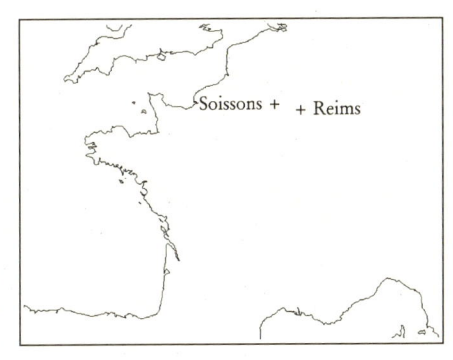

"He's more than a good shepherd, Vedastus," said Clovis one night, in response to one image the bishop had presented, "He's a great warrior too!"

Vedastus saw how little impressed Clovis was with the picture of Christ as the Good Shepherd and how important the image of a conquering king was to him. He humored his student and said, "Yes, Clovis, he is a great warrior."

"Tell me, though," said Clovis, "does he help those who follow him?"

"So he's promised."

"I'll welcome his strength in battle." Clovis poked at the coals with a stick, still captured by the picture of a hopeless battle transformed into victory. "If my Gods have turned away from me, it must be because they can no longer come to my aid." A rush of memories came to Clovis of his father assuring him that the Gods would assist him if he proved heroic. "Perhaps they're in their own battle," he said, wondering if his father was with the Gods, battling giants, even now.

"God is a God of power," said Vedastus, "and His power is greater than that of other gods."

"Yes, Vedastus, I'm convinced. But this Jesus...was he heroic?"

Vedastus had never thought of Jesus in such terms. But now he did, and after taking a moment to choose his words he said, "Heroic? I should say so—though many didn't think so. He never fought in battle."

"I've been taught that a coward thinks he'll live forever if he can avoid battle."

"Oh but Clovis, there's so much more to being heroic—so much more! Our Lord knew he would die. And he faced death heroically, going willingly to the cross."

Clovis didn't try to hide his confusion. It was a look Vedastus had seen numerous times in these last few days,. Clovis was clearly interested in who Jesus was, but the theological concepts were stretching him. The bishop knew it was time to teach again.

"You've heard about our Lord's birth and about what he taught his disciples. But you haven't heard how the people received his words."

"They were good words. I would think the people were impressed," said Clovis.

"True. But not all of the impressions were favorable. Not everyone saw them as good words. The chief priests and scribes were threatened by what he had to say and plotted with Judas, one of the disciples, to have Jesus killed."

"Truly?"

"Yes. And eventually, he was killed. Crucified...nailed on a cross of wood."

Clovis came to his feet. He struggled to comprehend the injustice. His eyes shifted back and forth as he looked for meaning in the killing of this Jesus. Sacrifice was understandable, familiar, but only to a reasonable purpose. For a man to die there had to be more—an offense, a crime, or a kingdom to win. He assumed his most commanding posture.

"If I and my men had been there, we would have avenged his death!" he spouted.

Vedastus looked up at the indignant Clovis and smiled in warm amusement.

"Pope Symmachus would be pleased with your enthusiasm."

The two traveled on toward Soissons, and Vedastus taught Clovis what he could about faith and the scriptures, about the Lord Jesus and the Apostle Paul. The story of the blinding light Paul experienced on the road to Damascus intrigued Clovis.

"Perhaps I'll see that light someday."

"Possibly," replied Vedastus. He'd heard that particular hope expressed by more than a few new Christians. Rarely was the hope fulfilled.

They talked about baptism, and Vedastus, inwardly humbled that he was playing a part in the King's life, agreed to speak to Remigius about baptism for Clovis.

By the time they made Soissons, Clovis had heard about the soul, heaven, salvation, and the Trinity. "Augustine says that the Trinity is

Chapter 19 *Baptism: 504-505 CE*

like he who loves, that which is loved, and the power of love," said Vedastus. Clovis took it all in. But what interested him most was what he learned of God's might. His questions to Vedastus about God's power were nearly endless. With such a omnipotent ally, Clovis wondered, would he ever face defeat again?

Clotild could scarcely believe the words that had come from her husband's mouth, "I'm going to be baptized," he'd said, "Your God is greater than my Gods." She turned the words over and over in her head, "I'm going to be baptized." She made certain she was awake, that these words were not the trick of a dream. He related the story of his victory over the Alemanni, adding details she'd not yet heard. He told her of his prayer on the field of battle, and she listened with all her attention. When he told her of his discussions with Vedastus, though, Clotild barely heard the tale, lost in an ecstasy deeper than any sleep, more profound than any dream.

Her continual prayers had not been in vain, and the thanks she offered now was more fervent than any prayer she'd ever voiced. Years of anxiety, born in a marriage to a non-believer, now knew relief. In spite of the assurances of Avitus and Remigius, only now did Clotild release the fears she'd held for her husband's soul and the questions she held about the fate of her own. Her prayers now flowed in a bright, fresh stream of gratitude.

Clotild brought her attention back to her husband only when she heard him say, "Vedastus has agreed to speak with Remigius about the baptism." The simple statement caused Clotild to realize the urgency of this moment. The distractions of a king are many and this change of heart might soon dissolve in a melange of state matters. Her attention to her husband was sincere now, but accompanied by necessary planning. At the first opportunity, Clotild composed a message to Remigius urging haste, lest her husband's resolve fade.

Clovis continued to talk of the battle. He talked with Aurelian, his mother, and his sisters. He told the story to Tranquillinus, who nodded politely throughout the telling but seemed unsure about the tale's significance. The story Clovis told of his prayer, and of the victory that followed, was soon common knowledge in the streets of Soissons. The Christians in the town spoke of "the miracle" while Franks who still believed in the Gods of their ancestors murmured about the news with serious reservation. Basina listened to her son's report, pondering what it might mean, but kept her reservations to herself. She watched her son closely, quietly, looking for any suggestion that his true feelings, his first motivations, might be other than spiritual.

The church in Soissons was too small for the baptism of a king. Plans were made to hold the rite in the Church of St. Martin, in Reims, on Christmas Day. Though the day of baptism was nearly a month away, Clovis went with Clotild to Reims, to meet with the bishop.

Remigius looked well. It was a good day for him and his joints were less painful than usual. Clearly, though, he had much on his mind, and he tried to dispense quickly with the amenities, only to have Clovis present him with the gift of an exquisite silver bowl, tiny, though crafted in the finest detail, ribbed, lustrous and lovely.

"No damaged goods this time," said a smiling king.

Remigius took the bowl and turned to gaze out the window. He turned over the bowl in his hands, several times, taking in each detail. Then he spoke.

"When Vedastus informed me of your desire to be baptized," he said, "we began to make arrangements immediately." He turned around to face the king, smiling grandly at Clovis. "And I will use this bowl at your baptism." Clovis smiled his appreciation but said nothing. Remigius walked toward the new convert and continued. "You must know, Clovis, that with your baptism, you'll gain new support from the Church. Many of the people of Gaul, those who are believers, are already celebrating. I have no doubt that this will prove to be a good thing for you," He paused and stroked his chin before adding, "...and a blessing for us."

Remigius let his thoughts drift back through the years that had passed since he'd walked along the river Eure with Avitus, making plans that seemed too far-fetched to consider seriously. For thirteen years he'd hoped and waited, encouraged others and sought encouragement himself. During those years the Church had survived the challenges of the Arian Church. And now, the most powerful ruler in Gaul was prepared to take the one step that would fulfill the dream Remigius had held onto for so long. He took in a deep breath and his smile faded. "But I am concerned about one thing." He looked at the floor and frowned before looking back up at Clovis, "I'm concerned about your own men." Remigius walked back to his desk and sat. "You're their leader, Clovis. Will they follow you when you no longer follow their gods?"

Chapter 19 *Baptism: 504-505 CE*

Clovis hadn't even considered the possibility that his men wouldn't follow him. "I've always allowed them to believe as they wished," he said slowly, wondering how his men might be dealing with his conversion. "I hope their loyalty won't end when I enter the Church, but I can't assure you that my men will follow me."

"They will," said Clotild. She stroked her husband's arm. "They trust you."

"If they don't,..." Remigius tried to be realistic while still hopeful. He thought about the thousands of souls that could be brought to right belief, adding to the strength of the Church. But such thoughts were being overshadowed by the possibility of failure. Might these warriors really rebel against this man for converting to the Christian faith? Remigius frowned slightly, scratched his cheek with his long index finger and, his voice softer, ended his sentence, "...may God be with us all."

The day of baptism brought crowds to the streets of Reims. Soldiers paraded and children marched beside them, mimicking their every move and gesture, using sticks for swords. The faithful were celebrating Christmas but the baptism of the king added immeasurably to the festivities. The weather was always a question this time of year, but God was smiling on the people of Reims. The sky was clear, the wind low, and the chill slight, all serving to swell the already substantial crowd.

The events moved people toward the Cathedral. A procession of clergy led the way, moving slowly from the residence of the bishop. They processed with the Gospels, with the Cross, and with banners. They sang songs praising God, heightening the fervor of the crowds.

Remigius held the King's hand. Since early morning he'd been with Clovis, encouraging him with last minute words of instruction. Now, seeing the enormity of the celebration, Clovis asked, "Remigius, is the Kingdom of Heaven being delivered to me today?"

"No, my King," said Remigius, smiling, "only an entrance to the road that leads there."

They entered the Cathedral and walked toward the altar, keeping time to the chanting voices of the choir:

"Rejoice and be glad, Thou delight of the angels,
"Rejoice Virgin of the Lord, Thou joy of the Prophets,
"Rejoice, Blessed Lady, the Lord is with Thee."

Dressed in his most elaborate priestly raiment, striking in its colors of gold and burgundy, warmed in its bulky layers, Remigius stood before the baptistery. His heart beat faster as he looked out over the many notables who had gathered from remote places in Gaul. His brother, Principius, was there of course, as was Solemnus of Chartres and Eleutherius of Tournai. Lupus of Bayeux was present and so was Gallicinus of Bordeaux, who was accompanied by Bishop Ruricius, an old and kindly man, who had recently been exiled from Limoges by the Visigoths. Count Arnoul of Reims joined them as well. Without a doubt it was a distinguished collection of dignitaries. And they were all conscious of the importance of this particular baptism.

The choir continued to chant:

"Rejoice, for the angel told Thee of the joy of the world,
"Rejoice, for Thou didst bear the maker and Lord,
"Rejoice, for Thou art worthy to be the Mother of Christ."

White curtains and canopies were hanging throughout the Cathedral, lending it a further air of celebration. There were tapestries as well, showing the story of Creation and the life of Kings David and Solomon. The Baptism of Christ, the Crucifixion, and the Apocalypse were also depicted in the woven works of art. Candles burned and the smell of incense confused some, delighted others, but interested all, for it was the first time they'd experienced this innovation in Christian worship.

"The sea saw the Lord and was afraid;
"The waves came to meet him and adored Him.
"When he saw this, Peter cried: 'God have mercy upon me!'"

With the last lines of the chant, at the direction of Remigius, Clovis stepped forward toward the font. He wore a long white tunic; his hair hung loose around his shoulders. Clotild walked beside him and Albofleda and Lantechild followed, both looking pale and frightened. Basina chose to stay back and observe.

Gerard was next and then came, to the great surprise of Remigius, a seemingly endless line of Frankish soldiers, filling in behind their king from their places inside and outside of the Cathedral.

Clovis waited, face to face with the bishop, as the warriors continued to file into the nave. Looking above the crowd, Remigius could not see the end of the line. Amazed at what he saw, the bishop stepped forward toward the king and whispered,

Chapter 19 *Baptism: 504-505 CE*

"Have all your men come to be baptized?"

"No Father, only the trustis, my home guard. We met and I asked for their support. They've forsaken their Gods to accept the God of Jesus. But only half are here. Some declined and some have gone north to be with my cousin, Ragnachar."

"But half have come with you!" said the bishop. "Remarkable!"

Remigius stepped back and raised himself to his full height once again. The soldiers finally stopped moving, their line stretching to the door of the Church and beyond. The bishop looked at the guests and then at those awaiting the baptism, cleared his throat and began to speak.

"Welcome brothers and sisters in our Lord Jesus Christ. Peace be to all."

"And to thy spirit," responded the people.

"We give Thee thanks, yea more than thanks, O Lord our God, the Father of our Lord and God and Savior Jesus Christ, for all Thy goodness..."

Remigius offered the liturgy of the baptism, his voice strong enough to reach to the back of the Cathedral, asking questions of the king that assured everyone, Clovis was indeed a believer. And when the bishop was done, he motioned Clovis forward. Clovis stepped to the side of the baptistery and descended two steps to where he awaited the Bishop's next words.

"Bend your neck, Sicamber," Remigius said, "Worship what you have burned and burn what you have worshipped. You are a new creature now and the old one has passed away."

As Clovis bowed his head he thought how strange it was to hear the word "Sicamber" again. The Franks had descended from those called Sicambers, but not since before his father's death had he heard the name of that most ancient tribe.

In the bowl he'd received from Clovis, Remigius lifted water from the font and slowly poured it over the long hair of this man in whom he'd place so many hopes. The water drained through the King's hair and dripped into the baptistry, splashing away the silence which had fallen over those present. Remigius watched as the miracle of baptism cleansed the soul of a king and gave new hope to the Church. Then he touched Clovis on the shoulder and lifted him up.

"Welcome, Clovis," he said.

"Thank you, Father," returned Clovis as he pulled his hair back from his face. He squeezed the water from his locks as he pivoted back toward his wife and stopped his motion when he saw her. Her face carried him back to a visit with Genevieve when he'd first seen

Clotild in the glow of what could only be called 'ecstasy'. It seemed as though his entry into the Christian faith had released a woman bathed in love and pride for her husband and new bliss in the face of God's power. Clovis smiled at his queen and watched a tear roll down her cheek. Clotild choked back a joyous sob and embraced her husband.

Remigius invited the king and queen to stand with him as he baptized Albofleda and Lantechild, both of whom still looked pale. Albofleda stumbled as she approached the font and Lantechild had to help her stand for the baptism. Once the two sisters were baptized, 3000 soldiers, led by Gerard, filed forward. With a blanket pronouncement of baptism for the soldiers and nearly continuous movement, it took nearly three hours to baptize them all.

When the last soldier had undergone the rite, a tired Remigius pronounced a benediction and Clovis led the way out of the church.

In spite of a cold Christmas Day, a large crowd gathered outside the church doors to wish their newly baptized ruler well. Clovis stopped at the door and smiled broadly, waving. From within the crowd a peasant woman approached the king and placed in his hand an iris, hand-carved in wood, and said apologetically, "There are no real flowers this time of year, my lord. Long live the king!"

Clovis, amazed at the workmanship, thanked the woman with all sincerity. The title of 'King' sounded better than it ever had before. He was a Christian now, and the title seemed more appropriate, somehow.

For a few moments Clovis lingered, enjoying the crowd's cheers. Then, chilled by rising winds, Clotild said, "My love, it's cold. Can we go?"

"Yes, please," echoed Lantechild who stood shivering with her sister, Albofleda. "We're freezing!"

Clovis gave in to their pleading. As he descended the steps of the church, the crowd parted to let him pass. They fell in behind the king as he and his family made their way to the great hall of the Governor's palace, where the Christmas table was already spread.

Albofleda and Lantechild both fell ill before the feasting was done. Shaking with chills and both vomiting, they left the hall and suffered through the evening as Basina packed for a hurried journey back to Soissons. Late the next day, upon their arrival home, Tranquillinus was summoned immediately.

Chapter 19 *Baptism: 504-505 CE*

Clovis blamed himself for not having considered how the baptism might affect his sisters' health. He was certain he and his men were also at risk. He kept his concerns inside, waiting patiently for Tranquillinus to arrive. Clotild stood with him, fully aware that he was remembering their first born's fate.

The news of the baptism brought correspondence from many of the bishops of the Church. Germerius wrote to Clovis, as did Verus. From Burgundy, Avitus wrote, "My dear King Clovis, I beg your forgiveness for not attending your baptism. The day of our Lord's birth was also your day. Your ancestors have prepared the way for you. A great destiny awaits, and your decision will open the way to an even greater future for your children. Your faith is our Church's triumph: every battle you fight is a victory for us. Constantinople can boast of a ruler of persuasion. But she's no longer alone in possessing such a bright light. The Western empire now shares in that light."

Even Pope Symmachus wrote to the new convert, saying, "We thank our Lord and God in heaven that He has provided such a helmet of salvation for the Church."

Clovis received the letters graciously but with only the slightest pleasure. His more immediate concern was with his sisters.

Within a week of receiving the letter of Pope Symmachus, Albofleda died. Basina nearly lost herself in mourning, taking only slight comfort from Tranquillinus. Lantechild remained sick and a grieving Clovis held little hope for her. Bishop Principius wasted no time in informing Remigius of Albofleda's death, reminding his brother of Ingomer's death years before. Remigius in return, sent a hasty letter to the king.

Maccolus was again the messenger and Clovis received him warmly.

"Maccolus! I haven't seen you in such a long time. I'm glad to know that you're still with Remigius. I hope you're doing well."

"I am. And I thank you for your welcome. It's not been so long since I've seen you, though. I witnessed your baptism," He paused, awkwardly, "and I'm sorry about your sister's death."

"Thank you." Clovis closed his eyes and heaved a sigh.

Maccolus could think of no comfort to offer and said only, "I have a message from Remigius."

"Yes, of course. What does he have to say?"

Maccolus pulled the letter from his satchel and began to read, "I am deeply grieved by the sorrow you bear over the death of your sister, Albofleda. But we can be consoled, because she who departed from this life ought to be remembered rather than mourned. Such was her life that we believe she was taken up and chosen by God for heaven. She lives that you might have faith."

Clovis was again beginning to doubt the value of the Christian faith. His anger was beginning to rise. Maccolus continued:

"There remains the duty of administering your kingdom and, under God's auspices, you are the head of the people and hold the direction of the realm. Let those who are accustomed to see happy things through you, not see you afflicted by grief. You must be their consoler. Don't let sadness cover the brilliance of your mind and heart. As for your sister's recent passing, she's joined to the choirs of virgins and, in so believing, the King rejoices in heaven."

The letter went on expressing the Bishop's apology for not bringing his words in person, but sending Maccolus instead, "Nevertheless, if you bid me come through this messenger, I'll put aside my work and heed not the severity of winter nor the difficulty of the way, so that with God's help, I can hasten to you."

Clovis let the words settle in his mind. He understood the sentiments and the opportunities, but he wanted nothing from the Church just now.

"Convey my thanks to Remigius, if you would, Maccolus."

"Of course."

"Tell him there's no need for him to make the journey here. I doubt that I would enjoy a visit. Maybe after a while."

"I'll tell him." Maccolus knew his job was done for now. All that was left for him was a return trip to Reims.

Clovis saw to it that Maccolus was fed, but chose not to join him. He was beginning to feel ill.

Chapter 20

A King Renewed
505-506 CE

+ Soissons

"I'm going to die."

"Nonsense," said the aging physician, Tranquillinus. He stood over Clovis, laying another blanket atop the shivering man. "You have a fever, and no wonder, considering all you've been through: warring in the snow, though that was long enough ago that I don't suppose it would be of great importance now…but a baptism of no small significance it seems, and the death of your dear sister, Lord bless her soul. Your veins are a little dried out, that's all. You need to drink fluids and rest."

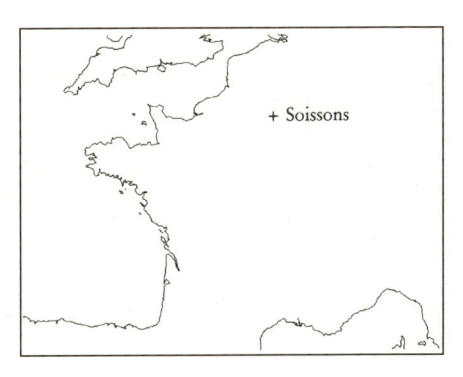

"I'm going to die," repeated Clovis. "It's the baptism. First my son, then my sister and now me."

"If you keep this up, my King, not only will you die, but you'll make me look like a bad physician as well. Think a moment. Your wife, Clotild, is healthy and she's been baptized. Chlodomer too. And Lantechild has recovered. You've simply caught a fever."

Tranquillinus laid yet another blanket upon Clovis, who was still shivering, and then proceeded to administer a dose of hydromel.

"This is what our great Hippocrates calls for," he said. "Now drink it, all of it."

Clovis was not convinced that baptism was harmless, but he did wonder why some sickened and died following the rite while others did not. He drank the hydromel obediently and handed the goblet back to Aurelian.

The potion did its job in short order, evacuating the King's bowel, but his condition over the next day did not improve noticeably.

"We'll have to bleed you some, I think," said the doctor on the following morning, "and maybe administer a clyster."

Clovis was too weak to argue with the doctor and didn't flinch as he was cut for the bleeding. The procedure effected no change in the King's condition. Eventually, Clovis asked Tranquillinus to leave him alone.

Clovis refused the food he was brought and grieved in silence over the loss of Albofleda. He remembered the joy she took in life, and her death infuriated him. He cursed God.

The business of the Franks was being handled. Aurelian set aside his business in Melun to give more time to the administrative needs of his king. As they related to the Alemanni, all of the decisions regarding tribute, assurances of shared glory in battle and shared protection in war, were finalized. There was a slight skirmish with Alaric, but Gerard dealt with it. A short campaign across the Loire brought the Visigoths back to their senses.

Clovis, was fortunate that he could trust his men to act competently. For the time being, he wanted little to do with the affairs of state.

Clotild watched her husband's worsening mood and diminishing energy, and worried more with each day. She was at a loss as to how she might help her husband and turned to Tranquillinus.

"Beyond prayers I can think of little you might do," said the physician. "Prayer is the most powerful medicine. God will not fail our king."

"My prayers are endless, Tranquillinus. But…" Clotild's eyes reddened and began to spill tears. The physician put his arms around her and wiped her face with a towel.

"Come child," he said in his most comforting voice, "think of what your prayers have already done. Don't think your petitions have lost their power."

Even as Tranquillinus spoke, though, he worried. He'd seen patients sicken and die often, and he knew there was a chance that Clovis would actually succumb to this illness. It was the King's mind that was causing his condition to worsen—his fear over his fate, now that he'd been baptized. Until that perceived threat was removed, there would be little anyone could do.

Basina busied herself in the kitchen, not really helping, but occupying herself so she wouldn't think of her son's illness quite so much. The cooks couldn't send her out of the kitchen but they maneuvered Basina in such a way that she didn't interfere in their work. When Tranquillinus found her, she stood by the raised hearth stirring the large black cauldron that hung from the trivet.

"Ah, here you are," said the physician.

Basina tensed upon seeing him, stirring faster, fearing the worst.

"I've been looking for you to assure you that your son is holding his own. I thought you'd want to know."

Chapter 20 *A King Renewed: 505-506 CE*

"Thank you, Tranquillinus. I'm so worried for him." She allowed herself to relax and stopped stirring the stew in favor of wringing her hands. "Do you think he'll recover? Do you really think this baptism has cursed him?"

"Yes, my lady...I mean no, my lady...I mean," Tranquillinus looked at the workers that stood around and, with a pleading look and a tilt of his head, asked them to give them a moment in private. When they were gone, he walked to where Basina was, embraced her lightly and said, "I mean, my dear Basina, I don't believe Clovis has been cursed. And I will do all I can to speed his recovery."

"Thank you," said Basina, her voice hopeful.

There was little more to say. They stood quietly in their embrace until the stew began to boil over.

Theuderic, now fifteen years old, had not visited with his father since the week of the royal baptism. Nearly six months had passed since then—time Theuderic had spent in Tournai, seeing friends and establishing his position as a prince. Now he was summoned by his father.

Theuderic had been told of his father's illness but spared the details. What he'd heard had not concerned him greatly. One report would be cautious, the next hopeful. One would give account of a vital and busy ruler, the next, news of a relapse. He entered the King's bedchamber, expecting to see a strong man who was merely tired or uncomfortable. He expected to see him weak but not emaciated. He was shocked by what awaited him. His father's cheeks were sunken, his color ashen and it looked as though he could barely open his eyes.

"Father?" Theuderic said, his voice shaky.

Clovis opened his eyes and motioned with a roll of his head to a chair near the foot of the bed. Theuderic seated himself, smiling bravely, saying nothing.

"It appears as though we need to talk," said Clovis. Theuderic raised his eyebrows fearfully, his respiration quickened, and he waited for his father's next words.

"We've never spoken about what it means to be a king."

"No father, but is it necessary now?" Theuderic was instantly uncomfortable—more so than he'd been since he could remember. Already this felt like a farewell.

"I want to talk about it now."

"Shouldn't you be resting?"

"No. We need to talk." Theuderic acquiesced. Clovis went on, "My father, your grandfather, was a great chief, Theuderic."

"Yes, father, and so are you!"

Clovis pretended not to hear but took quiet pleasure in his son's compliment. "And his father before him. Merovech, my grandfather, fought against Attila and his Huns."

"Yes," said Theuderic, he heard the stories before, "they were great chiefs."

"Do you know what that means, to be a great chief?"

"To be a great warrior!"

"Yes. But there's..." he coughed a long wheezing cough, "...there's more. There are many great warriors among our people. Gerard, for example. You won't find a greater warrior anywhere, but that doesn't make him a chief." It was difficult for him to carry on the conversation. Theuderic helped his father to a drink. "A chief, Theuderic, must be heroic but he must also be honorable. My father, for a time, lost sight of honor. He lost his land and his people because of it. A chief must be honorable."

Clovis lay his head back on his pillows to catch his breath. Theuderic could see his father's fatigue. Leaning forward from his chair, he touched his father's hand. it was hot from fever.

"You're honorable, father."

"And now, Theuderic, I am a Christian. That makes me more than a chief. It makes me a king, like the people have been calling me. It makes me a king, like the great King, Jesus." Clovis coughed again and thought about Ingomer and Albofleda and looked at his own weakened frame. "But as you can see by looking at me, that fact may not be serving me as well as I could hope."

"Are you dying?" asked Theuderic, choking back a sob.

"I'm afraid I am. Then you will be chief along with Chlodomer and Childebert and Chlotar, your brothers. You're the oldest, though. I hope you'll be the wisest. I was barely older than you when my father died..." His eyes rolled up into his head and his voice trailed off.

"If this is your time to die, father, I'm ready to be chief."

Clovis opened his eyes and he smiled weakly at his son. Theuderic looked a great deal like Nathalie. "How is you mother," he asked.

"She's well. She works hard, but she's well."

"She's a good woman, your mother. I know I hurt her."

"Yes." Theuderic carried his mother's pain with him. Though he loved and admired his father, he had seen his mother cry too many

Chapter 20 *A King Renewed: 505-506 CE*

times at the loss of her one great love not to hold some resentment of his own.

"Surely she understood."

"I don't know," said Theuderic.

Clovis was not listening closely enough to hear the conflict in his son's voice. He had ventured too deeply into his memories. He remembered the early years with Nathalie. They had been good years. But things were different now. He brought his thoughts back to the present.

"You must remember to be honorable, my son…honorable in the eyes of your people and treacherous in the eyes of your enemies. Then you'll have the respect of them both."

"I'll remember, father."

Clovis took a deep breath. "I'm tired. Let me rest."

"Yes father." Theuderic had watched the energy drain from his father's body as they'd spoken. He stood and clasped his father's hand. As he left, Theuderic wiped a tear from his own cheek, a tear that flowed from the struggle between love and anger, between respect and hatred.

Clovis drifted into sleep before Theuderic was out of the door. He dreamt about Nathalie. She was young again, and happy.

Delivering deep bows of courtesy, Tranquillinus came into the study of Bishop Principius and as concisely as he could, stated his concern for the king.

"But how can I help?" asked Principius after hearing the story Tranquillinus brought. "You're the physician."

"Yes," said Tranquillinus, "I am the physician. But as I've said, my efforts are proving less than effective. I find myself unable to help further. It's been nearly a year since my king first fell ill. Some days are better than other days—some weeks better than others. Sometimes he's up and about his business. But he keeps returning to his sick-bed, and, as I've said, I've done all that I know to do. I've come to the place where, knowing no other path, I seek out your help, and the Church's."

"We'll certainly do what we can," said Principius. "Do you have something specific in mind?"

Tranquillinus nodded. "Good Principius, you're aware of the abbot of St. Maurice in Agaunum?"

"Severinus? Yes." Principius was beginning to understand what had drawn the physician here.

"You may or may not be aware that he's gaining a reputation for his healing powers."

"Yes," said the bishop, "he's becoming something of a celebrity."

"I thought it would be wise to see if he could heal our king. Little else seems to be working."

"Severinus, you say." Principius stroked his chin. "Of course, we must do what we can. He is a long way from here. Agaunum is south of Bordeaux...but yes, certainly. I'll summon him immediately. May God be with our king and keep him alive until Severinus comes!"

"Indeed, my lord," said Tranquillinus, uncertain as to the language of the Church. "May God treat him well."

Principius did summon Severinus, but he would not see his arrival. On the same night he sent for the abbot of Agaunum, Principius died in his sleep.

"See, he's still weak after all this time!"

Peeking around the corner of the door, the physician saw nothing new. His king lay weak and despondent, as he had lain so frequently over the course of nearly two years. Abbot Severinus, still wearing his cloak, trying to shake off the chill of outside, stood full in the doorway as he looked upon the king for the first time.

"Will you introduce us?" he said softly to Tranquillinus.

"Oh, certainly, indeed. Come, I'll introduce you!" The physician strutted into the bed chamber and gave a loud "Ahem!" to be sure that Clovis was awake. The king had been awake for some time and said quietly,

"Yes, Tranquillinus, what is it?"

"Someone to see you, my lord."

Clovis opened his eyes, saying, "Business this early in the day?" Though business had continued, only critical issues, or ones that might amuse the king, were brought to him now.

"Not exactly, my lord. The abbot of Agaunum is here at my request. I thought, perhaps, he might be able to help you in your illness. I've informed him of your condition, you see." Tranquillinus reached down and touched his king's forehead, affirming, to the physician's dismay, that the latest fever was still with his patient.

Clovis frowned and said, "Welcome, Abbot. As you can see, I'm dying."

Severinus hummed and looked down upon the emaciated Clovis. With a slight turn, he nodded to Tranquillinus that he could now leave.

Chapter 20 *A King Renewed: 505-506 CE*

Tranquillinus nodded back, not catching the hint. Again, Severinus made the gesture. This time the physician understood and began to bluster and look all around him as if he had lost something.

"Oh, my, there is, my lord…that is…there are things I must be doing, so I'll just excuse myself, yes that's it. So, good-bye. I leave you in the care of the abbot." He nodded and bowed all the way out of the room, leaving Severinus to minister to the king in privacy. The abbot pulled a chair up to the side of the bed and seated himself.

"Quite an interesting physician," said Severinus, smiling.

"Yes," said Clovis, "but I don't doubt his skills…even now."

"That speaks well of him…and of you."

Both men were silent for a moment, Clovis, because of his weakness, and Severinus, in his care to speak the right words. Having no better place to begin, in a voice that was neither weak nor overbearing, Severinus said, "Dying, you say?"

Clovis opened his eyes at the question. "Yes, Abbot, dying. I've been baptized and so I must die. It just takes so long."

"I see. Then perhaps we still have time to talk?"

"If you wish."

"At least your salvation is secure, now that you've been baptized. That must be some comfort to you."

"It doesn't seem to lighten my mood, if I may say so, Abbot."

"And your kingdom seems to be strong and healthy."

"Yes, at least that much is true."

"I'm from Agaunum, under Alaric's rule, you know."

"Agaunum?" said Clovis weakly.

"Things aren't so secure there. Certainly not for the Church. But I've just had a visit from a priest in Burgundy. From what I hear, things are changing there these days."

"Yes?"

"Yes. From what I gather, Gundobad seems to be doing fine, recovered from his war with you and his brother." Severinus was lighter now, almost casual. "His health is good and he seems to be secure." Severinus paused to see if Clovis was still awake. He was, so he continued. "The people have been pleased with him, so I'm told." Severinus paused again. "Of course his new laws aren't hurting either, giving his people a chance to make a better life. And they're responding to that, oh yes."

"Yes, I've heard about his laws," said Clovis, mildly interested. "I've begun something similar regarding the law among the Franks."

"Really?"

"Yes, but I don't know.…"

Severinus could see Clovis was tiring. Still, now was the time to talk. He decided to try something more bold. Perhaps if order was not a reason to live, a fight would be.

"I don't imagine Gundobad will ever have trouble raising an army," said the abbot.

Clovis started in his bed, his eyes opened wide.

"Is he planning to do that? Have you heard something?"

"Oh me, no. I just meant that his growing popularity is certain to help him if he ever needs to rally his troops. I am sorry, I didn't mean to upset you. On the other hand, I do know that Alaric's trying to build an army."

Clovis shivered and he pulled the blanket up to his neck. "I have a chill…and I'm so tired. I must sleep now, forgive me, Abbot."

Severinus watched as the King's eyes closed. Once more Clovis shivered, violently; so violently that Severinus stood and took off his cloak and spread it out over the bed. Clovis relaxed a bit, as if an immediate warmth had embraced him.

As the abbot re-seated himself, Clotild entered the room. Her carriage was tentative and she asked, quietly, "Am I interrupting, Father?"

"No, my child. He's sleeping." He looked at the king as he spoke, "It's good for him and not a bad idea. I'm looking forward to some sleep myself."

"A room is prepared for you next to where Tranquillinus sleeps. I can show you there, if you wish."

"Thank you, daughter, but I'd like to stay with your husband a little longer."

"Of course," said Clotild. She gave Severinus directions to his room, and offered her thanks by way of a kiss on his cheek.

The abbot assured the queen that he understood the directions, and bid her goodnight. When she'd gone, Severinus turned back to face the King's bed. Lowering his head, he began to pray, asking God to heal Clovis. The prayer was never completed. While mouthing his silent petitions, Severinus, his head bowing even further, fell into a deep and much needed sleep.

"Hellooo…Hellooo." Tranquillinus took in the sight of Clovis in bed and Severinus, still asleep in the chair.

"Are you going to sleep until the day is spent? It's a lovely day outside and you should be enjoying it!" The physician walked to the window and gazed out, a look of surrender coming to his face. "Actu-

Chapter 20 *A King Renewed: 505-506 CE*

ally, it's cold and miserable..." he turned back from the window, "...but you should be up anyway."

Severinus opened his eyes widely taking a moment to remember where he was. He closed his eyes, rubbed them and flinched as he tried to stretch. Having slept upright, his head bobbing, his neck was stiff and sore. He moaned as he rolled his head around.

Clovis opened his eyes and turned his head so he could see Tranquillinus standing by the window. Then he frowned and said, "I'm soaked...I am soaked."

"So you are," said Tranquillinus, noncommittally as he approached the bed. Then he saw that this was no mild complaint. "So you are!" he said.

Severinus was up at the bedside in an instant to confirm what he was hearing. "Yes!" he said, "You're sweating!"

"I know I'm sweating! Get me out of this bath," said Clovis, irritably. "And get me something to drink, I'm thirsty. Breakfast too!" A note of command entered his voice that had long been absent.

"Yes, my lord, right away!" said Tranquillinus and he practically danced out of the room singing, "He's hungry, he's hungry! He's sweating, he's sweating!"

Severinus picked up his cloak from the bed and draped it over the chair and rubbed his eyes again.

"Were you here all night, Abbot?"

"I fell asleep in the chair. I remember beginning a prayer for you...though I don't know that I finished it."

Clovis chuckled. "I am grateful for your efforts, Father. Perhaps I'm going to live after all."

"I believe so, my lord. My experience says that baptism is rarely fatal. Death is more often the result of a sinful act than of a blessed one."

"I hope you're correct." Clovis pulled himself up in bed until he was sitting up. He felt better than he had in almost a year. And there was no question in his mind that it was the man before him that had performed what was clearly a miracle.

Conversation was cut short as food arrived and new clothes were brought in for the king. Clovis ate with a hearty appetite. Food tasted good again.

Watching her husband eat, a grateful Clotild nearly overflowed with joy and thanked the abbot profusely, certain that his prayers had healed her husband. All this only made the abbot embarrassed and anxious to leave. At the request of the king, however, Severinus stayed another night. Clovis tried to get out of bed only once during the day, but feeling the weakness in his legs, chose to remain in bed. From there he conversed and slept, talking with Severinus about his monastery, the faith, and kings.

The next morning, as Clovis slept a healing sleep, Tranquillinus and Aurelian said farewells as the abbot of Agaunum set out from the residence of the king.

It was several months before Clovis was himself again. He worked for short spans of time with Aurelian, who tried to update the king on the details of recent events. When he was not working or resting, Clovis played with his children. Chlotar was four years old now and wanted to play constantly. Clotild had to admonish him on occasion so his father could get some rest. He tired Clovis the most, though there were no regrets about the time spent with his youngest son. The other children better understood the need for quiet around the bedchamber.

Throughout his recovery, in the back of his mind, Clovis was troubled by the fact that he had not been able to reward Severinus in some material way. The nagging concern stayed with him until one day, as he sat in the quiet of the garden, he recalled the words of the abbot, "Thanks be to God, not me," and so Clovis began to thank God.

He parceled more land to the churches at Soissons, Tournai, and Cambrai. Another gift of silver went to Remigius at Reims. It wasn't, however, until Clovis decided to found a monastery, remembering how fondly Severinus had spoken of his own abbey, that he began to feel he was showing sufficient gratitude to God for his renewed health.

With a simple, matter of fact command to Aurelian, Clovis founded the monastery at Micy and, upon the recommendation of Vedastus, named the priest, Mesmin, as its first abbot. When Clovis had the chance to meet with the young priest, he was please to find that Mesmin reminded him of Severinus. It seemed more than appropriate to Clovis, and he began to believe God had been properly thanked.

Chapter 21

The Visigoths
507 CE

Since the day of the King's baptism, times had been peaceful in Gaul. Gundobad showed no desire to battle again. He was more concerned with improving the lot of his people than with enlarging his domain. The Thuringians, Alemmani, and Armoricans were on stable terms with the Franks. Alaric was too frightened to attack Clovis, honoring the peace pact with only the rarest of exceptions. Little skirmishes threatened the agreement occasionally, but they were settled quickly, the largest having been resolved by Gerard early on, shortly after Clovis first became sick.

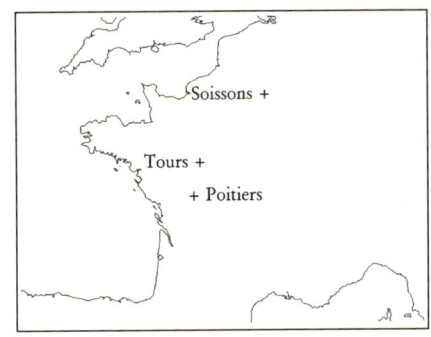

Now recovered from his illness, Clovis was grateful for these quiet times. He reveled in watching his children grow, and they were growing fast. Theuderic was seventeen, a man now, married to a Frankish girl, by whom he'd fathered his first child, Theudebert, the first grandchild of Clovis, a grandchild he was yet to see; Chlodomer was eleven; Clotild, ten, and was as beautiful as her mother; Childebert, nine; and Chlothar was nearly six. Clotild was wonderful with the children, and Clovis enjoyed watching his queen fuss over them, and play with them showing a devotion he could only hope to equal.

Clotild was most proficient, or so it seemed to Clovis, in inspiring the children to good hearted mischief. It was an inspiration that seemed to come all too easily. Chlothar, at his tender age, was already especially devious and laughed the hardest of all whenever the children were able to trick their father in one way or another.

There was ample time for the children to plan their jokes, for part of each day found Clovis away from the family as he tended to business.

One autumn day, in that season when young hearts are inspired by crisp weather, the boys fixed a chair so it would collapse when more than the slightest weight was applied to it.

Their father, keeping to the routine of recent days, appeared in the dining room late in the afternoon and promptly called for dinner.

"I'm hungry!" he said with eager anticipation and he began to sit in a chair that was still reliable.

"No, father, I want that chair!" said Childebert.

"Won't another chair do just as well?"

"No please, I want that one."

"Yes, father, sit here. This is a better chair," said Chlothar.

To have one boy wanting a particular chair was not especially unusual, but the politeness of Chlothar struck Clovis as odd. He prepared for the worst.

"I suppose I could sit there," he said. "Here, Childebert, you sit in this place." He offered the chair, much to the boy's satisfaction, and took the seat Chlothar was holding for him. He sat down gingerly after checking the seat for sharp objects. The thought crossed his mind that the chair might buckle, but as his weight settled in the chair, it's construction seemed sturdy enough. As he sat, Clotild, who had been out with her daughter, entered the room and greeted her husband. At that precise instant, Clovis heard an urgent and suspicious creak. The next thing he knew, he was on his back with pieces of chair strewn about him and the children were laughing. Clotild was worried until her husband shot her a look she understood, a look which the children might think was anger but which she knew concealed a smile. She said, "My dear, you have been looking a little rounder."

"It's not funny," he said loudly, just before he growled fiercely and grabbed at the perpetrators of the crime. Shouts of glee led to dinner and a night of playfulness.

"A message from the Council of Bishops at Adge is next, my lord." Aurelian was trying to complete the business more quickly than usual. He had plans to visit his wife's family near Amiens and wanted to get an early start on the journey.

"Yes, what does it say?" asked Clovis.

"Uhm...Caesarius sends us greetings and salutations..." Aurelian read silently for a moment, looking for any pertinent information. "The bishop of Rodez, Quintianus, is having some difficulty it seems...yes...here...my, this looks like it could be troublesome." There was resignation in his tone.

"What is it Aurelian?"

"Oh, I'm sorry." The secretary shook his head at his own behavior, "The bishop of Rodez has been exiled...apparently because he supports you. Alaric's men were going to execute him, but he escaped to…I lost my place, oh…here, to Clermont. Not only that, but Verus of Tours was also suspected of being loyal to you and has been exiled as well."

"Verus too? Exiled?" Aurelian could see that Clovis was disturbed by the news. The king stepped down from his throne and paced the width of the room in silence. Then he stopped in front of his advisor.

"These bishops…Verus and what was the other's name?"

"Quintianus."

"Have they been loyal to me?"

"The suggestion's there. They're both Catholic."

"Why would the bishops want to inform me of this?" His face twisted into a frown and he returned to his throne.

"It's difficult to say for certain. I can imagine, though, that they're hoping you'll take action against Alaric."

"That's exactly what it is, Aurelian." Clovis rubbed his brow and clenched his teeth. His fingers began to tap against the arm of his throne. He was silent long enough that Aurelian began to shift his weight from one foot to the other, impatiently. "The question is, why? I need to consider this for a while, Aurelian. Can the rest of our business wait?"

Surprised by this stroke of luck, Aurelian gave a laugh of wonder at his good fortune and then checked it as Clovis looked up at him.

"I'm sorry, my lord. I just didn't expect to be finished so soon."

"Plans?"

"My wife's family."

"Can the rest wait?"

"Yes, sir," Aurelian said, going through the mental notes he'd made, "I believe the rest can wait for awhile."

"Then feel free to go," said Clovis. His smile was pasted on his face, his thoughts already centered on the Church's dilemma, a dilemma that he feared was quickly becoming his own.

———

The children were asleep and Clovis lay in bed holding his wife. He pulled her warmth to him, bending his knees in behind her's. He stroked the curve of her hip and sighed deeply.

"What's that for?" asked Clotild.

Clovis sighed again. "I need to make a decision."

"You do that well," she said as she patted his hand. "What is it?"

"Alaric has exiled two bishops—he was going to kill one of them—and they both support me."

"What's the decision?"

Clovis rolled over on his back and put his hands behind his head. "Whether or not to make war on Alaric."

Clotild turned to face her husband and propped her head on her arm so she looked down upon him.

"But you have a peace pact with the Visigoths."

"That's the problem. I keep wondering, when Alaric attacks the Church, does he attack me? Has the pact, been broken, even if he doesn't know it?" He sighed again. "The Church seems to want me to be its protector, even in lands that aren't my own. And I don't know if that's what I want to be doing."

A long silence followed. Clotild had no idea what the proper path might be, but she wanted to encourage her husband. "You're a wise man, Clovis. You'll do what pleases God." Clotild kissed her husband's head lightly, a kiss that he absentmindedly returned. "Now, get some sleep."

Clotild turned her back to her husband again and quieted for her own night's rest. Clovis stared into the dark for a long while, wondering if he should be angry at the Church for their presumption, or praying for God's guidance.

The men weren't sure why they'd been summoned, but they had all come, some making a full week's journey to Soissons. The commanders of the king's army milled about, trying to find one of their own who knew what this meeting was about. Theuderic was there, standing with Gerard, the nearest thing he had to an uncle. He knew no more than the others did and waited anxiously. The warriors had only a few minutes to wonder before Clovis entered the Great Hall and took his throne.

He looked around the room and made brief eye contact with Gerard.

"I want you to remember the peace pact made with Alaric, the Visigoth. It's been five years since that agreement was reached." He shifted his weight in the throne and spoke more softly. "I want you to hear what the bishops of the Church have told me." He then filled his men in on the details of Alaric's actions against the Church. Following the recital of facts he turned to his right, looking now at his secretary as he spoke, "Aurelian will lay out the situation regarding the Visigoth's current activity."

The king's advisor came to the side of the throne, raised his slight build to its full stature and spoke with his most authoritative voice. It was a voice that usually amused the soldiers. High pitched and thin,

Chapter 21 *The Visigoths: 507 CE*

it was difficult to take seriously. But today it was not hard. There was too much uncertainty in the moment. The commanders listened carefully.

"First of all," Aurelian said, "be aware that Alaric is gathering an army near Poitiers. Also know that he's doing it in the face of some rather substantial difficulties. His economy is suffering badly, he's devalued his money, and our scouts tell us that because of it, many of his best men have moved into Spain. It's not likely he'll field a strong army."

He continued on, completing a report that included details of exiled bishops and challenged territories. When he was done, Aurelian stepped back and looked to Clovis, anticipating his concluding remarks.

"You've heard the situation," said the king. "It goes very much against the grain with me that these Arians should hold any part of Gaul. Prepare yourselves to march on them, and with God's help, we'll overthrow Alaric, and make the land of the Visigoth the land of the Frank."

The battle starved soldiers shouted their approval in unison. The time was long overdue for a good fight and the prospect excited them. Even Gerard approved, much to his own surprise. Though he'd been enjoying the thought that his warring days were over, now the excitement of combat was suddenly stirring inside him again.

Clovis sent a call for help to his allies, including the recently converted Gundobad, and the wheels of war were put into motion.

Ragnachar and Chararic, kinsmen of Clovis from Cambrai and Tongres, respectively, offered only token troops. The Armoricans offered what help they could. Melanius, the bishop of Rennes had helped convince them of the wisdom in honoring their agreement and coming to the aid of Clovis. It was more than Clovis had expected, and it pleased him. Even though the Armorican frontier had remained peaceful, relations had never been amicable. Siegbert, unable to fight because of his injured foot, (the wound he had suffered in the battle against the Alemmani had never healed properly) sent his son, Chloderic, at the head of a large army. With the added possibility of Gundobad's assistance, a possibility Clovis could barely tolerate, the King of the Franks was confident he could go ahead with his plan. First, however, he went to Reims to seek the blessing of the Church.

The king's request was reasonable and proper, and it excited Remigius. This was the first battle Clovis was undertaking in the name of the Church and Remigius knew it to be a turning point. He also knew that he'd give the blessing Clovis was seeking.

"Before I offer the blessing of the Church," said Remigius, "there are some things I must insist upon." Remigius had earned the trust of the king, and though the bishop knew that this battle was particularly important for the Church in Gaul, he could not neglect his obligation to protect the Church in any way he could.

"In the past, you've not hesitated to add to your wealth by plundering churches as you've traveled the land. Your men must eat, I understand that, but promise me you won't plunder any churches or monasteries."

"If that's your wish," answered Clovis.

"It is. And it applies especially to the area surrounding Tours and the Abbey of Marmoutier. That's the territory of our dear St. Martin."

Clovis kneeled in obedience. "You have my promise," he said. "In fact, my respect for St. Martin grows everyday and I'll soon be asking for his blessing as well. I won't plunder his land."

"I'm certain your efforts will be rewarded," said Remigius as he looked down upon the king. "I'll see that the Church does what she can to provide for your men along the way. May God be with you, Clovis, and may you take comfort in the blessing of the Church."

Remigius laid his hand on the head of the king as he pronounced his blessing.

Clovis wasted no time in seeking the blessing of St. Martin. Envoys were sent to Tours. And when they returned, their news was good.

Two men came before the throne of Clovis with their report.

"We went seeking an omen, as you asked," said one envoy. "We entered the Basilica of St. Martin's at the time of service and the singer sang these words: 'Thou hast girded me, O Lord, with strength unto the battle; thou hast subdued under me those that rose up against me, and hast made mine enemies turn their backs unto me and thou hast utterly destroyed them that hated me."

Clovis listened and pondered the account for only a moment. The message was clear. "St. Martin has blessed us!" he said.

Chapter 21 *The Visigoths: 507 CE*

The Franks assembled, ready to fight again. Their lances were polished; their axes sharpened; their swords ready at their sides. It had been too long since battle had invigorated them. As the soldiers waited, their commanders joined with Clovis in a final meeting before the march on Alaric.

Clovis looked at his men. They were in a jovial mood, eager for battle. He raised his hands to quiet them but said nothing for a long moment. He looked into the faces of his men, seeing loyalty and confidence. There was no reason to delay them longer.

"As you've already heard," he said, "Alaric is in Poitiers, building an army. The Church has declined to offer Alaric their support. He's surrounded by Catholic believers and he's frightened." The men were quiet now. They knew their king well enough to know he didn't offer irrelevant information. "Since he signed the peace pact with us, he hasn't kept a full attack army because there's been no need. Now he's trying to put something together, which says to me we dare not waste time. The more disorganized they are, the more successful we'll be."

The commanders nodded their agreement.

"But as we go to war, and out of respect for St. Martin, hear this command: we will not take anything from the country that St. Martin oversaw, except grass and water. I have promised our God, the Church, and St. Martin himself, that we will respect the people and the land." The king looked sternly at his men. "This order will be followed—nothing but grass and water from the territory of Touraine. Understood?"

One of the commanders asked, "Where will we get food, my lord?"

"I have an assurance from the Church that they'll do what they can to provide food for us as we march south." It seemed to be a satisfactory response. Aware of the need to clear up all questions at the start, Clovis asked, "Is there anything else?"

There was only silence.

"Then," continued Clovis, "It's time! First, to Tours, to pay our respects to St. Martin, then on to defeat Alaric!"

Heading south, by Paris, the Franks came to Orléans and there crossed the Loire into land that was officially understood to be Alaric's. Only once did they encounter a company of Visigothic soldiers. The people in the region said most of them had gone to Poitiers.

The Franks had an easy time as they followed the Loire into Tours. There, as evening fell, Clovis met with the new bishop, Licinius, who had replaced the recently ousted bishop, Verus.

At first Clovis was cautious. He had no way of knowing if this man might be a supporter of Alaric, a weak man chosen to support a throne instead of a God. It was not so. Verus had been chosen by the people, accepted by the Church, and was a strong supporter of Clovis.

Indeed, Licinius was especially glad to see the king, glad to have the security of his army. Clovis sought a further blessing, which the bishop was only too glad to proffer, but he had something additional for Clovis: a message from Emperor Anastasius.

"The emperor?" said Clovis.

"Yes, the message missed you in Soissons, so a rider was sent here. It only just arrived. Please, allow me…" Licinius cleared his throat, lifted the dispatch and said, "Let me see…the main thrust is that Anastasius, our emperor, wishes you well, as you are a champion for the Church of our Lord, Jesus Christ. It seemed good to bring such a message to you as you go into battle…. In general he says that, as now you are a Christian, he can officially encourage you in all you do."

"Thank you, Father. I welcome any encouragement. With the help of the Church and St. Martin, I'm certain we'll defeat Alaric."

"I don't doubt it, Clovis," said the bishop, "but your journey's been a long one and you'll be fighting soon enough. We've gathered food to feed your men, Bishop Remigius said you'd be needing it, and I imagine your men could use a good night's sleep as well."

Supplies were carted out to the men who were encamped south of the city. After their hunger was satisfied, a peaceful night allowed soldiers to sleep.

In the morning, Clovis asked Bishop Licinius to escort him to the Shrine of St. Martin's at the Abbey Marmoutier. The pilgrimage, short as it was, took them back over the Loire up to the craggy rock face that looked out over the river and the city of Tours itself. There was strength here. Clovis could feel it. Buildings constructed into the rock lifted nearly thirty feet high, looming over the river. The venerated battle cloak of the dear Saint was here. Martin, the most beloved Saint of the people, had been a warrior himself. In his youth he'd fought as a soldier, giving his pay to the poor and distressed. His life of service endeared him to the people. Even now, Clovis watched sick and crippled people coming to the shrine to be healed. He was moved by their faith.

"Does this happen among the Arians?" he asked Licinius.

The bishop shook his head slowly, silently.

Chapter 21 *The Visigoths: 507 CE*

On the shrine, the inscription read: "Here lies Martin the bishop, of holy memory, whose soul is in the hand of God; but he is fully here, present and made plain in miracles of every kind."

Clovis knelt and murmured, "Saint Martin, I pray for your arm in our battle, I pray for a victory against Alaric, and I promise you a share in the spoils, God granting us the victory."

Then, after offering thanks to Licinius, Clovis and his army departed.

The three day journey to Poitiers stretched into four days and then five. The troops had a late start and were further slowed by torrential rains. The dirt roads were quickly saturated, and marching on firm roads soon became trudging through thick mud. Only four leagues were traversed before they stopped to set up camp the first night.

No sooner had Clovis dried out under the protection of his tent than a soldier was brought before him, charged with roughing up a farmer outside of Tours in order to procure some hay for the horses that pulled one of the supply wagons.

After the charges had been stated, Clovis asked the soldier, "What's this you've done?"

"Your command, my lord, was to take nothing but grass. Isn't hay grass?"

His tone was casual, almost flippant, and at his words Clovis turned red with anger.

"You heard my command to respect the land of St. Martin and yet you did violence to a man to steal his hay?"

"I thought there would be no harm in taking a little hay, my King." The soldier was beginning to realize that his actions might bring more than a token reprimand.

"Where will our hope of victory be if we offend the blessed Martin? I will not hear of it!"

Clovis grabbed his sword from the small table next to him and, taking one long step toward the soldier, thrust it through the man's heart.

"I'll not hear of it!" he repeated as the man sagged, dying. "Take this corpse away and return to the man who lost the hay. Take him gifts and make up his loss." The king turned his back and didn't see the looks of shock on the faces of his commanders. They'd known discipline, but never before had they seen such a price paid for stealing hay. Who was this St. Martin that Clovis so wanted his favor? They were silent as they went out into the rain to do their King's bidding.

Eventually the rain began to subside. Soon thereafter, the clouds broke, the warmth of sunlight encouraging them on. They were approaching the region around Poitiers and the thought of battling in mud didn't set well with any of the Franks.

Though the rains had stopped, the river Vienne was swollen to heights not seen in over a generation. That fact forced the troops further south than they'd planned to go. Their intention was to cross due east of Poitiers. Now they went south in an attempt to find a place where they might safely ford the river.

The people in the village of Chauvigny told the Franks they'd never seen the river this high. Since the water had risen, most crossings known to them had become unusable. "But," said one old man to the soldiers, "there is a bend in the river south of town where the river widens. You might find passage there."

It was not to be. As dusk drew near, the Franks still had not found a way to cross the Vienne. They set up camp and slept, hoping to find a crossing the next day.

In the early morning light, just before the order was given to resume the southward march, Gerard touched the arm of his king and pointed to the river.

"Look!" he whispered. Following the line that Gerard's arm made, Clovis saw a large hart, unusually light and creamy golden in color, sniffing the air 200 yards in front of them. It was a magnificent beast, larger than any buck either of them had ever seen. He carried a rack still covered with velvet and his bearing was proud. "It would be good meat for your table tonight, wouldn't it?"

Clovis watched the hart's movement. The buck's tail flicked and his skin twitched. Quickly Clovis whispered a command for complete silence, a whisper that sounded like wind in the trees as it passed through the ranks. Assuming the order meant that the enemy was near, it was instantly obeyed.

"Gerard," breathed Clovis, "he may have something more to offer us."

As they watched, the hart moved slowly toward the river's edge looked up the river and down, then lowered his head to drink. After satisfying his thirst, the buck stepped into the river and walked across with only one hesitant step.

"Our ford! He gives us our ford!" shouted Clovis. The buck, bolted at the shout, bounding up the opposite bank and away, as word passed back to the soldiers that they would be crossing to the opposite shore.

Chapter 21 *The Visigoths: 507 CE*

Southwest of the city of Poitiers, along the shores of the Clain River, Alaric's army of 50,000 men was gathered. That compared to the 30,000 who marched with Clovis. Word came that Clovis had finally crossed the Vienne and Alaric called his commanders together to determine their next move. It soon became clear that there were two major schools of thought regarding their strategy.

On one hand, there were those uncertain about the battle, represented most articulately by the loud voiced Gaius, a long time commander under Alaric.

"With all respect, Alaric, I'm surprised we're considering this attack at all. Isn't Theodoric sending emissaries to Clovis to stop his campaign?"

The intentions of Clovis had reached Theodoric by way of spies in Gundobad's court, and it was common knowledge, at least among the commanders of Alaric's army, that the Italian king was trying to end this war before it began.

Alaric still remembered the content of Theodoric's letter: "Surrounded as you are by an innumerable multitude of subjects, and strong in the remembrance of their having turned back Attila, still do not fight with Clovis. War is a terrible thing and a terrible risk." And though Alaric was angered by Theodoric's presumption, he knew that Theodoric was correct on one count. "The long peace may have softened the hearts of your people, and your soldiers, from want of practice, may have lost the habit of working together on the battlefield." It was a severe concern, there was no doubt. Theodoric had said more, "Before blood is shed, draw back if possible. We're sending ambassadors to the King of the Franks to try to prevent this war." Alaric hoped Clovis would respond.

Gaius continued, "But if we must fight, sir, our troops should avoid meeting the Franks early in the day and, instead, retreat at a pace that would cause Clovis to come upon us late in the day after a long march." He didn't think the strategy especially strong, but there was always the chance that Theodoric's message would yet reach Clovis and battle could be avoided altogether.

On the other side of the argument, were those who wanted to engage Clovis as soon as possible. These were the younger warriors, less seasoned, but more enthusiastic about the prospect of battle. Julius, the son of Syagrius, had grown up with Alaric. He looked like his father and still remembered the last time Syagrius had held him. He carried a personal grudge against Clovis. His single-mindedness earned him the position of spokesman for soldiers eager to fight.

"Would you run from this Frank?" he asked Alaric. "We're stronger than he is...more numerous. Even your own scouts tell you that."

"We may have more troops," said Gaius, "but perhaps you believe that you're stronger than you truly are. Have you ever fought against the Franks?"

Julius tightened his lips and looked at Gaius.

"We shouldn't give them the honor of seeing us flee."

Gaius raised his voice in anger, "We are not speaking of fleeing! We're talking about strategy! Anything we can do to improve our chances for victory should be done!"

"Except battle, it seems."

Gaius jumped from his chair at the remark, only to be quieted by Alaric's hand, held up in a gesture demanding decorum.

Julius turned to the other commanders present. "Our position is a good one and we outnumber the enemy. I say we fight here!"

Alaric listened carefully as the debate carried on into the night.

Another dusk arrived. As the Franks set up camp and built their campfires, a scout reported to his king.

"The Goths are less than a day away, sir. They're camped south of Poitiers, on the river Clain."

"Closer than I'd expected," said Clovis, his eyebrows rising at the news.

An estimate of their strength was given and, even as Alaric, near Poitiers, listened to his commanders argue, Clovis met with his commanders to plan their attack in light of new information.

The reports were encouraging but Clovis was concerned about the natural barrier of the Clain river. Any delay would lessen the surprise, and surprise was their best weapon. The decision was made to let the men get a few hours sleep and then awaken them at midnight to march in darkness. Each commander went back to his own men to make certain they would be ready to move on short notice.

Clovis walked to a clearing that gave him a view to the west. There he sat on the ground alone, his back to a rock, looking toward Poitiers. He picked up a stick and began to peel off the bark. In spite of the omen from the Basilica of St. Martin, Clovis was uneasy about this campaign. While he sat, contemplating, a bright meteor fell across the sky leaving a green streak in the heavens. A resolute smile came to the King's face. "Yes," he thought, "another omen. We'll face Alaric and win!" The sharp crack of a stick made him whirl about, his hand reaching for his short sword.

"You should get some sleep too," said Gerard. He'd watched his friend depart from the camp and had followed to assure the safety of his king. "There are only a few hours to midnight."

"Yes, Gerard. Quite right." Clovis grabbed his friend's wrist and came to his feet. He turned to look back at the sky, his hand still on Gerard's wrist and asked, "Did you see it?"

"See what?" asked Gerard as he looked up into the sky.

Clovis shook his head. "Nothing."

"What?" repeated Gerard.

"Never mind."

Clovis looked at the sky for a long moment, well aware that Gerard was content to remain silent with him. It was a good friendship, one Clovis cherished.

"How do you see the battle, Gerard?"

"I think we'll win."

"Do you?"

"We'll lose good men, but I think we'll defeat Alaric." Gerard looked to the west with Clovis and breathed in deeply.

Quiet for a few more moments, Clovis finally gave in to his fatigue, saying only, "Well."

The men returned to camp and parted for their own tents. Clovis picked up his shield. It was still graced with the decoration that Clotild had applied to it. He looked at it, imagining how it might be used in the morning. He laid it by the door of his tent and placed his ax beside it. Then he slept.

A bleary-eyed and angry Alaric made a decision that was long overdue. The Franks were less than a day's march away. His commanders were deadlocked and relieved that Alaric was taking a stand at last. "We won't wait for Theodoric." he said. "It may be that Clovis has heard from him and rejected his call for peace. We'll make a slow retreat in the morning so that if and when we do battle, we'll be facing tired troops. Our scouts know where they're camped and their march tomorrow will be significant. If we give them more ground to cover, they'll be less eager to fight."

The compromise seemed fair on the surface but it satisfied no one.

"We'll only become tired too," said Julius.

"We've already been through that," said Gaius, "let it rest." He thought to himself, though, that if they were going to fight anyway, their current position was as good as they could hope for. He would not admit it out loud, but Julius had been correct about that.

Alaric continued, "Let the men get a good night's sleep and then in the morning we'll begin to move south, toward Angoulême."

It was barely daylight when the Franks first saw the masses of men Alaric had assembled. It quickly became evident that the men were not ready for battle, but instead, were preparing to leave. Clovis and his commanders could scarcely believe their eyes. Gerard looked at the numbers of men and confirmed for himself that the battle would not be easy. Still, it appeared that surprise remained on their side. Advance troops had stolen into the territory and killed nearly a dozen sentries. Clovis was amazed that not one had returned to warn Alaric. He was also impressed at the stealth that could be exercised by thousands of men. Those quiet men now stood ready to descend upon the Visigoths, barely breathing, crouching low, eyeing their targets.

The commanders knew there would be no opportunity like the present one. An order was passed and, with screams that chilled the blood of the unorganized Visigoths, Franks charged into Alaric's camp.

The surprised Visigoths scrambled like ants to regain an advantage, but before the Franks actually arrived, almost half of Alaric's men were on the run. Those who remained faced a swarm of incoming axes and lances covering them before they could hurl their own weapons. Instantly, Franks engaged the Visigoths, quickly gaining the advantage.

The battle lasted only a short while, but for many of the warriors it was a lifetime. Scores died before they could get their hands on their weapons. Others ran without trying to fight, hoping another chance for battle would present itself someday in the future. The screams of Alaric's men, however, could not drown out the cries of triumph that came from the conquering Franks.

After the initial burst of carnage, the Visigoths who were lucky enough to have camped away from the river, now made a stand, led by Alaric himself. A line of men met the Franks, fighting valiantly but fruitlessly as the Franks stormed in upon them, overwhelming them, breaking the line into units of isolated warriors who were quickly dispatched or dispersed.

As the battle began to slow, Clovis found himself, by chance, face to face with Alaric. The Visigoth had taken his helmet off and was kneeling over his commander, Gaius, who had fallen next to him. When he heard Clovis bring up his horse, he turned to look at him.

Chapter 21 *The Visigoths: 507 CE*

He reached for his headgear and stood to face his enemy. Clovis noticed that Alaric's hair had thinned.

"Alaric." The King of the Franks looked grim, but spoke in a tone that was matter-of-fact.

"Will you fight me from your horse or on an equal footing?" said Alaric, challenge in his voice.

Clovis looked coldly at his adversary. Without saying a word, he climbed off his horse, bounced his ax in his hand to check for balance and walked toward his ready opponent.

Alaric lifted his sword and circled to the left. Nearby, soldiers stopped their own battling, hands to their opponent's wrists in mutual constraint, to watch what was transpiring. Clovis didn't draw his sword immediately. He kept Alaric at a distance with his ax while Alaric kept Clovis off balance by constant circling. Now and then he would thrust his sword at the Frank only to have Clovis bat it away with his ax.

The moving target irritated Clovis and, uttering a loud and angry cry, he threw his ax at Alaric, grabbed his sword and began to charge his opponent. In avoiding the ax, Alaric stumbled and those watching thought it spelled his death. A quick reflex, though, allowed him to recover in time to block the first slashing blows of Clovis.

The Visigoth jumped aside and Clovis followed. It took only a few moments for Clovis to spot his opportunity. He moved to his right and the Visigoth moved to the left, circling around an imaginary point between them. Again he moved right and Alaric moved left.

Testing his idea, Clovis stepped to the right once more, Alaric responding with another move to the left. Consistency was the flaw in his style. Clovis pursued the Visigoth again and again, steering him next to the steed he'd just dismounted, offering a thrust of the sword here, or a slash in the air there, to keep Alaric thinking of defense. The maneuvering complete, Clovis offered another obvious step to the right. For the shortest instant Alaric's leftward circling retreat was blocked by his opponent's horse and it was enough. In the brief instant of confusion, with a quick, close thrust, Clovis killed Alaric.

The blow signaled the resumption of fighting on the field and the Franks quickly took an upper hand.

Clovis removed his sword and looked around him to see how the battle was proceeding. He could see Theuderic, looking proficient. He would be a good commander someday, Clovis thought. Watching his son, however, he let his own guard down for a moment. He didn't notice one of Alaric's young soldiers approaching him from behind, until it was too late. When he heard movement he turned in time to see, but not in time to react to a javelin being thrust at him. It hit him in the left side and knocked him back. He was able to swing his sword and avoid a second blow, but for a moment he feared he had been seriously wounded. Tiny plates of iron, sewn to his leather corslet, an idea taken from the armor of Roman soldiers, did their job and stopped the point of the javelin short of flesh. A bruise was his only injury. Encouraged by his narrow escape, he rallied and attacked the soldier, sending him running.

Clovis then rushed to his horse, mounted, and turned to where the fading battle was the thickest. As he turned, another of the Visigoths came at him from the right with his lance. It was Julius, the son of Syagrius, but Clovis had no way of knowing. Digging his heels into the ribs of his horse, Clovis was off before Julius could do any harm.

The Visigoths fled south to Vivonne where they regrouped for another battle. No one had yet assumed command of the fleeing men and their chaotic effort resulted in another retreat, this time to Champagne St. Hilaire. There, still without a leader, the Visigothic forces were broken.

That night, Clovis reviewed the day and it was clear that the Franks had beaten the Visigoths soundly. Theuderic had proven himself to be a fine warrior, and that was gratifying to Clovis. But his pleasure was overshadowed by the painful news that Gerard had fallen.

Siegbert's son, Chloderic, who stood with Gerard and Theuderic in the battle, told how he watched Gerard fight heroically, killing no less than five of the enemy, before a thrown ax plowed into the back of his neck. Theuderic confirmed the account.

It was a good death, thought Clovis, the kind of heroic death that would have pleased Gerard. It seemed little comfort, though, and in truth there was still work to be done. Even though the Visigoths were scattering, a large number of them had gone southeast, with others aiming themselves south, to the Visigothic capital of Bordeaux. Clovis decided to follow those who were making their way south.

"Tomorrow we'll avenge Gerard's death," he said, "and make the land of the Visigoth our own. But that's tomorrow. Tonight…sleep."

The commanders were excused, and Clovis went to his tent to mourn his friend's loss. The years he and Gerard had stood and fought side by side came back to him, times more valuable than gold, the Alemmani, the Thuringians, and Burgundians, and his memories were seasoned by the salt of his own tears—a bitterness he'd not tasted

Chapter 21 *The Visigoths: 507 CE*

since his father had died. It was a taste that was only as it could be, appropriate, necessary, natural. Clovis was both grateful and shamed by his quiet sobbing. Finally, late in the night, weary with grief, the King of the Franks slept.

Chapter 22
Theodoric Draws a Line
507-508 CE

As they marched to the city of Bordeaux, the Franks were more brutal than usual. Clear of the lands of St. Martin, they felt free to ravage at will, burning peasant's cottages, raping women and taking property and provisions.

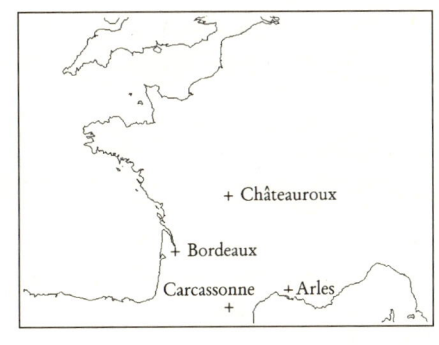

Clovis made no attempt to control his men. On the whole, they were decent men, prone to stop short of murder. The raping was rarely in anger, more the price the soldiers exacted for risking their lives, for watching death, for needing to remind themselves that they were still alive. Though Clovis was now content to rest when there was time to be had, in earlier days, as a young warrior, he'd shared heartily in the same sins.

After the victory at Champagne St. Hilaire, the Visigoths scattered. Most turned east, hoping Clovis would go on to Bordeaux, their capital. In that much they were correct. But Clovis wanted more than plunder; he was not going to make the same mistake he'd made with Gundobad. The Visigoths would not be a threat to him again. He sent more than half of his men, under Theuderic's command, to follow the eastward bound Visigoths. Clovis led the rest of his troops south, meeting resistance in only one place, Angoulême. The battle there was brief and bloody, another victory for the Franks.

With autumn nearly over, Clovis decided to winter in one of Alaric's resort homes, the Bordeaux residence. As he waited for word from Theuderic, he took stock of what the late king had left behind: sumptuous accommodations in a building more rambling and open than the palace in Soissons, which made him wonder what the palace in Toulouse must look like. The stores of food were abundant. With such a supply, Clovis made it a point to entertain his commanders and provide for his troops. Two weeks of gluttony and indulgence rewarded the men. Foods they'd never known, wine, better than any they'd tasted before. Cheeses, that nearly caused fights when supplies ran low, delighted soldiers who would normally have settled for much less. Soon, though, their victory celebrations were done, and the quest began for further diversions that would carry them through the winter.

Clovis kept busy with pleas from the people of Bordeaux, who came to him hoping for his favor so they could retain their businesses or property. It was work that made him wish Aurelian was with him.

The main part of the Visigoths were continuing east, hoping to come under Theodoric's protection before the Franks caught up with them. It was an unwarranted worry. Burdened by a greater army, Theuderic was slowly falling behind. He continued on, knowing that if they should meet Alaric's men, they would win, and if the Visigoths left Gaul before they could engage them, there would be no shame.

Soon the Franks were in Albi and then Rodez. The reports of scouts repeatedly confirmed that the Visigoths were outdistancing the Franks. Theuderic and Chloderic were ready to resume the pursuit when word reached them that Gundobad, the King of Burgundy, was in Clermont, to the north, ready to join them if there was a need.

"Another ally," said Theuderic. "Should we meet Gundobad before we go on?"

"Numbers never hurt in a fight," answered Chloderic.

A decision was made. With fall deepening into the first frosts of winter, Theuderic, Chloderic, and their troops turned north and made their way to Clermont where they would spend the next few weeks of winter, if not more. As they moved to meet Gundobad, the Visigoths continued on to the Rhône river and the fortress city of Arles. The two armies would face each other soon enough.

Spring did not come quickly enough, but now it was imminent, and Clovis was feeling the need to be about a more active business. He'd taken the winter months to secure the territory he'd conquered. He'd also written to the bishops of the area, assuring them that his desire was that no harm come to the Church. It was important work, but not very exciting. Now, he prepared for a move on Toulouse, Alaric's capital and treasury. Clovis expected some resistance, but nothing insurmountable. He remembered facing the walls of Toulouse after defeating Syagrius. They had been imposing then, but with Alaric dead, and with no substantial armies to defend the city, he felt certain it would fall quickly.

Chapter 22 *Theodoric Draws a Line: 507-508 CE*

There was only a token unit of soldiers guarding the treasury and their defeat was swift. With victory, Clovis gained a hoard of gold and silver coins of the Empire, as well as a small collection of plunder, which had accumulated over time. In this one place was great wealth, but Clovis knew the treasury should contain more. Coins and the small collection of jewelry and treasures would be only a part of the riches Alaric held.

To discover where the remainder of Alaric's treasures were hidden, one of the guards who had survived the attack on the treasury was threatened with torture. Once the man was bound and shown a glowing ember near his genitals, he eagerly revealed that the bulk of Alaric's wealth was kept in a heavily guarded treasury in Carcassonne.

Leaving Clermont as spring arrived, Theuderic, Chloderic, and Gundobad implemented a plan to begin annexing the Visigothic cities that lay in the Rhône Valley.

Theuderic was glad to have the advantage of Gundobad's army, but he couldn't avoid noticing a certain uneasiness on the part of his new ally. Gundobad showed no inclination to talk and offered no explanations. Theuderic held his tongue but decided to keep a watchful eye on this uncertain friend. The assessment was more exact than he knew.

In recent months, in the city of Vienne, Bishop Avitus had pressured Gundobad to dissolve or at least weaken his ties with Theoderic so he might join the cause of the Franks. Now Gundobad was regretting the decisions he'd made in deference to the bishop. He was willing to be the warrior king in central Gaul, but now, as they headed further south, Gundobad knew the ground was growing more dangerous. He knew that Theoderic would not want his northern border challenged nor vulnerable.

Even as Gundobad worried, Theoderic learned of the plight of the Visigoths. General Ibbas, a trusted and accomplished general, was sent toward Arles with orders to protect Italy's northern frontier.

Caesarius, the bishop of Arles, served the faithful in that great port city, where the first Constantine lived, where walls, aqueducts and amphitheaters still spoke of the influence Arles enjoyed when Rome was strong.

It was no secret that Caesarius and his followers would have preferred the rule of a Catholic, like Clovis or Gundobad, over that of the Arian, Alaric. Now, however, as what was left of Alaric's troops gathered within the walls of Arles, the bishop was content to keep his thoughts to himself. With the arrival of the retreating Visigoths, the days in Arles became days fraught with suspicion and paranoia. The Visigoths were frustrated and not inclined to tolerate half-hearted support. Gisalic, the bastard son of Alaric, assumed leadership. Not only was he trying to survive along with the rest of the men, but he was also trying to consolidate his support among the troops. Many of the Visigoths believed that the only true ruler was Alaric's legitimate son, the infant, Amalaric. But an infant couldn't command, and besides, the child was in Spain for safe keeping, so Gisalic's claim went unchallenged, except in quiet and very private conversations. Even so, all grumbling ceased when the men of Gisalic joined the residents of Arles in watching the armies of Theuderic, Chloderic, and Gundobad assemble outside the walls.

The next day it was discovered that a priest, named Valerius, had lowered himself down a rope, slipping outside the walls of the city, and had gone to the Franks. The truth of the incident, along with the rumor that the priest had betrayed the city, passed among the people. Caesarius was dragged from his bed and imprisoned along with other clerics, but his imprisonment proved short-lived. Those who knew Valerius insisted that the young priest had only wanted to escape the siege. He had no intention whatsoever of betraying the city. The contention was not believed until it was learned that a Jew, named Jareb, had, in fact, tried to strike a deal with the Franks.

Seeing the size of the Frankish army, Jareb had decided to help speed the inevitable, on the condition that all of the Jews of the city be spared. Jews were tolerated, even respected in Arles, but stories of persecutions frightened him. Composing a note in which he proposed his plan, he tied it around a rock and hurled it over the city walls at the Franks. To his misfortune, and that of all the Jews in Arles, the rock fell short. It was found the next day, proving who had been the real traitor. Jareb was jailed, along with a number of his Jewish friends, and Bishop Caesarius was released, as were the other priests who had been imprisoned. The bishop emerged from his cell in time to see Theodoric's troops arrive. It was a sight he would rather not have seen.

One column of the Italian Army drove due west, engaging the Franks and Burgundians head on. A second force followed the valley of the Durance river and attacked from the north. Like a great mortar and pestle the two columns of Theodoric's men ground their enemies to powder.

Chapter 22 *Theodoric Draws a Line: 507-508 CE*

Caesarius watched and wept as the Franks and Burgundians scattered and ran. Thousands of men would never see another sunrise, cut down in the battle, destined to have their bodies piled with their dead companions and burned. Hundreds of Franks were captured, and those others who survived crossed the Rhône and began a hurried retreat to the north. General Ibbas followed.

To the west, the siege of Carcassonne was not going well either. The fortress was the strongest Clovis had ever seen, and spring rains were not helping matters. Rock walls, soaked and glistening, rose from the plateau, standing insolently, daring any aggressor to attempt an assault. It was a frustrated king who received news of the defeat at Arles.

"Theuderic?" he asked the runner.

"He survived. But many men were lost and the rest are running for Châteauroux. Theodoric's army's in pursuit."

No time was lost. The detachments of Franks that had been posted in Bordeaux and Angoulême were instructed to maintain control in those cities. There was less hope of keeping a grip on the more southern towns, but a contingent was left in Toulouse just the same. Thus secured, Clovis lifted the siege of Carcassonne, withdrawing in order to assist his son.

As soon as it was learned that Clovis was moving north, General Ibbas called off the pursuit, at Theodoric's instruction. Only a small delegation of Ostrogoths continued on to meet with the Franks at Châteauroux. They brought with them a truce as well as a warning from Theodoric that said, "Go no further." There was no need for explanation, nor discussion. Alaric had been defeated and so had the Franks. There had been enough fighting for now. Agreements were signed, and Theodoric's armies returned to Italy, reclaiming, along the way, land that had fallen to the Franks and Burgundians. It was a worried Gundobad, a weak king concerned about his future as a neighbor of Theodoric, who began his return to Vienne, following the armies of General Ibbas.

Eventually, Alaric's bastard son, Gisalic, was pushed back into Spain and Theodoric made arrangements to rule the Visigothic lands himself, until Amalaric, his grandson and legitimate successor to Alaric, was of age. Knowing that there is no substitute for land as protection, Theodoric added the land south of the Durance river to his domain, from the Alps to the Rhône. He resolved that, never again would his northern border be vulnerable.

The Franks, now reunited, took time to recover in Châteauroux and reflected upon the campaign. Despite the defeat at Arles, Clovis, Theuderic, and Chloderic agreed that their overall campaign had been a success. Alaric was dead, and the Visigoths no longer held southern Gaul. Their own losses had been significant, but they were returning victors, nonetheless.

Clovis remembered the words of Remigius, words sent to encourage him when his sister died: don't let the people see your grief. Clovis saw the wisdom as it applied to his soldiers as well. When he was with his men there was no talk of Gerard, the man, nor of Gerard, the fallen warrior, nor of the many dead. Still, in private, he grieved.

A messenger, sent to Soissons, encouraged Clotild and Remigius and a host of others to come to Tours where the conquerors intended to bring gifts honoring St. Martin. Two weeks in Châteauroux allowed the men sufficient time to regain their strength. With wounds bound and spirits rising at the prospect of seeing their homes and families again, the Franks began a five day march to Tours.

Chapter 23

Consul
508 CE

St. Martin's Basilica was full. Shoulder to shoulder, in front of windows, behind columns, and between soldiers, the people of Tours struggled to get a better view. Children ducked between legs and avoided shuffling feet to see the raised chancel before them. Seated in front were the bishops: Remigius, Eleutherius and Vedastus, among others. Septimus, representative of the Emperor Anastasius, had begun his journey from Constantinople the moment news reached the Emperor that Clovis had defeated Alaric. He'd gone straight to Soissons expecting to find Clovis, only to discover the King's plans to celebrate his victory in Tours. Making the last leg of his journey with Clotild and Aurelian, he sat with them now. Behind them sat Basina, Tranquillinus and Lantechild. Clovis, Theuderic and Chloderic were seated in front of them all.

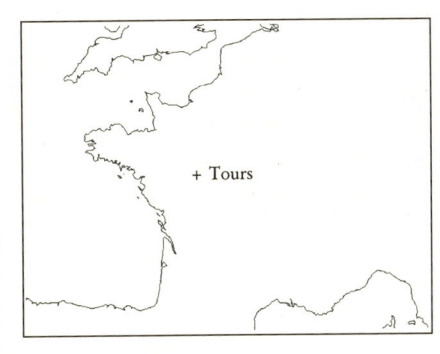

It was difficult for Clovis to look at Clotild. She'd arrived in Tours, glad to see him, but wounded to her soul. A single embrace was all they offered one another before they shared their news. Gerard was dead. Genevieve was dead, found in her bed just after Clovis had departed to face Alaric. Now they both grieved quietly and ached for one another.

The bishop of Tours, Licinius, distracted Clovis from his melancholy, offering a prayer for what was about to take place. Then, by way of explanation the bishop said, "Children, we are here to bring honor to a great king and conqueror, a defender of the faith and a generous advocate of the Church." He turned and gestured to gifts that covered a large portion of the chancel. Clovis had returned from battle with statues and jewelry for St. Martin, his patron in battle. "St. Martin and our Lord Jesus Christ, the Virgin Mary and God Almighty have blessed us greatly," continued the bishop. "And now Emperor Anastasius sends his blessings too." Licinius invited Septimus, the symbol of the Emperor, to stand next to him. "His legate comes to confer on King Clovis the title of Consul."

A great shout of approval went up in the church and Clovis rose to approach the chancel. From his portion of the spoils of battle, Clovis held back only one item from St. Martin: a diamond studded gold diadem that he carried with him now.

With Clovis standing before him, the bishop concluded his part. "In the name of the Father, the Son, and the Holy Spirit, amen." Then he deferred to the legate who held the purple robe granted to all called Consul. Traditionally, it was worn by those in the Empire who were appointed to look after the commercial interests of the Emperor. Anastasius had followed the news of Clovis since before his baptism, hoping that ultimately, the King of the Franks would defeat Theodoric, thus opening the door to a re-united Empire. It was prudent to honor powerful leaders…especially those who might, one day, prove to be a threat themselves.

Septimus, the tall, lanky, hairless representative of the Emperor stepped forward. He cleared his throat and in a low stately tone said, "In the name of Emperor Anastasius, I call you Consul." He placed the robe on the shoulders of the king, pausing to give him time to pin the garment securely and then handed Clovis a scroll that carried the official decree of the honor.

Clovis received the robe and scroll with visible pride. He quietly thanked Septimus, who accepted the thanks and then moved back a step.

Clovis turned to Bishop Licinius. "If you would, Father." He held out to Licinius the diadem and his intentions were clear. This was now a coronation. There was no chance to discuss the matter and the king stood waiting. Licinius tried to disguise his discomfort at the idea of being party to a king crowning himself, but he felt his face burn with shame as he accepted the crown and watched Clovis bow before him. In a moment the deed was done, and with diadem in place, the king faced his people.

From the crowd, a voice arose shouting the name "Augustus!" and once the name had been spoken, it was repeated by the people. A chant arose, "Augustus! Augustus! Augustus!" filling the Basilica.

The chant offered a suggestion, which the people gladly accepted: Clovis was not merely an official of the Emperor, but the Emperor himself. Septimus lowered his head and chose not to contradict the implication. He knew how weak Anastasius was in Gaul.

Clovis stepped down from the chancel and slowly walked the length of the aisle of the Basilica, relishing the cheers and applause. As he passed by where Clotild sat, she came to his side to walk with him. Eleutherius, who sat next to Remigius whispered, "The diadem makes him look silly."

Chapter 23 *Consul: 508 CE*

Remigius smiled slightly and nodded in an almost imperceptible way but thought to himself, Silly or not, we're more secure now than we've been in my lifetime…if his pride doesn't ruin him…or us. His slight smile slid into a subtle frown.

Clovis exited the church, stepped into the daylight, and looked at the people who lined the streets. At the bottom of the stairs before him, a priest stood, holding the reins of the horse Clovis had ridden into battle. He'd given his horse to St. Martin as a gift, but now asked if he might buy the horse back. He offered a hundred solidi.

The priest who had been given charge of the gift said, "Is that an appropriate price, my King? Remember that it was St. Martin who gave you victory."

Clovis increased the price another fifty solidi. He could see by the look on the priest's face that he wished for more. So he offered yet another fifty and the priest smiled and handed over the reins.

Accepting them Clovis said, "St. Martin is an expensive friend, eh? Good in his help and careful in his business!"

The priest smiled, said nothing more, and turned to leave. Aurelian came through the crowded church and to the side of his king. A satchel filled with coins was in his hand. Clovis took the bag from his friend.

"It's a great blessing, isn't it, Aurelian, that God has seen me worthy for such honor?"

"Yes, my King—a great honor. Now mount your horse. Your people are waiting for you."

Seeing first that Clotild was given a place of honor in a carriage, Clovis mounted his stallion. With carriages and chariots following behind, he made his way through the streets of Tours, from the Basilica of St. Martin toward the Cathedral of St. Gatien, named for the first bishop of Tours. As cheers and shouts erupted saying, "Consul Clovis!" and "Hail Augustus!" Clovis smiled, waved, and tossed coins to the people.

Remigius took the arm of Bishop Eleutherius, holding on for support as they descended the steps of the Basilica. Licinius walked with them as they watched Clovis go on his way. The slight steady rise of the road led straight to the Cathedral and offered an unobstructed view of the new consul's ride.

Shaking his head, Licinius said, "May God help us all!"

Remigius responded, "Yes, indeed."

Eleutherius agreed, offering only a silent nod.

"And yet," continued Remigius, after a rather long pause during which they watched Clovis proceed, "he rules Gaul now, and he is Catholic. That helps us."

"He's Catholic in name only, my friend," said Licinius, who had heard too many stories of churches sacked by the Franks.

"No different than most of Gaul," returned Remigius. "But Clovis will keep the land secure."

"And now he has the Empire behind him," offered Eleutherius.

"He doesn't belong to the Empire," said Remigius. "He's ours. He belongs to the Church. Thank the Blessed Virgin for that!"

The other bishops murmured "Amen" quietly as they all watched Clovis ride on. He was still waving and throwing coins.

Clotild watched Clovis, still wearing his purple tunic, as he began to relax at the end of the day. He was eating a late meal of venison, bread, fruit and wine and was still reviewing the day with Aurelian, whom he'd insisted must join him for the meal.

"But really, the title doesn't mean much," said Clovis.

"Oh?" said Clotild. "Have you already forgotten the cheers of the people?"

"No, no, not yet! And I agree, the title means something to the people. But I think they remember a different Rome than exists in fact. Don't you think so, Aurelian?" He paused barely long enough to allow his friend to nod his head once and then said, "Still, their cheers were exciting, weren't they?"

"Yes," said Aurelian, a smile crossing his face, "they were at that."

"But understand what I mean," said Clovis. "I don't expect Anastasius to offer me anything more than kind words. The Empire's voice can reach here, but its arms aren't that long. In a time of trouble I'll be on my own."

"Mmmm," murmured Aurelian through a bite of cheese. "I suspect you're right."

"Anastasius may think I belong to him now. But he's wrong. I don't belong to anyone. I rule Gaul alone now and no one can challenge me!" Clovis picked up a small bunch of grapes and pulled off one. "Not Alaric," and he chewed the grape. He plucked another, "Not Gundobad," and he chewed again. "Not Theodoric," popping a third grape into his mouth. Then, as he pulled one last grape free of the stem, he said, "Not even Anastasius." Clovis bit down on the fruit slowly, feeling its skin burst in his mouth. "Thank you, St. Martin!" he shouted. Then he leaned back, kicked his feet up on the table, pulled his wife to him and let forth with a loud laugh.

Chapter 24

Rulers Confer
508 CE

"I'll be leaving in the morning."

In a gesture of the mildest curiosity, Clovis raised an eyebrow at Chloderic's declaration.

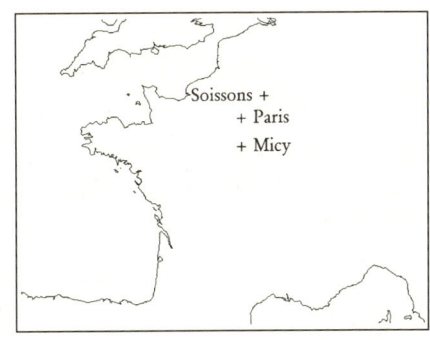

The two stood next to a window that opened out onto the streets of Soissons. Watching the life of the city, they could see that the spirit of celebration the Franks had enjoyed in Tours was still alive. Chloderic and his men had shared in the festive mood willingly. Once in Soissons, however, the celebrations took on a different flavor, as soldiers not only boasted of victory, but also returned home to those they loved. Those who resided in Soissons were quickly back in their homes, while those who lived in surrounding areas, even as far as Tournai, dispersed over a matter of days, eager to be home again. The desire was shared equally by Chloderic's men who still faced the return journey to Cologne.

"I've appreciated your help," said Clovis.

The two were silent as their attention was captured by an old man passing by, leading his family toward the market. Their cart was filled with a harvest of turnips and onions, but no one even imagined that the return on their efforts would be sufficient to meet the family's needs for the winter. No one appeared more aware of this than the old man himself. He strained against the weight of the cart, looking as if he was bearing the weight of the world. Clovis and Chloderic watched, intrigued, unfamiliar with such a struggle, not especially saddened by the family's plight. The same scene could be observed in nearly every town either of them had ever known. They watched in silence until the family was out of view.

"Will you carry my greetings to your father?" asked Clovis.

"Certainly. He'll be glad to hear from you."

"I was sorry he couldn't join us," said Clovis. "He's a good warrior."

Chloderic shook his head. "No, not so good anymore. He's still lame from his injury and it gets worse every year. His mind is good, but he's getting old."

"I understand," said Clovis. He flexed his knee, producing a grinding sound. "It happens to us all."

The both of them smiled, admitting to the pains that are brought on with long years. As they reflected on their own aches, a deeper reflection for Clovis than for Chloderic, a thought occurred to Clovis that caused him to look at his younger companion with a new intensity. Chloderic couldn't help but notice.

"What is it?"

"Nothing. Nothing really." Clovis shook the look off his face, still captured by the realization that Chloderic was a competent man and that his competence might actually be a threat. Even though he now ruled most of Gaul, Clovis knew this was no time to drop his guard. "I was just thinking of your father," he said.

"Do I look like him? People say I do."

"Yes, but that's not what I was thinking. I was thinking that he is, as you say, getting on in years. Siegbert wasn't a young man when we defeated the Alemmani." There was a long silence, or at least Chloderic thought so. Clovis stared out of the window and chose his words carefully before he continued. "He'll die one day, you know. Then it will be up to you to lead," He faced his cousin squarely and said, "Chloderic, I do believe you're ready for that."

"Thank you." Chloderic appreciated the encouragement. "I agree. I believe I'm ready to take my father's place."

"Does it frustrate you to wait for the kingdom…and the riches?"

Chloderic pursed his lips and his eyes narrowed as he thought over the years since he'd first seen his father weak and limping. "Sometimes it frustrates me, yes."

"I'm not surprised," said Clovis. "Every year that Siegbert lives is a year you must deny your own instincts. That's nothing against Siegbert, it's only that you have your own ideas, I'm sure."

"Yes, I do."

"And, be assured, our alliance will stand firm when your father does die. You won't need to worry about that."

"It's good to know." Chloderic looked back into the room and shook his head. "Sometimes I swear he'll live forever!" Defiance grew in him as he considered uncertain possibilities of days to come. Clovis watched him closely and the slightest hint of a smile grew on his face.

"You've led your men well in battle. They've seen how capable you are."

Neither man said more.

On the next morning, Chloderic faced Clovis one last time, before leading his men back to Cologne. Clovis was glad to conclude his most recent campaign.

"I wish you a safe journey, Chloderic," said Clovis. "Please carry my best wishes to your father."

"He will be pleased to receive them."

Clovis noticed, or imagined, or hoped, he wasn't certain which, that Chloderic sounded something less than sincere. At best, this young prince seemed preoccupied.

"I thank you again for your help."

Chloderic smiled and bowed, saying, "It was a good campaign. I was honored to share it with you, Consul."

At the title, Clovis returned the smile. He shook Chloderic's hand and the men parted, each to their own homes, each to their own work.

The autumn sky was clear and the air cool, invigorating Clovis as he sat looking over his new capital, the walled island city of Paris. Aurelian had recommended the move to Paris for the simple reason that the city offered more efficient access to a larger part of Gaul. Clovis had agreed. The Roman roads and the Seine had lifted Paris to a place of superiority in terms of trade. Even the poor were a sign of affluence. They came to Paris looking for a better life. Most didn't find one, but some did—enough to maintain the city's position as a financial center and enough to show visitors a hopeful city, made so by the presence of a king.

The island city, though it needed some work, was still impressive, growing steadily on the southern bank of the Seine, while the northern bank, more prone to flooding, remained relatively clear of new structures. The markets were busier than ever and sellers were bringing their goods from Chartres, Amiens, Reims and other regions, hoping for higher profits than one would find elsewhere in Gaul; certainly better than one found in Soissons. The aqueduct, the Forum, the baths, all found on the south bank, were sumptuous, still marked by the best sculptures and mosaics in northern Gaul. On the island itself, only the church and palace were in good repair. Other buildings had been neglected and often scavenged for stone walls elsewhere.

It had taken nearly two months for the move to be made, but now, on the porch of the new royal residence, Clovis appreciated the wisdom of Aurelian.

He noticed he was tapping his fingers, clicking his nails, on the banister before him. He fought the nervous habit, clenching a fist as he watched the activity of the city. The traffic, North and South, was heavy through Paris. Heavier than usual. Trade was growing. Clovis told himself he should be happy, but he could only fidget.

Clotild had never seen her husband this nervous. She was familiar with the tension that came before battle, but this was different. And the normally calm Aurelian was a shambles. For weeks he'd been making sure that celebrations were planned, lodgings were prepared, and servants were prompted. They'd been in the new palace only two months and Theodoric, the King of the Ostrogoths, was due to arrive from Italy in less than two days.

Theodoric was the one of the few names that conjured for Clovis a figure larger than life.

"Please! You're making me nervous." Clotild laughed at her husband.

Clovis gave an exaggerated shrug and smiled sheepishly.

"Everything will be fine!" said Clotild. "Aurelian has all the details in hand." She stroked her husband's hair and lightly kissed his cheek. "And your sister, Audofleda, will be here. You'll see, everything will be fine."

It was late afternoon when Theodoric's carriage crossed the bridge that brought him inside the walls of Paris. Aurelian had fully orchestrated the event, deciding where the carriage would stop, when the horns would blow their welcome, and where the king and queen would receive their visitors. He'd even planned where the spectators would stand. He would have preferred no onlookers but for such an event they were unavoidable. Now all he could do was hope the meeting went well.

The sound of carriage crossing stone came into the courtyard, preceding the carriage itself by only a few brief seconds, drumming the arrival of Theodoric. Clovis, Clotild, Lantechild, Aurelian, and Tranquillinus, standing alongside a nearly bursting Basina, hushed. The gathered citizens rustled quietly as they fought for better views of the King of the Ostrogoths. Horns sounded on Aurelian's com-

Chapter 24 *Rulers Confer: 508 CE*

mand, and the procession, guided by a row of barrels, stopped precisely where Aurelian hoped it would.

There was silence for a few anxious seconds before the door on the carriage was opened by a handsome Italian servant, allowing a tall man dressed in royal robes, red, green, and gold, to step out. Theodoric was a rugged looking man with a strong jaw, a scarred nose, and inquisitive eyes. He was beginning to turn gray around his temples. He took one quick look at his surroundings, then helped a smiling Audofleda down from the carriage. She held a small dog in her arms that looked out and wiggled its nose. Audofleda took just a moment to smooth her dress, juggling the dog from one arm to the other as she straightened herself, and then the two walked the few steps needed to face their hosts. Theodoric looked Clovis up and down and smiled warmly.

"So, this is the 'New Constantine.' I'm pleased to meet you at last, brother Clovis."

The title, "brother," surprised Clovis for a moment, striking him more forcefully than that of "New Constantine." Throughout the years his sister had been married to this man, he'd never thought to consider him as his brother. Rumors had come to Clovis that some were calling him the New Constantine, but that Theodoric had heard the name was remarkable. "Welcome, Theodoric," he said, choosing not to comment on the unofficial title. "We've waited too long for this meeting." He turned and put his arm around his queen's waist, bringing her forward. "My wife, Clotild."

Theodoric bowed and kissed her hand, then, rising, turned and reciprocated with, "My wife, Audofleda."

"Of course," said Clovis as he embraced and kissed his sister. Her dog squirmed and gave a friendly growl. Audofleda set the puppy down and gave her brother a full hug. The years had hardly changed her. She remained the Audofleda he remembered, though Clovis could see she walked taller now, with more confidence. Her time with Theodoric had been good for her.

Audofleda returned the kiss and looked at the gray in her brother's hair. She brushed it lightly and smiled. "I have missed you!" she said, joyous at the reunion, a tear breaking free to run down her cheek.

It was the tear that broke Basina's resolve to have a seemly reunion. She choked back a sob and cried, "Audofleda!" and pushed past her son to embrace the Queen of Italy. Clovis gave Theodoric a look of kind resignation, a look that brought an understanding smile to the Goth. Aurelian tried to look dignified as this change in plans sent him inwardly reeling. The mother and daughter cried and laughed in their embrace, swaying, ignorant of their witnesses, relishing each other's warmth. "Oh my!" was all the more Basina could say, while "Mother!" summed up Audofleda's exclamation. They broke from their embrace and looked at one another, saying more with their eyes than anyone else understood, sharing pain and joy as well as the knowledge that later was the time for talk.

Without a word, Basina stepped aside, stroking her son's arm as she passed by him, and Audofleda embraced a waiting Lantechild who also remained in silent but rich communication with her. It was only after Lantechild separated from her sister, at Basina's urging, that Audofleda turned her attentions to Clotild. At this first glance she was impressed with her brother's wife in a way that caused her neither jealousy nor resentment. Rather, she found herself genuinely moved by Clotild's radiance. "I've heard a great deal about you," she said.

"And I, you," Clotild replied.

Uncertain as to how they might continue the conversation, not knowing what the other knew, Clotild and Audofleda smiled awkwardly at one another.

Aurelian, continuing obsessively in his role as overseer of the festivities and glad to have a lapse in conversation, stepped forward to begin the transition from this ceremony to another, inside.

"Good Kings and Queens," said Aurelian in his most formal voice. Audofleda smiled at Aurelian, thinking that he hadn't changed much in the years since she'd last seen him, though his formal attire seemed overmuch. Theodoric, unsure who this man was looked at him in curiosity.

Clovis saw the look and interjected, "My secretary," hoping that this piece of information would explain Aurelian's involvement, "and the Count of Melun."

"Ah," said Theodoric, "this is Aurelian, then."

"Yes, sir," said Aurelian, flattered that Theodoric would know his name.

"Your letters are most eloquent."

A slight bow spoke Aurelian's appreciation of the complement. Clovis wasn't certain, but thought he saw a slight blush come to his secretary's face. Aurelian said, "A room is awaiting us, if you'll come this way." He gestured to the door of the palace.

Clovis looked in wonder at his secretary's red face once more, then, along with the others, walked by the beckoning Aurelian, past the crowd, and under the Roman arch that framed the front doors of the residence which was now the center of Gaul's official and political

Chapter 24 *Rulers Confer: 508 CE*

life. At Theodoric's command, two servants, carrying a substantial box made of cane, followed them.

When the last of them passed inside, Aurelian signaled servants to take care of the visitors' belongings. Then he rushed in after the guests, directing the two royal couples, and the others present, into the main hall of the castle; a room lined with pillars, floored with tile and filled with the scent of years.

"Rome knows how to build palaces don't they?" asked Theodoric, looking around as he sat where Aurelian invited him to sit.

"It is a remarkable building," replied Clovis, "but in recent years it's known some carelessness."

Theodoric nodded, familiar with what time and negligence can do to a structure.

Aurelian cleared his throat loudly, drawing the attention of everyone in the room.

"It is our wish," he said, including Clovis with a tilt of his head, "that we might pursue peace together and enjoy relations that serve the people of both our lands. And to emphasize our sincere hope that we will continue as allies, please accept these gifts."

A wave of the hand brought servants carrying a variety of gifts, ranging from tapestries to candle sticks, but of most interest to Theodoric, a jewel encrusted goblet, gold with garnets and sapphires.

"I thank you, Aurelian," said Theodoric as he stood. He was clearly familiar with many such moments of greeting. "And I thank you too, Clovis, for such kindnesses. Please," he signaled his servants, who still bore the box, to come forward, "accept these gifts."

Opening the box, the servants lifted out spices, jewelry, most of which Audofleda had chosen herself, jars of olive oil, and a striking silver platter that made both Clotild and Basina moan at its beauty.

"Generous gifts, Theodoric," said Clovis. "We're grateful to you as well, though I think the most precious gift you bring is my sister."

It was the ensuing cheer from the family which caused Aurelian to resign himself to a less formal time than he'd imagined. He raised his voice only long enough to offer an invitation to dinner.

Over the meal of venison and late harvest vegetables, Audofleda, Basina, and Lantechild dominated the conversation, a family at home, together again, free to talk as in no other place.

"What are the men like?" asked Lantechild, unable to stop herself.

Basina gasped at the question, Lantechild blushed and then they both broke into laughter, Audofleda joining in.

Clotild was happy to keep silent and celebrate the gathering by her willing presence alone. Tranquillinus joined her in silence but was unable to avoid detection.

"I know you, don't I?" asked Theodoric, eventually, after long moments staring at the physician.

"Well, I…"

"This is my doctor, Tranquillinus," said Clovis, "whom you sent to me and who is surely one of the great doctors in all the world!"

"Well, I…" sputtered Tranquillinus, only to be cut off by Basina.

"Indeed he is!" she said proudly, taking his hand in her own as she spoke.

Theodoric watched the shower of praise fall on Tranquillinus. "I fear I should have kept you with me, physician."

"Tranquillinus, if you please, sir," replied the good doctor and he bowed as the others chuckled.

Clovis and Theodoric listened and laughed mostly, but did take time, later in the evening, to indulged themselves in making plans for a hunting trip to begin on the next day.

"There is a forest near here, I've established a monastery there, I know the area, and the hunting is superb!"

Aurelian was included in the discussion so he could make the appropriate arrangements, familiar work which he welcomed, now that Theodoric and Audofleda seemed comfortable.

The meal finished and a song from the harper, who had also been a gift from Theodoric, led to a final toast from the king of Italy. He raised his glass, inviting the others to join him, and said, "To our family, our friends, our hosts, a good night's rest and long life!"

"To you as well," said Clovis and they all drank before parting for their rooms.

Their destination, the woods near Micy, northeast of Orléans, was a four-day journey from Paris, and in spite of the Roman road that paved the way, Clotild had a difficult time. Throughout the summer, feigning mild illnesses, and helped by the distractions that came with the move to Paris and the hectic preparations for Theodoric's visit, she had managed to conceal the fact that she was pregnant. She was nearly four months along, now, but chose to keep her pregnancy secret so that nothing would interfere with Theodoric's visit. Basina knew, but was sworn to secrecy; Audofleda suspected, was almost certain, but chose to say nothing while in the company of the others.

Chapter 24 *Rulers Confer: 508 CE*

Out of concern for Clotild, the party rested a day in a country house near Orléans before continuing on.

She was better after the respite, and rejoined the group as they made their way into Orléans for a few last minute preparations. Supplies were acquired and weapons checked. Theodoric purchased a new lance, an event which pleased him greatly and bored the women.

Riding on horseback, Clovis and Theodoric led the group out of Orléans, into the forest that held some of the best stag and boar hunting in Gaul.

The morning was glorious, and the women, in carriages still, took particular pleasure in the good crisp air and brilliant rich sunshine, admiring the deep sapphire blue sky. By midday the men had dropped their first buck and were jubilant. They stopped for a light meal in a clearing, and it was a pale and sweating Clotild that grasped her husband's hand as she emerged from her carriage.

"Clovis, I'm not well. Find me a place to rest." There was pleading in her voice.

It was not like Clotild to complain, so Clovis took her request seriously.

"We're close to the monastery. Mesmin will have a bed for you." Clovis stroked her brow lightly.

Since Clovis had placed Mesmin in charge of the monastery built in gratitude to God after Severinus had healed the king, only one visit had brought Clovis there. Now he hoped he could find the place.

The short trip seemed endless, for as they began, Clotild screamed and clutched her stomach. There was little anyone could do to keep her comfortable as they slowly made their way to Micy. She was flushed and covered with sweat. His concern for his wife distracted Clovis, and on two occasions he made wrong turns, cursing himself for his ineptitude.

At last they rode clear of the trees and saw the monastery capping a small rise. Its brown stone walls spoke of solitude, but Clovis felt only relief. Minutes after their first sighting of the monastery, Clotild was in bed and Mesmin had provided towels and water and prayers. Audofleda and Theodoric were doing quite well in looking after Clotild, so Mesmin concluded it would be safe, for the time being, to leave her in their care. He asked Clovis to follow him, which the king obediently did.

"She doesn't look well."

"No, Mesmin, she doesn't. I'm afraid for her."

"God will do what God has planned, my King. Our prayers may be all we can offer, aside from the bed." Then there was silence. Clovis chewed his lip and tapped his fingers. Mesmin tried to divert Clovis from his worry.

"Leonard is back."

"Leonard?" asked Clovis, "My godson?"

"Yes, the same. He's visiting his old abbot," Mesmin gestured to himself, "and I'm certain he would want to see you."

"Yes, I'd like to see him too."

"Let me fetch him."

Mesmin patted Clovis on the shoulder, invited him to sit on a bench and then set about to retrieve Leonard. In moments, with Mesmin by his side, the smiling and robust hermit approached. Time had given Leonard a certain roundness, but it didn't seem to slow him down. His life as a hermit was suiting him. When he saw his godfather, he unashamedly embraced the king. "What brings you to Micy, my Lord?" he said.

Clovis related the story of the hunt and Clotild's condition and Leonard could see the growing concern in his king's eyes and hear it in his voice. He seated himself next to the king.

"I'm sorry," he said, "My prayers are with you. May our Lord Jesus heal the queen."

"My thanks, Leonard," said Clovis distantly, as he turned his head back toward where Clotild lay. He sighed deeply, stood and started back toward her room, Mesmin and Leonard following.

She was nearly delirious now, her writhing body soaked in sweat and her moans continuing as she winced from the pains in her abdomen.

Theodoric arose as the men entered. Audofleda looked toward them but still held Clotild's hand.

"My godson, Leonard," said Clovis. Then, for Leonard's sake, "Theodoric and Audofleda, King and Queen of Italy."

Leonard looked only at Clotild, barely acknowledging the introduction. He went to the bedside, practically pushing Queen Audofleda out of the way. He grabbed Clotild's hand and knelt beside the bed. He cried openly and remained on his knees.

The others watched for a long while before Mesmin touched their arms and encouraged them to leave Leonard and Clotild alone.

They bowed to Mesmin's suggestion, though Audofleda more reluctantly than the men, and were led to the cloister where they sat in silence. The vibrant palette of wildflowers in the courtyard was not noticed. They remained lost in their own thoughts for nearly an hour, until Leonard reappeared. He looked worn and haggard, drenched in his own sweat.

Chapter 24 *Rulers Confer: 508 CE*

"I've offered what prayers are in me."

Clovis looked at the fatigued figure before him. "Leonard..." and before he could finish his sentence, a scream came from Clotild's room. The whole lot of them ran to her. Audofleda, seeing the situation and recognizing the signs of childbirth, commanded the men out. Her authority was so surprising that the men obeyed without questioning her reasons. It was the authority of womanhood, sisterhood, that would not be challenged by men of wisdom. Once the room was cleared, Audofleda helped Clotild deliver her still-born child.

Outside the room, Clovis stood listening to the sounds. Unable to help, he resorted to finishing what he had begun to say to his godson.

"Leonard, I was about to say, I won't forget your efforts."

"I could do nothing more, nor less, than what I did," said Leonard. His tone was not encouraging.

Their attempt to carry on a conversation failed, and they were silent for nearly an hour. After the screaming stopped, Audofleda opened the door and called to her brother. He came instantly.

Clovis entered the room, taking a few moments to let his eyes adjust to the dimness. Initially he only saw the shadow of his sister, unable to see what she held. Softly, so no others could hear, Audofleda lifted a small bundle she carried in one hand and told him the news.

"Your wife has lost a baby."

"A baby?" Clovis looked at his sister and then at the proof. It was a girl.

"You didn't know, did you?"

"No."

"I thought as much."

"Is she all right?" Clovis asked, looking past Audofleda toward the motionless figure of Clotild.

"I believe Leonard's prayers helped. I think she's going to recover." Clovis made for his wife's bed and Audofleda grabbed his arm. "She's quiet now, Clovis. She needs the rest badly." The worried look in her brother's eyes was not lost on her and she released her grip on his arm. "Take a moment, but no more. Then go take a walk...take my husband and go for a walk. I'll stay and watch over her." She stroked her brother's arm and said, "Relax if you can."

"Yes, yes, all right," he said, his tension easing little at her comforting. Then, moving past her, Clovis went to his wife.

Clotild didn't speak, but as Clovis squeezed her hand, he thought, or imagined, that she returned the gesture. He caressed her forehead and noticed how much she looked like she did when he first met her. Her perspiration had been because of her nerves, then, her blush, because of embarrassment. She was still the most beautiful woman he had ever seen. The lines added by the years only accented her beauty and strength.

"Rest, my love," he said. He lifted her hand and kissed it. Then, walking slowly backwards, watching Clotild, wishing for a more encouraging sign that did not come, he left.

"It's been a good life." Reflecting on his past, Clovis found few days to regret. "I'm tired of war, though. So is Clotild."

The kings strolled slowly around the perimeter of the monastery. They both realized a friendship was developing. Politics would demand that it be distant, inconsequential when matters of state intruded. Still, a friendship founded in family and in common concern was taking shape.

"There does come a time when the glory wears thin," said Theodoric.

"Yes," agreed Clovis, "and there's always an enemy who wants to do battle, isn't there?"

"Competitors can be dispatched."

Clovis slowed his pace. "Competitors?" he said, carefully.

"Oh, not you, at least not yet. I mean those who try to claim your throne."

"But I might try to claim your throne one day," said Clovis.

"Then you would have to be dispatched, wouldn't you?"

Clovis smiled. He didn't feel a threat in this man. Power, yes; authority, yes; ability, yes; threat, no.

The two were nearly a third of the way around the monastery. It had become overcast in the last hour and a chilly wind was rustling the leaves above them. Squirrels followed the two kings, darting among the trees and bushes that stood outside the monastery walls.

"I have a grandson now," said Clovis.

"Oh?" Theodoric raised an eyebrow.

"Yes, Theudebert is his name. He's a handsome boy."

Theodoric smiled.

Clovis sighed. "I suspect Theudebert will fight wars too."

"Mmm," punctuated with a nod, was Theodoric's only response. He thought of his own grandson, Amalaric, now back in Italy, and wondered if these two grandchildren would fight each other one day.

Chapter 24 *Rulers Confer: 508 CE*

They walked on, contemplating the blood they'd seen and the blood they'd shed. Hopes of a less violent world reminded Clovis of what Gundobad was trying to do in Burgundy.

"Have you heard about Gundobad's law?" asked Clovis.

"Gundobad's a fool!"

"Maybe. But he's a stronger fool than he was a year ago. Have you heard of this law of his?"

"Only a little. I get some information through my emissaries."

"I think there may be some value in what he's doing. There are so many misunderstandings these days. When I was in Tournai, customs were enough, but now, with so much land, with so many people, a written code would clear up many things. I was beginning to do something like it, myself, but the war with Alaric…" He was sorry he'd mentioned the campaign he'd waged against Theodoric's son-in-law and let his voice trail off.

Theodoric didn't reply.

They walked further, with Clovis silently considering the law. A law in writing would make the consequences of crimes uniform throughout Gaul. His father had never known such a code, nor his father before him. It would be a good thing, a code of laws, and he decided it was time to resume work on it.

"Gundobad *is* a fool you know," said Theodoric.

"Hmm?"

"A fool…Gundobad. He can't decide upon his loyalties and his armies are ineffective at best."

"Yes, I suppose," said Clovis, leaving his thoughts of law behind for a moment, and beginning to wonder what Theodoric was getting at.

"In fact," continued the Italian king, "I don't think he deserves the land he gained while fighting with your son."

"But there's not much of that left. Your men took most of it back."

"Not all of it," said Theodoric, smiling.

Clovis stopped and faced the man.

"Just what are you proposing?"

"Taking that land back from Gundobad." Theodoric spoke with a nonchalance that Clovis found almost charming.

"Seriously?"

"And what, my good Clovis, could he do? He's sacrificed his alliances with everyone but you. Since Aridius died he's lost much of his cunning. If we both came against him, he could only surrender."

Clovis smiled at Theodoric's reasoning, knowing full well that he was right. When Gundobad's advisor succumbed to pneumonia, Burgundy lost a great deal of influence.

"You're a vicious man," said Clovis, good naturedly.

"Some say so." Theodoric returned the smile.

"And I am interested," continued Clovis. He imagined Clotild would celebrate any campaign against Gundobad, and with the thought of Clotild, more immediate concerns came back to his mind. "We can talk about this later," he said, "I'm anxious about Clotild."

"Certainly," said Theodoric as they started back toward the gate of the monastery. "And Clovis..." he said, stopping again, "I truly hope your wife will be well."

"Thank you," said Clovis as he put his hand on Theodoric's shoulder. "She's a good woman."

They walked on and the squirrels continued to stalk them.

"Leonard, you must be rewarded." Clotild was well on the way to recovery, and Clovis was convinced that Leonard's prayers were decisive in it. The hermit was making last minute preparations to return to his hermitage in Noblac to the south, and Clovis stood with Mesmin as they watched Leonard tie his few provisions on the back of his donkey. "I've not forgotten what you did for my wife," said Clovis.

Leonard blushed and looked at his godfather.

"A reward's really not necessary."

"Yes it is!" said Clovis. "And here's what I'll do. I'll have a Bishopric conferred upon you."

"No!" Leonard blurted insistently. He stepped away from his donkey. "Please, don't do that. You'd take me away from my home...my place."

"No? Your home is so important, Leonard?"

"Yes, it is...truly."

"Then, Leonard..." said Clovis, quickly enough to make Leonard realize the king never expected him to accept the bishopric; he'd already conceived of an alternative plan, "...this is what I will do: an offer of land." Encouraged by Leonard's silence, Clovis went on. "As much as you can ride around in the course of one night on your donkey." Clovis patted the animal's flanks.

"It's a generous offer, my lord." Leonard was flattered by the compliment. The offer of land seemed very possible. "A monastery could go on the land," he continued. "I accept your offer. But," he held up a finger for emphasis, "may my night's ride be done where I live…at Noblac?"

"Certainly!" Clovis was glad that this gift was acceptable.

"Well then," said Leonard, "I accept and I give you my thanks."

"I'll have Aurelian make the arrangements," said Clovis.

Leonard bowed to him, embraced him, and after offering his farewells to Mesmin, mounted his donkey and began his journey home.

Clotild was not ready to travel for more than a week after Leonard's departure. Theodoric and Clovis used the time together well. The two kings crafted their plans to take what was left of Gundobad's most recently acquired land very much as two little boys might plot to steal cake from a kitchen.

"If all goes well," said Theodoric, "our plans could be fulfilled before winter's done."

"You don't think that's a little ambitious?"

"You'd gain more land, which I'm sure you'd welcome, and," continued Theodoric, "I would add territory to the defensive buffer around Italy. That could serve us both. Gundobad would retain his kingdom, but it would be of little consequence."

The plans grew and changed, the expectations fluctuated and in the meantime, Clotild recovered enough to travel. The hunting party journeyed back to Paris. Clovis was gratified with his wife's reclaimed health. As they traveled, his concerns over Clotild eased and he found his thoughts turning to other recent events.

He'd gained a new respect for Theodoric, founded in familiarity and not fear. He admired Theodoric's ability to protect his kingdom without emotion, and knew that however friendly he became with his brother-in-law, he would never let down his guard.

Clovis thought again about what value there might be in establishing laws for the Franks. But these thoughts were soon crowded from his mind, as a more important matter, entered in, a concern Theodoric had mentioned, one that Clovis had yet to address: the matter of competitors.

Chapter 25
One King for Gaul
509 CE

Aurelian understood what his king was doing, but he didn't like it. Nor did he think the deception necessary. Still, he knew that, with or without his approval, with or without this ploy, Clovis would ultimately succeed in gaining the territory of his relatives.

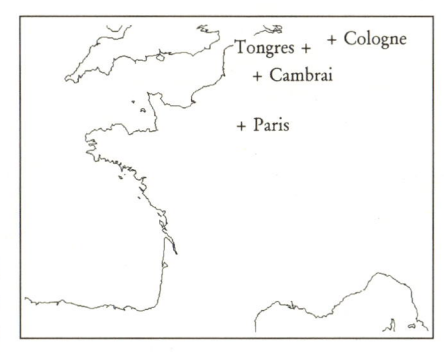

Simon, a goldsmith from the south bank of the Loire, was setting up shop in the palace, after being summoned by Clovis. Out of sight of any curious eyes, bronze and copper armlets and belts were being gilded so they appeared gold. As he supervised the delivery of equipment, Aurelian felt a twinge of regret that he'd ever conveyed the message to Clovis that Ragnachar and his man, Farron, were falling out of favor with their own people. The unashamed and unabashed debauchery the two enjoyed was disgusting not only the common people under Ragnachar's rule, but also the commanders who had served him for so long. The gilded brass jewelry was being prepared for those men, as a bribe, so they might deliver their wretched king to Clovis. There was no mistaking the intent of the plan. The jewelry was payment to those who would betray Ragnachar, false jewelry for false friends. But that would be later.

After the return to Cologne, and the celebrations that followed, Chloderic took the winter to contemplate how he would deal with his father, King Siegbert. At one point, he thought the problem would take care of itself when Siegbert caught a terrible cold that put him in bed for nearly a month, but he recovered. Chloderic began considering again, what he might do to gain the kingdom his father had so handily and considerately maintained. It was time for him to assume the throne, time for Siegbert to pass into memory.

Spring brought opportunity. A rejuvenated Siegbert made plans to camp in the woods near Duisburg, two days journey north of Cologne. Years before, he'd camped in the same woods with his son.

They used to go there in the summer, for weeks at a time, just the two of them. It was there that Chloderic, under his father's watchful eye, had first learned how to wield a sword. Now, because of his health and his age, a half-day's journey was all Siegbert could tolerate. Chloderic knew where his father would camp the first night.

Soon after midday, on the second day of Siegbert's trip, the king limped to a nearby tree.

"Here," he said, waving to his entourage, "I need a rest." Supporting himself against the tree with one arm, he used his other to stir the leaves on the ground with his walking stick, assuring that his bed would be free of animals. He groaned as he crouched to his knees and then turned over to his back, settling for a nap in the shade of the forest canopy.

Two of Siegbert's attendants followed their king's example, falling asleep shortly after they themselves found soft ground, free of rocks. No one was expecting battle. No one was prepared to fight. The servants who traveled with Siegbert were ready to fetch and carry, to do their King's bidding. They were not at war and the men who approached them in the late afternoon, were familiar in any case, men of Cologne, Franks known in Siegbert's court. Approaching openly and slowly, presenting no obvious threat, the men, now in Chloderic's employ, kept a respectful silence.

"Greetings," said the one attendant who remained awake. He spoke softly and lifted a finger to his mouth before pointing to the men around him. "What brings you this way?"

Quietly, in feigned courtesy, one of Chloderic's men came to the guard and whispered, "We've come for the king." With that he quickly brought his left hand up to the man's mouth as he stabbed him with the short sword he drew with his right hand. The guards eyes widened in surprise before they glazed over and he slumped to the ground.

The other assassins took their cue and quickly ended the snoring of the other guards. Then, fulfilling their charge from Chloderic, they stabbed Siegbert to death with one merciful thrust to the heart.

The leader wiped his blade on the leaves beside Siegbert and said, "There. I don't think we woke anyone."

"Yes, Aurelian, what is it?" Clovis was tired after a long day's work.

Aurelian heard the note of annoyance in his king's voice, but continued just the same.

"Siegbert the lame is dead."

"How?"

Chapter 25 *One King for Gaul: 509 CE*

Aurelian noticed the lack of emotion in his king's voice, though he couldn't be sure if it was due to fatigue or some other cause.

"Chloderic sent word that…well, I'll read it, "My father is dead and I have his treasures in my possession—as well as his kingdom. Send men to me and I shall gladly transmit to you from his treasures whatever pleases you." And it's signed by Chloderic himself."

"Things change, eh Aurelian? Things change."

It was the look in his king's eyes, distant and cunning, that convinced Aurelian that Clovis knew more of this than he was letting on.

"Yes, my Lord," he said.

"Take down my response, Aurelian." Clovis thought a moment. "I thank you for your goodwill. Indeed, I will send men to you. Please feel free to show them the extent of your new found wealth, but keep it for yourself. You are deserving of it." Clovis pursed his lips and then nodded, satisfied that the message was sufficient.

It was still a full day's march to Cologne when the army of the Franks stopped. A small contingent of soldiers was sent ahead carrying the note that Clovis had dictated to Aurelian. The men knew their orders.

They arrived in Chloderic's court offering greetings from their king, Clovis. Chloderic heard the generous and gracious words of his friend and couldn't hide his pleasure.

"Good, good," he said. "I'm pleased you could come. Please, come and see our riches. After all, I did promise to show them to you." Leading the men into the heart of the castle of Cologne, into a formidable stronghold, Chloderic came to the treasury, a room near the center of the castle, a room with no windows, lit only from a grate in the ceiling, which let in daylight, and by the glow from three oil lamps. The lamps were lit before the men arrived and sat now on small shelves around the room. Ushering the men into the chamber so ceremoniously that it was nearly comical, with wide waves of his arms and a gaping grin, Chloderic began showing them the spoils that his father had collected. Swords, chalices, sculptures, and jewelry filled the room. The Franks followed their guide, their sense of awe growing as they took in the abundance around them.

Gloating over the treasures of his family, Chloderic came, finally, to a chest that stood at the end of the room. He turned and faced his visitors.

"It was in this chest," and he patted the iron-clad box that stood nearly waist high, "that my father used to put all the gold coins he acquired."

"Could we see, my lord?" asked one of the soldiers, rather indiscreetly.

Chloderic laughed at the directness. "Of course," he said.

With no small effort, he lifted the heavy lid of the chest and revealed the hoard of solidi that filled the coffer.

One of the men saw this as a chance to fulfill the orders Clovis had given them and asked, "Chloderic, tell us, how deep is the chest? Are you sure there's no false bottom to deceive us?" The Franks laughed.

Chloderic was delighted by the question and said, lightly, "Let's find out!" He reached his hand into the center of the chest, groping until his fingertips touched the bottom.

"There!" he said.

He had no chance to say more or even withdraw his arm. As Chloderic had reached for the bottom of the chest, one of his guests quietly drew a battle ax and raised it. Just as Chloderic exclaimed that he had reached bottom, the blade came down onto the back of his head. Gold, blood, and brains mixed, and once again the Franks of Cologne were without a king.

"We'll wait another two days," said Clovis to his new commander, Adalhard. "I don't want them thinking this was planned. We're already running the risk of this appearing too convenient."

Only when the king was convinced that a reasonable amount of time had passed, did the Franks enter Cologne so Clovis might arrange a meeting with the leaders of the city. The city was in an uproar and when the people of Cologne saw Clovis, a cry went up, "That's the killer! It was his men!"

A show of strength was enough to quell the leaderless people of Cologne, and Clovis quickly arranged to meet with the advisors and commanders of the late Siegbert and Chloderic.

Their sorrow was obvious as they struggled to cope with the loss, not only of Siegbert, but also of his heir, Chloderic. Clovis met with them in counsel and began his words with counterfeit compassion.

"I understand your grief. You know better than I do what's happened. Siegbert, my cousin, has been murdered.

"He stood with me against the Alemmani. And his son, Chloderic, stood with me against Alaric. Their loss is a great one. But you must

Chapter 25 *One King for Gaul: 509 CE*

know something. I've learned that it was Chloderic, himself, who sent assassins to kill his father, Siegbert."

Clovis continued to talk over the gasp that came from the elders. "Indeed, Chloderic told me some months ago that he planned to kill his father." Clovis started to pace, slowly, back and forth in front of the men who were now shocked even beyond gasping. "But, I'm sorry to say that I didn't take him seriously. I thought it was only talk. But he was serious. And his plot turned against him, and someone killed him; we don't know who."

"Your men did!" shouted one of the commanders.

"I've heard that as well, but you should know, if renegade Franks did this deed, it was not at my bidding," Clovis lied. "You can believe me or not, but the simple fact is that since this has all happened, you've become a people without a leader." Clovis stopped his pacing. "I offer you this: if you find it acceptable: look to me as your king and I will keep you under my protection."

The room was quiet. Counselor looked at advisor, who looked at commander, who looked at counselor. Clovis knew there would be discussion, and he understood that dissenting voices would need privacy. He turned toward the door and spoke as he walked away from them, "I leave you to confer."

It was a deliberation that did not take long. Soon the leaders were calling for the people of the city to gather together. Word begin to spread that Clovis was in Cologne as a true friend, not as the usurper some thought.

Vachel, a respected elder in Cologne, one of Siegbert's long time advisors, arranged to meet Clovis at the steps of the town hall. They stood together, silently, as a crowd gathered. Vachel's history among the people of Cologne was long enough and respected enough that when there was a prospect of him speaking, a ready ear would turn his way. When the square was full, he stepped forward and raised a hand to quiet the people. Their murmur settled into quiet and he spoke, softly.

"My friends, you know our recent trials. We are without a leader. Clovis, King of the Franks of Tournai, offers his protection and we, the elders and commanders agree with him. It was not through his doing that Chloderic met his fate. Clovis has proven himself our friend. Chloderic had no son and Clovis is his kinsman. So from now on, we look to Clovis as our king!"

Respecting Vachel's wisdom, and remembering how Clovis helped them against the Alemmani, the crowd cheered. The cheer began slowly, but the affirmation grew. The sight of the elders shouting inspired the townspeople to cheer. Soldiers saw the cheering of their commanders and started to bang their shields together. A group close to Clovis lifted him on a shield. It was their highest compliment. He was their new chief. He was their king.

Clovis had not laid eyes on his cousin Chararic since he had defeated Syagrius at Soissons. There had been infrequent correspondence between them and the few soldiers Chararic sent for the campaign against the Visigoths, but nothing more. Clovis approached his cousin's home in Tongres. There was no reason for Chararic to be expecting an attack, but Clovis took no chances and kept his army out of sight. Taking a small entourage and leaving behind specific orders for a sunrise attack, he made his way into town and to Chararic's court.

"Welcome, Clovis!" said Chararic as Clovis was presented, "What brings you to Tongres?"

"Greetings, cousin," said Clovis, bowing slightly, "I've been on business in Cologne, and it seemed convenient to visit you and our cousin Ragnachar as I returned home."

"It's bad business going on in Cologne, isn't it?"

"They'll survive," was the only reply.

Chararic had no reason to suspect a malicious motive on the part of Clovis. He called for a feast, and food was brought as soon as it could be prepared. They ate and drank well into the night and told stories of battle. Chararic was especially interested in the victory against the Visigoths.

"My son," Chararic tilted his head to the young man who sat beside him, "learned the story of your victory from our soldiers. He tells me that Alaric had at least 20,000 more men than you. Were you really outnumbered by that many?"

"Yes, it's true," said Clovis, "God was with us."

"Or the 'Gods', eh?" said Chararic's son through his thin smiling lips. Aksel had remained quiet throughout dinner as he tried to size up this man, Clovis. Though he'd heard a great deal about him, this was the first time he'd seen him. Now he sought a small test.

"No, young Aksel. Not the 'Gods'. They left me—or, rather, I left them—some time ago. The God of Jesus Christ is now my God...a God of power."

"My apologies," said Aksel, sarcastically. "I thought you still worshipped the Gods of our ancestors."

"No longer," said Clovis, challenge rising in his voice.

Chapter 25 *One King for Gaul: 509 CE*

"Enough!" interrupted Chararic. "There are more enjoyable topics of conversation! We have a fire here!" He waved at the hearth and looked at his son, admonishing him with his eyes. "We don't need any more heat." He looked back at Clovis and smiled indulgently. "Tell me, cousin, was Alaric's treasury a full one?"

"Not full enough," said Clovis, "the bulk of it escaped me, I'm sad to say."

The conversation continued, without much contribution from Aksel, until bleary eyes and prolonged yawns convinced them all that it was time to sleep. Clovis and his men were made comfortable and the house of Chararic fell into a deep slumber-filled silence.

Morning arrived, accompanied by the sounds of soldiers shouting orders and others running to their posts. Clovis and his men wasted no time. At the first sounds they subdued the surprised guards who were standing by in the palace hallways. Then, with frightening efficiency, they took Chararic and Aksel captive and led them to the throne room.

"What is this?" said Chararic. He'd not yet shaken off the fog of sleep.

"You're my prisoners," said Clovis with a smug smile.

"Prisoners? In my own palace? Clovis have you gone mad?"

"Not at all. That noise," he used his scramasax to point toward the window, "is my army. I rule Tongres now."

Aksel, awake now, understood his situation all too clearly. "Are we going to be killed?" he asked nervously, his mouth dry.

"No, Aksel. You're my kinsman. It wouldn't be right for me to kill you." Clovis knew that he would kill this impertinent young man himself if he had to, but he didn't think it necessary just yet. "Instead," he said, remembering Aksel's disdain of his Lord, "I think it would be good for you to serve my God."

Aksel looked into the face of the one who now ruled his fate. Clovis looked back, showing the smirk of one who believes, for the moment at least, that he is the master of all fates.

Soon the battle outside was over, the Franks of Clovis victorious over Chararic's overwhelmed forces. When the palace was secure, Clovis removed Chararic and his son, Aksel, to prison where, before the day was out, they underwent tonsure, as Falco, the bishop of Tongres, fearfully obeyed the order of Clovis and made preparations to ordain Chararic, priest, and Aksel, deacon.

Chararic sat with his back against the cell wall, watching his son pace and kick straw. "If my people see me like this…" he said indignantly, "…such dishonor!" Chararic rubbed his hand over his bare scalp and then put his head on his knees in dismay. Long hair, the mark of a king, now gone.

Aksel stopped his pacing and looked down at his father. The top of Chararic's shaved head reflected the light in their cell. He moved his hand over his own bare head and simultaneously felt his father's humiliation. Aksel's love for his father and his hatred for Clovis grew in the same moment.

"Our hair will grow back, father; there's still sap in these trees," he patted his chest with both hands, "and our hair will grow back as quickly and as thickly as ever," he looked toward the grate on the door, and beyond, toward where he imagined Clovis was working his treachery, and with loathing in his voice, said, "and may he who put us here perish as swiftly!"

"Aksel!" snapped Chararic, "The guards!" But it was too late. The threat could not be unspoken. Now their only hope was that the guard hadn't heard, or that the guard was a traitor to Clovis. But both hopes were futile.

Clovis was informed of the threat, and took it at face value. It was more justification than he needed, but one he was glad to have. Without hesitation, Clovis gave the order to execute the men. Father and son were beheaded without trial or comment. Clovis bothered himself no further with it, choosing to be absent as the sentence was administered. When he was informed that the execution had been carried out he nonchalantly accepted the news and, when the messenger was gone, he looked to the south, thinking, now,…Ragnachar.

Throughout Ragnachar's reign, the people of Cambrai had become more and more offended at the wantonness of their king and that of his friend, Farron. The years had taught neither of them restraint, and their appetites for debauchery had only grown to include even incest. Some wondered how far the excesses could go. In recent months, Ricchar, Ragnachar's younger brother, had risen to a place of power, but with no greater success in gaining the people's affection. His own weakness and indecision had become a source of embarrassment to the people of Cambrai. So the people were less than enthusiastic when Ragnachar, Farron and Ricchar stood before them calling upon them to defend Cambrai against the armies of Clovis.

Chapter 25 *One King for Gaul: 509 CE*

The approach of Clovis came as no surprise. Men escaping from Tongres had related the tale of Chararic's downfall. As soon as this information came to light, Ragnachar sent out spies to learn the strength that Clovis was bringing to bear upon him, a task easy enough in the land around Cambrai, a terrain that denied any secrecy in approach. The reports that came back were encouraging. "Your numbers are more than enough to overpower them, my lord; your army is strong enough," was the deliberate and consistently erroneous response his commanders relayed to him. Ragnachar waited several days as Clovis and his men drew nearer, and at last decided the time was right to fight.

Once on the field of battle, Ragnachar and his men stood looking out at the attacking army in utter horror. For now, the truth became clear. All, including Ragnachar, saw that the army of Clovis far outnumbered the army of Cambrai.

There was a small group of soldiers, however, who watched Ragnachar more closely than they watched Clovis. They watched as Ragnachar sat sweating on his steed. They watched his brother, Ricchar, and his man, Farron, as they awaited the first assaults.

When they came, they came from Clovis, and were vicious. It was only a matter of moments before the men of Cambrai scattered and Ragnachar realized he was beaten. He turned to run, followed by his brother and his friend, but the effort was short-lived.

When the group watching Ragnachar and his companions saw them bolt, they pursued them and pulled them from their horses. Farron was killed in the process, run through by a soldier who was unable to control his anger. Ragnachar and Ricchar, apprehended by men who were more restrained, were bound for delivery to Clovis.

Those few men who remained loyal to Ragnachar were crushed. The others, the bulk of Ragnachar's army, laid down their weapons, unwilling to fight a losing battle for a chief they abhorred. Now, with the battle complete, Ragnachar, his hands still tied behind his back, stood before Clovis.

"You're a sad excuse for a Frank, Ragnachar! Why have you humiliated our family in letting yourself be bound?" Clovis looked down on his cousin who hung his head in shame and resignation. "It would have been better for you to die in battle."

Ragnachar began to cry. Clovis half-feigned indignation and then swiftly raised his ax and brought it down against his cousin's bowed head. Ragnachar's lifeless form fell to the floor.

Ricchar gasped as he watched his brother die and then looked at Clovis with fear in his eyes, "Now me?"

As if to justify what he was about to do, Clovis said, "If you'd helped your brother, he wouldn't have faced the indignity of being bound."

Again Clovis raised his ax and brought Ricchar's body down next to Ragnachar's. The soldiers who had delivered the two brothers stood and watched, pleased they had helped bring the fall of Ragnachar. A celebration followed the executions, with no regrets or grief over a king brought down.

The men who had worked for Clovis ate and drank, bragging about their part in Ragnachar's downfall and waving gold jewelry over their heads. A careless hand dropped a bracelet on the stone floor and it's landing was scarcely heard. The bracelet clanged and began to roll away from the soldier who'd let it fall. A quick step and a foot on the bracelet ground it into the stone and brought it to a stop. The soldier stooped to picked it up, noticing copper looking out from behind a thin gilding, now partially worn away. He gave a yell of surprise and anger. This outburst was heard and it quieted the room.

Lifting the bracelet over his head and moving toward the king's table, the soldier asked, "Good Clovis, what is this?"

Clovis looked at the man and the bracelet, pausing long enough for some other soldiers to check their gifts. Then, looking around, with an air of authority the men had never seen from their own king, he said, "It's only right that this kind of gold comes to those who willingly bring their own master to death! You should be glad that you haven't been tortured and executed as traitors!"

The soldiers recoiled at the words, asking pardon, and very quickly, the festivities were over.

Two weeks later, one last remaining cousin of Clovis, Rignomer of Le Mans, an especially quiet and unambitious man, was killed as he slept. Clovis continued in his efforts, seeking any distant relations that might prove a threat, but there were none left. The lands and treasures of all the Franks became the property of Clovis.

A dutiful Aurelian began a morning's business with the confirmation of Rignomer's death.

Clovis smiled from his throne. He began to rock back and forth in obvious satisfaction, looking, first at Aurelian, then through him, then upward and outward seeing a vision of a changed world. "Can anyone challenge me now?" he said, "Gaul is mine!"

Chapter 26
One Church
510 CE

Remigius looked at the bishops who were meeting in Reims at his request. The group included Adventinus, who had succeeded Solemnus as bishop of Chartres; Avitus of Vienne; Heraclius of Paris; Germerius, who was now the bishop of Toulouse; Eleutherius of Tournai and young Carentinus of the newly established church in Cologne. Vedastus was also present, recently made the bishop of Arras and Cambrai, joining Eleutherius in the task of instructing Franks who had become baptized.

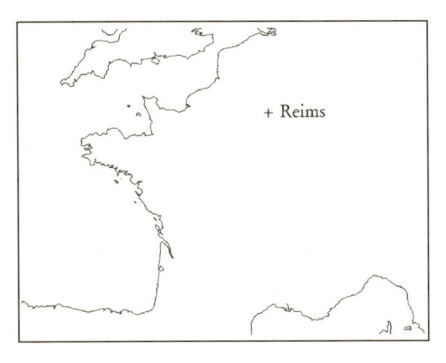

In calling them together, Remigius made his agenda clear. They were to discuss the security of the Church in Gaul. Now they sat, waiting for their convener to begin, nibbling at the food provided for them: hare, fruit, bread, and a thin wine.

"My brothers," said Remigius, when he finally started, "circumstances for the Church have shifted dramatically in the past ten years. Wouldn't you agree?" All the bishops nodded their heads. "It's only right that we should consider where the Church stands at this moment. And I've asked you, specifically, because you represent the whole of Gaul. Also," he cleared his throat loudly, "you've had contact with our king in varied circumstances, and to a significant degree, I believe, the state of the Church today is dependent upon the impact Clovis has had up to now and will have in the future.

"I suspect that our perspectives are all different. And they will all be heard. I'll ask Eleutherius to begin, because he's spent the longest time among the Franks."

Eleutherius bowed in acknowledgment to Remigius, still chewing a bite of apple. Remigius thought the bishop of Tournai was not the same man he'd been when he first met Clovis. Nearly a quarter of a century had passed since then. Good relationships with the Chieftain-turned-king had blessed Eleutherius abundantly. He was more worldly now, too fond of good food and drink. He wiped his face and stood to speak.

"Thank you Remigius," he said through his food, and then swallowed. "As you know, Clovis now makes his capital in Paris. But a large number of Franks still live in and around Soissons and Tournai. As far as I can tell, they remain loyal to Clovis. And, as you also know, many are now Christian, though more so in Soissons than in Tournai. Ever since the King's baptism it's been popular to be Christian.

"The Franks who lived under the ill-begotten guidance of Ragnachar are coming along more slowly. But it appears that the Church is gaining influence among them, now that Clovis has removed the wretch. From my perspective, I believe there's good reason to be encouraged for the Church. She grows in strength, thanks be to God!"

Eleutherius seated himself and Remigius nodded his thanks, while saying, "Next, I would ask Germerius to speak about the south of Gaul."

It was common knowledge that Clovis had recently granted Germerius lands in the district of Dux, near Toulouse. The grant had come from the lands of Alaric and were substantial. The bishops expected Germerius to give a favorable report.

The young bishop came slowly to his feet—more slowly than even drama would have required. The look on his handsome face told the other bishops that he was still considering what he would say. They waited patiently.

"The south of Gaul is weak," he began. "Clovis did wonderful things for the Church there, but it is weak. The Visigoths have been driven south, nearly to the Pyrenees but the Arians are still plentiful. The influence of Alaric will not fade quickly.

"It's true that many people welcomed Clovis when he defeated Alaric. And I, myself, have benefited from his kindness. But Arians have been in prominent positions there for years, and many remain today. That being the case, progress for the Church is rather slow.

"On the other hand," he said in a more conciliatory tone, "Clovis is helping the Church. At his command a new monastery was founded near Limoges. If that sort of thing continues, there will be reason to be hopeful. So, we are weak, but things are improving." He paused and sucked at a piece of food wedged in his teeth and said, "Yes, things are improving."

Germerius took his seat as the others affirmed their understanding by nodding in unison. Remigius called next upon Avitus.

"Things are better in Burgundy," said the bishop from Vienne. "I tell you nothing new when I mention the conversion of Gundobad.

Chapter 26 *One Church: 510 CE*

With his conversion the Church has been making long strides forward. Arians are becoming more difficult to find, and, barring the unexpected, which we ought not entirely do, I believe the Church will prevail in Burgundy."

Adventinus of Chartres was the next bishop to report. He was a young bishop, nervous in this gathering, and it showed. Avitus remembered a similar meeting, that took place years before, and he looked over at Remigius. The smile on the elder Bishop's face showed that they were sharing the same memory of a young and uncertain Avitus.

"I'm pleased to tell you that the Loire is secure," said Adventinus. "Actually, thanks in large part to the work of Bishop Solemnus, it's been secure for some time. But with Clovis removing the Visigoths from the region, it's become even stronger. The people believe in the Trinity, with only a few exceptions, as far as I can tell, and it will take more than I can imagine for the Church to lose her hold in my region."

"Good!" said Remigius with a note of affirming kindness in his voice. "It's always nice to hear of strongholds." The bishop of Reims smiled at the young bishop, then encouraged him to take his seat, which Adventinus did, relieved that his part was done. Remigius focused his attention next on the bishop of Cologne.

"Carentinus."

"Thank you, Father." As had his peers, Carentinus stood to speak. "The situation in the portion of Gaul I serve is not secure. It's not substantially different from the south that Germerius described a moment ago. The difference is that pagans, and not Arians, live where I serve." Carentinus reached for his goblet and took a drink, reluctant to say what had to be said. "There is, however, a more dangerous threat that we have not yet mentioned. I believe the Church is well on the way to being secured against the threat of Arianism. Were that to happen, though," he hesitated momentarily, "I'm not so certain that the Church could survive an attack from Clovis himself."

There was a hush from the bishops. Finally Germerius blurted, "What are you saying?"

But before Carentinus could answer, Avitus said, "I know one ruler in Burgundy who doesn't trust Clovis."

His tone was even as he said the words, but Eleutherius didn't hear anything other than attack. "Is Gundobad any more trustworthy?" he said in his King's defense. "Clovis has confessed his sins to me, and I'm convinced his remorse is real."

"And Gundobad's confessed to me," returned Avitus, his voice raised now, slightly. "I could say the same thing about him!"

"Clovis hasn't proven himself to be beyond reproach in the north, that much is certain," said Carentinus, regaining the floor. "I know the official word is that renegade Franks killed Chloderic, but the people are still asking questions about Clovis, asking if he didn't arrange the murder."

"But he has no reason to turn against the Church," said Remigius, reasonableness in his voice. "We all know he'll do what he has to, as any king trying to increase his lands would, but he has every reason to remain allied with the Church. He's spoken to me recently of calling a Council of Bishops in Orléans."

"I don't understand your concern, Carentinus," Adventinus interjected. "Are you saying that we should we be afraid of Clovis?"

Carentinus allowed his tone to soften. "I hope we don't have to be. Whatever happened in Cologne, we know that he turned on his own family, killing his cousins in Tongres and Cambrai, to strengthen his own position. I would worry for the Church if Clovis ever sees it as a hindrance to his power!"

Still feeling that he must defend Clovis, Eleutherius raised his voice, "That warning should go for Gundobad as well!"

Then Remigius, not relishing the possibility of a battle between the bishops, brought his hand up sharply, which was enough to bring a halt to the discussion.

"Carentinus," he said, breaking the silence he'd imposed, "there's no reason to be concerned about that sort of history. Our task, now, is to ascertain how strong the Church is at this instant. And on the whole, it does appear to be doing well. We should remember that it's because of Clovis that we have the position we now enjoy. It's because of Clovis that the roads are open again. Not only is that helping the trade of Gaul, but it's speeding the message of our Lord. Missionaries are journeying to the north regularly these days." Remigius hacked violently. "Excuse me." He cleared the phlegm from his throat before going on. "I'm convinced that there are reasons to be optimistic. Don't you Heraclius?"

All eyes turned to the bishop of Paris. Heraclius had been bishop of the island city, and for the growing Parisian community, for almost as long as Remigius had been in Reims. He worked quietly for the Church, trying to balance his desire to be on good terms with Clovis, against his need to manage the direction of Church life in Paris.

Chapter 26 *One Church: 510 CE*

"I continue to be optimistic. Clovis supports the work of the Church in Paris, though sometimes he tries to direct it. Occasionally he succeeds. Usually he heeds my advice, though. Yes, I'm optimistic."

His words were spoken with conviction but Remigius heard a note of hesitation, a hint of reservation that concerned him.

At least in principle, the bishops agreed with Remigius that Clovis was not a danger to the Church at the present moment. With only Carentinus taking exception, the bishops judged that it was premature and counter-productive to imagine Clovis a threat. The topic was dropped.

The bishops filled three days with talk as they tried to arrive at a consensus about which steps ought to be taken to strengthen the Church, ranging from doctrinal emphases to the most advantageous locations for new churches. A banquet closed the meetings and during the feast, the bishops thanked God for lifting the true Church to such a place of predominance.

"What is it?" Eleutherius asked.

Personal business had caused him to remain in Reims long after the other bishops had departed. Now, two weeks later, as he, himself, prepared to leave, a worried Remigius stood before him, a letter in his hands.

"Maybe Carentinus was right," said Remigius, "Listen to this. It's from Clovis:

"Greetings and salutations! It is with joy that this correspondence is prepared for you as I believe I have information that will be of interest. As you wield power in the Church throughout Gaul, your words carrying great weight in the appointing of bishops and priests, I offer a name for your consideration.

"Claudius, who resides in Paris, has become known to me and would be of use to the work and goals of the Church.

"I humbly request that you confer upon Claudius orders to serve the Church as a priest. The location I leave to your good judgment. As we work together to make our lands secure, I'm certain appointments like this will be of value. I await your favorable response and remain, your servant, Clovis."

"Damn!" said Remigius as he slapped his hands together, crushing the letter. "What put the idea in his head that we would appoint a priest at the recommendation of someone outside the Church? Good Lord!"

The two bishops sat in silence letting the shock wear off. The issues were clear, but they were in conflict. On one hand, it was against Canon Law to appoint a priest in such a fashion. On the other hand, the bishops of Gaul had already committed themselves, earlier in secret, and now openly, to Clovis.

"Claudius!" said Remigius, shaking his head. "It would be bad enough if he was asking us to appoint someone respectable. But if this is the Claudius that's been a thorn in our side for the last four years...!"

"Maybe we could explain the problem to him," offered Eleutherius. "If this is that same Claudius, surely Clovis would understand if we told him about the man's lechery."

"Perhaps. Perhaps. And yet, when it comes right down to it, I think I'd rather gain a bad priest than lose Clovis as an ally."

"But we can't compromise the integrity of the Church for him."

"No, of course not," said Remigius as he leaned back in his chair. He mused a long moment. "Bishop Falco in Tongres did bow to the King's wishes when Chararic was defeated. There is a precedent, I suppose."

"But that was war," said Eleutherius, "It's altogether a different case."

"And Falco has no backbone anyway," added Remigius. He began to tap his finger on his lips, "Then again..." he said, stretching out the words as long as he could, "...we might turn our backs on procedure for a moment...using that precedent, I mean. I believe I'm willing to risk that much if we must."

Eleutherius made no secret of his concern. "We could pay for this kind of thinking, Remigius. Heraclius certainly won't approve. He's the one who's had to put up with Claudius."

"I know...I know," said Remigius. He thought back to the Bishop's meeting and remembered the note of odd hesitation he detected in the voice of Heraclius. It caused him to wonder if this request on the behalf of Claudius wasn't already at work then. He shook his head. "I can't see that we have any choice. If we refuse Clovis and he decides we're his enemy..." Even as he spoke, Remigius knew he'd do what Clovis asked, and he frowned at the thought. He'd be insulting Heraclius, as bishop of Paris, in the process, besides flying in the face of Canon Law. For the first time he wondered if Clovis might actually do the Church more harm than good.

Chapter 27
One Love
510-511 CE

The law of the Salian Franks was finally taking shape. Clovis knew it was pointless to attempt a code that covered every facet of the law, but he was pleased at what work was getting done, nonetheless. Started as a project before the war with Alaric, but dropped for years, a written law of the Franks was finally being realized. The laws being collected were the ones most commonly exercised, along with those which gave rise to the most confusion when they were utilized without a sufficient clarity of purpose. The code covered a broad range of subjects. Everything from crime to inheritance to court procedures was being addressed. Clovis, in his royal garb, and Aurelian, with quill in hand, were working together, supervising a team of lawyers who had been selected for this formidable task. As Clovis and Aurelian spoke, the lawyers labored, taking notes that would be transcribed later.

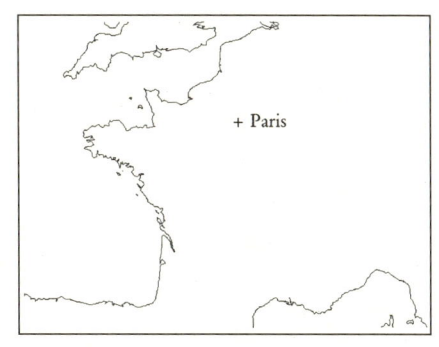

"The wergeld..." Clovis hesitated, taking care to choose his words well. "To redeem oneself for various crimes," he said, continuing, "a wergeld must be paid." The wergeld was a system of fines he'd come to know well. He found it equitable and functional. "Not only to repay the individual harmed," said Clovis, "but also the community. One third of the wergeld will go to the state and two-thirds to the victim or their family. Now, the specifics." He turned and looked at his secretary. "We can put these in order later. For now let's just name them as they come to us."

"Of course," said Aurelian. He knew that putting this document together was going to be a lengthy process.

"If a Frank assaults and robs a Roman," began Clovis, "the fine will be 1200 denarii. The testimony of twenty people on his behalf can release him of any wrongdoing. But if a Roman commits the same crime against a Frank, it will take the testimony of twenty-five people to clear him of his crime. And if he cannot be cleared, his fine will be 2500 denarii." He paused to make certain that his words were being noted. "If anyone kills a Frank they'll pay 8000 denarii. Anyone killing a Roman, as long as he's not one of my officials, will pay 4000 denarii, but if he is one of my officials it will be 12,000..."

The work of detailing the code stretched to fill days and then weeks, with considerations of one statute requiring another to be expressed. The work fed Clovis.

With her husband involved in compiling the law, and with the children growing, Clotild was finding more time to be involved with the work of the Church. Chlotar, now nine, was sometimes brought along when Clotild went to work among the poor. More often, though, Basina would watch the children at home. Tranquillinus helped her, and in those moments proved himself to be more capable with children than anyone might have envisioned. That especially delighted Basina. "He's certainly no Childeric," she said, when people asked about their relationship, "but then," she would add with a smile, "Childeric was no Tranquillinus, either." It was clear, to anyone who cared to notice, that Basina and Tranquillinus were devoted to one another.

Whether or not her son joined her, Clotild continued to enjoy serving the needs of the poor. Still, it was not the same without her dear Genevieve. It had been over four years since Genevieve had received the gift of a peaceful death. She was found lifeless in her bed, her hands crossed over her heart and a smile gracing her face. Clotild thought of her nearly every day. Around her neck she wore Genevieve's necklace, which she'd admired the day she met Genevieve. The people of Paris gave it to Clotild, a gift in memory of their beloved friend, and Clotild wore it always.

At first, Clotild's grief had been so great that her husband worried for her health. He offered to help in any way he could and, for reasons Clotild could only ascribe to God, she asked for a church—a church in which to bury Genevieve. The request was granted instantly.

Houses were cleared, families were displaced, surveyors set about marking the foundation of the place of worship so the work could begin at a hilltop sight on the southern bank of the Seine. Genevieve was buried temporarily, near the grave of Bishop Prudentius, a predecessor of Heraclius, to be moved to her final resting place when it was ready for her.

A sarcophagus for Genevieve's remains was ordered from Ravenna, a city renowned for its stonework. It was delivered to Paris shortly before Christmas, and brought at once to the palace so Clovis and

Chapter 27 *One Love: 510-511 CE*

Clotild could inspect it. On a cold and drizzling day the king and queen walked from the palace to the stable, where the wagon carrying the sarcophagus was to be viewed. The walls of the casket were a handbreadth thick and it lay open now, and empty, waiting to be filled and then capped with the gently rounded cover which rested on the wagon next to the box. Carvings, crosses grouped in threes, symbolizing the blessed Trinity, covered the outside. It seemed the proper resting place for their friend. Clotild cried at the sight.

As the main part of the church began to take shape, Clotild found it easier to bear the loss. Newly cut steps were put in place and Clotild watched the work, imagining Genevieve reaching out to those in need, there on the steps. The image warmed her heart.

As rumor and Remigius had said, Clovis issued a call for a council of bishops to be held in the city of Orléans. The call itself was encouraging to the leaders of the Church, an indication of support from the king. No such council had been called for the Arian bishops. Bishops from all over Gaul were invited, Goths and Franks alike. Cyprian of Bordeaux, formerly under the sway of Alaric, presided at the council. Still, there was some anxiety, for included with the call was an agenda, set by Clovis himself.

As the preparations for the council neared their fulfillment, Clovis left the work of the law in the hands of Aurelian, freeing himself to join with the leaders of the Church. Thirty-two bishops met with the king on the 10th of July and delved into the issues Clovis had charged them to address.

In the Cathedral at Orléans, the meeting convened with the bishops seated in a circle. Remigius stayed quiet, for the most part, nervous as he pondered the idea that a king might grow to have too much power. One canon that Clovis suggested for the council's approval was especially bothersome to Remigius. It began, "No layman is to be ordained a cleric except by the command of the king...." In spite of his concern over the implications of such an idea, Remigius was pleased at the restraint Clovis exhibited in the Council. The king limited his participation to greetings and listening, speaking only when asked a question, and was absent for sufficient amounts of time to allow the bishops honest and frank discussion.

Initially, the bishops were offended at the very idea that Clovis would presume to understand their needs as clergy. But his words proved impressive, both on paper and in defense of his suggestions. Early in the proceedings, Remigius resigned himself to the decisions he knew the council would make, and became anxious for the gathering to end. He distanced himself from the conversations, waved off questions, generally ignored the debate, and realized he wanted to be with his birds. Ultimately, the bishops adopted the regulations their king suggested, thirty-one in all. It became clear to Remigius: Clovis did indeed rule in Gaul.

"Of Salic land, no portion of the inheritance shall go to a woman, but shall go to a man…" Aurelian repeated the inheritance rule back to Clovis, making certain the copyists were hearing it correctly. There was little chance for error. Since anyone, anywhere, could remember, it was through the male that property had passed. It was decided to include this particular and obvious statute in the law lest someone contest the custom on the basis of omission from the law. It was too important to leave such a possibility to chance. "Yes, that's fine," said Clovis, and the copyists scribbled the words.

"A lengthy task, eh Aurelian?"

"My hand will never be the same," said his friend, shaking his left hand and massaging it with his right. He was leaving the bulk of the work to the copyists, but taking notes throughout the process.

Clovis smiled. "Another day or two should complete it."

Aurelian continued to rub his hand. "I look forward to having it done."

In the shadow cast by the church, Clovis and Clotild stood arm in arm, watching the construction as it progressed. With the dusk, the swifts were out, their shrill whistle piercing the air. The two watched the birds swoop and dive around the walls, racing to catch the most insects. Genevieve loved the swifts, Clovis remembered. He continued to look at the birds and let memories of Genevieve come back to him: the first time he heard her name from his frustrated father, the first time he saw her and she recognized him as Childeric's son, the way Clotild looked in her company. He remembered the look in Clotild's eyes after she'd spent that first day working with her. He knew he would always be grateful to Genevieve for that.

He considered the life he'd shared with the woman he held and a warmth flowed through his body. He tilted his head so that it touched Clotild's and he recalled the day she crossed the frontier of Burgundy, into the land of the Franks—into his life. Marveling that their paths

Chapter 27 *One Love: 510-511 CE*

had ever crossed at all, he offered a prayer of thanks. Prayers were coming easier to him these days.

Workers carrying scraps of materials away from the building caught his attention. The church was imposing; a full forty feet longer than St. Martin's Basilica in Tours. Its marble columns topped with ornate carvings were dramatic. And soon, there would be mosaics inside that would be the glory of Paris.

"It's a good church, Clovis," said Clotild as she patted his hand.

"Yes," he said, "it is a good church. Genevieve would have liked it, I think."

"Yes, I think she would have."

Past the construction, between two buildings, Clovis could just catch a glimpse of the island where Genevieve had so diligently served her Lord. It was her domain, small, but loyal. As he remembered Genevieve, he realized she'd never wanted a domain, not like his father, Childeric, had desired. She only wanted to serve. Clovis allowed an image of the Gaul he ruled to pass through his mind. It was a nation now, the Franks were a people united, not simply a group of tribes. That would have pleased his father.

He pulled his wife closer to him, feeling her warmth as she burrowed into his embrace, and in the deepening dusk he thought about his father…and wondered about God.

Epilogue

Clovis did not live long after the completion of the Church of the Holy Apostles and the Lex Salica. He died of unknown causes in the year 511—some sources say on November 27. By the time Clovis was buried in the Church he had helped to build, it had already been renamed for St. Genevieve.

Upon his death, Gaul was divided between his four sons with Theuderic becoming ruler over the kingdom of Metz, Chlodomer ruling over the kingdom of Orléans, Childebert ruling the kingdom of Paris, and Chlothar ruling over the kingdom of Soissons. Such a dispersal would prove unfortunate, for while the line of Merovingian kings continued into the 700's, the glory that Gaul had known under Clovis would not be repeated until after the Carolingian line of kings was in place, with Pepin the Short, in the year 751 CE.

History quotes the epitaph of Clovis, attributed to Remigius, as follows:

"Rich in resources, powerful in virtue, illustrious in triumph, King Clovis founded this realm. Ever an eminent nobleman, his life was resplendent with honor. Full of love of God, he despised belief in a thousand gods who caused terror by various portents. Cleansed in water and reborn in the font of Christ, his fragrant hair was anointed with chrism. He gave an example which great crowds of heathen people followed, and spurning the error of their ways honored God as creator and true parent. By his merits Clovis surpassed the exploits of his ancestors. He was always to be feared in council, in camp, and in war. A leader, fluent in exhortation and strong of heart, he stood in the first line of battle."

Following her husband's death, Clotild went to Tours to lead a life of holiness and perhaps some bitterness. Eventually, says Gregory, she pushed her sons to attack Sigismond, the son of her parent's murderer, Gundobad.

Clotild died in Tours in the year 545. Her body was brought to Paris so that it might be laid to rest next to that of her husband. She was later canonized by the Roman Catholic Church.

Family Tree 325

THE FAMILY OF CLOVIS

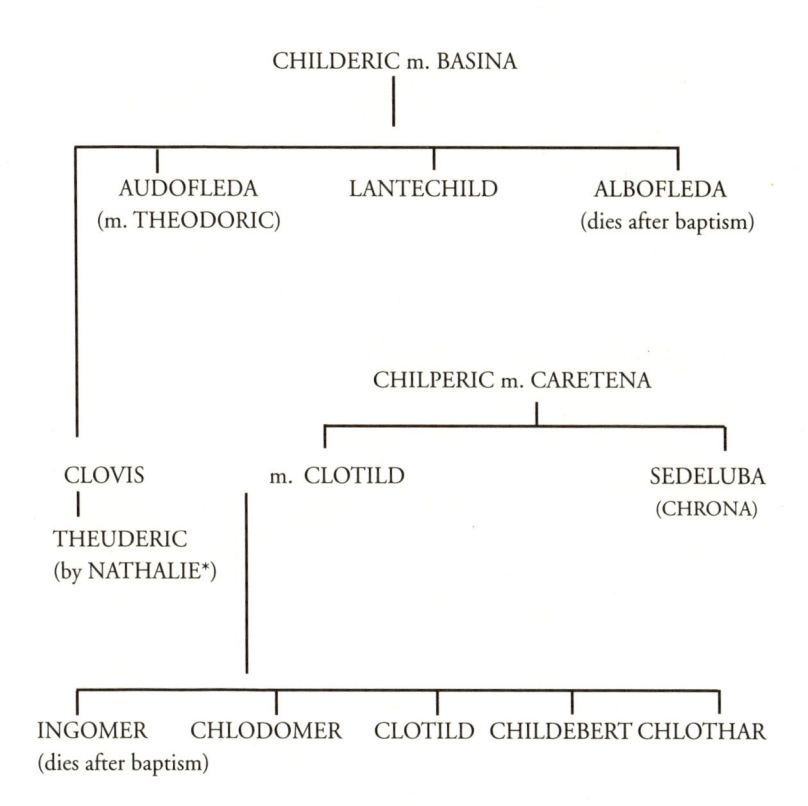

```
                    CHILDERIC m. BASINA
        ┌──────────────────┼──────────────────┐
    AUDOFLEDA          LANTECHILD          ALBOFLEDA
   (m. THEODORIC)                        (dies after baptism)


                              CHILPERIC m. CARETENA
                         ┌─────────────┴─────────────┐
    CLOVIS         m. CLOTILD                    SEDELUBA
      │                                          (CHRONA)
   THEUDERIC
   (by NATHALIE*)
      │
   ┌──────────┬──────────┬──────────┬──────────┐
 INGOMER  CHLODOMER   CLOTILD   CHILDEBERT  CHLOTHAR
(dies after baptism)
```

* name fictitious

GLOSSARY OF NAMES

Alaric II - King of the Visigoths

Albofleda - Sister of Clovis, who died after being baptised

Aridius - Roman advisor to Gundobad

Audofleda - Sister of Clovis and wife of Theodoric

Aurelian - Advisor to the Roman ruler, Syagrius and, later, to Clovis

Avitus - Bishop of Vienne in Burgundy

Basina - Mother of Clovis

Caretena - Mother of Clotild, murdered by Gundobad

Chararic - Chief of the Franks in Tongres

Childebert - Son of Clovis and Clotild

Childeric - Father of Clovis

Chilperic - Father of Clotild

Chloderic - Son of Siegbert of Cologne

Chlodomer - Son of Clovis and Clotild

Chlothar - Son of Clovis and Clotild

Clotild - Daughter of the Burgundian king, Chilperic, destined to be the bride of Clovis. Also the name of one daughter of Clovis and Clotild

Clovis - King of the Franks

Eleutherius - Bishop of Tournai

Glossary of Names

Genevieve - Saintly friend of Clovis and Clotild, help to the poor of Paris

Gerard - Oldest friend of Clovis and First Commander of the home guard (name fictitious)

Godegesil - Brother of Gundobad

Gundobad - King of Burgundy

Lantechild - Sister of Clovis

Nathalie - Concubine who gave Clovis his first son, Thierry (name fictitious)

Principius - Bishop of Soissons and brother of Remigius

Ragnachar - Chief of the Franks in Cambrai

Remigius - Bishop of Reims, known for wise and intelligent sermons

Siegbert - Chief of the Franks in Cologne

Solemnus - Bishop of Chartres

Theuderic - Son of Clovis and Nathalie

Theodoric - Arian king of Ostrogothic Italy

Tranquillinus - Court physician to Clovis

BIBLIOGRAPHY

Ambrosianischer Choral. A recording of Ambrosian Chants by Capella Musicale Del Duomo Di Milano. English translation of Latin Lyric by Hans Heimler. Milan: Archiv Produktion, 1975.

Anderson, Robert Gordon. *The Biography of a Cathedral.* New York: Longmans, Green and Co., 1945.

Ante-Nicene Christian Library: Translations of the Writings of the Fathers down to A.D. 325. ed. Rev. Alexander Roberts, D.D., & James Donaldson, Ll. D. Vol. XXIV, Early Liturgies and other Documents. Edinburgh: T.& T. Clark, 1872.

Bachrach, Bernard S. "Was The Marchfield Part of the Frankish Constitution?" *Mediaeval Studies* vol. XXXVI, 1974.

Bainton, Roland H. *Christendom.* vol. 1. New York: Harper Colophon Books, 1966.

Baring-Gould, Rev. S. *The Lives of the Saints.* Edinburgh: John Grant, 1914.

Bateman, J.C. *Ierne of Armorica: A Tale of the Time of Chlovis.* London: Burns and Oates, 1873.

Beale, S. Sophia. *The Churches of Paris From Clovis to Charles X.* London: W.H. Allen & Co. Limited, 1983.

The Bible. Revised Standard Version.

The Book of Saints. A Dictionary of Servants of God Canonized by the Catholic Church: extracted from the Roman and other Martyrologies. Compiled by the Benedictine Monks of St. Augustine's Abbey, Ramsgate. New York: The Macmillan Co., 1947.

Bovini, Guiseppe. *Ravenna.* trans., Robert Erich Wolf. New York: Harry N. Abrams, Inc., 1971.

Brittain, Alfred and Carroll, Mitchell. *Women of Early Christianity.* Woman in all ages and in all countries. Philadelphia: The Rittenhouse Press, 1908.

Brown, Peter. *The Cult of the Saints.* Chicago: The University of Chicago Press, 1981.

Bussy, George Moir and Gaspey, Thomas. *The Pictoral History of France and of the French People; from the Establishment of the Franks in Gaul, to the Period of the French Revolution.* London, W.S. Orr and Co., 1843.

Butler's Lives of the Saints. ed. Herbert Thurston, S.J. and Donald Attwater. New York: P.J. Kennedy and Sons, 1956.

The Cambridge Economic History of Europe. vol. III, Economic Organization and Policies in the Middle Ages. ed. M.M. Postan, E.E. Rich and Edward Miller. Cambridge: University Press, 1965.

The Cambridge Medieval History. vol. II, The Rise of the Saracens and the Foundation of the Western Empire. ed. H.M. Gwatkin and J.P. Whitney. Cambridge: University Press, 1967.

Cassiodorus, The Letters of. London Henry Frowde, 1886.

The Catholic Encyclopaedia. New York: Encyclopaedia Press, 1907-1950.

Chevallier, Raymond. *Roman Roads.* trans. N.H. Field. Los Angeles: University of California Press, 1976.

Childeric - Clovis; 1500e Anniversaire, 482-1982. Tournai: 1982.

Clerq, Carlo De. *La Legislation Religieuse Franque De Clovis à Charlemagne.* Paris: Univeristy de Louvain, 1936.

Delany, John J. *Dictionary of Saints.* Garden City, NY: Doubleday & Co., Inc., 1980.

Dill, Sir Samuel. *Roman Society in Gaul in the Merovingian Age.* London: Macmillan and Company, Ltd., 1926.

Drew, Katherine Fischer. *The Laws of the Salian Franks.* Philadelphia: University of Pennsylvania Press, 1991.

Dupuy, Colonel Trevor N. *The Evolution of Weapons and Warfare.* Indianapolis: The Bobbs-Merrill Company, Inc., 1980.

Durant, Will. *The Age of Faith.* New York: Simon and Schuster, 1950.

Duchesne, L. *Fastes Episcopaux de L'Ancienne Gaule.* vol. 1-3 ed. Albert Fontemoing. Paris: Ancienne Librarie Thorin et Fils, 1907.

Etudes Merovingiennes, Actes des Journees de Poitiers. Paris: Editions A. et J. Picard, 1953.

Funck-Brentano, Fr. *The National History of France: The Earliest Times.* trans. E.F. Buckley. New York: G.P. Putnam's Sons, 1927.

Geary, Patrick J. *Before France and Germany: The Creation and Transformation of the Merovingian World.* New York: Oxford University Press, 1988.

Gibbon, Edward. *The Decline and Fall of the Roman Empire.* Chicago: Encyclopaedia Britannica, Inc., 1952.

Gies, Frances and Joseph. *Marriage and Family in the Middle Ages.* New York: Harper & Row, 1987.

Goffart, Walter. *Barbarians and Romans, A.D. 418-584.* Princeton: Princeton University Press, 1980.

Goffart, Walter. *The Narrators of Barbarians History, (A.D. 550-800).* Princeton: Princeton University Press, 1988.

Gorce, M.M. *Clovis, 465-511.* Paris: Payot, 1935.

Gregory, Bishop of Tours. *History of the Franks.* trans., Ernest Brehaut. New York: W.W. Norton and Company, Inc., 1969.

Grisar, Hartmann. *History of Rome and the Popes in the Middle Ages.* St. Louis: B. Herder, 1912.

Grun, Bernard. *The Timetables of History.* New York: Simon & Schuster, 1979.

Guizot, Francois Pierre. *A Popular History of France, From the Earliest Times.* trans., Robert Black. Boston: Dana Estes and Charles E. Lauriat, c. 1869.

Hamilton, Edith. *Mythology.* New York: New American Library, 1969.

Headlam, Charles. *The Story of Chartres.* Nendeln, Liechtenstein: Kraus Reprint, 1971.

Hefele, Charles Joseph. *A History of the Councils of the Church, From the Original Documents.* trans., William R. Clark. Edinburgh: T.& T. Clark, 1895.

Heiberg, J. L. *Science and Mathematics in Classical Antiquity.* trans., D.C. Macgregor. Chapters in the History of Science, gen ed., Charles Singer. London: Oxford University Press, 1922.

Hippocratic Writings. Chicago: Encylopaedia Britannica, Inc., 1952.

Histoire de la Bourgogne. Publiée sous la direction del Jean Richard (Universe de la France edt des pays Francophones) ed. Edouard Privat. Toulouse, 1978.

Histoire Littéraire de la France. Paris: Imprimerie Nationale, 1733.

Hodgkin, Thomas. *Theodoric the Goth.* The Barbarian Champion of Civilization. New York: G.P. Putnam's Sons, 1894.

Holmes, T. Scott. *The Origin and Development of the Christian Church in Gaul During the First Six Centuries of the Christian Era.* London: Macmillan and Company, Ltd., 1911.

Huttmann, Maude Aline. *The Establishment of Christianity and the Proscription of Paganism.* New York: Columbia University, 1914.

Hutton, Edward. *The Story of Ravenna.* London: J.M. Dent & Sons, Ltd., 1926.

James, Edward. *The Franks.* Oxford: Basil Blackwell, 1988.

James, Edward. *The Origins of France: From Clovis to the Capetians, 500-1000.* New York: St. Martin's Press, 1982.

Jones, A.H.M. *The Later Roman Empire 284-602, A Social Economic and Administrative Survey.* Norman, Oklahoma: University of Oklahoma Press, 1964.

Keary, A. & E. *The Heros of Asgaard.* Tales from Scandinavian Mythology. Now York: Macmillan & Co., 1979.

Kibler, Willian W. and Zinn, Grover A., ed. *Medieval France; an Encyclopedia.* New York: Garland Publishing, Inc. 1995.

Kurth, Godefroid. *Clovis.* Paris: Victor Retaux, Libraire-Editeur, 1901.

Kurth, Godefroid. *Histoire Poétique des Mérovingiens.* Geneva: Slatkine Reprints, 1968.

Kurth, Godefroi. *St. Clotild.* trans. V.M. Crawford. Chicago: Benziger, 1898.

Kurth, Godefroy. *What are the Middle Ages?.* trans. Victor Day. c. 1921.

Lasko, Peter. *The Kingdom of the Franks, North-West Europe Before Charlemagne.* New York: McGraw-Hill Book Company, 1971.

Latourette, Kenneth Scott. *A History of the Expansion of Christianity*. vol. I, The First Five Centuries. New York: Harper & Brothers Publishers, 1937.
The Letters of Sidonius. trans. O.M. Dalton, M.A. Oxford: Clarendon Press, 1915.
Liber Historiae Francorum. ed. and trans. Bernard S. Bachrach. Lawrence, KS: Coronado Press, 1973.
Lister, Margot. *Costume: An Illustrated Survey from Ancient Times to the Twentieth Century*. Boston: Plays, Inc., 1968.
The Medieval World: 300-1300. Ideas and Institutions in Western Civilization, series ed. Norman F. Cantor. New York: The Macmillan Company, 1968.
Miller, Malcolm. *Chartres Cathedral*. London: Pitkin Pictorals, 1985.
Monvmenta Germaniae Historica: Scriptorum Rerum Merovingicarum. Tomus III, ed. Bruno Krusch, 1896.
Morris, John. *The Age of Arthur*. New York: Charles Scribner's Sons, 1973.
Moss, H.St.L.B. *The Birth of the Middle Ages: 395-814*. Oxford: Oxford University Press, 1957.
New Catholic Encyclopaedia. New York: McGraw-Hill Book Company, 1967.
The New Schaff-Herzog Encyclopedia of Religious Knowledge. vol. ix ed. Samuel Jacobson. Grand Rapids: Baker Book House, 1964.
Norris, Herbert. *Church Vestments*. Their Origins and Development. London: J.M. Dent & Sons, Ltd., 1949.
Ogg, Frederick Austin, ed. *A Source Book of Mediaeval History*. Chicago: American Book Company, 1907.
Oman, Charles. *The Dark Ages, 476-918*. London: Rivingtons, 1903.
Oppenheimer, Sir Francis. *Frankish Themes and Problems*. London: Faber and Faber Limited, 1952.
Paris Mérovingien. Bulletin du Musée Carnavalet. Paris: 1980.
Patrologiae. vol. 65 ed. J.P. Migne. Paris: Apud Garnier Fratres, no date.
Pinchemel, Philippe. *France: A Geographical Survey*. trans., Trollope, Christine and Hunt, Arthur J. London: G. Bell and Sons Ltd., 1969.
Porter, H.B. Jr. *The Ordination Prayers of the Ancient Western Churches*. London: SPCK, 1967.
Prah-Perochon, Anne. "Clovis devient roi des Francs," Journal Français D'Amérique, 12-25 février 1988, p. 5.
Quennell, Marjorie & C.H.B. *Everyday Life in Roman and Anglo-Saxon Times*. New York: G.P. Putnam's Sons, 1959.
Randers-Pehrson, Justine Davis. *Barbarians and Romans*. Norman: University of Oklahoma Press, 1983.
Scherman, Katherine. *The Birth of France: Warriors, Bishops and Long-Haired Kings*. New York: Random House, 1987.

Schoenfeld, Hermann. *Women of the Teutonic Nations*. Woman in all ages and in all countries. Philadephia: The Rittenhouse Press, 1908.
Sergeant, Lewis. *The Franks*. New York: G.P. Putnam's Sons, 1898.
Sitwell, N.H.H. *Roman Roads of Europe*. New York: St. Martin's Press, 1981.
Tannahill, Reay. *Food in History*. New York: Stein and Day, 1973.
Tessier, Georges. *Le Baptême de Clovis, 25 décembre*. Paris: Gallimard, 1964.
Tixeront, Rev. J. *Holy Orders and Ordination: a Study in the History of Dogma*. trans., Raemers, Rev. S.A. St. Louis: B. Herder Book Co., 1928.
The Trinitarian Controversy. Sources of Early Christian Thought, series ed., trans., William G. Rusch. Philadelphia: Fortress Press, 1980.
Velay, Philippe. *From Lutetia to Paris; The Island and the Two Banks*. Paris: Presses du CNRS, 1992.
Villette, Jean. *Chartres and its Cathedral*. trans. M. Th. Olano and Ian Robertson. France: Librairie Arthaud, 1979.
Viorst, Milton. *The Great Documents of Western Civilization*. Philadelphia: Chilton Books, 1965.
Walker, Williston. *A History of the Christian Church*. 3rd ed. New York: Charles Scribner's Sons, 1970.
Wallace-Hadrill, J.M. *The Long-Haired Kings*. London: Methuen & Co. Ltd., 1962.
Weiss, Rolf. *Chlodwigs Taufe: Reims 508*. Bern und Frankfurt/M.: Verlag Herbert Lang & Cie AG, 1971.
Wemple, Suzanne Fonay. *Women in Frankish Society; Marriage and the Cloister 500 to 900*. Philadelphia: University of Pennsylvania Press, 1990.
The Westminster Dictionary of Church History. ed. Jerald C. Brauer. Philadelphia: The Westminster Press, 1971.
Wood, I.N. "Gregory of Tours and Clovis," Revue Belge de Philologie et d'Histoire, 63 (1985), pp. 249-272.
Wood, I.N. "Kings, Kingdoms and Consent" in *Early Medieval Kingship*. ed. P.H. Sawyer and I.N. Wood. Published under the auspices of The School of History University of Leeds, 1977.
Wood, Ian. *The Merovingian Kingdoms, 450-751*. New York: Longman Publishing, 1994.